JAMES FENIMORE COOPER was born in Burlington, New Jersey, in 1789; his family moved to Cooperstown, New York, while he was still an infant. He attended Yale College but was expelled. Sailing before the mast, he saw Europe for the first time on a merchant vessel. In 1808 he became a midshipman in the U. S. Navy. He resigned in 1811 and married. Cooper lived, at various periods, in Westchester and New York City, but spent his later years in Cooperstown. From 1826 to 1833 he traveled extensively in Europe. The Leatherstocking Tales were published during the period from 1823 to 1841. Arranged according to the chronology of their hero, Natty Bumppo, who appears under various sobriquets in all five romances, the sequence is *The Deerslayer* (age 22–24?), *The Last of the Mohicans* (age 35–37?), *The Pathfinder* (age 37–39), *The Pioneers* (age 71–72), *The Prairie* (age 80–83). With his story *The Pilot* (1823) Cooper set the style for a new genre of sea fiction. A caustic social critic, he wrote *The American Democrat* (1838) as a critique of American civilization at that time. His works have been translated into numerous languages and have been enthusiastically received because of their vigor and robust narration. Never able to ignore a challenge, Cooper spent much of his later life in disputes with and suits against various journals. He died in 1851 at his home in Cooperstown.

James Fenimore Cooper

THE PRAIRIE
A TALE

Mark his condition and th' event; then tell me
If this might be a brother. The Tempest

With an Afterword by
JOHN WILLIAM WARD

A SIGNET CLASSIC from
NEW AMERICAN LIBRARY
TIMES MIRROR
New York and Scarborough, Ontario
The New English Library Limited, London

SIGNET CLASSIC TRADEMARK REG. U.S. PAT. OFF. AND FOREIGN COUNTRIES
REGISTERED TRADEMARK—MARCA REGISTRADA
HECHO EN CHICAGO, U.S.A.

SIGNET, SIGNET CLASSICS, MENTOR, PLUME AND MERIDIAN BOOKS
are published *in the United States* by
The New American Library, Inc.,
1301 Avenue of the Americas, New York, New York 10019,
in Canada by The New American Library of Canada Limited,
81 Mack Avenue, Scarborough, 704, Ontario,
in the United Kingdom by The New English Library Limited,
Barnard's Inn, Holborn, London, E.C. 1, England

First Printing, May, 1964

6 7 8 9 10 11 12 13 14

PRINTED IN THE UNITED STATES OF AMERICA

INTRODUCTION

THE GEOLOGICAL FORMATION of that portion of the American Union which lies between the Alleghenies and the Rocky Mountains has given rise to many ingenious theories. Virtually the whole of this immense region is a plain. For a distance extending nearly fifteen hundred miles east and west, and six hundred north and south, there is scarcely an elevation worthy to be called a mountain. Even hills are not common, though a good deal of the face of the country has more or less of that "rolling" character, which is described in the opening pages of this work.

There is much reason to believe that the territory which now composes Ohio, Illinois, Indiana, Michigan, and a large portion of the country west of the Mississippi lay formerly under water. The soil of all the former states has the appearance of an alluvial deposit, and isolated rocks have been found of a nature and in situations which render it difficult to refute the opinion that they have been transferred to their present beds by floating ice. This theory assumes that the Great Lakes were the deep pools of one immense body of freshwater which lay too low to be drained by the irruption that laid bare the land.

It will be remembered that the French, when masters of the Canadas and Louisiana, claimed the whole of the territory in question. Their hunters and advanced troops held the first communications with the savage occupants, and the earliest written accounts we possess of these vast regions are from the pens of their missionaries. Many French words have, consequently, become of local use in this quarter of America, and not a few names given in that language have been perpetuated. When the adventurers who first penetrated these wilds met in the center of the forests, immense plains covered with rich verdure or rank grasses, they naturally gave them the appellation of meadows. As the English succeeded the French and found a peculiarity of nature differing from all they had yet seen on the continent already distinguished by a word that did not express anything in their own language, they left these natural meadows in possession of their title of convention. In this manner has the word "prairie" been adopted into the English tongue.

The American prairies are of two kinds. Those which lie east of the Mississippi are comparatively small, are exceedingly fertile, and are always surrounded by forests. They are susceptible of high cultivation and are fast becoming settled. They abound in Ohio, Michigan, Illinois, and Indiana. They labor under the disadvantages of a scarcity of wood and water—evils of a serious character until art has had time to supply the deficiencies of nature. As coal is said to abound in all that region and wells are generally successful, the enterprise of the emigrants is gradually prevailing against these difficulties.

The second description of these natural meadows lies west of the Mississippi at a distance of a few hundred miles from that river, and is called the Great Prairies. They resemble the steppes of Tartary more than any other known portion of the world, being in fact a vast country incapable of sustaining a dense population in the absence of the two great necessaries already named. Rivers abound, it is true; but this region is nearly destitute of brooks and the smaller watercourses which tend so much to comfort and fertility.

The origin and date of the Great American Prairies form one of nature's most majestic mysteries. The general character of the United States, of the Canadas, and of Mexico is that of luxuriant fertility. It would be difficult to find another portion of the world, of the same extent, which has so little useless land as the inhabited parts of the American Union. Most of the mountains are arable, and even the prairies in this section of the republic are of deep alluvion. The same is true between the Rocky Mountains and the Pacific. Between the two lies the broad belt of comparative desert which is the scene of this tale, appearing to interpose a barrier to the progress of the American people westward. Since the original publication of this book, however, the boundaries of the republic have been carried to the Pacific, and the "settler," preceded by the "trapper," has already established himself on the shores of that vast sea.

The Great Prairies appear to be the final gathering place of the red men. The remnants of the Mohicans and the Delawares, of the Creeks, Choctaws, and Cherokees, are destined to fulfill their time on these vast plains. The entire number of the Indians within the Union is differently computed at between one and five hundred thousand souls. Most of them inhabit the country west of the Mississippi. At the period of the tale they dwelt in open hostility, national feuds passing from generation to generation. The power of the republic has done much to restore peace to these wild scenes, and it is now possible to travel in security where civilized man did not dare to pass unprotected five and twenty years ago.

Recent events have brought the Grand Prairies into familiar notice, and we now read of journeys across them as half a century since we perused the narratives of the emigrants to Ohio and Louisiana. It is a singular commentary on the times that places for railroads across these vast plains are in active discussion and that men have ceased to regard the project as chimerical.

This book closes the career of Leatherstocking. Pressed upon by time, he had ceased to be the hunter and the warrior and has become a trapper of the great West. The sound of the ax has driven him from his beloved forests to seek a refuge, by a species of desperate resignation, on the denuded plains that stretch to the Rocky Mountains. Here he passes the few closing years of his life, dying as he had lived, a philosopher of the wilderness, with few of the failings, none of the vices, and all the nature and truth of his position.

his own. The other two decisions were answered as the basis in respect to inhabitants constitution from the constitution, the audience

CHAPTER 1

I pray thee, shepherd, if that love, or gold
Can in this desert place buy entertainment,
Bring us where we may rest ourselves and feed.
                                      As You Like It

MUCH WAS SAID and written at the time concerning the policy of adding the vast regions of Louisiana to the already immense and but half-tenanted territories of the United States. As the warmth of controversy, however, subsided and party considerations gave place to more liberal views, the wisdom of the measure began to be generally conceded. It soon became apparent to the meanest capacity that while nature had placed a barrier of desert to the extension of our population in the West, the measure had made us the masters of a belt of fertile country which, in the revolutions of the day, might have become the property of a rival nation. It gave us the sole command of the great thoroughfare of the interior and placed the countless tribes of savages who lay along our borders entirely within our control; it reconciled conflicting rights and quieted national distrusts; it opened a thousand avenues to the inland trade and to the waters of the Pacific; and if ever time or necessity shall require a peaceful division of this vast empire, it assures us of a neighbor that will possess our language, our religion, our institutions, and it is also to be hoped, our sense of political justice.

Although the purchase was made in 1803, the spring of the succeeding year was permitted to open before the official prudence of the Spaniard, who held the province for his European master, admitted the authority or even the entrance of its new proprietors. But the forms of the transfer were no sooner completed and the new government acknowledged than swarms of that restless people which is ever found hovering on the skirts of American society plunged into the thickets that fringed the right bank of the Mississippi, with the same careless hardihood that had already sustained so many of them in their toilsome progress from the Atlantic states to the eastern shores of the "father of rivers." *

Time was necessary to blend the numerous and affluent colonists of the lower province with their new compatriots; but the thinner and more humble population above was almost immediately swallowed in the vortex which attended the tide of instant emigration. The inroad from the East was a new and sudden outbreaking of a people who had endured a momentary restraint after having been rendered nearly resistless by success. The toils and hazards of former undertakings were forgotten as these endless and unexplored regions, with all their fancied as well as real advantages, were laid open to their enterprise. The consequences were such as might easily have been anticipated from so tempting an offering, placed as it was before the eyes of a race long trained in adventure and nurtured in difficulties.

Thousands of the elders of what were then called the *New* States † broke up from the enjoyment of their hard-earned indulgences and were to be seen leading long files of descendants, born and reared in the forests of Ohio and Kentucky, deeper into the land in quest of that which might be termed, without the aid of poetry, their natural and more congenial atmosphere. The distinguished and resolute forester who first penetrated the wilds of the latter state was of the number. This adventurous and venerable patriarch was now seen making his last remove, placing the endless river between him and the multitude his own success had drawn around him and seeking for the renewal of enjoyments which were rendered worthless in his eyes when trammeled by the forms of human institutions.*

In the pursuit of adventures such as these, men are ordi-

---

* The Mississippi is thus termed in several of the Indian languages. The reader will gain a more just idea of the importance of this stream if he recalls to mind the fact that the Missouri and the Mississippi are properly the same river. Their united lengths cannot be greatly short of four thousand miles.

† All the states admitted to the American Union since the revolution are called New States, with the exception of Vermont; that had claims before the war, which were not, however, admitted until a later day.

* Colonel Boone, the patriarch of Kentucky. This venerable and hardy pioneer of civilization emigrated to an estate three hundred miles west of the Mississippi in his ninety-second year because he found a population of ten to the square mile inconveniently crowded!

narily governed by their habits or deluded by their wishes. A few, led by the phantoms of hope and ambitious of sudden affluence, sought the mines of the virgin territory; but by far the greater portion of the emigrants were satisfied to establish themselves along the margins of the larger watercourses, content with the rich returns that the generous alluvial bottoms of the rivers never fail to bestow on the most desultory industry. In this manner were communities formed with magical rapidity; and most of those who witnessed the purchase of the empty empire have lived to see already a populous and sovereign state parceled from its inhabitants and received into the bosom of the national Union on terms of political equality.

The incidents and scenes which are connected with this legend occurred in the earliest periods of the enterprises which have led to so great and so speedy a result.

The harvest of the first year of our possession had long been passed, and the fading foliage of a few scattered trees was already beginning to exhibit the hues and tints of autumn when a train of wagons issued from the bed of a dry rivulet to pursue its course across the undulating surface of what, in the language of the country of which we write, is called a "rolling prairie." The vehicles, loaded with household goods and implements of husbandry, the few straggling sheep and cattle that were herded in the rear, and the rugged appearance and careless mien of the sturdy men who loitered at the sides of the lingering teams united to announce a band of emigrants seeking for the Eldorado of the West. Contrary to the usual practice of the men of their caste, this party had left the fertile bottoms of the low country and had found its way, by means only known to such adventurers, across glen and torrent, over deep morasses and arid wastes, to a point far beyond the usual limits of civilized habitations. In their front were stretched those broad plains which extend with so little diversity of character to the bases of the Rocky Mountains, and many long and dreary miles in their rear foamed the swift and turbid waters of La Platte.

The appearance of such a train in that bleak and solitary place was rendered the more remarkable by the fact that the surrounding country offered so little that was tempting to the cupidity of speculation, and if possible, still less that was flattering to the hopes of an ordinary settler of new lands.

The meager herbage of the prairie promised nothing in favor of a hard and unyielding soil over which the wheels of the vehicles rattled as lightly as if they traveled on a beaten road, neither wagons nor beasts making any deeper impression than to mark that bruised and withered grass which the cattle plucked from time to time, and as often rejected as food too sour for even hunger to render palatable.

Whatever might be the final destination of these adventurers or the secret causes of their apparent security in so remote and unprotected a situation, there was no visible sign of uneasiness, uncertainty, or alarm among them. Including both sexes, and every age, the number of the party exceeded twenty.

At some little distance in front of the whole marched the individual who by his position and air appeared to be the leader of the band. He was a tall, sunburnt man, past the middle age, of a dull countenance and listless manner. His frame appeared loose and flexible, but it was vast and in reality of prodigious power. It was only at moments, however, as some slight impediment opposed itself to his loitering progress that his person, which, in its ordinary gait seemed so lounging and nerveless, displayed any of those energies which lay latent in his system, like the slumbering and unwieldy, but terrible, strength of the elephant. The inferior lineaments of his countenance were coarse, extended, and vacant, while the superior, or those nobler parts which are thought to affect the intellectual being, were low, receding, and mean.

The dress of this individual was a mixture of the coarsest vestments of a husbandman with the leathern garments that fashion as well as use had in some degree rendered necessary to one engaged in his present pursuits. There was, however, a singular and wild display of prodigal and ill-judged ornaments blended with his motley attire. In place of the usual deerskin belt, he wore around his body a tarnished silken sash of the most gaudy colors; the buckhorn haft of his knife was profusely decorated with plates of silver; the marten's fur of his cap was of a fineness and shadowing that a queen might covet; the buttons of his rude and soiled blanket-coat were of the glittering coinage of Mexico; the stock of his rifle was of beautiful mahogany riveted and banded with the same precious metal; and the trinkets of no less than three worthless watches dangled from different parts of his person. In addition to the pack and the rifle which were slung at his back, together with the well-filled and carefully guarded pouch and horn, he had carelessly cast a keen and bright wood-ax across his shoulder, sustaining the weight of the whole with as much apparent ease as if he moved unfettered in limb and free from encumbrance.

A short distance in the rear of this man came a group of youths very similarly attired and bearing sufficient resemblance to each other and to their leader to distinguish them as the children of one family. Though the youngest of their number could not much have passed the period that in the nicer judgment of the law is called the age of discretion, he had proved himself so far worthy of his progenitors as to have reared already his aspiring person to the standard height of his race. There were one or two others, of different mold, whose descriptions must, however, be referred to the regular course of the narrative.

Of the females, there were but two who had arrived at womanhood, though several white-headed, olive-skinned faces were peering out of the foremost wagon of the train with eyes of lively curiosity and characteristic animation. The elder of the two adults was the sallow and wrinkled mother of most of the party, and the younger was a sprightly, active girl of eighteen who in figure, dress, and mien seemed to belong to a station in society several gradations above that of any one of her visible associates. The second vehicle was covered with a top of cloth so tightly drawn as to conceal its contents with the nicest care. The remaining wagons were loaded with such rude furniture and other personal effects as might be supposed to belong to one ready at any moment to change his abode without reference to season or distance.

Perhaps there was little in this train or in the appearance of its proprietors that is not daily to be encountered on the highways of this changeable and moving country. But the solitary and peculiar scenery in which it was so unexpectedly exhibited gave to the party a marked character of wildness and adventure.

In the little valleys which, in the regular formation of the land, occurred at every mile of their progress, the view was bounded on two of the sides by the gradual and low elevations which give name to the description of prairie we have

mentioned; while on the others, the meager prospect ran off
in long, narrow, barren perspectives but slightly relieved by
a pitiful show of coarse though somewhat luxuriant vegetation. From the summits of the swells, the eye became fa-
tigued with the sameness and chilling dreariness of the landscape. The earth was not unlike the ocean when its restless
waters are heaving heavily after the agitation and fury of
the tempest have begun to lessen. There was the same waving and regular surface, the same absence of foreign objects,
and the same boundless extent to the view. Indeed so very
striking was the resemblance between the water and the
land that however much the geologist might sneer at so simple a theory, it would have been difficult for a poet not to
have felt that the formation of the one had been produced
by the subsiding dominion of the other. Here and there a
tall tree rose out of the bottoms, stretching its naked
branches abroad like some solitary vessel; and to strengthen
the delusion, far in the distance appeared two or three
rounded thickets looming in the misty horizon like islands
resting on the waters. It is unnecessary to warn the practiced reader that the sameness of the surface and the low
stands of the spectators exaggerated the distances, but as
swell appeared after swell and island succeeded island, there
was a disheartening assurance that long and seemingly interminable tracts of territory must be passed before the
wishes of the humblest agriculturist could be realized.

Still, the leader of the emigrants steadily pursued his way,
with no other guide than the sun, turning his back resolutely
on the abodes of civilization and plunging at each step more
deeply, if not irretrievably, into the haunts of the barbarous
and savage occupants of the country. As the day drew nigher
to a close, however, his mind, which was, perhaps, incapable
of maturing any connected system of forethought beyond
that which related to the interests of the present moment,
became in some slight degree troubled with the care of providing for the wants of the hours of darkness.

On reaching the crest of a swell that was a little higher
than the usual elevations, he lingered a minute and cast a
half-curious eye on either hand in quest of those well-known
signs which might indicate a place where the three grand
requisites of water, fuel, and fodder were to be obtained in
conjunction.

It would seem that his search was fruitless, for after a

few moments of indolent and listless examination, he suffered his huge frame to descend the gentle declivity in the same sluggish manner that an overfatted beast would have yielded to the downward pressure.

His example was silently followed by those who succeeded him, though not until the young men had manifested much more of interest, if not of concern, in the brief inquiry which each in his turn made on gaining the same lookout. It was now evident by the tardy movements both of beasts and men that the time of necessary rest was not far distant. The matted grass of the lower land presented obstacles which fatigue began to render formidable, and the whip was becoming necessary to urge the lingering teams to their labor. At this moment, when, with the exception of the principal individual, a general lassitude was getting the mastery of the travelers and every eye was cast by a sort of common impulse wistfully forward, the whole party was brought to a halt by a spectacle as sudden as it was unexpected.

The sun had fallen below the crest of the nearest wave of the prairie, leaving the usual rich and glowing train on its track. In the center of this flood of fiery light a human form appeared, drawn against the gilded background as distinctly, and seemingly as palpable, as though it would come within the grasp of any extended hand. The figure was colossal, the attitude musing and melancholy, and the situation directly in the route of the travelers. But embedded as it was in its setting of garish light, it was impossible to distinguish its just proportions or true character.

The effect of such a spectacle was instantaneous and powerful. The man in front of the emigrants came to a stand and remained gazing at the mysterious object with a dull interest that soon quickened into superstitious awe. His sons, so soon as the first emotions of surprise had a little abated, drew slowly around him, and as they who governed the teams gradually followed their example, the whole party was soon condensed in one silent and wondering group. Notwithstanding the impression of a supernatural agency was very general among the travelers, the ticking of gunlocks was heard, and one or two of the bolder youths cast their rifles forward in readiness for service.

"Send the boys off to the right," exclaimed the resolute wife and mother in a sharp, dissonant voice; "I warrant me

Asa or Abner will give some account of the creature!"

"It may be well enough to try the rifle," muttered a dull-looking man whose features, both in outline and expression, bore no small resemblance to the first speaker and who loosened the stock of his piece and brought it dexterously to the front while delivering this opinion. "The Pawnee Loups are said to be hunting by hundreds in the plains; if so, they'll never miss a single man from their tribe."

"Stay!" exclaimed a soft-toned but alarmed female voice which was easily to be traced to the trembling lips of the younger of the two women. "We are not all together; it may be a friend!"

"Who is scouting now?" demanded the father, scanning at the same time the cluster of his stout sons with a displeased and sullen eye. "Put by the piece, put by the piece," he continued, diverting the other's aim with the finger of a giant and with the air of one it might be dangerous to deny. "My job is not yet ended; let us finish the little that remains in peace."

The man who had manifested so hostile an intention appeared to understand the other's allusion and suffered himself to be diverted from his object. The sons turned their inquiring looks on the girl who had so eagerly spoken, to require an explanation; but as if content with the respite she had obtained for the stranger, she sank back in her seat and chose to affect a maidenly silence.

In the meantime the hues of the heavens had often changed. In place of the brightness which had dazzled the eye, a gray and more sober light had succeeded, and as the setting lost its brilliancy, the proportions of the fanciful form became less exaggerated, and finally distinct. Ashamed to hesitate now that the truth was no longer doubtful, the leader of the party resumed his journey, using the precaution, as he ascended the slight acclivity, to release his own rifle from the strap and to cast it into a situation more convenient for sudden use.

There was little apparent necessity, however, for such watchfulness. From the moment when it had thus unaccountably appeared, as it were, between the heavens and the earth, the stranger's figure had neither moved nor given the smallest evidence of hostility. Had he harbored any such evil intention, the individual who now came plainly into view seemed but little qualified to execute them.

A frame that had endured the hardships of more than eighty seasons was not qualified to awaken apprehension in the breast of one as powerful as the emigrant. Notwithstanding his years and his look of emaciation, if not of suffering, there was that about this solitary being, however, which said that time, and not disease, had laid his hand heavily on him. His form had withered, but it was not wasted. The sinews and muscles, which had once denoted great strength, though shrunken, were still visible; and his whole figure had attained an appearance of induration, which, if it were not for the well-known frailty of humanity, would have seemed to bid defiance to the further approaches of decay. His dress was chiefly of skins, worn with the hair to the weather; a pouch and horn were suspended from his shoulders; and he leaned on a rifle of uncommon length, but which, like its owner, exhibited the wear of long and hard service.

As the party drew nigher to this solitary being and came within a distance to be heard, a low growl issued from the grass at his feet, and then a tall, gaunt, toothless hound arose lazily from his lair, and shaking himself, made some show of resisting the nearer approach of the travelers.

"Down, Hector, down," said his master in a voice that was a little tremulous and hollow with age. "What have ye to do, pup, with men who journey on their lawful callings?"

"Stranger, if you are much acquainted in this country," said the leader of the emigrants, "can you tell a traveler where he may find necessaries for the night?"

"Is the land filled on the other side of the big river?" demanded the old man solemnly and without appearing to hearken to the other's question; "or why do I see a sight I had never thought to behold again?"

"Why, there is country left, it is true, for such as have money and are not particular in the choice," returned the emigrant; "but to my taste, it is getting crowdy. What may a man call the distance from this place to the nighest point on the main river?"

"A hunted deer could not cool his sides in the Mississippi without traveling a weary five hundred miles."

"And what may you name the district hereaway?"

"By what name," returned the old man, pointing significantly upwards, "would you call the spot where you see yonder cloud?"

The emigrant looked at the other like one who did not comprehend his meaning and who half suspected he was trifled with; but he contented himself by saying, "You are but a new inhabitant, like myself, I reckon, stranger, or otherwise you would not be backward in helping a traveler to some advice; words cost but little, and sometimes lead to friendships."

"Advice is not a gift, but a debt that the old owe to the young. What would you wish to know?"

"Where I may camp for the night. I'm no great difficulty maker as to bed and board; but all old journeyers like myself know the virtue of sweet water and a good browse for the cattle."

"Come, then, with me, and you shall be master of both; and little more is it that I can offer on this hungry prairie."

As the old man was speaking, he raised his heavy rifle to his shoulder with a facility a little remarkable for his years and appearance, and without further words led the way over the acclivity to the adjacent bottom.

CHAPTER 2

> Up with my tent: here will I lie tonight,
> But where tomorrow?—Well, all's one for that.
>   RICHARD THE THIRD

THE TRAVELERS SOON discovered the usual and unerring evidences that the several articles necessary to their situation were not far distant. A clear and gurgling spring burst out of the side of the declivity, and joining its waters to those of other similar little fountains in its vicinity, their united contributions formed a run which was easily to be traced for miles along the prairie by the scattering foliage and verdure which occasionally grew within the influence of its moisture. Hither, then, the stranger held his way, eagerly followed by the willing teams, whose instinct gave them a prescience of refreshment and rest.

On reaching what he deemed a suitable spot, the old man halted, and with an inquiring look, he seemed to demand if it possessed the needed conveniences. The leader of the emigrants cast his eyes understandingly about him and examined the place with the keenness of one competent to judge of so nice a question, though in that dilatory and heavy manner which rarely permitted him to betray precipitation.

"Aye, this may do," he said when satisfied with his scrutiny; "boys, you have seen the last of the sun; be stirring."

The young men manifested a characteristic obedience. The order, for such in tone and manner it was, in truth, was received with respect; but the utmost movement was the falling of an ax or two from the shoulder to the ground, while their owners continued to regard the place with listless and incurious eyes. In the meantime, the elder traveler, as if familiar with the nature of the impulses by which his children were governed, disencumbered himself of his pack and rifle, and, assisted by the man already mentioned as disposed to appeal so promptly to the rifle, he quietly proceeded to release the cattle from the gears.

At length the eldest of the sons stepped heavily forward, and, without any apparent effort, he buried his ax to the eye in the soft body of a cottonwood tree. He stood a moment regarding the effect of the blow, with that sort of contempt with which a giant might be supposed to contemplate the puny resistance of a dwarf, and then flourishing the implement above his head, with the grace and dexterity with which a master of the art of offense would wield his nobler though less useful weapon, he quickly severed the trunk of the tree, bringing its tall top crashing to the earth in submission to his prowess. His companions regarded the operation with indolent curiosity until they saw the prostrate trunk stretched on the ground, when, as if a signal for a general attack had been given, they advanced in a body to the work; and in a space of time, and with a neatness of execution that would have astonished an ignorant spectator, they stripped a small but suitable spot of its burden of forest as effectually and almost as promptly as if a whirlwind had passed along the place.

The stranger had been a silent but attentive observer of their progress. As tree after tree came whistling down, he cast his eyes upwards at the vacancies they left in the heavens, with a melancholy gaze, and finally turned away muttering to himself with a bitter smile, like one who disdained giving a more audible utterance to his discontent. Pressing through the group of active and busy children who had already lighted a cheerful fire, the attention of the old man became next fixed on the movements of the leader of the emigrants and of his savage-looking assistant.

These two had already liberated the cattle, which were eagerly browsing the grateful and nutritious extremities of the fallen trees and were now employed about the wagon, which has been described as having its contents concealed with so much apparent care. Notwithstanding this particular conveyance appeared to be as silent and as tenantless as the rest of the vehicles, the men applied their strength to its wheels and rolled it apart from the others to a dry and elevated spot near the edge of the thicket. Here they brought certain poles which had seemingly been long employed in such a service, and fastening their larger ends firmly in the ground, the smaller were attached to the hoops that supported the covering of the wagon. Large folds of cloth were next drawn out of the vehicle, and after being spread around the whole, were pegged to the earth in such a manner as to form a tolerably capacious and an exceedingly convenient tent. After surveying their work with inquisitive and perhaps jealous eyes, arranging a fold here and driving a peg more firmly there, the men once more applied their strength to the wagon, pulling it by its projecting tongue from the center of the canopy until it appeared in the open air deprived of its covering and destitute of any other freight than a few light articles of furniture. The latter were immediately removed by the traveler into the tent with his own hands, as though to enter it were a privilege to which even his bosom companion was not entitled.

Curiosity is a passion that is rather quickened than destroyed by seclusion, and the old inhabitant of the prairies did not view these precautionary and mysterious movements without experiencing some of its impulses. He approached the tent and was about to sever two of its folds, with the very obvious intention of examining more closely into the nature of its contents, when the man who had once already placed his life in jeopardy seized him by the arm and with a rude exercise of his strength threw him from the spot he had selected as the one most convenient for his object.

"It's an honest regulation, friend," the fellow drily observed, though with an eye that threatened volumes, "and sometimes it is a safe one, which says mind your own business."

"Men seldom bring anything to be concealed into these

deserts," returned the old man as if willing and yet a little ignorant how to apologize for the liberty he had been about to take, "and I had hoped no offense in examining your comforts."

"They seldom bring themselves, I reckon; though this has the look of an old country, to my eye it seems not to be overly peopled."

"The land is as aged as the rest of the works of the Lord, I believe; but you say true concerning its inhabitants. Many months have passed since I have laid eyes on a face of my own color before your own. I say again, friend, I meant no harm; I did not know but there was something behind the cloth that might bring former days to my mind."

As the stranger ended his simple explanation he walked meekly away like one who felt the deepest sense of the right which every man has to the quiet enjoyment of his own, without any troublesome interference on the part of his neighbor, a wholesome and a just principle that he had also most probably imbibed from the habits of his secluded life. As he passed towards the little encampment of the emigrants, for such the place had now become, he heard the voice of the leader calling aloud in its hoarse tones, the name of Ellen Wade.

The girl who has been already introduced to the reader and who was occupied with the others of her sex around the fires sprang willingly forward at this summons, and passing the stranger with the activity of a young antelope, she was instantly lost behind the forbidden folds of the tent. Neither her sudden disappearance nor any of the arrangements we have mentioned seemed, however, to excite the smallest surprise among the remainder of the party. The young men, who had already completed their tasks with the ax, were all engaged after their lounging and listless manner, some in bestowing equitable portions of the fodder among the different animals, others in plying the heavy pestle of a movable hominy mortar,* and one or two in wheeling the remainder of the wagons aside and arranging them in such a manner as to form a sort of outwork for their otherwise defenseless bivouac.

These several duties were soon performed, and as darkness now began to conceal the objects on the surrounding prairie, the shrill-toned termagant whose voice since the halt had

---

* Hominy is a dish composed chiefly of cracked corn, or maize.

been diligently exercised among her idle and drowsy off-spring announced in tones that might have been heard at a dangerous distance that the evening meal waited only for the approach of those who were to consume it. Whatever may be the other qualities of a borderman, he is seldom deficient in the virtue of hospitality. The emigrant no sooner heard the sharp call of his wife than he cast his eyes about him in quest of the stranger in order to offer him the place of distinction in the rude entertainment to which they were so unceremoniously summoned.

"I thank you, friend," the old man replied to the rough invitation to take a seat nigh the smoking kettle; "you have my hearty thanks; but I have eaten for the day and am not one of them who dig their graves with their teeth. Well, as you wish it, I will take a place, for it is long sin' I have seen people of my color eating their daily bread."

"You are an old settler in these districts, then?" the emigrant rather remarked than inquired, with a mouth filled nearly to overflowing with the delicious hominy, prepared by his skillful though repulsive spouse. "They told us below we should find settlers something thinnish hereaway, and I must say the report was mainly true, for unless we count the Canada traders on the big river, you are the first white face I have met in a good five hundred miles; that is, calculating according to your own reckoning."

"Though I have spent some years in this quarter, I can hardly be called a settler, seeing that I have no regular abode and seldom pass more than a month at a time on the same range."

"A hunter, I reckon?" the other continued, glancing his eyes aside as if to examine the equipments of his new acquaintance; "your fixen seem none of the best for such a calling."

"They are old and nearly ready to be laid aside, like their master," said the old man, regarding his rifle with a look in which affection and regret were singularly blended; "and I may say they are but little needed too. You are mistaken, friend, in calling me a hunter; I am nothing better than a trapper." *

---

* It is scarcely necessary to say that this American word means one who takes his game in a trap. It is of general use on the frontiers. The beaver, an animal too sagacious to be easily killed, is oftener taken in this way than in any other.

"If you are much of the one, I'm bold to say you are something of the other, for the two callings go mainly together in these districts."

"To the shame of the man who is able to follow the first be it so said!" returned the trapper, whom in future we shall choose to designate by his pursuit. "For more than fifty years did I carry my rifle in the wilderness without so much as setting a snare for even a bird that flies the heavens, much less a beast that has nothing but legs for its gifts."

"I see but little difference whether a man gets his peltry by the rifle or by the trap," said the ill-looking companion of the emigrant in his rough manner. "The 'arth was made for our comfort; and, for that matter, so are its creatur's."

"You seem to have but little plunder,* stranger, for one who is far abroad," bluntly interrupted the emigrant as if he had a reason for wishing to change the conversation. "I hope you are better off for skins."

"I make but little use of either," the trapper quietly replied. "At my time of life, food and clothing be all that is needed; and I have little occasion for what you call plunder, unless it may be now and then to barter for a horn of powder or a bar of lead."

"You are not, then, of these parts by natur', friend," the emigrant continued, having in his mind the exception which the other had taken to the very equivocal word, which he himself, according to the custom of the country, had used for "baggage," or "effects."

"I was born on the seashore, though most of my life has been passed in the woods."

The whole party now looked up at him as men are apt to turn their eyes on some unexpected object of general interest. One or two of the young men repeated the word "seashore," and the woman tendered him one of those civilities with which, uncouth as they were, she was little accustomed to grace her hospitality, as if in deference to the traveled dignity of her guest. After a long and seemingly a meditating silence, the emigrant, who had, however, seen no apparent

---

* The cant word for luggage in the Western states of America is "plunder." The term might easily mislead one as to the character of the people, who, notwithstanding their pleasant use of so expressive a word, are, like the inhabitants of all new settlements, hospitable and honest. Knavery of the description conveyed by "plunder" is chiefly found in regions more civilized.

necessity to suspend the functions of his masticating powers, resumed the discourse.

"It is a long road, as I have heard, from the waters of the West to the shores of the main sea?"

"It is a weary path indeed, friend; and much have I seen, and something have I suffered in journeying over it."

"A man would see a good deal of hard travel in going its length!"

"Seventy and five years have I been upon the road; and there are not half that number of leagues in the whole distance, after you leave the Hudson, on which I have not tasted venison of my own killing. But this is vain boasting. Of what use are former deeds when time draws to an end?"

"I once met a man that had boated on the river he names," observed the eldest son, speaking in a low tone of voice like one who distrusted his knowledge and deemed it prudent to assume a becoming diffidence in the presence of a man who had seen so much. "From his tell, it must be a considerable stream, and deep enough for a keelboat from top to bottom."

"It is a wide and deep watercourse, and many sightly towns are there growing on its banks," returned the trapper; "and yet it is but a brook to the waters of the endless river!"

"I call nothing a stream that a man can travel round," exclaimed the ill-looking associate of the emigrant; "a real river must be crossed, not headed like a bear in a county hunt." *

"Have you been far towards the sundown, friend?" interrupted the emigrant as if he desired to keep his rough companion as much as possible out of the discourse. "I find it is a wide tract of clearing, this into which I have fallen."

"You may travel weeks and you will see it the same. I often think the Lord has placed this barren belt of prairie behind the States to warn men to what their folly may yet bring the land! Aye, weeks, if not months, may you journey in these open fields, in which there is neither dwelling nor

---

* There is a practice in the new countries to assemble the men of a large district, sometimes of an entire county, to exterminate the beasts of prey. They form themselves into a circle of several miles in extent and gradually draw nearer, killing all before them. The allusion is to this custom, in which the hunted beast is turned from one to another.

habitation for man or beast. Even the savage animals travel miles on miles to seek their dens; and yet the wind seldom blows from the east, but I conceit the sound of axes and the crash of falling trees are in my ears."

As the old man spoke with the seriousness and dignity that age seldom fails to communicate even to less striking sentiments, his auditors were deeply attentive and as silent as the grave. Indeed the trapper was left to renew the dialogue himself, which he soon did by asking a question in the indirect manner so much in use by the border inhabitants.

"You found it no easy matter to ford the watercourses and to make your way so deep into the prairies, friend, with teams of horses and herds of horned beasts?"

"I kept the left bank of the main river," the emigrant replied, "until I found the stream leading too much to the north, when we rafted ourselves across without any great suffering. The woman lost a fleece or two from the next year's shearing, and the girls have one cow less to their dairy. Since then we have done bravely by bridging a creek every day or two."

"It is likely you will continue west until you come to land more suitable for a settlement?"

"Until I see reason to stop or to turn ag'in," the emigrant bluntly answered, rising at the same time and cutting short the dialogue by the suddenness of the movement. His example was followed by the trapper, as well as the rest of the party; and then, without much deference to the presence of their guest, the travelers proceeded to make their dispositions to pass the night. Several little bowers, or rather huts, had already been formed of the tops of trees, blankets of coarse country manufacture and the skins of buffaloes united without much reference to any other object than temporary comfort. Into these covers the children, with their mother, soon drew themselves, where, it is more than possible, they were all speedily lost in the oblivion of sleep. Before the men, however, could seek their rest, they had sundry little duties to perform, such as completing their works of defense, carefully concealing the fires, replenishing the fodder of their cattle, and setting the watch that was to protect the party in the approaching hours of night.

The former was effected by dragging the trunks of a few trees into the intervals left by the wagons and along the open space between the vehicles and the thicket, on which, in military language, the encampment would be said to have rested, thus forming a sort of chevaux-de-frise on three sides of the position. Within these narrow limits, with the exception of what the tent contained, both man and beast were now collected, the latter being far too happy in resting their weary limbs to give any undue annoyance to their scarcely more intelligent associates. Two of the young men took their rifles, and first renewing the priming and examining the flints with the utmost care, they proceeded, the one to the extreme right, and the other to the left of the encampment, where they posted themselves within the shadows of the thicket, but in such positions as enabled each to overlook a portion of the prairie.

The trapper loitered about the place, declining to share the straw of the emigrant, until the whole arrangement was completed; and then, without the ceremony of an adieu, he slowly retired from the spot.

It was now in the first watch of the night; and the pale, quivering, and deceptive light from a new moon was playing over the endless waves of the prairie, tipping the swells with gleams of brightness and leaving the interval land in deep shadow. Accustomed to scenes of solitude like the present, the old man, as he left the encampment, proceeded alone into the waste like a bold vessel leaving its haven to enter on the trackless field of the ocean. He appeared to move for some time without object or, indeed, without any apparent consciousness whither his limbs were carrying him. At length, on reaching the rise of one of the undulations, he came to a stand, and for the first time since leaving the band who had caused such a flood of reflections and recollections to crowd upon his mind, the old man became aware of his present situation. Throwing one end of his rifle to the earth, he stood leaning on the other, again lost in deep contemplation for several minutes, during which time his hound came and crouched at his feet. A deep, menacing growl from the faithful animal first aroused him from his musing.

"What now, dog?" he said, looking down at his companion as if he addressed a being of an intelligence equal to his own, and speaking in a voice of great affection. "What is it, pup? Ha! Hector, what is it nosing now? It won't do, dog; it won't do; the very fa'ans play in open view of us without minding so worn-out curs as you and I. Instinct is their gift,

Hector, and they have found out how little we are to be feared, they have!"

The dog stretched his head upwards and responded to the words of his master by a long and plaintive whine, which he even continued after he had again buried his head in the grass, as if he held an intelligent communication with one who so well knew how to interpret dumb discourse.

"This is a manifest warning, Hector!" the trapper continued, dropping his voice to the tones of caution and looking warily about him. "What is it, pup; speak plainer, dog; what is it?"

The hound had, however, already laid his nose to the earth, and was silent, appearing to slumber. But the keen, quick glances of his master soon caught a glimpse of a distant figure which seemed, through the deceptive light, floating along the very elevation on which he had placed himself. Presently its proportions became more distinct, and then an airy female form appeared to hesitate, as if considering whether it would be prudent to advance. Though the eyes of the dog were now to be seen glancing in the rays of the moon, opening and shutting lazily, he gave no further signs of displeasure.

"Come nigher; we are friends," said the trapper, associating himself with his companion by long use, and probably through the strength of the secret tie that connected them together; "we are your friends; none will harm you."

Encouraged by the mild tones of his voice, and perhaps led on by the earnestness of her purpose, the female approached until she stood at his side, when the old man perceived his visitor to be the young woman with whom the reader has already become acquainted by the name of Ellen Wade.

"I had thought you were gone," she said, looking timidly and anxiously around. "They said you were gone and that we should never see you again. I did not think it was you!"

"Men are no common objects in these empty fields," returned the trapper, "and I humbly hope, though I have so long consorted with the beasts of the wilderness, that I have not yet lost the look of my kind."

"Oh! I knew you to be a man, and I thought I knew the whine of the hound too," she answered hastily, as if willing to explain she knew not what, and then checking herself like one fearful of having already said too much.

"I saw no dogs among the teams of your father," the trapper remarked.

"Father!" exclaimed the girl feelingly. "I have no father! I had nearly said no friend."

The old man turned towards her with a look of kindness and interest that was even more conciliating than the ordinary upright and benevolent expression of his weatherbeaten countenance.

"Why then do you venture in a place where none but the strong should come?" he demanded. "Did you not know that when you crossed the big river you left a friend behind you that is always bound to look to the young and feeble like yourself?"

"Of whom do you speak?"

"The law—'tis bad to have it, but I sometimes think it is worse to be entirely without it. Age and weakness has brought me to feel such weakness at times. Yes—yes, the law is needed when such as have not the gifts of strength and wisdom are to be taken care of. I hope, young woman, if you have no father you have at least a brother."

The maiden felt the tacit reproach conveyed in this covert question, and for a moment she remained in an embarrassed silence. But catching a glimpse of the mild and serious features of her companion as he continued to gaze on her with a look of interest, she replied firmly and in a manner that left no doubt she comprehended his meaning, "Heaven forbid that any such as you have seen should be a brother of mine or anything else near or dear to me! But tell me, do you then actually live alone in this desert district, old man; is there really none here besides yourself?"

"There are hundreds, nay, thousands of the rightful owners of the country roving about the plains, but few of our own color."

"And have you then met none who are white but us?" interrupted the girl like one too impatient to await the tardy explanations of age and deliberation.

"Not in many days. Hush, Hector, hush," he added in reply to a low and nearly inaudible growl from his hound. "The dog scents mischief in the wind! The black bears from the mountains sometimes make their way even lower than this. The pup is not apt to complain of the harmless game. I am not so ready and true with the piece as I used to could be, yet I have struck even the fiercest animals of the prairie in my time; so you have little reason for fear, young woman."

The girl raised her eyes in that peculiar manner which is so often practiced by her sex when they commence their glances by examining the earth at their feet and terminate them by noting everything within the power of human vision; but she rather manifested the quality of impatience than any feeling of alarm.

A short bark from the dog, however, soon gave a new direction to the looks of both, and then the real object of his second warning became dimly visible.

CHAPTER 3

Come, come, thou art as hot a Jack in thy mood as any in Italy; and as soon moved to be moody, and as soon moody to be moved.

ROMEO AND JULIET

THOUGH THE TRAPPER manifested some surprise when he perceived that another human figure was approaching him, and that too from a direction opposite to the place where the emigrant had made his encampment, it was with the steadiness of one long accustomed to scenes of danger.

"This is a man," he said; "and one who has white blood in his veins, or his step would be lighter. It will be well to be ready for the worst, as the half-and-halfs * that one meets in these distant districts are altogether more barbarous than the real savage."

He raised his rifle while he spoke and assured himself of the state of its flint, as well as of the priming, by manual examination. But his arm was arrested while in the act of throwing forward the muzzle of the piece by the eager and trembling hands of his companion.

"For God's sake be not too hasty," she said; "it may be a friend—an acquaintance—a neighbor!"

"A friend!" the old man repeated, deliberately releasing himself at the same time from her grasp. "Friends are rare in any land, and less in this perhaps than in another; and the neighborhood is too thinly settled to make it likely that he who comes towards us is even an acquaintance."

* Half-breeds; men born of Indian women by white fathers. This race has much of the depravity of civilization without the virtues of the savage.

"But though a stranger, you would not seek his blood!"

The trapper earnestly regarded her anxious and frightened features, and then he dropped the butt of his rifle on the ground like one whose purpose had undergone a sudden change.

"No," he said, speaking rather to himself than to his companion, "she is right; blood is not to be spilt to save the life of one so useless and so near his time. Let him come on; my skins, my traps, and even my rifle shall be his if he sees fit to demand them."

"He will ask for neither; he wants neither," returned the girl; "if he be an honest man, he will surely be content with his own and ask for nothing that is the property of another."

The trapper had not time to express the surprise he felt at this incoherent and contradictory language, for the man who was advancing was already within fifty feet of the place where they stood. In the meantime Hector had not been an indifferent witness of what was passing. At the sound of the distant footsteps, he had arisen from his warm bed at the feet of his master; and now, as the stranger appeared in open view, he stalked slowly towards him, crouching to the earth like a panther about to take his leap.

"Call in your dog," said a firm, deep, manly voice in tones of friendship rather than of menace; "I love a hound and should be sorry to do an injury to the animal."

"You hear what is said about you, pup?" the trapper answered. "Come hither, fool. His growl and his bark are all that is left him now; you may come on, friend; the hound is toothless."

The stranger profited by the intelligence. He sprang eagerly forward and at the next instant stood at the side of Ellen Wade. After assuring himself of the identity of the latter by a hasty but keen glance, he turned his attention, with a quickness and impatience that proved the interest he took in the result, to a similar examination of her companion.

"From what cloud have you fallen, my good old man?" he said in a careless, offhand, heedless manner that seemed too natural to be assumed. "Or do you actually live, hereaway, in the prairies?"

"I have been long on earth, and never I hope nigher to heaven than I am at this moment," returned the trapper; "my dwelling, if dwelling I may be said to have, is not far distant. Now may I take the liberty with you that you are so willing to take with others? Whence do you come, and where is your home?"

"Softly, softly; when I have done with my catechism, it will be time to begin with yours. What sport is this you follow by moonlight? You are not dodging the buffaloes at such an hour!"

"I am, as you see, going from an encampment of travelers which lies over yonder swell in the land to my own wigwam; in doing so, I wrong no man."

"All fair and true. And you got this young woman to show you the way because she knows it so well and you know so little about it yourself!"

"I met her, as I have met you, by accident. For ten tiresome years have I dwelt on these open fields, and never before tonight have I found human beings with white skins on them at this hour. If my presence here gives offense, I am sorry and will go my way. It is more than likely that when your young friend has told her story, you will be better given to believe mine."

"Friend," said the youth, lifting a cap of skins from his head and running his fingers leisurely through a dense mass of black and shaggy locks, "if I have ever laid eyes on the girl before tonight, may I——"

"You've said enough, Paul," interrupted the female, laying her hand on his mouth with a familiarity that gave something very like the lie direct to his intended asseveration. "Our secret will be safe with this honest old man. I know it by his looks and kind words."

"Our secret. Ellen, have you forgot——"

"Nothing. I have not forgotten anything I should remember. But still I say we are safe with this honest trapper."

"Trapper! Is he then a trapper? Give me your hand, Father; our trades should bring us acquainted."

"There is little call for handicrafts in this region," returned the other, examining the athletic and active form of the youth as he leaned carelessly and not ungracefully on his rifle; "the art of taking the creatur's of God in traps and nets is one that needs more cunning than manhood; and yet am I brought to practice it in my age! But it would be quite as seemly in one like you to follow a pursuit better becoming your years and courage."

"I! I never took even a slinking mink or a paddling muskrat in a cage, though I admit having peppered a few of the dark-skinned devils when I had much better have kept my powder in the horn and the lead in its pouch. Not I, old man; nothing that crawls the earth is for my sport."

"What then may you do for a living, friend? For little profit is to be made in these districts if a man denies himself his lawful right in the beasts of the fields."

"I deny myself nothing. If a bear crosses my path, he is soon the mere ghost of Bruin. The deer begin to nose me; and as for the buffalo, I have killed more beef, old stranger, than the largest butcher in all Kentuck."

"You can shoot then!" demanded the trapper with a glow of latent fire glimmering about his eyes. "Is your hand true and your look quick?"

"The first is like a steel trap, and the last nimbler than a buckshot. I wish it was hot noon now, grand'ther, and that there was an acre or two of your white swans or of black feathered ducks going south over our heads; you or Ellen here might set your heart on the finest in the flock, and my character against a horn of powder, that the bird would be hanging head downwards in five minutes, and that too with a single ball. I scorn a shotgun! No man can say he ever knew me carry one a rod."

"The lad has good in him! I see it plainly by his manner," said the trapper, turning to Ellen with an encouraging air; "I will take it on myself to say that you are not unwise in meeting him as you do. Tell me, lad, did you ever strike a leaping buck atwixt the antlers? Hector; quiet, pup; quiet. The very name of venison quickens the blood of the cur; did you ever take an animal in that fashion on the long leap?"

"You might just as well ask me, Did you ever eat. There is no fashion, old stranger, that a deer has not been touched by my hand, unless it was when asleep."

"Aye, aye; you have a long and a happy—aye, and an honest life afore you! I am old, and I suppose I might also say worn out and useless; but if it was given me to choose my time and place again—as such things are not and ought not ever to be given to the will of man—though if such a gift was to be given me I would say, twenty and the wilderness! But tell me; how do you part with the peltry?"

"With my pelts! I never took a skin from a buck nor a quill from a goose in my life! I knock them over now and then for a meal, and sometimes to keep my finger true to the touch; but when hunger is satisfied the prairie wolves get the remainder. No—no—I keep to my calling, which pays me better than all the fur I could sell on the other side of the big river."

The old man appeared to ponder a little, but shaking his head, he soon continued, "I know of but one business that can be followed here with profit——"

He was interrupted by the youth, who raised a small cup of tin which dangled at his neck before the other's eyes, and springing its lid, the delicious odor of the finest flavored honey diffused itself over the organs of the trapper.

"A bee hunter!" observed the latter with a readiness that proved he understood the nature of the occupation, though not without some little surprise at discovering one of the other's spirited mien engaged in so humble a pursuit. "It pays well in the skirts of the settlements, but I should call it a doubtful trade in the more open districts."

"You think a tree is wanting for a swarm to settle in! But I know differently; and so I have stretched out a few hundred miles further west than common to taste your honey. And now I have bated your curiosity, stranger, you will just move aside while I tell the remainder of my story to this young woman."

"It is not necessary, I'm sure it is not necessary, that he should leave us," said Ellen with a haste that implied some little consciousness of the singularity if not of the impropriety of the request. "You can have nothing to say that the whole world might not hear."

"No! Well, may I be stung to death by drones if I understand the buzzings of a woman's mind. For my part, Ellen, I care for nothing nor anybody and am just as ready to go down to the place where your uncle, if uncle you can call one who I'll swear is no relation, has hobbled his teams, and tell the old man my mind now, as I shall be a year hence. You have only to say a single word and the thing is done, let him like it or not."

"You are ever so hasty and rash, Paul Hover, that I seldom know when I am safe with you. How can you who know the danger of our being seen together speak of going before my uncle and his sons?"

"Has he done that of which he has reason to be ashamed?" demanded the trapper, who had not moved an inch from the place he first occupied.

"Heaven forbid! But there are reasons why he should not be seen just now, that could do him no harm if known, but which may not yet be told. And so if you will wait, Father, near yonder willow bush until I have heard what Paul can possibly have to say, I shall be sure to come and wish you a good night before I return to the camp."

The trapper drew slowly aside, as if satisfied with the somewhat incoherent reason Ellen had given why he should retire. When completely out of earshot of the earnest and hurried dialogue that instantly commenced between the two he had left, the old man again paused, and patiently awaited the moment when he might renew his conversation with beings in whom he felt a growing interest, no less from the mysterious character of their intercourse than from a natural sympathy in the welfare of a pair so young, and who, as in the simplicity of his heart he was also fain to believe, were also so deserving. He was accompanied by his indolent but attached dog, who once more made his bed at the feet of his master and soon lay slumbering as usual, with his head nearly buried in the dense fog of the prairie grass.

It was a spectacle so unusual to see the human form amid the solitude in which he dwelt that the trapper bent his eyes on the dim figures of his new acquaintances with sensations to which he had long been a stranger. Their presence awakened recollections and emotions to which his sturdy but honest nature had latterly paid but little homage, and his thoughts began to wander over the varied scenes of a life of hardships that had been strangely blended with scenes of wild and peculiar enjoyment. The train taken by his thoughts had already conducted him in imagination far into an ideal world, when he was once more suddenly recalled to the reality of his situation by the movements of the faithful hound.

The dog, who in submission to his years and infirmities had manifested such a decided propensity to sleep, now arose and stalked from out the shadow cast by the tall person of his master and looked abroad into the prairie, as if his instinct apprised him of the presence of still another visitor. Then, seemingly content with his examination, he returned to his comfortable post and disposed of his weary limbs with the deliberation and care of one who was no novice in the art of self-preservation.

"What; again, Hector!" said the trapper in a soothing voice, which he had the caution, however, to utter in an undertone. "What is it, dog? Tell it all to his master, pup; what is it?"

Hector answered with another growl, but was content to continue in his lair. These were evidences of intelligence and distrust to which one as practiced as the trapper could not turn an inattentive ear. He again spoke to the dog, encouraging him to watchfulness by a low, guarded whistle. The animal, however, as if conscious of having already discharged his duty, obstinately refused to raise his head from the grass.

"A hint from such a friend is far better than man's advice!" muttered the trapper as he slowly moved towards the couple who were yet too earnestly and abstractedly engaged in their own discourse to notice his approach; "and none but a conceited settler would hear it and not respect it as he ought. Children," he added when nigh enough to address his companions, "we are not alone in these dreary fields; there are others stirring, and therefore, to the shame of our kind be it said, danger is nigh."

"If one of the lazy sons of skirting Ishmael is prowling out of his camp tonight," said the young bee hunter with great vivacity, and in tones that might easily have been excited to a menace, "he may have an end put to his journey sooner than either he or his father is dreaming!"

"My life on it they are all with the teams," hurriedly answered the girl. "I saw the whole of them asleep myself, except the two on watch; and their natures have greatly changed if they too are not both dreaming of a turkey hunt or a courthouse fight at this very moment."

"Some beast with a strong scent has passed between the wind and the hound, Father, and it makes him uneasy; or perhaps he too is dreaming. I had a pup of my own in Kentuck, that would start upon a long chase from a deep sleep, and all upon the fancy of some dream. Go to him and pinch his ear, that the beast may feel the life within him."

"Not so—not so," returned the trapper, shaking his head as one who better understood the qualities of his dog. "Youth sleeps, aye, and dreams too; but age is awake and watchful. The pup is never false with his nose, and long experience tells me to heed his warnings."

"Did you ever run him upon the trail of carrion?"

"Why, I must say that the ravenous beasts have sometimes tempted me to let him loose, for they are as greedy as men after the venison in its season; but then I know the reason of the dog would tell him the object! No—no, Hector is an animal known in the ways of man and will never strike a false trail when a true one is to be followed!"

"Aye, aye, the secret is out! You have run the hound on the track of a wolf, and his nose has a better memory than his master!" said the bee hunter, laughing.

"I have seen the creatur' sleep for hours with pack after pack in open view. A wolf might eat out of his tray without a snarl unless there was a scarcity; then, indeed, Hector would be apt to claim his own."

"There are panthers down from the mountains; I saw one make a leap at a sick deer as the sun was setting. Go—go you back to the dog, and tell him the truth—Father; in a minute, I——"

He was interrupted by a long, loud, and piteous howl from the hound, which rose on the air of the evening like the wailing of some spirit of the place and passed off into the prairie in cadences that rose and fell like its own undulating surface. The trapper was impressively silent, listening intently. Even the reckless bee hunter was struck with the wailing wildness of the sounds. After a short pause the former whistled the dog to his side, and turning to his companions, he said with the seriousness which in his opinion the occasion demanded, "They who think man enjoys all the knowledge of the creatur's of God will live to be disappointed if they reach, as I have done, the age of fourscore years. I will not take upon myself to say what mischief is brewing, nor will I vouch that even the hound himself knows so much; but that evil is nigh and that wisdom invites us to avoid it, I have heard from the mouth of one who never lies. I did think the pup had become unused to the footsteps of man and that your presence made him uneasy, but his nose has been on a long scent the whole evening, and what I mistook as a notice of your coming has been intended for something more serious. If the advice of an old man is, then, worth hearkening to, children, you will quickly go different ways to your places of shelter and safety."

"If I quit Ellen at such a moment," exclaimed the youth, "may I——"

"You've said enough!" the girl interrupted, by again interposing a hand that might both by its delicacy and color have graced a far more elevated station in life; "my time is out, and we must part at all events—so good night, Paul—Father—good night."

"Hist!" said the youth, seizing her arm as she was in the very act of tripping from his side. "Hist! Do you hear nothing? There are buffaloes playing their pranks at no great distance. That sound beats the earth like a herd of the mad scampering devils!"

His two companions listened, as people in their situation would be apt to lend their faculties to discover the meaning of any doubtful noises, especially when heard after so many and such startling warnings. The unusual sounds were unequivocally, though still faintly, audible. The youth and his female companion had made several hurried and vacillating conjectures concerning their nature when a current of the night air brought the rush of trampling footsteps too sensibly to their ears to render mistake any longer possible.

"I am right!" said the bee hunter. "A panther is driving a herd before him, or maybe there is a battle among the beasts."

"Your ears are cheats," returned the old man, who, from the moment his own organs had been able to catch the distant sounds, stood like a statue made to represent deep attention; "the leaps are too long for the buffalo and too regular for terror. Hist! Now they are in a bottom where the grass is high and the sound is deadened! Aye, there they go on the hard earth! And now they come up the swell, dead upon us; they will be here afore you can find a cover!"

"Come, Ellen," cried the youth, seizing his companion by the hand, "let us make a trial for the encampment."

"Too late! Too late," exclaimed the trapper, "for the creatur's are in open view; and a bloody band of accursed Siouxes they are, by their thieving look and the random fashion in which they ride!"

"Siouxes or devils, they shall find *us* men!" said the bee hunter with a mien as fierce as if he led a party of superior strength and of a courage equal to his own. "You have a piece, old man, and will pull a trigger in behalf of a helpless Christian girl!"

"Down, down into the grass—down with ye both," whispered the trapper, intimating to them to turn aside to the tall weeds, which grew in a denser body than common near the place where they stood. "You've not the time to fly, nor the numbers to fight, foolish boy. Down into the grass, if you prize the young woman or value the gift of life!"

His remonstrance, seconded as it was by a prompt and energetic action, did not fail to produce the submission to his order which the occasion seemed, indeed, imperiously to require. The moon had fallen behind a sheet of thin, fleecy clouds which skirted the horizon, leaving just enough of its faint and fluctuating light to render objects visible, dimly revealing their forms and proportions. The trapper, by exercising that species of influence over his companions which experience and decision usually assert in cases of emergency, had effectually succeeded in concealing them in the grass; and by the aid of the feeble rays of the luminary, he was enabled to scan the disorderly party which was riding, like so many madmen, directly upon them.

A band of beings who resembled demons rather than men, sporting in their nightly revels across the bleak plain, was in truth approaching at a fearful rate, and in a direction to leave little hope that someone among them, at least, would not pass over the spot where the trapper and his companions lay. At intervals the clattering of hoofs was borne along by the night wind, quite audibly in their front, and then again their progress through the fog of the autumnal grass was swift and silent, adding to the unearthly appearance of the spectacle. The trapper, who had called in his hound and bidden him crouch at his side, now kneeled in the cover also and kept a keen and watchful eye on the route of the band, soothing the fears of the girl and restraining the impatience of the youth in the same breath.

"If there's one, there's thirty of the miscreants!" he said in a sort of episode to his whispered comments. "Aye, aye; they are edging towards the river—peace, pup—peace—no, here they come this way again—the thieves don't seem to know their own errand! If there were just six of us, lad, what a beautiful ambushment we might make upon them from this very spot—it won't do, it won't do, boy; keep yourself closer, or your head will be seen—besides, I'm not altogether strong in the opinion it would be lawful, as they have done us no harm. There they bend again to the river— no; here they come up the swell, now is the moment to be as still as if the breath had done its duty and departed the body."

The old man sank into the grass while he was speaking,

as if the final separation to which he alluded had in his own case actually occurred, and at the next instant a band of wild horsemen whirled by them with the noiseless rapidity in which it might be imagined a troop of specters would pass. The dark and fleeting forms were already vanished when the trapper ventured again to raise his head to a level with the tops of the bending herbage, motioning at the same time to his companions to maintain their positions and their silence.

"They are going down the swell towards the encampment," he continued in his former guarded tones; "no, they halt in the bottom and are clustering together like deer in council. By the Lord, they are turning again, and we are not yet done with the reptiles!"

Once more he sought his friendly cover, and at the next instant the dark troop were to be seen riding in a disorderly manner on the very summit of the little elevation on which the trapper and his companions lay. It was now soon apparent that they had returned to avail themselves of the height of the ground in order to examine the dim horizon.

Some dismounted, while others rode to and fro like men engaged in a local inquiry of much interest. Happily for the hidden party, the grass in which they were concealed not only served to screen them from the eyes of the savages, but opposed an obstacle to prevent their horses, which were no less rude and untrained than their riders, from trampling on them in their irregular and wild paces.

At length an athletic and dark-looking Indian who, by his air of authority, would seem to be the leader summoned his chiefs about him to a consultation, which was held mounted. This body was collected on the very margin of that mass of herbage in which the trapper and his companions were hid. As the young man looked up and saw the fierce aspect of the group, which was increasing at each instant by the accession of some countenance and figure apparently more forbidding than any which had preceded it, he drew his rifle, by a very natural impulse, from beneath him and commenced putting it in a state for service. The female at his side buried her face in the grass by a feeling that was possibly quite as natural to her sex and habits, leaving him to follow the impulses of his hot blood; but his aged and more prudent adviser whispered sternly in his ear, "The tick of the lock is as well known to the knaves as the blast of a trumpet to a soldier! Lay down the piece —lay down the piece—should the moon touch the barrel, it could not fail to be seen by the devils, whose eyes are keener than the blackest snake's! The smallest motion now would be sure to bring an arrow among us."

The bee hunter so far obeyed as to continue immovable and silent. But there was still sufficient light to convince his companion, by the contracted brow and threatening eye of the young man, that a discovery would not bestow a bloodless victory on the savages. Finding his advice disregarded, the trapper took his measures accordingly and awaited the result with a resignation and calmness that were characteristic of the individual.

In the meantime, the Sioux (for the sagacity of the old man was not deceived in the character of his dangerous neighbors) had terminated their council and were again dispersed along the ridge of land as if they sought some hidden object.

"The imps have heard the hound," whispered the trapper, "and their ears are too true to be cheated in the distance. Keep close, lad, keep close; down with your head to the very earth, like a dog that sleeps."

"Let us rather take to our feet and trust to manhood," returned his impatient companion.

He would have proceeded, but feeling a hand laid rudely on his shoulder, he turned his eyes upwards and beheld the dark and savage countenance of an Indian gleaming full upon him. Notwithstanding the surprise and the disadvantage of his attitude, the youth was not disposed to become a captive so easily. Quicker than a flash of his own gun he sprang upon his feet and was throttling his opponent with a power that would soon have terminated the contest, when he felt the arms of the trapper thrown around his body, confining his exertions by a strength very little inferior to his own. Before he had time to reproach his comrade for this apparent treachery, a dozen Sioux were around them, and the whole party were compelled to yield themselves as prisoners.

CHAPTER 4

——With much more dismay
I view the fight, than those who make the fray.
THE MERCHANT OF VENICE

THE UNFORTUNATE BEE HUNTER and his companions had become the captives of a people who might, without exaggeration, be called the Ishmaelites of the American deserts. From time immemorial the hands of the Sioux had been turned against their neighbors of the prairies; and even at this day, when the influence and authority of a civilized government are beginning to be felt around them, they are considered a treacherous and dangerous race. At the period of our tale the case was far worse, few white men trusting themselves in the remote and unprotected regions where so false a tribe was known to dwell.

Notwithstanding the peaceable submission of the trapper, he was quite aware of the character of the band into whose hands he had fallen. It would have been difficult, however, for the nicest judge to have determined whether fear, policy, or resignation formed the secret motive of the old man in permitting himself to be plundered as he did, without a murmur. So far from opposing any remonstrance to the rude and violent manner in which his conquerors performed the customary office, he even anticipated their cupidity by tendering to the chiefs such articles as he thought might prove the most acceptable. On the other hand, Paul Hover, who had been literally a conquered man, manifested the strongest repugnance to submit to the violent liberties that were taken with his person and property. He even gave several exceedingly unequivocal demonstrations of his displeasure during the summary process and would more than once have broken out in open and desperate resistance but for the admonitions and entreaties of the trembling girl, who clung to his side in a manner so dependent as to show the youth that her hopes were now placed no less on his discretion than on his disposition to serve her.

The Indians had, however, no sooner deprived the captives of their arms and ammunition and stripped them of a few articles of dress of little use, and perhaps of less value,

41

than they appeared disposed to grant them a respite. Business of greater moment pressed on their hands and required their attention. Another consultation of the chiefs was convened, and it was apparent by the earnest and vehement manner of the few who spoke that the warriors conceived their success as yet to be far from complete.

"It will be well," whispered the trapper, who knew enough of the language he heard to comprehend perfectly the subject of the discussion, "if the travelers who lie near the willow brake are not awoke out of their sleep by a visit from these miscreants. They are too cunning to believe that a woman of the 'palefaces' is to be found so far from the settlements without having a white man's inventions and comforts at hand."

"If they will carry the tribe of wandering Ishmael to the Rocky Mountains," said the young bee hunter, laughing in his vexation with a sort of bitter merriment, "I may forgive the rascals."

"Paul! Paul!" exclaimed his companion in a tone of reproach. "You forget all! Think of the dreadful consequences!"

"Aye, it was thinking of what you call consequences, Ellen, that prevented me from putting the matter at once to yonder red devil and making it a real knock-down and drag-out! Old trapper, the sin of this cowardly business lies on your shoulders! But it is no more than your daily calling, I reckon, to take men, as well as beasts, in snares."

"I implore you, Paul, to be calm—to be patient."

"Well, since it is your wish, Ellen," returned the youth, endeavoring to swallow his spleen, "I will make the trial; though, as you ought to know, it is part of the religion of a Kentuckian to fret himself a little at a mischance."

"I fear your friends in the other bottom will not escape the eyes of the imps!" continued the trapper as coolly as though he had not heard a syllable of the intervening discourse. "They scent plunder; and it would be as hard to drive a hound from his game as to throw the varmints from its trail."

"Is there nothing to be done?" asked Ellen in an imploring manner which proved the sincerity of her concern.

"It would be an easy matter to call out, in so loud a voice as to make old Ishmael dream that the wolves were among his flock," Paul replied; "I can make myself heard a mile in these open fields, and his camp is but a short quarter from us."

"And get knocked on the head for your pains," returned the trapper. "No, no; cunning must match cunning, or the hounds will murder the whole family."

"Murder! No—no murder. Ishmael loves travel so well, there would be no harm in his having a look at the other sea, but the old fellow is in a bad condition to take the long journey! I would try a lock myself before he should be quite murdered."

"His party is strong in number, and well armed; do you think it will fight?"

"Look here, old trapper; few men love Ishmael Bush and his seven sledgehammer sons less than one Paul Hover, but I scorn to slander even a Tennessee shotgun. There is as much of the true stand-up courage among them as there is in any family that was ever raised in Kentuck itself. They are a long-sided and a double-jointed breed; and let me tell you, that he who takes the measure of one of them on the ground must be a workman at a hug."

"Hist! The savages have done their talk and are about to set their accursed devices in motion. Let us be patient; something may yet offer in favor of your friends."

"Friends! Call none of the race a friend of mine, trapper, if you have the smallest regard for my affection! What I say in their favor is less from love than honesty."

"I did not know but the young woman was of the kin," returned the other a little drily, "but no offense should be taken where none was intended."

The mouth of Paul was again stopped by the hand of Ellen, who took upon herself to reply in her conciliating tones, "We should be all of a family when it is in our power to serve each other. We depend entirely on your experience, honest old man, to discover the means to apprise our friends of their danger."

"There will be a real time of it," muttered the bee hunter, laughing, "if the boys get at work, in good earnest, with these redskins!"

He was interrupted by a general movement which took place among the band. The Indians dismounted to a man, giving their horses in charge to three or four of the party, who were also intrusted with the safekeeping of the prisoners. They then formed themselves in a circle around a warrior who appeared to possess the chief authority, and at a given signal the whole array moved slowly and cautiously from the center in straight and consequently in diverging lines. Most of their dark forms were soon blended with the brown covering of the prairie, though the captives, who watched the slightest movement of their enemies with vigilant eyes, were now and then enabled to discern a human figure drawn against the horizon as someone more eager than the rest rose to his greatest height in order to extend the limits of his view. But it was not long before even these fugitive glimpses of the moving and constantly increasing circle were lost, and uncertainty and conjecture were added to apprehension. In this manner passed many anxious and weary minutes, during the close of which the listeners expected at each moment to hear the whoop of the assailants and the shrieks of the assailed rising together on the stillness of the night. But it would seem that the search which was so evidently making was without a sufficient object, for at the expiration of half an hour the different individuals of the band began to return singly, gloomy and sullen, like men who were disappointed.

"Our time is at hand," observed the trapper, who noted the smallest incident or the slightest indication of hostility among the savages; "we are now to be questioned, and if I know anything of the policy of our case, I should say it would be wise to choose one among us to hold the discourse in order that our testimony may agree. And furthermore, if an opinion from one as old and as worthless as a hunter of fourscore is to be regarded, I would just venture to say that man should be the one most skilled in the natur' of an Indian and that he should also know something of their language. Are you acquainted with the tongue of the Siouxes, friend?"

"Swarm your own hive," returned the discontented bee hunter. "You are good at buzzing, old trapper, if you are good at nothing else."

" 'Tis the gift of youth to be rash and heady," the trapper calmly retorted. "The day has been, boy, when my blood was like your own, too swift and too hot to run quietly in my veins. But what will it profit to talk of silly risks and foolish acts at this time of life? A gray head should cover a brain of reason, and not the tongue of a boaster."

"True, true," whispered Ellen; "and we have other things

to attend to now! Here comes the Indian to put his questions."

The girl, whose apprehensions had quickened her senses, was not deceived. She was yet speaking when a tall, half-naked savage approached the spot where they stood, and after examining the whole party as closely as the dim light permitted, for more than a minute in perfect stillness, he gave the usual salutation in the harsh and guttural tones of his own language. The trapper replied as well as he could, which it seems was sufficiently well to be understood. In order to escape the imputation of pedantry we shall render the substance and, so far as it is possible, the form of the dialogue that succeeded into the English tongue.

"Have the palefaces eaten their own buffaloes and taken the skins from all their own beavers," continued the savage, allowing the usual moment of decorum to elapse after the words of greeting before he again spoke, "that they come to count how many are left among the Pawnees?"

"Some of us are here to buy, and some to sell," returned the trapper; "but none will follow if they hear it is not safe to come nigh the lodge of a Sioux."

"The Siouxes are thieves, and they live among the snow; why do we talk of a people who are so far, when we are in the country of the Pawnees?"

"If the Pawnees are the owners of this land, then white and red are here by equal right."

"Have not the palefaces stolen enough from the red men, that you come so far to carry a lie? I have said that this is a hunting ground of my tribe."

"My right to be here is equal to your own," the trapper rejoined with undisturbed coolness; "I do not speak as I might—it is better to be silent. The Pawnees and the white men are brothers, but a Sioux dare not show his face in the village of the Loups."

"The Dakotas are men!" exclaimed the savage fiercely, forgetting in his anger to maintain the character he had assumed and using the appellation of which his nation was most proud; "the Dakotas have no fear! Speak; what brings you so far from the villages of the palefaces?"

"I have seen the sun rise and set on many councils and have heard the words of wise men. Let your chiefs come, and my mouth shall not be shut."

"I am a great chief!" said the savage, affecting an air of

offended dignity. "Do you take me for an Assiniboin? Weucha is a warrior often named, and much believed!"

"Am I a fool not to know a burnt-wood Teton?" demanded the trapper with a steadiness that did great credit to his nerves. "Go; it is dark, and you do not see that my head is gray!"

The Indian now appeared convinced that he had adopted too shallow an artifice to deceive one so practiced as the man he addressed, and he was deliberating what fiction he should next invent in order to obtain his real object when a slight commotion among the band put an end at once to all his schemes. Casting his eyes behind him as if fearful of a speedy interruption, he said in tones much less pretending than those he had first resorted to, "Give Weucha the milk of the Long Knives, and he will sing your name in the ears of the great men of his tribe."

"Go," repeated the trapper, motioning him away with strong disgust. "Your young men are speaking of Mahtoree. My words are for the ears of a chief."

The savage cast a look on the other which, notwithstanding the dim light, was sufficiently indicative of implacable hostility. He then stole away among his fellows, anxious to conceal the counterfeit he had attempted to practice no less than the treachery he had contemplated against a fair division of the spoils from the man named by the trapper, whom he now also knew to be approaching by the manner in which his name passed from one to another in the band. He had hardly disappeared before a warrior of powerful frame advanced out of the dark circle and placed himself before the captives with that high and proud bearing for which a distinguished Indian chief is ever so remarkable. He was followed by all the party, who arranged themselves around his person in a deep and respectful silence.

"The earth is very large," the chief commenced after a pause of that true dignity which his counterfeit had so miserably affected; "why can the children of my great white father never find room on it?"

"Some among them have heard that their friends in the prairies are in want of many things," returned the trapper, "and they have come to see if it be true. Some want, in their turns, what the red men are willing to sell, and they come to make their friends rich with powder and blankets."

"Do traders cross the big river with empty hands?"

"Our hands are empty because your young men thought we were tired, and they have lightened us of our load. They were mistaken; I am old, but I am still strong."

"It cannot be. Your load has fallen in the prairies. Show my young men the place, that they may pick it up before the Pawnees find it."

"The path to the spot is crooked, and it is night. The hour is come for sleep," said the trapper with perfect composure. "Bid your warriors go over yonder hill; there is water and there is wood; let them light their fires and sleep with warm feet. When the sun comes again I will speak to you."

A low murmur, but one that was clearly indicative of dissatisfaction, passed among the attentive listeners and served to inform the old man that he had not been sufficiently wary in proposing a measure that he intended should notify the travelers in the brake of the presence of their dangerous neighbors. Mahtoree, however, without betraying in the slightest degree the excitement which was so strongly exhibited by his companions, continued the discourse in the same lofty manner as before.

"I know that my friend is rich," he said, "that he has many warriors not far off, and that horses are plentier with him than dogs among the redskins."

"You see my warriors and my horses."

"What! Has the woman the feet of a Dakota, that she can walk for thirty nights in the prairies and not fall! I know the red men of the woods make long marches on foot, but we, who live where the eye cannot see from one lodge to another, love our horses."

The trapper now hesitated, in his turn. He was perfectly aware that deception, if detected, might prove dangerous, and for one of his pursuits and character he was strongly troubled with an unaccommodating regard for the truth. But recollecting that he controlled the fate of others as well as of himself, he determined to let things take their course and to permit the Dakota chief to deceive himself if he would.

"The women of the Siouxes and of the white men are not of the same wigwam," he answered evasively. "Would a Teton warrior make his wife greater than himself? I know he would not; and yet my ears have heard that there are lands where the councils are held by squaws."

Another slight movement in the dark circle apprised the

trapper that his declaration was not received without surprise, if entirely without distrust. The chief alone seemed unmoved, nor was he disposed to relax from the loftiness and high dignity of his air.

"My white fathers who live on the Great Lakes have declared," he said, "that their brothers towards the rising sun are not men; and now I know they did not lie! Go—what is a nation whose chief is a squaw! Are you the dog and not the husband of this woman?"

"I am neither. Never did I see her face before this day. She came into the prairies because they had told her a great and generous nation called the Dakotas lived there, and she wished to look on men. The women of the palefaces, like the women of the Siouxes, open their eyes to see things that are new; but she is poor, like myself, and she will want corn and buffaloes if you take away the little that she and her friend still have."

"My ears listen to many wicked lies!" exclaimed the Teton warrior in a voice so stern that it startled even his red auditors. "Am I a woman? Has not a Dakota eyes? Tell me, white hunter, who are the men of your color that sleep near the fallen trees?"

As he spoke, the indignant chief pointed in the direction of Ishmael's encampment, leaving the trapper no reason to doubt that the superior industry and sagacity of this man had effected a discovery which had eluded the search of the rest of his party. Notwithstanding his regret at an event that might prove fatal to the sleepers, and some little vexation at having been so completely outwitted in the dialogue just related, the old man continued to maintain his air of inflexible composure.

"It may be true," he answered, "that white men are sleeping in the prairie. If my brother says it, it is true; but what men thus trust to the generosity of the Tetons I cannot tell. If there be strangers asleep, send your young men to wake them up, and let them say why they are here; every paleface has a tongue."

The chief shook his head with a wild and fierce smile, answering abruptly as he turned away to put an end to the conference, "The Dakotas are a wise race, and Mahtoree is their chief! He will not call to the strangers, that they may rise and speak to him with their carbines. He will whisper softly

in their ears. When this is done, let the men of their own
color come and awake them!"

As he uttered these words and turned on his heel, a low
and approving laugh passed around the dark circle, which
instantly broke its order and followed him to a little distance from the stand of the captives, where those who might
presume to mingle opinions with so great a warrior again
gathered about him in consultation. Weucha profited by
this occasion to renew his importunities, but the trapper, who
had discovered how great a counterfeit he was, shook him
off in displeasure. An end was, however, more effectually
put to the annoyance of this malignant savage by a mandate
for the whole party, including men and beasts, to change
their positions. The movement was made in dead silence and
with an order that would have done credit to more enlightened beings. A halt, however, was soon made, and when
the captives had time to look about them, they found
they were in view of the low, dark outline of the copse
near which lay the slumbering party of Ishmael.

Here another short but grave and deliberative consultation
was held.

The beasts, which seemed trained to such covert and silent
attacks, were once more placed under the care of keepers,
who as before were charged with the duty of watching the
prisoners. The mind of the trapper was in no degree relieved from the uneasiness which was at each instant getting
a stronger possession of him when he found Weucha was
placed nearest to his own person, and as it appeared by the
air of triumph and authority he assumed, at the head of the
guard also. The savage, however, who doubtless had his
secret instructions, was content for the present with making
a significant gesture with his tomahawk, which menaced
death to Ellen. After admonishing in this expressive manner his male captives of the fate that would instantly attend
their female companion on the slightest alarm proceeding from any of the party, he was content to maintain a rigid silence. This unexpected forbearance on the
part of Weucha enabled the trapper and his two associates
to give their undivided attention to the little that might
be seen of the interesting movements which were passing
in their front.

Mahtoree took the entire disposition of the arrangements
on himself. He pointed out the precise situation he wished

each individual to occupy, like one intimately acquainted with the qualifications of his respective followers, and he was obeyed with the deference and promptitude with which an Indian warrior is wont to submit to the instructions of his chief in moments of trial. Some he dispatched to the right, and others to the left. Each man departed with the noiseless and quick step peculiar to the race until all had assumed their allotted stations, with the exception of two chosen warriors, who remained nigh the person of their leader. When the rest had disappeared, Mahtoree turned to these select companions and intimated by a sign that the critical moment had arrived when the enterprise he contemplated was to be put in execution.

Each man laid aside the light fowling piece which, under the name of a carbine, he carried in virtue of his rank, and divesting himself of every article of exterior or heavy clothing, he stood resembling a dark and fierce looking statue, in the attitude, and nearly in the garb, of nature. Mahtoree assured himself of the right position of his tomahawk, felt that his knife was secure in its sheath of skin, tightened his girdle of wampum, and saw that the lacing of his fringed and ornamented leggings was secure and likely to offer no impediment to his exertions. Thus prepared at all points, and ready for his desperate undertaking, the Teton gave the signal to proceed.

The three advanced in a line with the encampment of the travelers until, in the dim light by which they were seen, their dusky forms were nearly lost to the eyes of the prisoners. Here they paused, looking around them like men who deliberate and ponder long on the consequences before they take a desperate leap. Then sinking together, they became lost in the grass of the prairie.

It is not difficult to imagine the distress and anxiety of the different spectators of these threatening movements. Whatever might be the reasons of Ellen for entertaining so strong attachment to the family in which she has first been seen by the reader, the feelings of her sex and perhaps some lingering seeds of kindness predominated. More than once she felt tempted to brave the awful and instant danger that awaited such an offense and to raise her feeble and in truth impotent voice in warning. So strong, indeed, and so very natural was the inclination that she would most probably have put it into execution but for the often-repeated, though whispered remonstrances of Paul Hover. In the breast of the young bee hunter himself there was a singular union of emotions. His first and chiefest solicitude was certainly in behalf of his gentle and dependent companion; but the sense of her danger was mingled in the breast of the reckless woodsman with a consciousness of a high and wild, and by no means an unpleasant, excitement. Though united to the emigrants by ties still less binding than those of Ellen, he longed to hear the crack of their rifles, and, had occasion offered, he would gladly have been among the first to rush to their rescue. There were, in truth, moments when he felt in his turn an impulse that was nearly resistless to spring forward and awake the unconscious sleepers; but a glance at Ellen would serve to recall his tottering prudence and to admonish him of the consequences. The trapper alone remained calm and observant, as if nothing that involved his personal comfort or safety had occurred. His ever-moving, vigilant eyes watched the smallest change with the composure of one too long inured to scenes of danger to be easily moved, and with an expression of cool determination which denoted the intention he actually harbored of profiting by the smallest oversight on the part of the captors.

In the meantime the Teton warriors had not been idle. Profiting by the high fog which grew in the bottoms, they had wormed their way through the matted grass like so many treacherous serpents stealing on their prey, until the point was gained where an extraordinary caution became necessary to their further advance. Mahtoree alone had occasionally elevated his dark, grim countenance above the herbage, straining his eyeballs to penetrate the gloom which skirted the border of the brake. In these momentary glances he gained sufficient knowledge, added to that he had obtained in his former search, to be the perfect master of the position of his intended victims, though he was still profoundly ignorant of their numbers and of their means of defense.

His efforts to possess himself of the requisite knowledge concerning these two latter and essential points were, however, completely baffled by the stillness of the camp, which lay in a quiet as deep as if it were literally a place of the dead. Too wary and distrustful to rely, in circumstances of so much doubt, on the discretion of any less firm and crafty than himself, the Dakota bade his companions remain where they lay, and pursued the adventure alone.

The progress of Mahtoree was now slow, and to one less accustomed to such a species of exercise, it would have proved painfully laborious. But the advance of the wily snake itself is not more certain or noiseless than was his approach. He drew his form, foot by foot, through the bending grass, pausing at each movement to catch the smallest sound that might betray any knowledge on the part of the travelers of his proximity. He succeeded at length in dragging himself out of the sickly light of the moon into the shadows of the brake, where not only his own dark person was much less liable to be seen, but where the surrounding objects became more distinctly visible to his keen and active glances.

Here the Teton paused long and wearily to make his observations before he ventured further. His position enabled him to bring the whole encampment, with its tent, wagons, and lodges, into a dark but clearly marked profile, furnishing a clue by which the practiced warrior was led to a tolerably accurate estimate of the force he was about to encounter. Still an unnatural silence pervaded the spot, as if men suppressed even the quiet breathings of sleep in order to render the appearance of their confidence more evident. The chief bent his head to the earth and listened intently. He was about to raise it again in disappointment when the long-drawn and trembling respiration of one who slumbered imperfectly met his ear. The Indian was too well skilled in all the means of deception to become himself the victim of any common artifice. He knew the sound to be natural by its peculiar quivering, and he hesitated no longer.

A man of nerves less tried than those of the fierce and conquering Mahtoree would have been keenly sensible of all the hazard he incurred. The reputation of those hardy and powerful white adventurers who so often penetrated the wilds inhabited by his people was well known to him; but while he drew nigher with the respect and caution that a brave enemy never fails to inspire, it was with the vindictive animosity of a red man, jealous and resentful of the inroads of the stranger.

Turning from the line of his former route, the Teton dragged himself directly towards the margin of the thicket. When this material object was effected in safety, he arose to his seat and took a better survey of his situation. A single moment served to apprise him of the place where the unsuspecting traveler lay. The reader will readily anticipate that the savage had succeeded in gaining a dangerous proximity to one of those slothful sons of Ishmael who were deputed to watch over the isolated encampment of the travelers.

When certain that he was undiscovered, the Dakota raised his person again, and bending forward, he moved his dark visage above the face of the sleeper in that sort of wanton and subtle manner with which the reptile is seen to play about its victim before it strikes. Satisfied at length not only of the condition but of the character of the stranger, Mahtoree was in the act of withdrawing his head when a slight movement of the sleeper announced the symptoms of reviving consciousness. The savage seized the knife which hung at his girdle, and in an instant it was poised above the breast of the young emigrant. Then changing his purpose, with an action as rapid as his own flashing thoughts he sank back behind the trunk of the fallen tree against which the other reclined, and lay in its shadow, as dark, as motionless, and apparently as insensible as the wood itself.

The slothful sentinel opened his heavy eyes, and gazing upwards for a moment at the hazy heavens, he made an extraordinary exertion and raised his powerful frame from the support of the log. Then he looked about him with an air of something like watchfulness, suffering his dull glances to run over the misty objects of the encampment until they finally settled on the distant and dim field of the open prairie. Meeting with nothing more attractive than the same faint outlines of swell and interval which everywhere rose before his drowsy eyes, he changed his position so as completely to turn his back on his dangerous neighbor, and suffered his person to sink sluggishly down into its former recumbent attitude. A long and, on the part of the Teton, an anxious and painful silence succeeded before the deep breathing of the traveler again announced that he was indulging in his slumbers. The savage was, however, far too jealous of a counterfeit to trust to the first appearance of sleep. But the fatigues of a day of unusual toil lay too heavy on the sentinel to leave the other long in doubt. Still the motion with which Mahtoree again raised himself to his knees was so noiseless and guarded that even a vigilant observer might have hesitated to believe he stirred. The change was, however, at length effected, and the Dakota chief then bent again over his enemy, without having produced a noise louder than that of the cottonwood leaf which fluttered at his side in the currents of the passing air.

Mahtoree now felt himself master of the sleeper's fate. At the same time that he scanned the vast proportions and athletic limbs of the youth in that sort of admiration which physical excellence seldom fails to excite in the breast of a savage, he coolly prepared to extinguish the principle of vitality which could alone render them formidable. After making himself sure of the seat of life by gently removing the folds of the intervening cloth, he raised his keen weapon and was about to unite his strength and skill in the impending blow when the young man threw his brawny arm carelessly backwards, exhibiting in the action the vast volume of its muscles.

The sagacious and wary Teton paused. It struck his acute faculties that sleep was less dangerous to him at that moment than even death itself might prove. The smallest noise, the agony of struggling, with which such a frame would probably relinquish its hold of life suggested themselves to his rapid thoughts, and were all present to his experienced senses. He looked back into the encampment, turned his head into the thicket, and glanced his glowing eyes abroad into the wild and silent prairies. Bending once more over the respited victim, he assured himself that he was sleeping heavily, and then abandoned his immediate purpose in obedience alone to the suggestions of a more crafty policy.

The retreat of Mahtoree was as still and guarded as had been his approach. He now took the direction of the encampment, stealing along the margin of the brake as a cover into which he might easily plunge at the smallest alarm. The drapery of the solitary hut attracted his notice in passing. After examining the whole of its exterior and listening with painful intensity in order to gather counsel from his ears, the savage ventured to raise the cloth at the bottom and to thrust his dark visage beneath. It might have been a minute before the Teton chief drew back and seated himself with the whole of his form without the linen tenement. Here he sat, seemingly brooding over his discovery, for many moments, in rigid inaction. Then he resumed his crouching attitude and once more projected his visage beyond the covering of the tent. His second visit to the interior was longer and, if possible, more ominous than the first. But it had, like everything else, its termination, and the savage again withdrew his glaring eyes from the secrets of the place.

Mahtoree had drawn his person many yards from the spot in his slow progress towards the cluster of objects which pointed out the center of the position before he again stopped. He made another pause and looked back at the solitary little dwelling he had left, as if doubtful whether he should not return. But the chevaux-de-frise of branches now lay within reach of his arm, and the very appearance of precaution it presented, as it announced the value of the effects it encircled, tempted his cupidity and induced him to proceed.

The passage of the savage through the tender and brittle limbs of the cottonwood could be likened only to the sinuous and noiseless winding of the reptiles which he imitated. When he had effected his object and had taken an instant to become acquainted with the nature of the localities within the enclosure, the Teton used the precaution to open a way through which he might make a swift retreat. Then raising himself on his feet, he stalked through the encampment like the master of evil, seeking whom and what he should first devote to his fell purposes. He had already ascertained the contents of the lodge in which were collected the woman and her young children and had passed several gigantic frames stretched on different piles of brush which happily for him lay in unconscious helplessness, when he reached the spot occupied by Ishmael in person. It could not escape the sagacity of one like Mahtoree that he had now within his power the principal man among the travelers. He stood long hovering above the recumbent and herculean form of the emigrant, keenly debating in his own mind the chances of his enterprise and the most effectual means of reaping its richest harvest.

He sheathed the knife, which, under the hasty and burning impulse of his thoughts, he had been tempted to draw, and was passing on when Ishmael turned in his lair and demanded roughly who was moving before his half-opened eyes. Nothing short of the readiness and cunning of a savage could have evaded the crisis. Imitating the gruff tones and nearly unintelligible sounds he heard, Mahtoree threw his body heavily on the earth and appeared to dispose himself to sleep. Though the whole movement was seen by Ishmael in a sort of stupid observation, the artifice was too bold and too admirably executed to fail. The drowsy father closed his eyes and slept heavily, with this treacherous inmate in the very bosom of his family.

It was necessary for the Teton to maintain the position he had taken for many long and weary minutes in order to make sure that he was no longer watched. Though his body lay so motionless, his active mind was not idle. He profited by the delay to mature a plan which he intended should put the whole encampment, including both its effects and their proprietors, entirely at his mercy. The instant he could do so with safety, the indefatigable savage was again in motion. He took his way towards the slight pen which contained the domestic animals, worming himself along the ground in his former subtle and guarded manner.

The first animal he encountered among the beasts occasioned a long and hazardous delay. The weary creature, perhaps conscious through its secret instinct that in the endless wastes of the prairies its surest protector was to be found in man, was so exceedingly docile as quietly to submit to the close examination it was doomed to undergo. The hand of the wandering Teton passed over the downy coat, the meek countenance, and the slender limbs of the gentle creature with untiring curiosity; but he finally abandoned the prize as useless in his predatory expeditions and offering too little temptation to the appetite. As soon, however, as he found himself among the beasts of burden, his gratification was extreme, and it was with difficulty that he restrained the customary ejaculations of pleasure that were more than once on the point of bursting from his lips. Here he lost sight of the hazards by which he had gained access to his dangerous position, and the watchfulness of the wary and long-practiced warrior was momentarily forgotten in the exultation of the savage.

CHAPTER 5

Why, worthy father, what have we to lose?
　　　—The law
Protects us not. Then why should we be tender
To let an arrogant piece of flesh threat us!　
Play judge and executioner.

CYMBELINE

WHILE THE TETON thus enacted his subtle and characteristic part, not a sound broke the stillness of the surrounding prairie. The whole band lay at their several posts waiting with the well-known patience of the natives for the
signal which was to summon them to action. To the eyes
of the anxious spectators who occupied the little eminence,
already described as the position of the captives, the scene
presented the broad, solemn view of a waste, dimly lighted
by the glimmering rays of a clouded moon. The place of
the encampment was marked by a gloom deeper than that
which faintly shadowed out the courses of the bottoms, and
here and there a brighter streak tinged the rolling summits of the ridges. As for the rest, it was the deep, imposing quiet of a desert.

But to those who so well knew how much was brooding beneath this mantle of stillness and night, it was a scene
of high and wild excitement. Their anxiety gradually increased as minute after minute passed away and not the
smallest sound of life arose out of the calm and darkness
which enveloped the brake. The breathing of Paul grew louder
and deeper, and more than once Ellen trembled at she knew
not what as she felt the quivering of his active frame
while she leaned dependently on his arm for support.

The shallow honesty as well as the besetting infirmity of
Weucha have already been exhibited. The reader, therefore,
will not be surprised to learn that he was the first to forget
the regulations he had himself imposed. It was at the precise
moment when we left Mahtoree yielding to his nearly ungovernable delight as he surveyed the number and quality of
Ishmael's beasts of burden that the man he had selected to
watch his captives chose to indulge in the malignant pleasure of tormenting those it was his duty to protect. Bending his head nigh the ear of the trapper, the savage rather

muttered than whispered, "If the Tetons lose their great chief by the hands of the Long Knives,* old shall die as well as young!"

"Life is the gift of the Wahcondah," was the unmoved reply. "The burnt-wood warrior must submit to his laws, as well as his other children. Men only die when *He* chooses; and no Dakota can change the hour."

"Look!" returned the savage, thrusting the blade of his knife before the face of his captive. "Weucha is the Wahcondah of a dog."

The old man raised his eyes to the fierce visage of his keeper, and for a moment a gleam of honest and powerful disgust shot from their deep cells; but it instantly passed away, leaving in its place an expression of commiseration, if not of sorrow.

"Why should one made in the real image of God suffer his natur' to be provoked by a mere effigy of reason?" he said in English, and in tones much louder than those in which Weucha had chosen to pitch the conversation. The latter profited by the unintentional offense of his captive, and seizing him by the thin, gray locks that fell from beneath his cap, was on the point of passing the blade of his knife in malignant triumph around their roots when a long, shrill yell rent the air and was instantly echoed from the surrounding waste, as if a thousand demons opened their throats in common at the summons. Weucha relinquished his grasp and uttered a cry of exultation.

"Now!" shouted Paul, unable to control his impatience any longer. "Now, old Ishmael, is the time to show the native blood of Kentucky! Fire low, boys—level into the swales, for the redskins are settling to the very earth!"

His voice was, however, lost, or rather unheeded, in the midst of the shrieks, shouts, and yells that were by this time bursting from fifty mouths on every side of him. The guards still maintained their posts at the side of the captives, but it was with that sort of difficulty with which steeds are restrained at the starting post when expecting the signal to commence the trial of speed. They tossed their arms wildly in the air, leaping up and down more like exulting children than sober men, and continued to utter the most frantic cries.

---

* The whites are so called by the Indians, from their swords.

In the midst of this tumultuous disorder a rushing sound was heard, similar to that which might be expected to precede the passage of a flight of buffaloes, and then came the flocks and cattle of Ishmael in one confused and frightened drove.

"They have robbed the squatter of his beasts!" said the attentive trapper. "The reptiles have left him as hoofless as a beaver!" He was yet speaking when the whole body of the terrified animals rose the little acclivity and swept by the place where he stood, followed by a band of dusky and demonlike-looking figures who pressed madly on their rear.

The impulse was communicated to the Teton horses, long accustomed to sympathize in the untutored passions of their owners, and it was with difficulty that the keepers were enabled to restrain their impatience. At this moment, when all eyes were directed to the passing whirlwind of men and beasts, the trapper caught the knife from the hands of his inattentive keeper with a power that his age would have seemed to contradict and, at a single blow, severed the thong of hide which connected the whole of the drove. The wild animals snorted with joy and terror, and tearing the earth with their heels, they dashed away into the broad prairies in a dozen different directions.

Weucha turned upon his assailant with the ferocity and agility of a tiger. He felt for the weapon of which he had been so suddenly deprived, fumbled with impotent haste for the handle of his tomahawk, and at the same moment glanced his eyes after the flying cattle with the longings of a Western Indian. The struggle between thirst for vengeance and cupidity was severe but short. The latter quickly predominated in the bosom of one whose passions were proverbially groveling, and scarcely a moment intervened between the flight of the animals and the swift pursuit of the guards. The trapper had continued calmly facing his foe during the instant of suspense that succeeded his hardy act, and now that Weucha was seen following his companions, he pointed after the dark train, saying with his deep and nearly inaudible laugh, "Red natur' is red natur', let it show itself on a prairie or in a forest! A knock on the head would be the smallest reward to him who would take such a liberty with a Christian sentinel; but there goes the Teton after his horses as if he thought two legs as good as four in such a race! And yet the imps will have every hoof of them afore the day sets in, because it's reason ag'in instinct. Poor reason, I allow; but still there is a great deal of the man in the Indian. Ah's me! Your Delawares were the redskins of which America might boast; but few and scattered is that mighty people now! Well! The traveler may just make his pitch where he is; he has plenty of water, though natur' has cheated him of the pleasure of stripping the 'arth of its lawful trees. He has seen the last of his four-footed creatures, or I am but little skilled in Sioux cunning."

"Had we not better join the party of Ishmael?" said the bee hunter. "There will be a regular fight about this matter, or the old fellow has suddenly grown chickenhearted."

"No—no—no," hastily exclaimed Ellen.

She was stopped by the trapper, who laid his hand gently on her mouth as he answered, "Hist! Hist! The sound of voices might bring us into danger. Is your friend," he added, turning to Paul, "a man of spirit enough?"

"Don't call the squatter a friend of mine!" interrupted the youth. "I never yet harbored with one who could not show hand and seal for the land which fed him."

"Well—well. Let it then be acquaintance. Is he a man to maintain his own, stoutly, by dint of powder and lead?"

"His own! Aye, and that which is not his own too! Can you tell me, old trapper, who held the rifle that did the deed for the sheriff's deputy that thought to rout the unlawful settlers who had gathered nigh the Buffalo Lick in old Kentucky? I had lined a beautiful swarm that very day into the hollow of a dead beech, and there lay the people's officer at its roots, with a hole directly through the 'grace of God' which he carried in his jacket pocket covering his heart, as if he thought a bit of sheepskin was a breastplate against a squatter's bullet! Now, Ellen, you needn't be troubled, for it never strictly was brought home to him; and there were fifty others who had pitched in that neighborhood with just the same authority from the law."

The poor girl shuddered, struggling powerfully to suppress the sigh which arose in spite of her efforts, as if from the very bottom of her heart.

Thoroughly satisfied that he understood the character of the emigrants by the short but comprehensive description conveyed in Paul's reply, the old man raised no further question concerning the readiness of Ishmael to revenge his wrongs, but rather followed the train of thought which was suggested to his experience by the occasion.

"Each one knows the ties which bind him to his fellow creatures best," he answered. "Though it is greatly to be mourned that color, and property, and tongue, and l'arning should make so wide a difference in those who, after all, are but the children of one father! Howsomever," he continued by a transition not a little characteristic of the pursuits and feelings of the 'man, "as this a business in which there is much more likelihood of a fight than need for a sermon, it is best to be prepared for what may follow. Hush! There is a movement below; it is an equal chance that we are seen."

"The family is stirring," cried Ellen with a tremor that announced nearly as much terror at the approach of her friends as she had before manifested at the presence of her enemies. "Go, Paul, leave me. *You*, at least, must not be seen!"

"If I leave you, Ellen, in this desert before I see you safe in the care of old Ishmael at least, may I never hear the hum of another bee, or what is worse, fail in sight to line him to his hive!"

"You forget this good old man. He will not leave me. Though I am sure, Paul, we have parted before where there has been more of a desert than this."

"Never! These Indians may come whooping back, and then where are you! Halfway to the Rocky Mountains before a man can fairly strike the line of your flight. What think you, old trapper? How long may it be before these Tetons as you call them will be coming for the rest of old Ishmael's goods and chattels?"

"No fear of them," returned the old man, laughing in his own peculiar and silent manner; "I warrant me the devils will be scampering after their beasts these six hours yet! Listen! You may hear them in the willow bottoms at this very moment; aye, your real Sioux cattle will run like so many long-legged elks. Hist! Crouch again into the grass, down with ye both; as I'm a miserable piece of clay, I heard the clicking of a gunlock!"

The trapper did not allow his companions time to hesitate, but dragging them both after him, he nearly buried his own person in the fog of the prairie while he was speaking. It was fortunate that the senses of the aged hunter remained so acute and that he had lost none of his readiness of action. The three were scarcely bowed to the ground when their ears were saluted with the well-known, sharp, short reports of the western rifle, and instantly the whizzing of the ragged lead was heard, buzzing within dangerous proximity of their heads.

"Well done, young chips! Well done, old block!" whispered Paul, whose spirits no danger nor situation could entirely depress. "As pretty a volley as one would wish to hear on the wrong end of a rifle! What d'ye say, trapper! Here is likely to be a three-cornered war. Shall I give 'em as good as they send?"

"Give them nothing but fair words," returned the other hastily, "or you are both lost."

"I'm not certain it would much mend the matter if I were to speak with my tongue instead of the piece," said Paul in a tone half jocular, half bitter.

"For the sake of heaven, do not let them hear you!" cried Ellen. "Go, Paul, go; you can easily quit us now!"

Several shots in quick succession, each sending its dangerous messenger still nearer than the preceding discharge, cut short her speech, no less in prudence than in terror.

"This must end," said the trapper, rising with the dignity of one bent only on the importance of his object. "I know not what need ye may have, children, to fear those you should both love and honor, but something must be done to save your lives. A few hours more or less can never be missed from the time of one who has already numbered so many days; therefore, I will advance. Here is a clear space around you. Profit by it as you need, and may God bless and prosper each of you as ye deserve."

Without waiting for any reply, the trapper walked boldly down the declivity in his front, taking the direction of the encampment, neither quickening his pace in trepidation nor suffering it to be retarded by fear. The light of the moon fell brighter for a moment on his tall, gaunt form and served to warn the emigrants of his approach. Indifferent, however, to this unfavorable circumstance, he held his way silently and steadily towards the copse until a threatening voice met him with the challenge of, "Who comes; friend or foe?"

"Friend," was the reply; "one who has lived too long to disturb the close of life with quarrels."

"But not so long as to forget the tricks of his youth," said Ishmael, rearing his huge frame from beneath the slight covering of a low bush and meeting the trapper face to face; "old man, you have brought this tribe of red devils upon us, and tomorrow you will be sharing the booty."

"What have you lost?" calmly demanded the trapper.

"Eight as good mares as ever traveled in gears, besides a foal that is worth thirty of the brightest Mexicans that bear the face of the king of Spain. Then the woman has not a cloven hoof for her dairy or her loom, and I believe even the grunters, footsore as they be, are plowing the prairie. And now, stranger," he added, dropping the butt of his rifle on the hard earth with a violence and a clatter that would have intimidated one less firm than the man he addressed, "how many of these creatures may fall to your lot?"

"Horses have I never craved, nor even used, though few have journeyed over more of the wide lands of America than myself, old and feeble as I seem. But little use is there for a horse among the hills and woods of York—that is, as York was, but as I greatly fear York is no longer; as for woolen covering and cow's milk, I covet no such womanly fashions! The beasts of the field give me food and raiment. No, I crave no cloth better than the skin of a deer, nor any meat richer than his flesh."

The sincere manner of the trapper as he uttered this simple vindication was not entirely thrown away on the emigrant, whose dull nature was gradually quickening into a flame that might speedily have burst forth with dangerous violence. He listened like one who doubted, though not entirely convinced; and he muttered between his teeth the denunciation with which a moment before he intended to precede the summary vengeance he had certainly meditated.

"This is brave talking," he at length grumbled, "but to my judgment, too lawyerlike for a straightforward, fair-weather and foul-weather hunter."

"I claim to be no better than a trapper," the other meekly answered.

"Hunter or trapper—there is little difference. I have come, old man, into these districts because I found the law sitting too tight upon me and am not overfond of neighbors who can't settle a dispute without troubling a justice and twelve men; but I didn't come to be robbed of my plunder and then to say thankee to the man who did it!"

"He who ventures far into the prairie must abide by the ways of its owners."

"Owners!" echoed the squatter. "I am as rightful an owner of the land I stand on as any governor of the States! Can you tell me, stranger, where the law or the reason is to be found which says that one man shall have a section, or a town, or perhaps a county to his use and another have to beg for earth to make his grave in? This is not nature, and I deny that it is law. That is, your legal law."

"I cannot say that you are wrong," returned the trapper, whose opinions on this important topic, though drawn from very different premises, were in singular accordance with those of his companion, "and I have often thought and said as much when and where I have believed my voice could be heard. But your beasts are stolen by them who claim to be masters of all they find in the deserts."

"They had better not dispute that matter with a man who knows better," said the other in a portentous voice, though it seemed deep and sluggish as he who spoke. "I call myself a fair trader, and one who gives to his chaps as good as he receives. You saw the Indians?"

"I did—they held me a prisoner while they stole into your camp."

"It would have been more like a white man and a Christian to let me have known as much in better season," retorted Ishmael, casting another ominous sidelong glance at the trapper as if still meditating evil. "I am not much given to call every man I fall in with cousin, but color should be something when Christians meet in such a place as this. But what is done is done and cannot be mended by words. Come out of your ambush, boys; here is no one but the old man; he has eaten of my bread and should be our friend, though there is such good reason to suspect him of harboring with our enemies."

The trapper made no reply to the harsh suspicion which the other did not scruple to utter without the smallest delicacy notwithstanding the explanations and denials to which he had just listened. The summons of the unnurtured squatter brought an immediate accession to their party. Four or five of his sons made their appearance from beneath as many covers, where they had been posted, under the impression that the figures they had seen on the swell of the prairie were a part of the Sioux band. As each man approached and dropped his rifle into the hollow of his arm, he cast an indolent but inquiring glance at the stranger, though none of them expressed the least curiosity to know whence he had come or why he was there. This forbearance, however, proceeded only in part from the sluggishness of their common temper, for long and frequent experience in scenes of a similar character had taught them the virtue of discretion. The trapper endured their sullen scrutiny with the steadiness of one as practiced as themselves, and with the entire composure of innocence. Content with the momentary examination he had made, the eldest of the group, who was in truth the delinquent sentinel by whose remissness the wily Mahtoree had so well profited, turned towards his father and said bluntly, "If this man is all that is left of the party I saw on the upland yonder, we haven't altogether thrown away our ammunition."

"Asa, you are right," said the father, turning suddenly on the trapper, a lost idea being recalled by the hint of his son. "How is it, stranger; there were three of you just now, or there is no virtue in moonlight?"

"If you had seen the Tetons racing across the prairies like so many black-looking evil ones on the heels of your cattle, my friend, it would have been an easy matter to have fancied them a thousand."

"Aye, for a town-bred boy or a skeary woman; though, for that matter, there is old Esther; she has no more fear of a redskin than of a suckling cub or of a wolf pup. I'll warrant ye, had your thievish devils made their push by the light of the sun, the good woman would have been smartly at work among them, and the Siouxes would have found she was not given to part with her cheese and her butter without a price. But there'll come a time, stranger, right soon, when justice will have its dues, and that too without the help of what is called the law. We are of a slow breed, it may be said, and it is often said of us; but slow is sure; and there are few men living who can say they ever struck a blow that they did not get one as hard in return from Ishmael Bush."

"Then has Ishmael Bush followed the instinct of the beasts rather than the principle which ought to belong to his kind," returned the stubborn trapper. "I have struck many a blow myself, but never have I felt the same ease of mind that of right belongs to a man who follows his reason, after slaying even a fawn when there was no call for his meat or hide, as I have felt at leaving a Mingo unburied in the woods when following the trade of open and honest warfare."

"What, you have been a soldier, have you, trapper! I made a forage or two among the Cherokees when I was a lad my-

self; and I followed Mad Anthony * one season through the
beeches, but there was altogether too much tattooing and
regulating among his troops for me, so I left him without
calling on the paymaster to settle my arrearages. Though, as
Esther afterwards boasted, she had made such use of the
pay ticket that the states gained no great sum by the oversight.
You have heard of such a man as Mad Anthony if you tarried long among the soldiers."

"I fought my last battle, as I hope, under his orders," returned the trapper, a gleam of sunshine shooting from his
dim eyes, as if the event was recollected with pleasure, and
then a sudden shade of sorrow succeeding, as though he
felt a secret admonition against dwelling on the violent
scenes in which he had so often been an actor. "I was passing
from the states on the seashore into these far regions when I
crossed the trail of his army, and I fell in on his rear just
as a looker-on; but when they got to blows, the crack of
my rifle was heard among the rest, though to my shame it
may be said, I never knew the right of the quarrel as well
as a man of threescore and ten should know the reason of
his acts afore he takes mortal life, which is a gift he never
can return!"

"Come, stranger," said the emigrant, his rugged nature a
good deal softened when he found that they had fought on
the same side in the wild warfare of the West, "it is of small
account what may be the groundwork of the disturbance,
when it's a Christian ag'in a savage. We shall hear more of
this horse stealing tomorrow; tonight we can do no wiser or
safer thing than to sleep."

So saying, Ishmael deliberately led the way back towards
his rifled encampment and ushered the man whose life a few
minutes before had been in real jeopardy from his resentment into the presence of his family. Here, with a very few
words of explanation mingled with scarce but ominous
denunciations against the plunderers, he made his wife acquainted with the state of things on the prairie and announced his own determination to compensate himself for his

* Anthony Wayne, a Pennsylvanian distinguished in the war of the
revolution, and subsequently against the Indians of the West, for his
daring as a general, by which he gained from his followers the title of
Mad Anthony. General Wayne was the son of the person mentioned
in the life of West as commanding the regiment which excited his military ardor.

broken rest by devoting the remainder of the night to sleep.

The trapper gave his ready assent to the measure and adjusted his gaunt form on the pile of brush that was offered him with as much composure as a sovereign could resign himself to sleep in the security of his capital and surrounded by his armed protectors. The old man did not close his eyes, however, until he had assured himself that Ellen Wade was among the females of the family and that her relation or lover, whichever he might be, had observed the caution of keeping himself out of view, after which he slept, though with the peculiar watchfulness of one long accustomed to vigilance, even in the hours of deepest night.

CHAPTER 6

He is too picked, too spruce, too affected, too odd,
As it were too peregrinate, as I may call it.

SHAKESPEARE

THE ANGLO-AMERICAN is apt to boast, and not without reason, that his nation may claim a descent more truly honorable than that of any other people whose history is to be credited. Whatever might have been the weaknesses of the original colonists, their virtues have rarely been disputed. If they were superstitious, they were sincerely pious, and consequently, honest. The descendants of these simple and single-minded provincials have been content to reject the ordinary and artificial means by which honors have been perpetuated in families, and have substituted a standard which brings the individual himself to the ordeal of the public estimation, paying as little deference as may be to those who have gone before him. This forbearance, self-denial, or common sense, or by whatever term it may be thought proper to distinguish the measure, has subjected the nation to the imputation of having an ignoble origin. Were it worth the inquiry, it would be found that more than a just proportion of the renowned names of the mother country are, at this hour, to be found in her *ci-devant* colonies; and it is a fact well known to the few who have wasted sufficient time to become the masters of so unimportant a subject that the direct descendants of many a failing line, which the policy of England has seen fit to sustain by collateral supporters, are now discharging the simple duties of citizens in the bosom of this republic. The hive has remained stationary, and they who flutter around the venerable straw are wont to claim the empty distinction of antiquity, regardless alike of the frailty of their tenement and of the enjoyments of the numerous and vigorous swarms that are culling the fresher sweets of a virgin world. But as this is a subject which belongs rather to the politician and historian than to the humble narrator of the home-bred incidents we are about to reveal, we must confine our reflections to such matters as have an immediate relation to the subject of the tale.

Although the citizen of the United States may claim so just an ancestry, he is far from being exempt from the penalties of his fallen race. Like causes are well known to produce like effects. That tribute, which it would seem nations must ever pay, by way of a weary probation, around the shrine of Ceres before they can be indulged in her fullest favors, is in some measure exacted in America from the descendant instead of the ancestor. The march of civilization with us has a strong analogy to that of all coming events, which are known "to cast their shadows before." The gradations of society, from that state which is called refined to that which approaches as near barbarity as connection with an intelligent people will readily allow, are to be traced from the bosom of the States, where wealth, luxury, and the arts are beginning to seat themselves, to those distant and ever-receding borders which mark the skirts and announce the approach of the nation as moving mists precede the signs of the day.

Here, and here only, is to be found that widely spread though far from numerous class which may be at all likened to those who have paved the way for the intellectual progress of nations in the old world. The resemblance between the American borderer and his European prototype is singular though not always uniform. Both might be called without restraint, the one being above, the other beyond, the reach of the law—brave because they were inured to danger, proud because they were independent, and vindictive because each was the avenger of his own wrongs. It would be unjust to the borderer to pursue the parallel much further. He is irreligious because he has inherited the knowledge that religion does not exist in forms, and his reason rejects mockery. He is not a knight because he has not the power to bestow distinctions, and he has not the power because he is the offspring and not the parent of a system. In what manner these several qualities are exhibited in some of the most strongly marked of the latter class will be seen in the course of the ensuing narrative.

Ishmael Bush had passed the whole of a life of more than fifty years on the skirts of society. He boasted that he had never dwelt where he might not safely fell every tree he could view from his own threshold, that the law had rarely been known to enter his clearing, and that his ears had never willingly admitted the sound of a church bell. His exertions seldom exceeded his wants, which were peculiar to his class, and rarely failed of being supplied. He had no respect for any learning except that of the leech, because he was ignorant of the application of any other intelligence than such as met the senses. His deference to this particular branch of science had induced him to listen to the application of a medical man, whose thirst for natural history had led him to the desire of profiting by the migratory propensities of the squatter. This gentleman he had cordially received into his family, or rather under his protection, and they had journeyed together thus far through the prairies in perfect harmony, Ishmael often felicitating his wife on the possession of a companion who would be so serviceable in their new abode, wherever it might chance to be, until the family were thoroughly "acclimated." The pursuits of the naturalist frequently led him, however, for days at a time from the direct line of the route of the squatter, who rarely seemed to have any other guide than the sun. Most men would have deemed themselves fortunate to have been absent on the perilous occasion of the Sioux inroad, as was Obed Bat (or, as he was fond of hearing himself called, Battius), M.D. and fellow of several cis-Atlantic learned societies—the adventurous gentleman in question.

Although the sluggish nature of Ishmael was not actually awakened, it was sorely pricked by the liberties which had just been taken with his property. He slept, however, for it was the hour he had allotted to that refreshment, and because he knew how impotent any exertions to recover his effects must prove in the darkness of midnight. He also knew the danger of his present position too well to hazard what was left in pursuit of that which was lost. Much as the inhabitants of the prairie were known to love horses, their attachment to many other articles still in the possession of the travelers was equally well understood. It was a common artifice to scatter the herds and to profit by the confusion. But Mahtoree had, as it would seem, in this particular undervalued the acuteness of the man he had assailed. The phlegm with which the squatter learned his loss has already been seen, and it now remains to exhibit the results of his more matured determinations.

Though the encampment contained many an eye that was long unclosed and many an ear that listened greedily to catch the faintest evidence of any new alarm, it lay in deep quiet during the remainder of the night. Silence and fatigue finally performed their accustomed offices, and before morning all but the sentinels were again buried in sleep. How well these indolent watchers discharged their duties after the assault has never been known, inasmuch as nothing occurred to confirm or to disprove their subsequent vigilance.

Just as day, however, began to dawn, and a gray light was falling from the heavens on the dusky objects of the plain, the half-startled, anxious, and yet blooming countenance of Ellen Wade was reared above the confused mass of children among whom she had clustered on her stolen return to camp. Arising warily, she stepped lightly across the recumbent bodies and proceeded with the same caution to the utmost limits of the defenses of Ishmael. Here she listened, as if doubting the propriety of venturing further. The pause was only momentary, however, and long before the drowsy eyes of the sentinel who overlooked the spot where she stood had time to catch a glimpse of her active form, it had glided along the bottom and stood on the summit of the nearest eminence.

Ellen now listened, intently anxious to catch some other sound than the breathings of the morning air which faintly rustled the herbage at her feet. She was about to turn in disappointment from the inquiry when the tread of human feet making their way through the matted grass met her ear. Springing eagerly forward, she soon beheld the outlines of a figure advancing up the eminence on the side opposite to the camp. She had already uttered the name of Paul and was beginning to speak in the hurried and eager voice with which female affection is apt to greet a friend, when, drawing back, the disappointed girl closed her salutation by coldly adding, "I did not expect, doctor, to meet you at this unusual hour."

"All hours and all seasons are alike, my good Ellen, to the genuine lover of nature," returned a small, slightly made, but exceedingly active man dressed in an odd mixture of cloth and skins, a little past the middle age, and who advanced directly to her side with the familiarity of an old acquaintance; "and he who does not know how to find things to admire by this gray light is ignorant of a large portion of the blessings he enjoys."

"Very true," said Ellen, suddenly recollecting the necessity of accounting for her own appearance abroad at that unseasonable hour; "I know many who think the earth has a pleasanter look in the night than when seen by the brightest sunshine."

"Ah! Their organs of sight must be too convex! But the man who wishes to study the active habits of the feline race or the variety albinos must indeed be stirring at this hour. I dare say there are men who prefer even looking at objects by twilight for the simple reason that they see better at that time of the day."

"And is this the cause why you are so much abroad in the night?"

"I am abroad at night, my good girl, because the earth in its diurnal revolutions leaves the light of the sun but half the time on any given meridian, and because what I have to do cannot be performed in twelve or fifteen consecutive hours. Now have I been off two days from the family in search of a plant that is known to exist on the tributaries of La Platte, without seeing even a blade of grass that is not already enumerated and classed."

"You have been unfortunate, doctor, but——"

"Unfortunate!" echoed the little man, sidling nigher to his companion and producing his tablets with an air in which exultation struggled strangely with an affectation of self-abasement. "No, no, Ellen, I am anything but unfortunate! Unless, indeed, a man may be so called whose fortune is made, whose fame may be said to be established forever, whose name will go down to posterity with that of Buffon. Buffon! A mere compiler, one who flourishes on the foundation of other men's labors. No; *pari passu* with Solander, who bought his knowledge with pain and privations."

"Have you discovered a mine, Doctor Bat?"

"More than a mine; a treasure coined, and fit for instant use, girl. Listen! I was making the angle necessary to intersect the line of your uncle's march after my fruitless search, when I heard sounds like the explosion produced by firearms——"

"Yes," exclaimed Ellen eagerly, "we had an alarm——"

"And thought I was lost," continued the man of science, too much bent on his own ideas to understand her interruption. "Little danger of that! I made my own base, knew the length of the perpendicular by calculation, and to draw the hypotenuse had nothing to do but to work my angle. I supposed the guns were fired for my benefit, and changed my course for the sounds—not that I think the senses more accurate, or even as accurate as a mathematical calculation, but I feared that some of the children might need my services."

"They are all happily——"

"Listen," interrupted the other, already forgetting his affected anxiety for his patients in the greater importance of the present subject. "I had crossed a large tract of prairie—for sound is conveyed far where there is little obstruction—when I heard the trampling of feet, as if bisons were beating the earth. Then I caught a distant view of a herd of quadrupeds rushing up and down the swells, animals which would have still remained unknown and undescribed had it not been for a most felicitous accident! One, and he a noble specimen of the whole, was running a little apart from the rest. The herd made an inclination in my direction, in which the solitary animal coincided, and this brought him within fifty yards of the spot where I stood. I profited by the opportunity, and by the aid of steel and taper I wrote his description on the spot. I would have given a thousand dollars, Ellen, for a single shot from the rifle of one of the boys!"

"You carry a pistol, doctor; why didn't you use it?" said the half-inattentive girl, anxiously examining the prairie, but still lingering where she stood, quite willing to be detained.

"Aye, but it carries nothing but the most minute particles of lead, adapted to the destruction of the larger insects and reptiles. No, I did better than to attempt waging a war in which I could not be the victor. I recorded the event, noting each particular with the precision necessary to science. You shall hear, Ellen, for you are a good and improving girl, and by retaining what you learn in this way, may be yet of great service to learning should any accident occur to me. Indeed, my worthy Ellen, mine is a pursuit which has its dangers as well as that of the warrior. This very night," he continued, glancing his eyes behind him, "this awful night, has the principle of life itself been in great danger of extinction!"

"By what?"

"By the monster I have discovered. It approached me often, and ever as I receded, it continued to advance. I believe nothing but the little lamp I carried was my protector. I kept it between us whilst I wrote, making it serve the double purpose of luminary and shield. But you shall hear the character of the beast, and you may then judge of the risks we promoters of science run in behalf of mankind."

The naturalist raised his tablets to the heavens and disposed himself to read as well as he could by the dim light they yet shed upon the plain, premising with saying, "Listen, girl, and you shall hear with what a treasure it has been my happy lot to enrich the pages of natural history!"

"Is it then a creature of your forming?" said Ellen, turning away from her fruitless examination with a sudden lighting of her sprightly blue eyes, that showed she knew how to play with the foible of her learned companion.

"Is the power to give life to inanimate matter the gift of man? I would it were! You should speedily see a *Historia naturalis americana* that would put the sneering imitators of the Frenchman De Buffon to shame! A great improvement might be made in the formation of all quadrupeds, especially those in which velocity is a virtue. Two of the inferior limbs should be on the principle of the lever, wheels perhaps as they are now formed, though I have not yet determined whether the improvement might better be applied to the anterior or posterior members, inasmuch as I am yet to learn whether dragging or shoving requires the greatest muscular exertion. A natural exudation of the animal might assist in overcoming the friction, and a powerful momentum be obtained. But all this is hopeless—at least for the present," he added, raising his tablets again to the light and reading aloud: "October 6, 1805, that's merely the date, which I dare say you know better than I—mem. Quadruped; seen by starlight and by the aid of a pocket lamp in the prairies of North America; see journal for latitude and meridian.

Genus, unknown, therefore named after the discoverer and from the happy coincidence of having been seen in the evening—*Vespertilio horribilis americanus*. Dimensions, by estimation—greatest length, eleven feet; height, six feet; head, erect; nostrils, expansive; eyes, expressive and fierce; teeth, serrated and abundant; tail, horizontal, waving, and slightly feline; feet, large and hairy; talons, long, curvated, dangerous; ears, inconspicuous; horns, elongated, diverging, and formidable; color, plumbeous-ashy with fiery spots; voice, sonorous, martial, and appalling; habits, gregarious, carnivorous, fierce, and fearless.

"There," exclaimed Obed when he had ended this sententious but comprehensive description, "there is an animal which will be likely to dispute with the lion his title to be called the king of the beasts!"

"I know not the meaning of all you have said, Dr. Battius," returned the quick-witted girl, who understood the weakness of the philosopher and often indulged him with a title he loved so well to hear, "but I shall think it dangerous to venture far from the camp if such monsters are prowling over the prairies."

"You may well call it prowling," returned the naturalist, nestling still closer to her side and dropping his voice to such low and undignified tones of confidence as conveyed a meaning still more pointed than he had intended. "I have never before experienced such a trial of the nervous system; there was a moment, I acknowledge, when the *fortiter in re* faltered before so terrible an enemy; but the love of natural science bore me up and brought me off in triumph!"

"You speak a language so different from that we use in Tennessee," said Ellen, struggling to conceal her laughter, "that I hardly know whether I understand your meaning. If I am right, you wish to say you were chickenhearted."

"An absurd simile drawn from the ignorance of the formation of the biped. The heart of a chicken has a just proportion to its other organs, and the domestic fowl is, in a state of nature, a gallant bird. Ellen," he added with a countenance so solemn as to produce an impression on the attentive girl, "I was pursued, hunted, and in a danger that I scorn to dwell on—what's that?"

Ellen started, for the earnestness and simple sincerity of her companion's manner had produced a certain degree of credulity even on her buoyant mind. Looking in the direction indicated by the doctor, she beheld, in fact, a beast coursing over the prairie and making a straight and rapid approach to the spot they occupied. The day was not yet sufficiently advanced to enable her to distinguish its form and character, though enough was discernible to induce her to imagine it a fierce and savage animal.

"It comes! It comes!" exclaimed the doctor, fumbling, by a sort of instinct, for his tablets, while he fairly tottered on his feet under the powerful efforts he made to maintain his ground. "Now, Ellen, has fortune given me an opportunity to correct the errors made by starlight—hold—ashy-plumbeous—no ears—horns, excessive." His voice and hand were both arrested by a roar, or rather a shriek, from the beast that was sufficiently terrific to appall even a stouter heart than that of the naturalist. The cries of the animal passed over the prairie in strange cadences, and then succeeded a deep and solemn silence that was only broken by an uncontrolled fit of merriment from the more musical voice of Ellen Wade. In the meantime the naturalist stood like a statue of amazement, permitting a well-grown ass, against whose approach he no longer offered his boasted shield of light, to smell about his person without comment or hindrance.

"It is your own ass," cried Ellen the instant she found breath for words; "your own patient, hard-working hack!"

The doctor rolled his eyes from the beast to the speaker, and from the speaker to the beast, but gave no audible expression of his wonder.

"Do you refuse to know an animal that has labored so long in your service?" continued the laughing girl. "A beast that I have heard you say a thousand times has served you well, and whom you loved like a brother!"

"*Asinus domesticus!*" ejaculated the doctor, drawing his breath like one who had been near suffocation. "There is no doubt of the genus, and I will always maintain that the animal is not of the species *equus*. This is undeniably *Asinus* himself, Ellen Wade; but this is not the *Vespertilio horribilis* of the prairies! Very different animals I can assure you, young woman, and differently characterized in every important particular. That, carnivorous," he continued, glancing his eye at the open page of his tablets; "this, granivorous; habits, fierce, dangerous; habits, patient, abstemious; ears, inconspicuous; ears, elongated; horns, diverging, etc.; horns, none!"

He was interrupted by another burst of merriment from Ellen, which served in some measure to recall him to his recollection.

"The image of the *Vespertilio* was on the retina," the astounded inquirer into the secrets of nature observed in a manner that seemed a little apologetic, "and I was silly enough to mistake my own faithful beast for the monster. Though even now I greatly marvel to see this animal running at large!"

Ellen then proceeded to explain the history of the attack and its results. She described, with an accuracy that might have raised suspicions of her own movements in the mind of one less simple than her auditor, the manner in which the beasts burst out of the encampment, and the headlong speed with which they had dispersed themselves over the open plain. Although she forbore to say as much in terms, she so managed as to present before the eyes of her listener the strong probability of having mistaken the frightened drove for savage beasts, and then terminated her account by a lamentation for their loss and some very natural remarks on the helpless condition in which it had left the family. The naturalist listened in silent wonder, neither interrupting her narrative nor suffering a single exclamation of surprise to escape him. The keen-eyed girl, however, saw that as she proceeded, the important leaf was torn from the tablets in a manner which showed that their owner had got rid of his delusion at the same instant. From that moment the world has heard no more of the *Vespertilio horribilis americanus*, and the natural sciences have irretrievably lost an important link in that great animated chain which is said to connect earth and heaven and in which man is thought to be so familiarly complicated with the monkey.

When Dr. Bat was put in full possession of all the circumstances of the inroad, his concern immediately took a different direction. He had left sundry folios and certain boxes well stored with botanical specimens and defunct animals under the good keeping of Ishmael, and it immediately struck his acute mind that marauders as subtle as the Siouxes would never neglect the opportunity to despoil him of these treasures. Nothing that Ellen could say to the contrary served to appease his apprehensions, and, consequently they

separated, he to relieve his doubts and fears together, and
she to glide, as swiftly and silently as she had just before
passed it, into the still and solitary tent.

CHAPTER 7

What! Fifty of my followers at a clap!

KING LEAR

THE DAY HAD now fairly opened on the seemingly interminable waste of the prairie. The entrance of Obed at such a
moment into the camp, accompanied as it was by vociferous
lamentations over his anticipated loss, did not fail to rouse
the drowsy family of the squatter. Ishmael and his sons,
together with the forbidding-looking brother of his wife,
were all speedily afoot; and then, as the sun began to shed
his light on the place, they became gradually apprised of the
extent of their loss.

Ishmael looked round upon the motionless and heavily
loaded vehicles with his teeth firmly compressed, cast a
glance at the amazed and helpless group of children, which
clustered around their sullen but desponding mother, and
walked out upon the open land as if he found the air of the
encampment too confined. He was followed by several of
the men, who were attentive observers, watching the dark
expression of his eye as the index of their own future movements. The whole proceeded in profound and moody silence to the summit of the nearest swell, whence they could
command an almost boundless view of the naked plains.
Here nothing was visible but a solitary buffalo, that gleaned
a meager subsistence from the decaying herbage at no great
distance, and the ass of the physician, who profited by his
freedom to enjoy a meal richer than common.

"Yonder is one of the creatures left by the villains to
mock us," said Ishmael, glancing his eye towards the latter, "and that the meanest of the stock. This is a hard country to make a crop in, boys; and yet food must be found to
fill many hungry mouths!"

"The rifle is better than the hoe in such a place as this,"
returned the eldest of his sons, kicking the hard and thirsty
soil on which he stood with an air of contempt. "It is good
for such as they who make their dinner better on beggars'

beans than hominy. A crow would shed tears if obliged by its errand to fly across the district."

"What say you, trapper?" returned the father, showing the slight impression his powerful heel had made on the compact earth and laughing with frightful ferocity. "Is this the quality of land a man would choose who never troubles the county clerk with title deeds?"

"There is richer soil in the bottoms," returned the old man calmly, "and you have passed millions of acres to get to this dreary spot, where he who loves to till the 'arth might have received bushels in return for pints, and that too at the cost of no very grievous labor. If you have come in search of land, you have journeyed hundreds of miles too far, or as many leagues too little."

"There is then a better choice towards the other ocean?" demanded the squatter, pointing in the direction of the Pacific.

"There is, and I have seen it all," was the answer of the other, who dropped his rifle to the earth and stood leaning on its barrel like one who recalled the scenes he had witnessed with melancholy pleasure. "I have seen the waters of the two seas! On one of them was I born and raised to be a lad like yonder tumbling boy. America has grown, my men, since the days of my youth to be a country larger than I once had thought the world itself to be. Near seventy years I dwelt in York, province and state together; you've been in York, 'tis like?"

"Not I—not I; I never visited the towns, but often have heard the place you speak of named. 'Tis a wide clearing there, I reckon."

"Too wide! Too wide! They scourge the very 'arth with their axes. Such hills and hunting grounds as I have seen stripped of the gifts of the Lord, without remorse or shame! I tarried till the mouths of my hounds were deafened by the blows of the chopper, and then I came west in search of quiet. It was a grievous journey that I made, a grievous toil to pass through falling timber and to breathe the thick air of smoky clearings week after week as I did! 'Tis a far country too, that state of York, from this!"

"It lies ag'in in the outer edge of old Kentuck, I reckon, though what the distance may be I never knew."

"A gull would have to fan a thousand miles of air to find the eastern sea. And yet it is no mighty reach to hunt across when shade and game are plenty! The time has been when I followed the deer in the mountains of the Delaware and Hudson and took the beaver on the streams of the upper lakes in the same season; but my eye was quick and certain at that day, and my limbs were like the legs of a moose! The dam of Hector"—dropping his look kindly to the aged hound that crouched at his feet—"was then a pup, and apt to open on the game the moment she struck the scent. She gave me a deal of trouble, that slut, she did!"

"Your hound is old, stranger, and a rap on the head would prove a mercy to the beast."

"The dog is like his master," returned the trapper without appearing to heed the brutal advice the other gave, "and will number his days when his work amongst the game is over, and not before. To my eye things seem ordered to meet each other in this creation. 'Tis not the swiftest-running deer that always throws off the hounds, nor the biggest arm that holds the truest rifle. Look around you, men; what will the Yankee choppers say when they have cut their path from the eastern to the western waters and find that a hand, which can lay the 'arth bare at a blow, has been here and swept the country in very mockery of their wickedness. They will turn on their tracks like a fox that doubles, and then the rank smell of their own footsteps will show them the madness of their waste. Howsomever, these are thoughts that are more likely to rise in him who has seen the folly of eighty seasons than to teach wisdom to men still bent on the pleasures of their kind! You have need yet of a stirring time if you think to escape the craft and hatred of the burnt-wood Indians. They claim to be the lawful owners of this country and seldom leave a white more than the skin he boasts of when once they get the power, as they always have the will, to do him harm."

"Old man," said Ishmael sternly, "to which people do you belong? You have the color and speech of a Christian, while it seems that your heart is with the redskins."

"To me there is little difference in nations. The people I loved most are scattered as the sands of the dry riverbeds fly before the fall hurricanes, and life is too short to make use and custom with strangers, as one can do with such as he has dwelt amongst for years. Still am I a man without the cross of Indian blood; and what is due from a warrior to his nation is owing by me to the people of the States, though little need have they, with their militia and their armed boats, of help from a single arm of fourscore."

"Since you own your kin, I may ask a simple question. Where are the Siouxes who have stolen my cattle?"

"Where is the herd of buffaloes which was chased by the panther across this plain no later than the morning of yesterday! It is as hard——"

"Friend," said Dr. Battius, who had hitherto been an attentive listener, but who now felt a sudden impulse to mingle in the discourse, "I am grieved when I find a venator, or hunter, of your experience and observation following the current of vulgar error. The animal you describe is in truth a species of the *Bos ferus* (or *Bos sylvestris*, as he has been happily called by the poets), but though of close affinity, it is altogether distinct from the common bubulus. Bison is the better word, and I would suggest the necessity of adopting it in future when you shall have occasion to allude to the species."

"Bison or buffalo, it makes but little matter. The creatur' is the same, call it by what name you will, and——"

"Pardon me, venerable venator; as classification is the very soul of the natural sciences, the animal or vegetable must of necessity be characterized by the peculiarities of its species, which is always indicated by the name——"

"Friend," said the trapper a little positively, "would the tail of a beaver make the worse dinner for calling it a mink; or could you eat of the wolf with relish because some bookish man had given it the name of venison?"

As these questions were put with no little earnestness and some spirit, there was every probability that a hot discussion would have succeeded between two men, of whom one was so purely practical and the other so much given to theory, had not Ishmael seen fit to terminate the dispute by bringing into view a subject that was much more important to his own immediate interests.

"Beavers' tails and minks' flesh may do to talk about before a maple fire and a quiet hearth," interrupted the squatter without the smallest deference to the interested feelings of the disputants, "but something more than foreign words, or words of any sort, is now needed. Tell me, trapper, where are your Siouxes skulking?"

"It would be as easy to tell you the colors of the hawk that is floating beneath yonder white cloud! When a redskin strikes his blow, he is not apt to wait until he is paid for the evil deed in lead."

"Will the beggarly savages believe they have enough when they find themselves masters of all the stock?"

"Natur' is much the same, let it be covered by what skin it may. Do you ever find your longings after riches less when you have made a good crop than before you were master of a kernel of corn? If you do, you differ from what the experience of a long life tells me is the common cravings of man."

"Speak plainly, old stranger," said the squatter, striking the butt of his rifle heavily on the earth, his dull capacity finding no pleasure in a discourse that was conducted in so obscure allusions; "I have asked a simple question, and one I know well that you can answer."

"You are right, you are right. I can answer, for I have too often seen the disposition of my kind to mistake it when evil is stirring. When the Siouxes have gathered in the beasts and have made sure that you are not upon their heels, they will be back nibbling like hungry wolves to take the bait they have left; or it may be, they'll show the temper of the great bears that are found at the falls of the Long River and strike at once with the paw, without stopping to nose their prey."

"You have then seen the animals you mention!" exclaimed Dr. Battius, who had now been thrown out of the conversation quite as long as his impatience could well brook, and who approached the subject with his tablets ready opened as a book of reference. "Can you tell me if what you encountered was of the species *Ursus horribilis*—with the ears rounded —front arquated—eyes destitute of the remarkable supplemental lid—with six incisors, one false, and four perfect molars——"

"Trapper, go on, for we are engaged in reasonable discourse," interrupted Ishmael; "you believe we shall see more of the robbers."

"Nay—nay—I do not call them robbers, for it is the usage of their people, and what may be called the prairie law."

"I have come five hundred miles to find a place where no man can ding the words of the law in my ears," said Ishmael fiercely, "and I am not in a humor to stand quietly at a bar while a redskin sits in judgment. I tell you, trapper, if another Sioux is seen prowling around my camp, wherever it may be, he shall feel the contents of old Kentuck"—slapping his rifle in a manner that could not be easily misconstrued—

"though he wore the medal of Washington * himself. I call the man a robber who takes that which is not his own."

"The Teton, and the Pawnee, and the Konza, and men of a dozen other tribes claim to own these naked fields."

"Natur' gives them the lie in their teeth. The air, the water, and the ground are free gifts to man, and no one has the power to portion them out in parcels. Man must drink, and breathe, and walk, and therefore each has a right to his share of 'arth. Why do not the surveyors of the States set their compasses and run their lines over our heads as well as beneath our feet? Why do they not cover their shining sheepskins with big words, giving to the landholder, or perhaps he should be called airholder, so many rods of heaven, with the use of such a star for a boundary mark, and such a cloud to turn a mill?"

As the squatter uttered his wild conceit, he laughed from the very bottom of his chest, in scorn. The deriding but frightful merriment passed from the mouth of one of his ponderous sons to that of the other until it had made the circuit of the whole family.

"Come, trapper," continued Ishmael in a tone of better humor, like a man who feels that he has triumphed, "neither of us, I reckon, has ever had much to do with title deeds, or county clerks, or blazed trees; therefore we will not waste words on fooleries. You are a man that has tarried long in this clearing; and now I ask your opinion face to face, without fear or favor, if you had the lead in my business, what would you do?"

The old man hesitated and seemed to give the required advice with deep reluctance. As every eye, however, was fastened on him, and whichever way he turned his face he encountered a look riveted on the lineaments of his own working countenance, he answered in a low, melancholy tone, "I have seen too much mortal blood poured out in empty quarrels to wish ever to hear an angry rifle again. Ten weary years have I sojourned alone on these naked plains waiting for my hour, and not a blow have I struck ag'in an enemy more humanized than the grizzly bear."

"*Ursus horribilis,*" muttered the doctor.

The speaker paused at the sound of the other's voice, but

---

* The American government creates chiefs among the western tribes, and decorates them with silver medals bearing the impression of the different presidents. That of Washington is the most prized.

perceiving it was no more than a sort of mental ejaculation, he continued in the same strain, "More humanized than the grizzly bear or the panther of the Rocky Mountains, unless the beaver, which is a wise and knowing animal, may be so reckoned. What would I advise? Even the female buffalo will fight for her young!"

"It never then shall be said that Ishmael Bush has less kindness for his children than the bear for her cubs!"

"And yet this is but a naked spot for a dozen men to make head in ag'in five hundred."

"Aye, it is so," returned the squatter, glancing his eye towards his humble camp; "but something might be done with the wagons and the cottonwood."

The trapper shook his head incredulously and pointed across the rolling plain in the direction of the west as he answered, "A rifle would send a bullet from these hills into your very sleeping cabins; nay, arrows from the thicket in your rear would keep you all burrowed, like so many prairie dogs; it wouldn't do, it wouldn't do. Three long miles from this spot is a place where, as I have often thought in passing across the desert, a stand might be made for days and weeks together if there were hearts and hands ready to engage in the bloody work."

Another low, deriding laugh passed among the young men, announcing, in a manner sufficiently intelligible, their readiness to undertake a task even more arduous. The squatter himself eagerly seized the hint which had been so reluctantly extorted from the trapper, who, by some singular process of reasoning, had evidently persuaded himself that it was his duty to be strictly neutral. A few direct and pertinent inquiries served to obtain the little additional information that was necessary in order to make the contemplated movement, and then Ishmael, who was on emergencies as terrifically energetic as he was sluggish in common, set about effecting his object without delay.

Notwithstanding the industry and zeal of all engaged, the task was one of great labor and difficulty. The loaded vehicles were to be drawn by hand across a wide distance of plain without track or guide of any sort except that which the trapper had furnished by communicating his knowledge of the cardinal points of the compass. In accomplishing this object, the gigantic strength of the men was taxed to the utmost, nor were the females or the children spared a heavy proportion of the toil. While the sons distributed themselves about the heavily loaded wagons and drew them by main strength up the neighboring swell, their mother and Ellen, surrounded by the amazed group of little ones, followed slowly in the rear, bending under the weight of such different articles as were suited to their several strengths.

Ishmael himself superintended and directed the whole, occasionally applying his colossal shoulder to some lagging vehicle until he saw that the chief difficulty, that of gaining the level of their intended route, was accomplished. Then he pointed out the required course, cautioning his sons to proceed in such a manner that they should not lose the advantage they had with so much labor obtained, and beckoning to the brother of his wife, they returned together to the empty camp.

Throughout the whole of this movement, which occupied an hour of time, the trapper had stood apart, leaning on his rifle, with the aged hound slumbering at his feet, a silent but attentive observer of all that passed. Occasionally a smile lighted his hard, muscular, but wasted features like a gleam of sunshine flitting across a ragged ruin, and betrayed the momentary pleasure he found in witnessing from time to time the vast power the youths discovered. Then, as the train drew slowly up the ascent, a cloud of thought and sorrow threw all into the shade again, leaving the expression of his countenance in its usual state of quiet melancholy. As vehicle after vehicle left the place of the encampment, he noted the change with increasing attention, seldom failing to cast an inquiring look at the little neglected tent, which, with its proper wagon, still remained as before, solitary and apparently forgotten. The summons of Ishmael to his gloomy associate had, however, as it would now seem, this hitherto neglected portion of his effects for its object.

First casting a cautious and suspicious glance on every side of him, the squatter and his companion advanced to the little wagon and caused it to enter within the folds of the cloth much in the manner that it had been extricated the preceding evening. They both then disappeared behind the drapery, and many moments of suspense succeeded, during which the old man, secretly urged by a burning desire to know the meaning of so much mystery, insensibly drew nigh to the place until he stood within a few yards of the proscribed spot. The agitation of the cloth betrayed the nature of the occupation of those whom it concealed, though their work was conducted in rigid silence. It would appear that long practice had made each of the two acquainted with his particular duty, for neither sign nor direction of any sort was necessary from Ishmael in order to apprise his surly associate of the manner in which he was to proceed. In less time than has been consumed in relating it, the interior portion of the arrangement was completed, when the men reappeared without the tent. Too busy with his occupation to heed the presence of the trapper, Ishmael began to release the folds of the cloth from the ground and to dispose of them in such a manner around the vehicle as to form a sweeping train to the new form the little pavilion had now assumed. The arched roof trembled with the occasional movement of the light vehicle, which, it was now apparent, once more supported its secret burden.

Just as the work was ended, the scowling eye of Ishmael's assistant caught a glimpse of the figure of the attentive observer of their movements. Dropping the shaft, which he had already lifted from the ground preparatory to occupying the place that was usually filled by an animal less reasoning and perhaps less dangerous than himself, he bluntly exclaimed, "I am a fool as you often say! But look for yourself. If that man is not an enemy, I will disgrace father and mother, call myself an Indian, and go hunt with the Siouxes!"

The cloud as it is about to discharge the subtle lightning is not more dark nor threatening than the look with which Ishmael greeted the intruder. He turned his head on every side of him as if seeking some engine sufficiently terrible to annihilate the offending trapper at a blow; and then, possibly recollecting the further occasion he might have for his counsel, he forced himself to say with an appearance of moderation that nearly choked him, "Stranger, I did believe this prying into the concerns of others was the business of women in the towns and settlements, and not the manner in which men who are used to live where each has room for himself deal with the secrets of their neighbors. To what lawyer or sheriff do you calculate to sell your news?"

"I hold but little discourse except with one, and then chiefly of my own affairs," returned the old man without the least observable apprehension, and pointing imposingly upward, "a Judge, and Judge of all. Little does he need knowledge from my hands, and but little will your wish to keep anything secret from him profit you, even in this desert."

The mounting tempers of his untutored listeners were rebuked by the simple, solemn manner of the trapper. Ishmael stood sullen and thoughtful, while his companion stole a furtive and involuntary glance at the placid sky which spread so wide and blue above his head as if he expected to see the Almighty eye itself beaming from the heavenly vault. But impressions of a serious character are seldom lasting on minds long indulged in forgetfulness. The hesitation of the squatter was consequently of short duration. The language, however, as well as the firm and collected air of the speaker were the means of preventing much subsequent abuse, if not violence.

"It would be showing more of the kindness of a friend and comrade," Ishmael returned in a tone sufficiently sullen to betray his humor, though it was no longer threatening, "had your shoulder been put to the wheel of one of yonder wagons, instead of edging itself in here where none are wanted but such as are invited."

"I can put the little strength that is left me," returned the trapper, "to this, as well as to another of your loads."

"Do you take us for boys!" exclaimed Ishmael, laughing, half in ferocity and half in derision, applying his powerful strength at the same time to the little vehicle, which rolled over the grass with as much seeming facility as if it were drawn by its usual team.

The trapper paused and followed the departing wagon with his eye, marveling greatly as to the nature of its concealed contents, until it had also gained the summit of the eminence and in its turn disappeared behind the swell of the land. Then he turned to gaze at the desolation of the scene around him. The absence of human forms would have scarce created a sensation in the bosom of one so long accustomed to solitude had not the site of the deserted camp furnished such strong memorial of its recent visitors, and as the old man was quick to detect, of their waste also. He cast his eye upward, with a shake of the head, at the vacant spot in the heavens which had so lately been filled by the branches of those trees that now lay stripped of their verdure, worthless and deserted logs at his feet.

"Aye," he muttered to himself, "I might have knowed it—I might have knowed it! Often have I seen the same before; and yet I brought them to the spot myself, and have now sent them to the only neighborhood of their kind within many long leagues of the spot where I stand. This is man's wish, and pride, and waste, and sinfulness! He tames the beasts of the field to feed his idle wants, and having robbed the brutes of their natural food, he teaches them to strip the 'arth of its trees to quiet their hunger."

A rustling in the low bushes which still grew, for some distance, along the swale that formed the thicket on which the camp of Ishmael had rested caught his ear at the moment and cut short the soliloquy. The habits of so many years spent in the wilderness caused the old man to bring his rifle to a poise, with something like the activity and promptitude of his youth, but suddenly recovering his recollection, he dropped it into the hollow of his arm again and resumed his air of melancholy resignation.

"Come forth, come forth!" he said aloud. "Be ye bird or be ye beast, ye are safe from these old hands. I have eaten and I have drunk; why should I take life when my wants call for no sacrifice? It will not be long afore the birds will peck at eyes that shall not see them, and perhaps light on my very bones; for if things like these are only made to perish, why am I to expect to live forever? Come forth, come forth; you are safe from harm at these weak hands."

"Thank you for the good word, old trapper!" cried Paul Hover, springing actively forward from his place of concealment. "There was an air about you when you threw forward the muzzle of your piece that I did not like, for it seemed to say that you were master of all the rest of the motions."

"You are right, you are right!" cried the trapper, laughing with inward self-complacency at the recollection of his former skill. "The day has been when few men knew the virtues of a long rifle like this I carry better than myself, old and useless as I now seem. You are right, young man; and the time was when it was dangerous to move a leaf within earshot of my stand; or," he added, dropping his voice and looking serious, "for a Red Mingo to show an eyeball from his ambushment. You have heard of the Red Mingoes?"

"I have heard of minks," said Paul, taking the old man by the arm and gently urging him towards the thicket as he spoke, while at the same time he cast quick and uneasy glances behind him in order to make sure he was not observed. "Of your common black minks; but none of any other color."

"Lord! Lord!" continued the trapper, shaking his head, and still laughing in his deep, but quiet manner. "The boy mistakes a brute for a man! Though a Mingo is little better than a beast; or for that matter, he is worse when rum and opportunity are placed before his eyes. There was that accursed Huron from the upper lakes that I knocked from his perch among the rocks in the hills back of the Hori—"

His voice was lost in the thicket into which he had suffered himself to be led by Paul while speaking, too much occupied by thoughts which dwelt on scenes and acts that had taken place half a century earlier in the history of the country to offer the smallest resistance.

CHAPTER 8

Now they are clapper clawing one another; I'll go look on. That dissembling abominable varlet, Diomed, has got that same scurvy, doting, foolish young knave in his helm.

TROILUS AND CRESSIDA

IT IS NECESSARY, in order that the thread of the narrative should not be spun to a length which might fatigue the reader, that he should imagine a week to have intervened between the scene with which the preceding chapter closed and the events with which it is our intention to resume its relation in this. The season was on the point of changing its character, the verdure of summer giving place more rapidly to the brown and parti-colored livery of the fall.* The heavens were clothed in driving clouds, piled in vast masses one above the other, which whirled violently in the gusts, opening occasionally to admit transient glimpses of the bright and glorious sight of the heavens, dwelling in a magnificence by far too grand and durable to be disturbed by the fitful efforts of the lower world. Beneath, the wind swept across the wild and naked prairies with a violence that is seldom witnessed in any section of the continent less open. It would have been easy to have imagined, in the ages of fable, that the god of the winds had permitted his subor-

---

* The Americans call the autumn the "fall" from the fall of the leaf.

dinate agents to escape from their den and that they now rioted in wantonness across wastes where neither tree, nor work of man, nor mountain, nor obstacle of any sort opposed itself to their gambols.

Though nakedness might, as usual, be given as the pervading character of the spot whither it is now necessary to transfer the scene of the tale, it was not entirely without the signs of human life. Amid the monotonous rolling of the prairie, a single naked and ragged rock arose on the margin of a little watercourse which found its way, after winding a vast distance through the plains, into one of the numerous tributaries of the father of rivers. A swale of lowland lay near the base of the eminence, and as it was still fringed with a thicket of alders and sumac, it bore the signs of having once nurtured a feeble growth of wood. The trees themselves had been transferred, however, to the summit and crags of the neighboring rocks. On this elevation the signs of man to which the allusion just made applies were to be found.

Seen from beneath, there were visible a breastwork of logs and stones intermingled in such a manner as to save all unnecessary labor, a few low roofs made of bark and boughs of trees, an occasional barrier constructed like the defenses on the summit and placed on such points of the acclivity as were easier of approach than the general face of the eminence; and a little dwelling of cloth, perched on the apex of a small pyramid that shot up on one angle of the rock, the white covering of which glimmered from a distance like a spot of snow, or, to make the simile more suitable to the rest of the subject, like a spotless and carefully guarded standard which was to be protected by the dearest blood of those who defended the citadel beneath. It is hardly necessary to add that this rude and characteristic fortress was the place where Ishmael Bush had taken refuge after the robbery of his flocks and herds.

On the day to which the narrative is advanced, the squatter was standing near the base of the rocks, leaning on his rifle and regarding the sterile soil that supported him with a look in which contempt and disappointment were strongly blended.

" 'Tis time to change our natur's," he observed to the brother of his wife, who was rarely far from his elbow, "and to become ruminators instead of people used to the fare of Christians and freemen. I reckon, Abiram, you could glean a living among the grasshoppers; you are an active man and might outrun the nimblest skipper of them all."

"The country will never do," returned the other, who relished but little the forced humor of his kinsman, "and it is well to remember that a lazy traveler makes a long journey."

"Would you have me draw a cart at my heels across this desert for weeks—aye, months?" retorted Ishmael, who like all of his class could labor with incredible efforts on emergencies, but who too seldom exerted continued industry on any occasion to brook a proposal that offered so little repose. "It may do for your people, who live in settlements, to hasten on to their houses; but, thank heaven, my farm is too big for its owner ever to want a resting-place."

"Since you like the plantation, then, you have only to make your crop."

"That is easier said than done on this corner of the estate. I tell you, Abiram, there is need of moving, for more reasons than one. You know I'm a man that very seldom enters into a bargain, but who always fulfills his agreements better than your dealers in wordy contracts written on rags of paper. If there's one mile, there are a hundred still needed to make up the distance for which you have my honor."

As he spoke, the squatter glanced his eye upward at the little tenement of cloth which crowned the summit of his ragged fortress. The look was understood and answered by the other; and by some secret influence, which operated either through their interests or feelings, it served to reestablish that harmony between them which had just been threatened with something like a momentary breach.

"I know it and feel it in every bone of my body. But I remember the reason why I have set myself on this accursed journey too well to forget the distance between me and the end. Neither you nor I will ever be the better for what we have done unless we thoroughly finish what is so well begun. Aye, that is the doctrine of the whole world, I judge; I heard a traveling preacher who was skirting it down the Ohio a time since say if a man should live up to the faith for a hundred years and then fall from his work a single day, he would find the settlement was to be made for the finishing blow that he had put to his job and that all the bad and none of the good would come into the final account."

"And you believed the hungry hypocrite!"

"Who said that I believed it?" retorted Abiram with a

bullying look that betrayed how much his fears had dwelt on the subject he affected to despise. "Is it believing to tell what a roguish— And yet, Ishmael, the man might have been honest after all! He told us that the world was, in truth, no better than a desert and that there was but one hand that could lead the most learned man through all its crooked windings. Now, if this be true of the whole, it may be true of a part."

"Abiram, out with your grievances like a man," interrupted the squatter with a hoarse laugh. "You want to pray! But of what use will it be, according to your own doctrine, to serve God five minutes and the devil an hour? Harkee, friend; I'm not much of a husbandman, but this I know to my cost: that to make a right good crop, even on the richest bottom, there must be hard labor; and your snufflers liken the 'arth to a field of corn, and the men who live on it to its yield. Now I tell you, Abiram, that you are no better than a thistle or a mullin; yea, ye are a wood of too open a pore to be good even to burn."

The malign glance which shot from the scowling eye of Abiram announced the angry character of his feelings; but as the furtive look quailed immediately before the unmoved, steady countenance of the squatter, it also betrayed how much the bolder spirit of the latter had obtained the mastery over his craven nature.

Content with his ascendancy, which was too apparent and had been too often exerted on similar occasions to leave him in any doubt of its extent, Ishmael coolly continued the discourse by adverting more directly to his future plans.

"You will own the justice of paying everyone in kind," he said; "I have been robbed of my stock, and I have a scheme to make myself as good as before by taking hoof for hoof; or for that matter, when a man is put to the trouble of bargaining for both sides, he is a fool if he don't pay himself something in the way of commission."

As the squatter made this declaration in a tone which was a little excited by the humor of the moment, four or five of his lounging sons, who had been leaning against the foot of the rock, came forward with the indolent step so common to the family.

"I have been calling Ellen Wade, who is on the rock keeping the lookout, to know if there is anything to be seen," observed the eldest of the young men, "and she shakes her head for an answer. Ellen is sparing of her words for a woman, and might be taught manners, at least, without spoiling her good looks."

Ishmael cast his eye upwards to the place where the offending but unconscious girl was holding her anxious watch. She was seated at the edge of the uppermost crag, by the side of the little tent and at least two hundred feet above the level of the plain. Little else was to be distinguished at that distance but the outline of her form, her fair hair streaming in the gusts beyond her shoulders and the steady and seemingly unchangeable look that she riveted on some remote point of the prairie.

"What is it, Nell?" cried Ishmael, lifting his powerful voice a little above the rushing of the element. "Have you got a glimpse of anything bigger than a burrowing barker?"

The lips of the attentive Ellen parted; she rose to the utmost height her small stature admitted, seeming still to regard the unknown object; but her voice, if she spoke at all, was not sufficiently loud to be heard amid the wind.

"It are a fact that the child sees something more uncommon than a buffalo or a prairie dog!" continued Ishmael. "Why, Nell girl, are ye deaf? Nell, I say; I hope it is an army of redskins she has in her eye, for I should relish the chance to pay them for their kindness under the favor of these logs and rocks!"

As the squatter accompanied his vaunt with corresponding gestures and directed his eyes to the circle of his equally confident sons while speaking, he drew their gaze from Ellen to himself; but now, when they turned together to note the succeeding movements of their female sentinel, the place which had so lately been occupied by her form was vacant.

"As I am a sinner," exclaimed Asa, usually one of the most phlegmatic of the youths, "the girl is blown away by the wind!"

Something like a sensation was exhibited among them, which might have denoted that the influence of the laughing blue eyes, flaxen hair, and glowing cheeks of Ellen had not been lost on the dull natures of the young men; and looks of amazement mingled slightly with concern passed from one to the other as they gazed in dull wonder at the point of the naked rock.

"It might well be!" added another. "She sat on a slivered stone, and I have been thinking of telling her she was in danger for more than an hour."

"Is that a ribbon of the child dangling from the corner of the hill below?" cried Ishmael. "Ha! Who is moving about the tent? Have I not told you all——"

"Ellen! 'Tis Ellen!" interrupted the whole body of his sons in a breath, and at that instant she reappeared to put an end to their different surmises and to relieve more than one sluggish nature from its unwonted excitement. As Ellen issued from beneath the folds of the tent, she advanced with a light and fearless step to her former giddy stand and pointed towards the prairie, appearing to speak in an eager and rapid voice to some invisible auditor.

"Nell is mad!" said Asa, half in contempt, and yet not a little in concern. "The girl is dreaming with her eyes open and thinks she sees some of them fierce creatur's with hard names with which the doctor fills her ears."

"Can it be that the child has found a scout of the Siouxes?" said Ishmael, bending his look towards the plain; but a low, significant whisper from Abiram drew his eyes quickly upwards again, where they were turned just in time to perceive that the cloth of the tent was agitated by a motion very evidently different from the quivering occasioned by the wind. "Let her, if she dare!" the squatter muttered in his teeth. "Abiram, they know my temper too well to play the prank with me!"

"Look for yourself! If the curtain is not lifted, I can see no better than the owl by daylight."

Ishmael struck the breech of his rifle violently on the earth and shouted in a voice that might easily have been heard by Ellen had not her attention still continued rapt on the object which so unaccountably attracted her eyes in the distance.

"Nell!" continued the squatter. "Away with you, fool! Will you bring down punishment on your own head? Why, Nell! She has forgotten her native speech; let us see if she can understand another language."

Ishmael threw his rifle to his shoulder, and at the next moment it was pointed upwards at the summit of the rock. Before time was given for a word of remonstrance, it had sent forth its contents in its usual streak of bright flame. Ellen started like the frightened chamois, and uttering a piercing scream, she darted into the tent with a swiftness that left it uncertain whether terror or actual injury had been the penalty of her offense.

The action of the squatter was too sudden and unexpected to admit of prevention; but the instant it was done, his sons manifested in an unequivocal manner the temper with which they witnessed the desperate measure. Angry and fierce glances were interchanged, and a murmur of disapprobation was uttered by the whole in common.

"What has Ellen done, Father," said Asa with a degree of spirit which was the more striking from being unusual, "that she should be shot at like a straggling deer or a hungry wolf?"

"Mischief," deliberately returned the squatter, but with a cool expression of defiance in his eye that showed how little he was moved by the ill-concealed humor of his children. "Mischief, boy, mischief! Take you heed that the disorder don't spread!"

"It would need a different treatment in a man than in yon screaming girl."

"Asa, you are a man, as you have often boasted; but remember, I am your father and your better."

"I know it well; and what sort of a father?"

"Harkee, boy; I more than half believe that your drowsy head let in the Siouxes. Be modest in speech, my watchful son, or you may have to answer yet for the mischief your own bad conduct has brought upon us."

"I'll stay no longer to be hectored like a child in petticoats. You talk of law as if you knew of none, and yet you keep me down as though I had not life and wants of my own. I'll stay no longer to be treated like one of your meanest cattle!"

"The world is wide, my gallant boy, and there's many a noble plantation on it without a tenant. Go; you have title deeds signed and sealed to your hand. Few fathers portion their children better than Ishmael Bush; you will say that for me at least when you get to be a wealthy landholder."

"Look! Father, look!" exclaimed several voices at once, seizing with avidity an opportunity to interrupt a dialogue which threatened to become more violent.

"Look!" repeated Abiram in a voice which sounded hollow and warning. "If you have time for anything but quarrels, Ishmael, look!"

The squatter turned slowly from his offending son and cast an eye that still lowered with deep resentment upward, but which, the instant it caught a view of the object that now attracted the attention of all around him, changed its expression to one of astonishment and dismay.

A female stood on the spot from which Ellen had been so fearfully expelled. Her person was of the smallest size that is believed to comport with beauty, and which poets and artists have chosen as the beau ideal of female loveliness. Her dress was of a dark and glossy silk and fluttered like gossamer around her form. Long, flowing, and curling tresses of hair, still blacker and more shining than her robe, fell at times about her shoulders, completely enveloping the whole of her delicate bust in their ringlets, or at others, streaming in the wind. The elevation at which she stood prevented a close examination of the lineaments of a countenance, which, however, it might be seen was youthful and at the moment of her unlooked-for appearance eloquent with feeling. So young indeed did this fair and fragile being appear that it might be doubted whether the age of childhood was entirely passed. One small and exquisitely molded hand was pressed on her heart, while with the other she made an impressive gesture which seemed to invite Ishmael, if further violence was meditated, to direct it against her bosom.

The silent wonder with which the group of borderers gazed upwards at so extraordinary a spectacle was only interrupted as the person of Ellen was seen emerging with timidity from the tent, as if equally urged by apprehensions in behalf of herself and the fears which she felt on account of her companion to remain concealed and to advance. She spoke, but her words were unheard by those below and unheeded by her to whom they were addressed. The latter, however, as if content with the offer she had made of herself as a victim to the resentment of Ishmael, now calmly retired, and the spot she had so lately occupied became vacant, leaving a sort of stupid impression on the spectators beneath, not unlike that which it might be supposed would have been created had they just been gazing at some supernatural vision.

More than a minute of profound silence succeeded, during which the sons of Ishmael still continued gazing at the naked rock in stupid wonder. Then, as eye met eye, an expression of novel intelligence passed from one to the other, indicating that to them, at least, the appearance of this extraordinary tenant of the pavilion was as unexpected as it was incomprehensible. At length Asa, in right of his years and moved by the rankling impulse of the recent quarrel, took on himself the office of interrogator. Instead, however, of braving the resentment of his father, of whose fierce nature, when aroused, he had had too frequent evidence to excite it wantonly, he turned upon the cowering person of Abiram, observing with a sneer, "This then is the beast you were bringing into the prairies for a decoy! I know you to be a man who seldom troubles truth when anything worse may answer, but I never knew you to outdo yourself so thoroughly before. The newspapers of Kentuck have called you a dealer in black flesh a hundred times, but little did they reckon that you drove the trade into white families."

"Who is a kidnapper?" demanded Abiram with a blustering show of resentment. "Am I to be called to account for every lie they put in print throughout the States? Look to your own family, boy; look to yourselves. The very stumps of Kentucky and Tennessee cry out ag'in ye. Aye, my tonguey gentleman, I have seen father and mother and three children, yourself for one, published on the logs and stubs of the settlements, with dollars enough for reward to have made an honest man rich, for——"

He was interrupted by a backhanded but violent blow on the mouth that caused him to totter and which left the impression of its weight in the starting blood and swelling lips.

"Asa," said the father, advancing with a portion of that dignity with which the hand of Nature seems to have invested the parental character, "you have struck the brother of your mother!"

"I have struck the abuser of the whole family," returned the angry youth, "and unless he teaches his tongue a wiser language, he had better part with it altogether, as the unruly member. I'm no great performer with the knife, but on an occasion could make out myself to cut off a slande——"

"Boy, twice have you forgotten yourself today. Be careful that it does not happen the third time. When the law of the land is weak, it is right the law of nature should be strong. You understand me, Asa; and you know me. As for you, Abiram, the child has done you wrong, and it is my place to see you righted. Remember; I tell you justice shall be done; it is enough. But you have said hard things ag'in me and my family. If the hounds of the law have put their bills on the trees and stumps of the clearings, it was for no act of dishonesty, as you know, but because we maintain the rule that 'arth is common property. No, Abiram; could I wash my hands of things done by your advice as easily as I can of the things done by the whisperings of the devil, my sleep would be quieter at night, and none who bear my name need blush to hear it mentioned. Peace, Asa, and you too, man; enough has been said. Let us all think well before anything is added that may make what is already so bad still more bitter."

Ishmael waved his hand with authority as he ended and turned away with the air of one who felt assured that those he had addressed would not have the temerity to dispute his commands. Asa evidently struggled with himself to compel the required obedience, but his heavy nature quietly sank into its ordinary repose and he soon appeared again the being he really was, dangerous only at moments, and one whose passions were too sluggish to be long maintained at the point of ferocity. Not so with Abiram. While there was an appearance of a personal conflict between him and his colossal nephew, his mien had expressed the infallible evidences of engrossing apprehension; but now that the authority as well as gigantic strength of the father were interposed between him and his assailant, his countenance changed from paleness to a livid hue that bespoke how deeply the injury he had received rankled in his breast. Like Asa, however, he acquiesced in the decision of the squatter; and the appearance, at least, of harmony was restored again among a set of beings who were restrained by no obligations more powerful than the frail web of authority with which Ishmael had been able to envelop his children.

One effect of the quarrel had been to divert the thoughts of the young man from their recent visitor. With the dispute that succeeded the disappearance of the fair stranger, all recollection of her existence appeared to have vanished. A few ominous and secret conferences, it is true, were held apart, during which the direction of the eyes of the different speakers betrayed their subject; but these threatening symptoms soon disappeared, and the whole party was again seen broken into its usual, listless, silent, and lounging groups.

"I will go upon the rock, boys, and look abroad for the savages," said Ishmael shortly after, advancing towards them with a mien which he intended should be conciliating, at the same time that it was authoritative. "If there is nothing to fear, we will go out on the plain; the day is too good to be lost in words, like women in the towns wrangling over their tea and sugared cakes."

Without waiting for approbation or dissent, the squatter advanced to the base of the rock, which formed a sort of perpendicular wall nearly twenty feet high around the whole acclivity. Ishmael, however, directed his footsteps to a point where an ascent might be made through a narrow cleft which he had taken the precaution to fortify with a breast-work of cottonwood logs and which in its turn was defended by a chevaux-de-frise of the branches of the same tree. Here an armed man was usually kept, as at the key of the whole position, and here one of the young men now stood, indolently leaning against the rock, ready to protect the pass if it should prove necessary until the whole party could be mustered at the several points of defense.

From this place the squatter found the ascent still difficult, partly by nature and partly by artificial impediments, until he reached a sort of terrace, or to speak more properly, the plain of the elevation, where he had established the huts in which the whole family dwelt. These tenements were, as already mentioned, of that class which are so often seen on the borders, and such as belonged to the infancy of architecture, being simply formed of logs, bark, and poles. The area on which they stood contained several hundred square feet and was sufficiently elevated above the plain greatly to lessen, if not to remove, all danger from Indian missiles. Here Ishmael believed he might leave his infants in comparative security under the protection of their spirited mother, and here he now found Esther engaged at her ordinary domestic employments, surrounded by her daughters, and lifting her voice in declamatory censure as one or another of the idle fry incurred her displeasure, and far too much engrossed with the tempest of her own conversation to know anything of the violent scene which had been passing below.

"A fine windy place you have chosen for the camp, Ishmael!" she commenced, or rather continued, by merely diverting the attack from a sobbing girl of ten at her elbow to her husband. "My word! If I haven't to count the young ones every ten minutes to see they are not flying away among the buzzards or the ducks. Why do ye all keep hovering round the rock like lolloping reptiles in the spring, when the heavens are beginning to be alive with birds, man!

D'ye think mouths can be filled and hunger satisfied by laziness and sleep!"

"You'll have your say, Eester," said the husband, using the provincial pronunciation of America for the name and regarding his noisy companions with a look of habitual tolerance rather than of affection. "But the birds you shall have if your own tongue don't frighten them to take too high a flight. Aye, woman," he continued, standing on the very spot whence he had so rudely banished Ellen, which he had by this time gained, "and buffalo too if my eye can tell the animal at the distance of a Spanish league."

"Come down; come down and be doing instead of talking. A talking man is no better than a barking dog. Nell shall hang out the cloth if any of the redskins show themselves, in time to give you notice. But, Ishmael, what have you been killing, my man, for it was your rifle I heard a few minutes agone, unless I have lost my skill in sounds."

"Poh! 'Twas to frighten the hawk you see sailing above the rock."

"Hawk, indeed! At your time of day to be shooting at hawks and buzzards, with eighteen open mouths to feed. Look at the bee and at the beaver, my good man, and learn to be a provider. Why, Ishmael! I believe my soul," she continued, dropping the tow she was twisting on a distaff, "the man is in that tent ag'in! More than half his time is spent about the worthless, good-for-nothing——"

The sudden reappearance of her husband closed the mouth of the wife; and as the former descended to the place where Esther had resumed her employment, she was content to grumble forth her dissatisfaction instead of expressing it in more audible terms.

The dialogue that now took place between the affectionate pair was sufficiently succinct and expressive. The woman was at first a little brief and sullen in her answers, but care for her family soon rendered her more complaisant. As the purport of the conversation was merely an engagement to hunt during the remainder of the day in order to provide the chief necessary of life, we shall not stop to record it.

With this resolution, then, the squatter descended to the plain and divided his forces into two parts, one of which was to remain as a guard with the fortress and the other to accompany him to the field. He warily included Asa and Abiram in his own party, well knowing that no authority short of his own was competent to repress the fierce disposition of his headlong son if fairly awakened. When these arrangements were completed, the hunters sallied forth, separating at no great distance from the rock in order to form a circle about the distant herd of buffaloes.

CHAPTER 9

Priscian a little scratched;
'Twill serve.   LOVE'S LABOR'S LOST

HAVING MADE THE reader acquainted with the manner in which Ishmael Bush had disposed of his family under circumstances that might have proved so embarrassing to most other men, we shall again shift the scene a few short miles from the place last described, preserving, however, the due and natural succession of time. At the very moment that the squatter and his sons departed in the manner mentioned in the preceding chapter, two men were intently occupied in a swale that lay along the borders of a little run just out of cannon-shot from the encampment discussing the merits of a savory bison's hump that had been prepared for their palates with the utmost attention to the particular merits of that description of food. The choice morsel had been judiciously separated from the adjoining and less worthy parts of the beast, and enveloped in the hairy coating provided by nature, it had duly undergone the heat of the customary subterranean oven and was now laid before its proprietors in all the culinary glory of the prairies. So far as richness, delicacy and wildness of flavor, and substantial nourishment were concerned, the viand might well have claimed a decided superiority over the meretricious cookery and labored compounds of the most renowned artist, though the service of the dainty was certainly achieved in a manner far from artificial. It would appear that the two fortunate mortals to whose happy lot it fell to enjoy a meal in which health and appetite lent so keen a relish to the exquisite food of the American deserts were far from being insensible of the advantage they possessed.

The one to whose knowledge in the culinary art the other was indebted for his banquet seemed the least disposed of the two to profit by his own skill. He ate, it is true, and with a relish, but it was always with the moderation with which age is apt to temper the appetite. No such restraint, however, was imposed on the inclination of his companion. In the very flower of his days and in the vigor of manhood, the homage that he paid to the work of his more aged friend's hands was of the most profound and engrossing character. As one delicious morsel succeeded another, he rolled his eyes towards his companion and seemed to express that gratitude which he had not speech to utter in looks of the most benignant nature.

"Cut more into the heart of it, lad," said the trapper, for it was the venerable inhabitant of those vast wastes who had served the bee hunter with the banquet in question; "cut more into the center of the piece; there you will find the genuine riches of natur', and that without need from spices or any of your biting mustard to give it a foreign relish."

"If I had but a cup of metheglin," said Paul, stopping to perform the necessary operation of breathing, "I should swear this was the strongest meal that was ever placed before the mouth of man!"

"Aye, aye, well you may call it strong!" returned the other, laughing after his peculiar manner in pure satisfaction at witnessing the infinite contentment of his companion. "Strong it is, and strong it makes him who eats it! Here, Hector" —tossing the patient hound, who was watching his eye with a wistful look, a portion of the meat—"you have need of strength, my friend, in your old days as well as your master. Now, lad, there is a dog that has eaten and slept wiser and better, aye, and that of richer food, than any king of them all! And why? Because he has used and not abused the gifts of his Maker. He was made a hound, and like a hound has he feasted. Them did He create men; but they have eaten like famished wolves. A good and prudent dog has Hector proved, and never have I found one of his breed false in nose or friendship. Do you know the difference between the cookery of the wilderness and that which is found in the settlements? No; I see plainly you don't, by your appetite; then I will tell you. The one follows man, the other natur'. One thinks he can add to the gifts of the Creator, while the other is humble enough to enjoy them; therein lies the secret."

"I tell you, trapper," said Paul, who was very little edified by the morality with which his associate saw fit to season their repast, "that every day while we are in this place, and they are likely to be many, I will shoot a buffalo and you shall cook his hump!"

"I cannot say that, I cannot say that. The beast is good, take him in what part you will, and it was to be food for man that he was fashioned; but I cannot say that I will be a witness and a helper to the waste of killing one daily."

"The devil a bit of waste shall there be, old man. If they all turn out as good as this, I will engage to eat them clean myself, even to the hoofs; how now, who comes here! Someone with a long nose, I will answer, and one that has led him on a true scent if he is following the trail of a dinner."

The individual who interrupted the conversation and who had elicited the foregoing remark of Paul was seen advancing along the margin of the run with a deliberate pace, in a direct line for the two revelers. As there was nothing formidable nor hostile in his appearance, the bee hunter, instead of suspending his operations, rather increased his efforts, in a manner which would seem to imply that he doubted whether the hump would suffice for the proper entertainment of all who were now likely to partake of the delicious morsel. With the trapper, however, the case was different. His more tempered appetite was already satisfied, and he faced the newcomer with a look of cordiality that plainly evinced how very opportune he considered his arrival.

"Come on, friend," he said, waving his hand as he observed the stranger to pause a moment, apparently in doubt. "Come on, I say; if hunger be your guide, it has led you to a fitting place. Here is meat, and this youth can give you corn, parched till it be whiter than the upland snow; come on, without fear. We are not ravenous beasts eating of each other, but Christian men receiving thankfully that which the Lord hath seen fit to give."

"Venerable hunter," returned the doctor, for it was no other than the naturalist on one of his daily exploring expeditions, "I rejoice greatly at this happy meeting; we are lovers of the same pursuits and should be friends."

"Lord, Lord," said the old man, laughing, without much deference to the rules of decorum, in the philosopher's very face, "it is the man who wanted to make me believe that a name could change the natur' of a beast! Come, friend, you are welcome, though your notions are a little blinded with reading too many books. Sit ye down, and after eating of this morsel, tell me, if you can, the name of the creatur' that has bestowed on you its flesh for a meal."

The eyes of Dr. Battius (for we deem it decorous to give the good man the appellation he most preferred)—the eyes of Dr. Battius sufficiently denoted the satisfaction with which he listened to this proposal. The exercise he had taken and the sharpness of the wind proved excellent stimulants, and Paul himself had hardly been in better plight to do credit to the trapper's cookery than was the lover of nature when the grateful invitation met his ears. Indulging in a small laugh, which his exertions to repress reduced nearly to a simper, he took the indicated seat by the old man's side and made the customary dispositions to commence his meal without further ceremony.

"I should be ashamed of my profession," he said, swallowing a morsel of the hump with evident delight, slyly endeavoring at the same time to distinguish the peculiarities of the singed and defaced skin, "I ought to be ashamed of my profession, were there beast or bird on the continent of America that I could not tell by some one of the many evidences which science has enlisted in her cause. This—then—the food is nutritious and savory—a mouthful of your corn, friend, if you please?"

Paul, who continued eating with increasing industry, looking askant not unlike a dog when engaged in the same agreeable pursuit, threw him his pouch without deeming it at all necessary to suspend his own labors.

"You were saying, friend, that you have many ways of telling the creatur'?" observed the attentive trapper.

"Many; many and infallible. Now, the animals that are carnivorous are known by their incisors."

"Their what?" demanded the trapper.

"The teeth with which nature has furnished them for defense, and in order to tear their food. Again——"

"Look you then for the teeth of this creatur'," interrupted the trapper, who was bent on convicting a man who had presumed to enter into competition with himself, in matters pertaining to the wilds, of gross ignorance; "turn the piece round and find your inside-overs."

The doctor complied, and of course without success, though he profited by the occasion to take another fruitless glance at the wrinkled hide.

"Well, friend, do you find the things you need before you can pronounce the creatur' a duck or a salmon?"

"I apprehend the entire animal is not here?"

"You may well say as much," cried Paul, who was now compelled to pause from pure repletion; "I will answer for some pounds of the fellow, weighed by the truest steelyards west of the Alleghenies. Still you may make out to keep soul and body together with what is left"—reluctantly eyeing a piece large enough to feed twenty men, but which he felt compelled to abandon from satiety; "cut in nigher to the heart, as the old man says, and you will find the riches of the piece."

"The heart!" exclaimed the doctor, inwardly delighted to learn there was a distinct organ to be submitted to his inspection. "Aye, let me see the heart—it will at once determine the character of the animal—certes this is not the core—aye, sure enough it is—the animal must be of the order *belluae,* from its obese habits!"

He was interrupted by a long and hearty but still a noiseless fit of merriment from the trapper, which was considered so ill-timed by the offended naturalist as to produce an instant cessation of speech, if not a stagnation of ideas.

"Listen to his beasts' habits and belly orders," said the old man, delighted with the evident embarrassment of his rival; "and then he says it is not the core! Why, man, you are further from the truth than you are from the settlements, with all your bookish larning and hard words, which I have, once for all, said cannot be understood by any tribe or nation east of the Rocky Mountains. Beastly habits or no beastly habits, the creatur's are to be seen cropping the prairies by tens of thousands, and the piece in your hand is the core of as juicy a buffalo hump as stomach need crave!"

"My aged companion," said Obed, struggling to keep down a rising irascibility that he conceived would ill comport with the dignity of his character, "your system is erroneous from the premises to the conclusion; and your classifications so faulty, as utterly to confound the distinctions of science. The buffalo is not gifted with a hump at all, nor is his flesh savory and wholesome, as I must acknowledge it would seem the subject before us may well be characterized——"

"There I'm dead against you, and clearly with the trapper,"

interrupted Paul Hover. "The man who denies that buffalo beef is good should scorn to eat it!" *

The doctor, whose observation of the bee hunter had hitherto been exceedingly cursory, stared at the new speaker with a look which denoted something like recognition.

"The principal characteristics of your countenance, friend," he said, "are familiar; either you or some other specimen of your class is known to me."

"I am the man you met in the woods east of the big river and whom you tried to persuade to line a yellow hornet to his nest, as if my eye was not too true to mistake any other animal for a honeybee in a clear day! We tarried together a week, as you may remember, you at your toads and lizards and I at my high-holes and hollow trees; and a good job we made of it between us! I filled my tubs with the sweetest honey I ever sent to the settlements, besides housing a dozen hives; and your bag was near bursting with a crawling museum. I never was bold enough to put the question to your face, stranger, but I reckon you are a keeper of curiosities?" †

"Aye! That is another of their wanton wickednesses!" exclaimed the trapper. "They slay the buck, and the moose, and the wildcat, and all the beasts that range the woods, and stuffing them with worthless rags, and placing eyes of glass into their heads, they set them up to be stared at, and call them the creatur's of the Lord, as if any mortal effigy could equal the works of his hand!"

"I know you well!" returned the doctor, on whom the plaint of the old man produced no visible impression. "I know you," offering his hand cordially to Paul; "it was a prolific week, as my herbal and catalogs shall one day prove. Aye, I remember you well, young man. You are of the class

---

* It is scarcely necessary to tell the reader that the animal so often alluded to in this book, and which is vulgarly called the buffalo, is in truth the bison; hence so many contretemps between the men of the prairies and the men of science.

† The pursuit of a bee hunter is not uncommon on the skirts of American society, though it is a little embellished here. When the bees are seen sucking the flowers, their pursuer contrives to capture one or two. He then chooses a proper spot, and suffering one to escape, the insect invariably takes its flight towards the hive. Changing his ground to a greater or less distance according to circumstances, the bee hunter then permits another to escape. Having watched the courses of the bees, which is technically called lining, he is enabled to calculate the intersecting angle of the two lines, which is the hive.

Mammalia, order Primates, genus Homo, species Kentucky." Pausing to smile at his own humor, the naturalist proceeded, "Since our separation, I have journeyed far, having entered into a compactum, or agreement, with a certain man named Ishmael——"

"Bush!" interrupted the impatient and reckless Paul. "By the Lord, trapper, this is the very bloodletter that Ellen told me of!"

"Then Nelly has not done me credit for what I trust I deserve," returned the single-minded doctor, "for I am not of the phlebotomizing school at all, greatly preferring the practice which purifies the blood instead of abstracting it."

"It was a blunder of mine, good stranger; the girl called you a skillful man."

"Therein she may have exceeded my merits," Dr. Battius continued, bowing with sufficient meekness. "But Ellen is a good, and a kind, and a spirited girl, too. A kind and a sweet girl I have ever found Nelly Wade to be!"

"The devil you have!" cried Paul, dropping the morsel he was sucking, from sheer reluctance to abandon the hump, and casting a fierce and direct look into the very teeth of the unconscious physician. "I reckon, stranger, you have a mind to bag Ellen too!"

"The riches of the whole vegetable and animal world united would not tempt me to harm a hair of her head! I love the child with what may be called amor naturalis—or rather paternus—the affection of a father."

"Aye—that indeed is more befitting the difference in your years," Paul coolly rejoined, stretching forth his hand to regain the rejected morsel. "You would be no better than a drone at your time of day, with a young hive to feed and swarm."

"Yes, there is reason because there is natur' in what he says," observed the trapper; "but, friend, you have said you were a dweller in the camp of one Ishmael Bush?"

"True; it is in virtue of a compactum——"

"I know but little of the virtue of packing, though I follow trapping, in my old age, for a livelihood. They tell me that skins are well kept in the new fashion, but it is long since I have left off killing more than I need for food and garments. I was an eyewitness myself of the manner in which the Siouxes broke into your encampment and drove off the cattle, stripping the poor man you call Ishmael of his smallest hoofs, counting even the cloven feet."

"*Asinus* excepted," muttered the doctor, who by this time was discussing his portion of the hump, in utter forgetfulness of all its scientific attributes. "*Asinus domesticus americanus* excepted."

"I am glad to hear that so many of them are saved, though I know not the value of the animals you name, which is nothing uncommon, seeing how long it is that I have been out of the settlements. But can you tell me, friend, what the traveler carries under the white cloth he guards with teeth as sharp as a wolf that quarrels for the carcass the hunter has left?"

"You've heard of it!" exclaimed the other, dropping the morsel he was conveying to his mouth in manifest surprise.

"Nay, I have heard nothing; but I have seen the cloth, and had like to have been bitten for no greater crime than wishing to know what it covered."

"Bitten! Then, after all, the animal must be carnivorous! It is too tranquil for the *Ursus horridus*; if it were the *Canis latrans*, the voice would betray it. Nor would Nelly Wade be so familiar with any of the genus Ferae. Venerable hunter! The solitary animal confined in that wagon by day and in the tent at night has occasioned me more perplexity of mind than the whole catalog of quadrupeds besides, and for this plain reason. I did not know how to class it."

"You think it a ravenous beast?"

"I know it to be a quadruped; your own danger proves it to be carnivorous."

During this broken explanation Paul Hover had sat silent and thoughtful, regarding each speaker with deep attention. But suddenly moved by the manner of the doctor, the latter had scarcely time to utter his positive assertion before the young man bluntly demanded, "And pray, friend, what may you call a quadruped?"

"A vagary of nature, wherein she has displayed less of her infinite wisdom than is usual. Could rotary levers be substituted for two of the limbs, agreeably to the improvement in my new order of phalangacrura, which might be rendered into the vernacular as lever-legged, there would be a delightful perfection and harmony in the construction. But as the quadruped is now formed, I call it a mere vagary of nature; no other than a vagary."

"Harkee, stranger! In Kentucky we are but small dealers in dictionaries. Vagary is as hard a word to turn into English as quadruped."

"A quadruped is an animal with four legs—a beast."

"A beast! Do you then reckon that Ishmael Bush travels with a beast caged in that wagon?"

"I know it; and lend me your ear, not literally, friend—" observing Paul to start and look surprised—"but figuratively, through its functions, and you shall hear. I have already made known that in virtue of a compactum I journey with the aforesaid Ishmael Bush; but though I am bound to perform certain duties while the journey lasts, there is no condition which says that the said journey shall be sempiternum, or eternal. Now, though this region may scarcely be said to be wedded to science, being to all intents a virgin territory as respects the inquirer into natural history, still it is greatly destitute of the treasures of the vegetable kingdom. I should, therefore, have tarried some hundreds of miles more to the eastward were it not for the inward propensity that I feel to have the beast in question inspected and suitably described and classed. For that matter," he continued, dropping his voice like one who imparts an important secret, "I am not without hopes of persuading Ishmael to let me dissect it."

"You have seen the creature?"

"Not with the organs of sight, but with much more infallible instruments of vision—the conclusions of reason and the deductions of scientific premises. I have watched the habits of the animal, young man, and can fearlessly pronounce, by evidence that would be thrown away on ordinary observers, that it is of vast dimensions, inactive, possibly torpid, of voracious appetite, and as it now appears by the direct testimony of this venerable hunter, ferocious and carnivorous!"

"I should be better pleased, stranger," said Paul, on whom the doctor's description was making a very sensible impression, "to be sure the creature was a beast at all."

"As to that, if I wanted evidence of a fact, which is abundantly apparent by the habits of the animal, I have the word of Ishmael himself. A reason can be given for my smallest deductions. I am not troubled, young man, with a vulgar and idle curiosity, but all my aspirations after knowledge, as I humbly believe, are first for the advancement of learning and secondly for the benefit of my fellow creatures. I pined greatly in secret to know the contents of the tent which Ishmael guarded so carefully and which he had covenanted that I should swear (jurare per deos) not to approach nigher than a defined number of cubits for a definite period of time. Your jusjurandum, or oath, is a serious matter, and not to be dealt in lightly; but as my expedition depended on complying, I consented to the act, reserving to myself at all times the power of distant observation. It is now some ten days since Ishmael, pitying the state in which he saw me, a humble lover of science, imparted the fact that the vehicle contained a beast which he was carrying into the prairies as a decoy, by which he intends to entrap others of the same genus, or perhaps species. Since then my task has been reduced simply to watch the habits of the animal and to record the results. When we reach a certain distance, where these beasts are said to abound, I am to have the liberal examination of the specimen."

Paul continued to listen in the most profound silence until the doctor concluded his singular but characteristic explanation; then the incredulous bee hunter shook his head and saw fit to reply by saying, "Stranger, old Ishmael has burrowed you in the very bottom of a hollow tree, where your eyes will be of no more use than the sting of a drone. I too know something of that very wagon, and I may say that I have lined the squatter down into a flat lie. Harkee, friend; do you think a girl like Ellen Wade would become the companion of a wild beast?"

"Why not? Why not?" repeated the naturalist. "Nelly has a taste and often listens with pleasure to the treasures that I am sometimes compelled to scatter in this desert. Why should she not study the habits of any animal, even though it were a rhinoceros?"

"Softly, softly," returned the equally positive, and though less scientific, certainly on this subject better-instructed bee hunter; "Ellen is a girl of spirit, and one too that knows her own mind, or I'm much mistaken; but with all her courage and brave looks, she is no better than a woman after all. Haven't I often had the girl crying——"

"You are an acquaintance, then, of Nelly's?"

"The devil a bit. But I know woman is woman, and all the books in Kentucky couldn't make Ellen Wade go into a tent alone with a ravenous beast!"

"It seems to me," the trapper calmly observed, "that there is something dark and hidden in this matter. I am a witness that the traveler likes none to look into the tent, and I have proof more sure than what either of you can lay claim to that the wagon does not carry the cage of a beast. Here is Hector, come of a breed with noses as true and faithful as a hand that is all-powerful has made any of their kind, and had there been a beast in the place, the hound would long since have told it to his master."

"Do you pretend to oppose a dog to a man, brutality to learning, instinct to reason!" exclaimed the doctor in some heat. "In what manner, prey, can a hound distinguish the habits, species, or even the genus of an animal, like reasoning, learned, scientific, triumphant man!"

"In what manner!" coolly repeated the veteran woodsman. "Listen; and if you believe that a schoolmaster can make a quicker wit than the Lord, you shall be made to see how much you're mistaken. Do you not hear something move in the brake? It has been cracking the twigs these five minutes. Now tell me what the creatur' is?"

"I hope nothing ferocious!" exclaimed the doctor, who still retained a lively impression of his rencounter with the *Vespertilio horribilis*. "You have rifles, friends; would it not be prudent to prime them? For this fowling piece of mine is little to be depended on."

"There may be reason in what he says," returned the trapper, so far complying as to take his piece from the place where it had lain during the repast and raising its muzzle in the air. "Now tell me the name of the creatur'."

"It exceeds the limits of earthly knowledge! Buffon himself could not tell whether the animal was a quadruped or of the order Serpens! A sheep, or a tiger!"

"Then was your buffoon a fool to my Hector! Here, pup! What is it, dog? Shall we run it down, pup, or shall we let it pass?"

The hound, which had already manifested to the experienced trapper by the tremulous motion of his ears his consciousness of the proximity of a strange animal, lifted his head from his forejaws and slightly parted his lips, as if about to show the remnants of his teeth. But suddenly abandoning his hostile purpose, he snuffed the air a moment, gaped heavily, shook himself, and peaceably resumed his recumbent attitude.

"Now, doctor," cried the trapper triumphantly, "I am well convinced there is neither game nor ravenous beast in the thicket; and that I call substantial knowledge to a man who is too old to be a spendthrift of his strength, and yet who would not wish to be a meal for a panther!"

The dog interrupted his master by a growl, but still kept his head crouched to the earth.

"It is a man!" exclaimed the trapper, rising. "It is a man, if I am a judge of the creatur's ways. There is but little said atwixt the hound and me, but we seldom mistake each other's meaning!"

Paul Hover sprang to his feet like lightning, and throwing forward his rifle, he cried in a voice of menace, "Come forward if a friend; if an enemy, stand ready for the worst!"

"A friend, a white man, and I hope, a Christian," returned a voice from the thicket, which opened at the same instant, and at the next the speaker made his appearance.

CHAPTER 10

Go apart, Adam, and thou shalt hear
How he will shake me up.
                    AS YOU LIKE IT

IT IS well known that even long before the immense regions of Louisiana changed their masters for the second, and, as it is to be hoped, for the last time, its unguarded territory was by no means safe from the inroads of white adventurers. The semibarbarous hunters from the Canadas, the same description of population, a little more enlightened, from the States, and the metifs, or half-breeds, who claimed to be ranked in the class of white men, were scattered among the different Indian tribes or gleaned a scanty livelihood in solitude amid the haunts of the beaver and the bison, or to adopt the popular nomenclature of the country —of the buffalo.*

---

* In addition to the scientific distinctions which mark the two species, it may be added, with due reverence to Dr. Battius, that a much more important particular is the fact that while the former of these animals is delicious and nourishing food, the latter is scarcely edible.

It was, therefore, no unusual thing for strangers to encounter each other in the endless wastes of the West. By signs which an unpracticed eye would pass unobserved, a borderer knew when one of his fellows was in his vicinity, and he avoided or approached the intruder as best comported with his feelings or his interests. Generally these interviews were pacific, for the whites had a common enemy to dread in the ancient and perhaps more lawful occupants of the country; but instances were not rare in which jealousy and cupidity had caused them to terminate in scenes of the most violent and ruthless treachery. The meeting of two hunters on the American desert, as we find it convenient sometimes to call this region, was consequently somewhat in the suspicious and wary manner in which two vessels draw together in a sea that is known to be infested with pirates. While neither party is willing to betray its weakness by exhibiting distrust, neither is disposed to commit itself by any acts of confidence from which it may be difficult to recede.

Such was, in some degree, the character of the present interview. The stranger drew nigh deliberately, keeping his eyes steadily fastened on the movements of the other party while he purposely created little difficulties to impede an approach which might prove too hasty. On the other hand, Paul stood playing with the lock of his rifle, too proud to let it appear that three men could manifest any apprehension of a solitary individual, and yet too prudent to omit entirely the customary precautions. The principal reason of the marked difference which the two legitimate proprietors of the banquet made in the receptions of their guests was to be explained by the entire difference which existed in their respective appearances.

While the exterior of the naturalist was decidedly pacific, not to say abstracted, that of the newcomer was distinguished by an air of vigor and a front and step which it would not have been difficult to have at once pronounced to be military.

He wore a forage cap of fine blue cloth from which depended a soiled tassel in gold and which was nearly buried in a mass of exuberant, curling, jet-black hair. Around his throat he had negligently fastened a stock of black silk. His body was enveloped in a hunting shirt of dark green trimmed with the yellow fringes and ornaments that were sometimes seen among the border troops of the Confederacy. Beneath this, however, were visible the collar and lapels of a jacket similar in color and cloth to the cap. His lower limbs were protected by buckskin leggings, and his feet by the ordinary Indian moccasins. A richly ornamented and exceedingly dangerous straight dirk was stuck in a sash of red-silk network; another girdle, or rather belt, of uncolored leather contained a pair of the smallest sized pistols in holsters nicely made to fit, and across his shoulder was thrown a short, heavy, military rifle, its horn and pouch occupying the usual places beneath his arms. At his back he bore a knapsack marked by the well-known initials that have since gained for the government of the United States the good-humored and quaint appellation of Uncle Sam.

"I come in amity," the stranger said, like one too much accustomed to the sight of arms to be startled at the ludicrously belligerent attitude which Dr. Battius had seen fit to assume. "I come as a friend and am one whose pursuits and wishes will not at all interfere with your own."

"Harkee, stranger," said Paul Hover bluntly; "do you understand lining a bee from this open place into a wood distant perhaps a dozen miles?"

"The bee is a bird I have never been compelled to seek," returned the other, laughing, "though I have too been something of a fowler in my time."

"I thought as much," exclaimed Paul, thrusting forth his hand frankly and with the true freedom of manner that marks an American borderer. "Let us cross fingers. You and I will never quarrel about the comb, since you set so little store by the honey. And now, if your stomach has an empty corner and you know how to relish a genuine dewdrop when it falls into your very mouth, there lies the exact morsel to put into it. Try it, stranger; and having tried it, if you don't call it as snug a fit as you have made since— How long are you from the settlements, pray?"

" 'Tis many weeks, and I fear it may be as many more before I can return. I will, however, gladly profit by your invitation, for I have fasted since the rising of yesterday's sun, and I know too well the merits of a bison's hump to reject the food."

"Ah! You are acquainted with the dish! Well, therein

you have the advantage of me, in setting out, though I think I may say we could now start on equal ground. I should be the happiest fellow between Kentucky and the Rocky Mountains if I had a snug cabin near some old wood that was filled with hollow trees, just such a hump every day as that for dinner, a load of fresh straw for hives, and little El—"

"Little what?" demanded the stranger, evidently amused with the communicative and frank disposition of the bee hunter.

"Something that I shall have one day, and which concerns nobody so much as myself," returned Paul, picking the flint of his rifle and beginning very cavalierly to whistle an air well known on the waters of the Mississippi.

During this preliminary discourse the stranger had taken his seat by the side of the hump and was already making a serious inroad on its relics. Dr. Battius, however, watched his movements with a jealousy still more striking than the cordial reception which the openhearted Paul had just exhibited.

But the doubts, or rather apprehensions, of the naturalist were of a character altogether different from the confidence of the bee hunter. He had been struck with the stranger's using the legitimate instead of the perverted name of the animal off which he was making his repast; and as he had been among the foremost himself to profit by the removal of the impediments which the policy of Spain had placed in the way of all explorers of her transatlantic dominions, whether bent on the purposes of commerce or like himself on the more laudable pursuits of science, he had a sufficiency of everyday philosophy to feel that the same motives which had so powerfully urged himself to his present undertaking might produce a like result on the mind of some other student of nature. Here, then, was the prospect of an alarming rivalry, which bade fair to strip him of at least a moiety of the just rewards of all his labors, privations, and dangers. Under these views of his character, therefore, it is not at all surprising that the native meekness of the naturalist's disposition was a little disturbed and that he watched the proceedings of the other with such a degree of vigilance as he believed best suited to detect his sinister designs.

"This is truly a delicious repast," observed the uncon-

scious young stranger, for both young and handsome he was
fairly entitled to be considered; "either hunger has given a
peculiar relish to the viand or the bison may lay claim to
be the finest of the ox family!"

"Naturalists, sir, are apt, when they speak familiarly, to
give the cow the credit of the genus," said Dr. Battius,
swelling with secret distrust and clearing his throat before
speaking, much in the manner that a duelist examines the
point of the weapon he is about to plunge into the body
of his foe. "The figure is more perfect; as the bos, meaning
the ox, is unable to perpetuate his kind; and the bos, in
its most extended meaning, or vaca, is altogether the
nobler animal of the two."

The doctor uttered this opinion with a certain air that
he intended should express his readiness to come at once to
any of the numerous points of difference which he doubted
not existed between them; and he now awaited the blow
of his antagonist, intending that his next thrust should
be still more vigorous. But the young stranger appeared
much better disposed to partake of the good cheer with
which he had been so providentially provided than to take
up the cudgels of argument on this or on any other of
the knotty points which are so apt to furnish the lovers of
science with the materials of a mental joust.

"I dare say you are very right, sir," he replied with a most
provoking indifference to the importance of the points he
conceded. "I dare say you are quite right, and that vaca
would have been the better word."

"Pardon me, sir; you are giving a very wrong construction
to my language if you suppose I include without many and
particular qualifications the *Bibulus americanus* in the family
of the vaca. For, as you well know, sir—or, as I presume
I should say, doctor—you have the medical diploma no
doubt?"

"You give me credit for an honor I cannot claim," interrupted the other.

"An undergraduate! Or perhaps your degrees have been
taken in some other of the liberal sciences?"

"Still wrong, I do assure you."

"Surely, young man, you have not entered on this important—I may say, this awful—service, without some evidence of your fitness for the task! Some commission by
which you can assert an authority to proceed or by which

you may claim an affinity and a communion with your fellow workers in the same beneficent pursuits!"

"I know not by what means or for what purposes you have made yourself master of my objects!" exclaimed the youth, reddening and rising with a quickness which manifested how little he regarded the grosser appetites when a subject nearer his heart was approached. "Still, sir, your language is incomprehensible. That pursuit which in another might perhaps be justly called beneficent is in me a dear and cherished duty; though why a commission should be demanded or needed is, I confess, no less a subject of surprise."

"It is customary to be provided with such a document," returned the doctor gravely, "and on all suitable occasions to produce it in order that congenial and friendly minds may at once reject unworthy suspicions, and stepping over what may be called the elements of discourse, come at once to those points which are desiderata to both."

"It is a strange request!" the youth muttered, turning his frowning eye from one to the other as if examining the characters of his companions with a view to weigh their physical powers. Then, putting his hand into his bosom, he drew forth a small box, and extending it with an air of dignity towards the doctor, he continued, "You will find by this, sir, that I have some right to travel in a country which is now the property of the American states."

"What have we here!" exclaimed the naturalist, opening the folds of a large parchment. "Why, this is the sign manual of the philosopher Jefferson! The seal of state! Countersigned by the minister of war! Why, this is a commission creating Duncan Uncas Middleton a captain of artillery!"

"Of whom? Of whom?" repeated the trapper, who had sat regarding the stranger during the whole discourse with eyes that seemed greedily to devour each lineament. "How is the name? Did you call him Uncas? Uncas! Was it Uncas?"

"Such is my name," returned the youth a little haughtily. "It is the appellation of a native chief, that both my uncle and myself bear with pride, for it is the memorial of an important service done my family by a warrior in the old wars of the provinces."

"Uncas! Did ye call him Uncas?" repeated the trapper, approaching the youth and parting the dark curls which clustered over his brow, without the slightest resistance on the part of their wondering owner. "Ah! My eyes are old and not so keen as when I was a warrior myself, but I can see the look of the father in the son! I saw it when he first came nigh, but so many things have since passed before my failing sight that I could not name the place where I had met his likeness! Tell me, lad, by what name is your father known?"

"He was an officer of the States in the war of the revolution, and of my own name of course; my mother's brother was called Duncan Uncas Heyward."

"Still Uncas! Still Uncas!" echoed the other, trembling with eagerness. "And *his* father?"

"Was called the same, without the appellation of the native chief. It was to him and to my grandmother that the service of which I have just spoken was rendered."

"I knowed it! I knowed it!" shouted the old man in his tremulous voice, his rigid features working powerfully, as if the names the other mentioned awakened some long-dormant emotions connected with the events of an anterior age. "I knowed it! Son or grandson, it is all the same; it is the blood, and 'tis the look! Tell me, is he they called Duncan, without the Uncas—is he living?"

The young man shook his head sorrowfully as he replied in the negative.

"He died full of days and of honors. Beloved, happy, and bestowing happiness!"

"Full of days!" repeated the trapper, looking down at his own meager but still muscular hands. "Ah! He lived in the settlements and was wise only after their fashions. But you have often seen him, and you have heard him discourse of Uncas and of the wilderness?"

"Often! He was then an officer of the king, but when the war took place between the crown and her colonies, my grandfather did not forget his birthplace, but threw off the empty allegiance of names and was true to his proper country; he fought on the side of liberty."

"There was reason in it, and what is better, there was natur'! Come, sit ye down beside me, lad; sit ye down and tell me of what your gran'ther used to speak when his mind dwelt on the wonders of the wilderness."

The youth smiled, no less at the importunity than at the interest manifested by the old man; but as he found there was no longer the least appearance of any violence being contemplated, he unhesitatingly complied.

"Give it all to the trapper, by rule, and by figures of speech," said Paul, very coolly taking his seat on the other side of the young soldier. "It is the fashion of old age to relish these anciènt traditions, and for that matter I can say that I don't dislike to listen to them myself."

Middleton smiled again, and perhaps with a slight air of derision; but good-naturedly turning to the trapper, he continued, "It is a long, and might prove a painful story. Bloodshed and all the horrors of Indian cruelty and of Indian warfare are fearfully mingled in the narrative."

"Aye, give it all to us, stranger," continued Paul; "we are used to these matters in Kentuck, and I must say I think a story none the worse for having a few scalps in it."

"But he told you of Uncas, did he?" resumed the trapper, without regarding the slight interruptions of the bee hunter, which amounted to no more than a sort of byplay. "And what thought he and said he of the lad, in his parlor, with the comforts and ease of the settlements at his elbow?"

"I doubt not he used a language similar to that he would have adopted in the woods, and had he stood face to face with his friend——"

"Did he call the savage his friend; the poor, naked, painted warrior? He was not too proud, then, to call the Indian his friend?"

"He even boasted of the connection, and as you have already heard, bestowed a name on his firstborn, which is likely to be handed down as an heirloom among the rest of his descendants."

"It was well done! Like a man. Aye! And like a Christian too! He used to say the Delaware was swift of foot; did he remember that?"

"As the antelope! Indeed, he often spoke of him by the appellation of Le Cerf Agile, a name he had obtained by his activity."

"And bold, and fearless, lad!" continued the trapper, looking up into the eyes of his companion with a wistfulness that bespoke the delight he received in listening to the praises of one whom it was so very evident he had once tenderly loved.

"Brave as a blooded hound! Without fear! He always quoted Uncas and his father—who from his wisdom was called the

Great Serpent—as models of heroism and constancy."

"He did them justice! He did them justice! Truer men were not to be found in tribe or nation, be their skins of what color they might. I see your gran'ther was just, and did his duty too by his offspring! 'Twas a perilous time he had of it, among them hills, and nobly did he play his own part! Tell me, lad, or officer, I should say, since officer you be, was this all?"

"Certainly not; it was, as I have said, a fearful tale full of moving incidents, and the memories both of my grandfather and of my grandmother——"

"Ah!" exclaimed the trapper, tossing a hand into the air as his whole countenance lighted with the recollections the name revived. "They called her Alice! Elsie or Alice, 'tis all the same. A laughing, playful child she was when happy, and tender and weeping in her misery! Her hair was shining and yellow as the coat of the young fawn, and her skin clearer than the purest water that drips from the rock. Well do I remember her! I remember her right well!"

The lip of the youth slightly curled, and he regarded the old man with an expression which might easily have been construed into a declaration that such were not his own recollections of his venerable and revered ancestor, though it would seem he did not think it necessary to say as much in words. He was content to answer, "They both retained impressions of the dangers they had passed, by far too vivid easily to lose the recollection of any of their fellow actors."

The trapper looked aside and seemed to struggle with some deeply innate feeling; then, turning again towards his companion, though his honest eyes no longer dwelt with the same open interest as before on the countenance of the other, he continued, "Did he tell you of them *all?* Were they *all* redskins but himself and the daughters of Munro?"

"No. There was a white man associated with the Delawares. A scout of the English army, but a native of the provinces."

"A drunken, worthless vagabond like most of his color who harbor with the savages, I warrant you!"

"Old man, your gray hairs should caution you against slander. The man I speak of was of great simplicity of mind, but of sterling worth. Unlike most of those who live a border life, he united the better instead of the worst qualities of the two people. He was a man endowed with the choicest and perhaps rarest gift of nature, that of distinguishing good from evil. His virtues were those of simplicity, because such were the fruits of his habits, as were indeed his very prejudices. In courage he was the equal of his red associates; in warlike skill, being better instructed, their superior. 'In short, he was a noble shoot from the stock of human nature which never could attain its proper elevation and importance, for no other reason than because it grew in the forest'; such, old hunter, were the very words of my grandfather when speaking of the man you imagine so worthless!"

The eyes of the trapper had sunk to the earth as the stranger delivered this character in the ardent tones of generous youth. He played with the ears of his hound, fingered his own rustic garment, and opened and shut the pan of his rifle with hands that trembled in a manner that would have implied their total unfitness to wield the weapon. When the other had concluded, he hoarsely added, "Your gran'ther didn't then entirely forget the white man!"

"So far from that, there are already three among us who have also names derived from that scout."

"A name, did you say?" exclaimed the old man, starting. "What, the name of the solitary, unlarned hunter? Do the great, and the rich, and the honored and, what is better still, the just—do they bear his very, actual name?"

"It is borne by my brother and by two of my cousins, whatever may be their titles to be described by the terms you have mentioned."

"Do you mean the actual name itself, spelt with the very same letters, beginning with an N and ending with an L?"

"Exactly the same," the youth smilingly replied. "No, no, we have forgotten nothing that was his. I have at this moment a dog brushing a deer, not far from this, who is come of a hound that very scout sent as a present after his friends, and which was of the stock he always used himself; a truer breed in nose and foot is not to be found in the wide Union."

"Hector!" said the old man, struggling to conquer an emotion that nearly suffocated him and speaking to his hound in the sort of tones he would have used to a child. "Do ye hear that, pup! Your kin and blood are in the prairies! A name—it is wonderful—very wonderful!"

Nature could endure no more. Overcome by a flood of unusual and extraordinary sensations and stimulated by tender and long-dormant recollections strangely and unexpectedly revived, the old man had just self-command enough to add in a voice that was hollow and unnatural through the efforts he made to command it, "Boy, I am that scout; a warrior once, a miserable trapper now!" When the tears broke over his wasted cheeks, out of fountains that had long been dried, and sinking his face between his knees, he covered it decently with his buckskin garment and sobbed aloud.

The spectacle produced correspondent emotions in his companions. Paul Hover had actually swallowed each syllable of the discourse as they fell alternately from the different speakers, his feelings keeping equal pace with the increasing interest of the scene. Unused to such strange sensations, he was turning his face on every side of him to avoid he knew not what, until he saw the tears and heard the sobs of the old man, when he sprang to his feet, and grappling his guest fiercely by the throat, he demanded by what authority he had made his aged companion weep. A flash of recollection crossing his brain at the same instant, he released his hold, and stretching forth an arm in the very wantonness of gratification, he seized the doctor by the hair, which instantly revealed its artificial formation by cleaving to his hand, leaving the white and shining poll of the naturalist with a covering no warmer than the skin.

"What think you of that, Mr. Bug Gatherer?" he rather shouted than cried. "Is not this a strange bee to line into his hole?"

" 'Tis remarkable! Wonderful! Edifying!" returned the lover of nature, good-humoredly recovering his wig, with twinkling eyes and a husky voice. " 'Tis rare and commendable! Though I doubt not in the exact order of causes and effects."

With this sudden outbreaking, however, the commotion instantly subsided, the three spectators clustering around the trapper with a species of awe at beholding the tears of one so aged.

"It must be so, or how could he be so familiar with a history that is little known beyond my own family," at length the youth observed, not ashamed to acknowledge how much he had been affected by unequivocally drying his own eyes.

"True!" echoed Paul. "If you want any more evidence, I

will swear to it! I know every word of it myself to be true as the gospel!"

"And yet we had long supposed him dead!" continued the soldier. "My grandfather had filled his days with honor, and he had believed himself the junior of the two."

"It is not often that youth has an opportunity of thus looking down on the weakness of age!" the trapper observed, raising his head and looking around him with composure and dignity. "That I am still here, young man, is the pleasure of the Lord, who has spared me until I have seen fourscore long and laborious years for his own secret ends. That I am the man I say, you need not doubt, for why should I go to my grave with so cheap a lie in my mouth?"

"I do not hesitate to believe; I only marvel that it should be so! But why do I find you, venerable and excellent friend of my parents, in these wastes, so far from the comforts and safety of the lower country?"

"I have come into these plains to escape the sound of the ax, for here, surely, the chopper can never follow! But I may put the like question to yourself. Are you of the party which the States have sent into their new purchase to look after the natur' of the bargain they have made?"

"I am not. Lewis is making his way up the river some hundreds of miles from this. I come on a private adventure."

"Though it is no cause of wonder that a man whose strength and eyes have failed him as a hunter should be seen nigh the haunts of the beaver, using a trap instead of a rifle, it is strange that one so young and prosperous and bearing the commission of the Great Father should be moving among the prairies without even a camp-colorman to do his biddings!"

"You would think my reasons sufficient did you know them, as know them you shall if you are disposed to listen to my story. I think you all honest, and men who would rather aid than betray one bent on a worthy object."

"Come, then, and tell us at your leisure," said the trapper, seating himself and beckoning to the youth to follow his example. The latter willingly complied; and after Paul and the doctor had disposed of themselves to their several likings, the newcomer entered into a narrative of the singular reasons which had led him so far into the deserts.

CHAPTER 11

So foul a sky clears not without a storm.

KING JOHN

IN THE MEANTIME, the industrious and irreclaimable hours continued their labors. The sun, which had been struggling through such masses of vapor throughout the day, fell slowly into a streak of clear sky and thence sank gloriously into the gloomy wastes, as he is wont to settle into the waters of the ocean. The vast herds which had been grazing among the wild pastures of the prairies gradually disappeared, and the endless flocks of aquatic birds that were pursuing their customary annual journey from the virgin lakes of the north towards the Gulf of Mexico ceased to fan that air, which had now become loaded with dew and vapor. In short, the shadows of night fell upon the rock, adding the mantle of darkness to the other dreary accompaniments of the place.

As the light began to fail, Esther collected her younger children at her side, and placing herself on a projecting point of her insulated fortress, she sat patiently awaiting the return of the hunters. Ellen Wade was at no great distance, seeming to keep a little aloof from the anxious circle, as if willing to mark the distinction which existed in their characters.

"Your uncle is, and always will be, a dull calculator, Nell," observed the mother after a long pause in a conversation that had turned on the labors of the day; "a lazy hand at figures and foreknowledge is that said Ishmael Bush! Here he sat lolloping about the rock from light till noon, doing nothing but scheme—scheme—scheme—with seven as noble boys at his elbows as woman ever gave to man; and what's the upshot? Why, night is setting in, and his needful work not yet ended."

"It is not prudent, certainly, Aunt," Ellen replied with a vacancy in her air that proved how little she knew what she was saying; "and it is setting a very bad example to his sons."

"Hoity-toity, girl! Who has reared you up as a judge over your elders, aye, and your betters too! I should like to see the man on the whole frontier who sets a more honest example to his children than this same Ishmael Bush! Show me, if you can, Miss Faultfinder, but not faultmender, a set of boys who will on occasion sooner chop a piece of logging and dress it for the crop than my own children, though I say it myself, who perhaps should be silent; or a cradler that knows better how to lead a gang of hands through a field of wheat, leaving a cleaner stubble in his track, than my own good man! Then, as a father, he is as generous as a lord, for his sons have only to name the spot where they would like to pitch, and he gives 'em a deed of the plantation, and no charge for papers is ever made!"

As the wife of the squatter concluded, she raised a hollow, taunting laugh that was echoed from the mouths of several juvenile imitators whom she was training to a life as shiftless and lawless as her own, but which, notwithstanding its uncertainty, was not without its secret charms.

"Holloa, old Eester!" shouted the well-known voice of her husband from the plain beneath. "Are you keeping your junkets while we are finding you in venison and buffalo beef? Come down; come down, old girl, with all your young, and lend us a hand to carry up the meat; why, what a frolic you are in, woman! Come down, come down, for the boys are at hand, and we have work here for double your number."

Ishmael might have spared his lungs more than a moiety of the effort they were compelled to make in order that he should be heard. He had hardly uttered the name of his wife before the whole of the crouching circle rose in a body, and tumbling over each other, they precipitated themselves down the dangerous passes of the rock with ungovernable impatience. Esther followed the young fry with a more measured gait; nor did Ellen deem it wise, or rather discreet, to remain behind. Consequently, the whole were soon assembled at the base of the citadel on the open plain.

Here the squatter was found staggering under the weight of a fine, fat buck, attended by one or two of his younger sons. Abiram quickly appeared, and before many minutes had elapsed most of the hunters dropped in, singly and in pairs, each man bringing with him some fruits of his prowess in the field.

"The plain is free from redskins, tonight at least," said Ishmael after the bustle of reception had a little subsided, "for I have scoured the prairie for many long miles on my own feet, and I call myself a judge of the print of an Indian moccasin. So, old woman, you can give us a few steaks of the venison, and then we will sleep on the day's work."

"I'll not swear there are no savages near us," said Abiram. "I too know something of the trail of a redskin, and unless my eyes have lost some of their sight, I would swear boldly that there are Indians at hand. But wait till Asa comes in. He passed the spot where I found the marks, and the boy knows something of such matters too."

"Aye, the boy knows too much of many things," returned Ishmael gloomily. "It will be better for him when he thinks he knows less. But what matters it, Hetty, if all the Sioux tribes west of the big river are within a mile of us; they will find it no easy matter to scale this rock in the teeth of ten bold men."

"Call 'em twelve at once, Ishmael; call 'em twelve!" cried his termagant assistant. "For if your moth-gathering, bug-hunting friend can be counted a man, I beg you will set me down as two. I will not turn my back to him with the rifle or the shotgun; and for courage, the yearling heifer that them skulking devils the Tetons stole was the biggest coward among us all, and after her came your driveling doctor. Ah! Ishmael, you rarely attempt a regular trade but you come out the loser; and this man, I reckon, is the hardest bargain among them all! Would you think it, the fellow ordered me a blister around my mouth because I complained of a pain in the foot?"

"It is a pity, Eester," the husband coolly answered, "that you did not take it; I reckon that it would have done considerably good. But, boys, if it should turn out as Abiram thinks, that there are Indians near us, we may have to scamper up the rock and lose our suppers after all; therefore, we will make sure of the game and talk over the performances of the doctor when we have nothing better to do."

The hint was taken, and in a few minutes the exposed situation in which the family was collected was exchanged for the more secure elevation of the rock. Here Esther busied herself, working and scolding with equal industry, until the repast was prepared, when she summoned her husband to his meal in a voice as sonorous as that with which the imam reminds the faithful of a more important duty.

When each had assumed his proper and customary place around the smoking viands, the squatter set the example by beginning to partake of a delicious venison steak, prepared like the hump of the bison, with a skill that rather increased than concealed its natural properties. A painter would gladly have seized the moment to transfer the wild and characteristic scene to the canvas.

The reader will remember that the citadel of Ishmael stood insulated, lofty, ragged, and nearly inaccessible. A bright, flashing fire that was burning on the center of its summit and around which the busy group was clustered lent it the appearance of some tall pharos placed in the center of the deserts to light such adventurers as wandered through their broad wastes. The flashing flame gleamed from one sunburnt countenance to another, exhibiting every variety of expression, from the juvenile simplicity of the children, mingled, as it was, with a shade of the wildness peculiar to their semibarbarous lives, to the dull and immovable apathy that dwelt on the features of the squatter when unexcited. Occasionally a gust of wind would fan the embers, and as a brighter light shot upwards, the little solitary tent was seen, as it were, suspended in the gloom of the upper air. All beyond was enveloped, as usual at that hour, in an impenetrable body of darkness.

"It is unaccountable that Asa should choose to be out of the way at such a time as this," Esther pettishly observed. "When all is finished and to rights, we shall have the boy coming up grumbling for his meal and hungry as a bear after his winter's nap. His stomach is as true as the best clock in Kentucky and seldom wants winding up to tell the time whether of day or night. A desperate eater is Asa when a-hungered by a little work!"

Ishmael looked sternly around the circle of his silent sons, as if to see whether any among them would presume to say aught in favor of the absent delinquent. But now, when no exciting causes existed to arouse their slumbering tempers, it seemed to be too great an effort to enter on the defense of their rebellious brother. Abiram, however, who since the pacification either felt or affected to feel a more generous interest in his late adversary, saw fit to express an anxiety to which the others were strangers, "It will be well if the boy has escaped the Tetons!" he muttered. "I should be sorry to have Asa, who is one of the stoutest of our party, both in heart and hand, fall into the power of the red devils."

"Look to yourself, Abiram; and spare your breath if you can use it only to frighten the woman and her huddling girls. You have whitened the face of Ellen Wade already, who looks as pale as if she was staring today at the very Indians you name when I was forced to speak to her through the rifle because I couldn't reach her ears with my tongue. How was it, Nell! You have never given the reason of your deafness?"

The color of Ellen's cheek changed as suddenly as the squatter's piece had flashed on the occasion to which he alluded, the burning glow suffusing her features until it even mantled her throat with its fine healthful tinge. She hung her head abashed but did not seem to think it needful to reply.

Ishmael, too sluggish to pursue the subject or content with the pointed allusion he had just made, rose from his seat on the rock, and stretching his heavy frame like a well-fed and fattened ox, he announced his intention to sleep. Among a race who lived chiefly for the indulgence of the natural wants, such a declaration could not fail of meeting with sympathetic dispositions. One after another disappeared, each seeking his or her rude dormitory; and before many minutes, Esther, who by this time had scolded the younger fry to sleep, found herself, if we except the usual watchman below, in solitary possession of the naked rock.

Whatever less valuable fruits had been produced in this uneducated woman by her migratory habits, the great principle of female nature was too deeply rooted ever to be entirely eradicated. Of a powerful, not to say fierce, temperament, her passions were violent and difficult to be smothered. But however she might and did abuse the accidental prerogatives of her situation, love for her offspring, while it often slumbered, could never be said to become extinct. She liked not the protracted absence of Asa. Too fearless herself to have hesitated an instant on her own account about crossing the dark abyss into which she now sat looking with longing eyes, her busy imagination, in obedience to this inextinguishable sentiment, began to conjure nameless evils on account of her son. It might be true, as Abiram had hinted, that he had become a captive to some of the tribes who were hunting the buffalo in that vicinity, or even a still more dreadful calamity might have befallen. So thought the mother, while silence and darkness lent their aid to the secret impulses of nature.

Agitated by these reflections, which put sleep at defiance, Esther continued at her post, listening with that sort of acuteness which is termed instinct in the animals a few degrees below her in the scale of intelligence for any of those noises which might indicate the approach of footsteps. At length her wishes had an appearance of being realized, for the long-desired sounds were distinctly audible, and presently she distinguished the dim form of a man at the base of the rock.

"Now, Asa, richly do you deserve to be left with an earthen bed this blessed night!" the woman began to mutter with a revolution in her feelings that will not be surprising to those who have made the contradictions that give variety to the human character a study. "And a hard one I've a mind it shall be! Why, Abner; Abner; you Abner; do you sleep? Let me not see you dare to open the hole till I get down. I will know who it is that wishes to disturb a peaceable, aye, and an honest family too at such a time in the night as this!"

"Woman!" exclaimed a voice that intended to bluster, while the speaker was manifestly a little apprehensive of the consequences. "Woman, I forbid you on pain of the law to project any of your infernal missiles. I am a citizen, and a freeholder, and a graduate of two universities; and I stand upon my rights! Beware of malice prepense, of chance medley, and of manslaughter. It is I—your amicus, a friend and inmate. I—Dr. Obed Battius."

"Who?" demanded Esther in a voice that nearly refused to convey her words to the ears of the anxious listener beneath. "Did you say it was not Asa?"

"Nay, I am neither Asa, nor Absalom, nor any of the Hebrew princes, but Obed, the root and stock of them all. Have I not said, woman, that you keep one in attendance who is entitled to a peaceable as well as an honorable admission? Do you take me for an animal of the class Amphibia, and that I can play with my lungs as a blacksmith does with his bellows?"

The naturalist might have expended his breath much longer without producing any desirable result had Esther been his only auditor. Disappointed and alarmed, the woman had already sought her pallet and was preparing with a sort of desperate indifference to compose herself to sleep. Abner, the sentinel below, however, had been aroused from an exceedingly equivocal situation by the outcry; and as he had now regained sufficient consciousness to recognize the voice of the physician, the latter was admitted with the least possible delay. Dr. Battius bustled through the narrow entrance with an air of singular impatience and was already beginning to mount the difficult ascent when, catching a view of the porter, he paused to observe with an air that he intended should be impressively admonitory, "Abner, there are dangerous symptoms of somnolency about thee! It is sufficiently exhibited in the tendency to hiation and may prove dangerous not only to yourself but to all thy father's family."

"You never made a greater mistake, doctor," returned the youth, gaping like an indolent lion; "I haven't a symptom, as you call it, about any part of me; and as to father and the children, I reckon the smallpox and the measles have been thoroughly through the breed these many months ago."

Content with his brief admonition, the naturalist had surmounted half the difficulties of the ascent before the deliberate Abner ended his justification. On the summit, Obed fully expected to encounter Esther, of whose linguacious powers he had too often been furnished with the most sinister proofs and of which he stood in an awe too salutary to covet a repetition of the attacks. The reader can foresee that he was to be agreeably disappointed. Treading lightly and looking timidly over his shoulder as if he apprehended a shower of something even more formidable than words, the doctor proceeded to the place which had been allotted to himself in the general disposition of the dormitories.

Instead of sleeping, the worthy naturalist sat ruminating over what he had both seen and heard that day, until the tossing and mutterings which proceeded from the cabin of Esther, who was his nearest neighbor, advertised him of the wakeful situation of its inmate. Perceiving the necessity of doing something to disarm this female Cerberus before his own purpose could be accomplished, the doctor, reluctant as he was to encounter her tongue, found himself compelled to invite a colloquial communication.

"You appear not to sleep, my very kind and worthy Mrs. Bush," he said, determined to commence his applications with a plaster that was usually found to adhere; "you appear to rest badly, my excellent hostess; can I administer to your ailings?"

"What would you give me, man?" grumbled Esther. "A blister to make me sleep?"

"Say rather a cataplasm. But if you are in pain, here are some cordial drops, which, taken in a glass of my own cognac, will give you rest, if I know aught of the materia medica."

The doctor, as he very well knew, had assailed Esther on her weak side; and as he doubted not to the acceptable quality of his prescription, he set himself at work, without unnecessary delay, to prepare it. When he made his offering, it was received in a snappish and threatening manner, but swallowed with a facility that sufficiently proclaimed how much it was relished. The woman muttered her thanks, and her leech reseated himself in silence to await the operation of the dose. In less than half an hour the breathing of Esther became so profound, and as the doctor himself might have termed it, so very abstracted, that had he not known how easy it was to ascribe this new instance of somnolency to the powerful dose of opium with which he had garnished the brandy, he might have seen reason to distrust his own prescription. With the sleep of the restless woman, the stillness became profound and general.

Then Dr. Battius saw fit to arise with the silence and caution of the midnight robber and to steal out of his own cabin, or rather kennel, for it deserved no better name, towards the adjoining dormitories. Here he took time to assure himself that all his neighbors were buried in deep sleep. Once advised of this important fact, he hesitated no longer, but commenced the difficult ascent which led to the upper pinnacle of the rock. His advance, though abundantly guarded, was not entirely noiseless; but while he was felicitating himself on having successfully effected his object, and he was in the very act of placing his foot on the highest ledge, a hand was laid upon the skirts of his coat, which as effectually put an end to his advance as if the gigantic strength of Ishmael himself had pinned him to the earth.

"Is there sickness in the tent," whispered a soft voice in his very ear, "that Dr. Battius is called to visit it at such an hour?"

So soon as the heart of the naturalist had returned from its hasty expedition into his throat, as one less skilled than Dr. Battius in the formation of the animal would have been apt to have accounted for the extraordinary sensation with which he received this unlooked-for interruption, he found resolution to reply, using, as much in terror as in prudence, the same precaution in the indulgence of his voice.

"My worthy Nelly! I am greatly rejoiced to find it is no other than thee. Hist, child, hist! Should Ishmael gain a knowledge of our plans, he would not hesitate to cast us both from this rock upon the plain beneath. Hist! Nelly, hist!"

As the doctor delivered his injunctions between the intervals of his ascent, by the time they were concluded, both he and his auditor had gained the upper level.

"And how, Dr. Battius," the girl gravely demanded, "may I know the reason why you have run so great a risk of flying from this place without wings and at the certain expense of your neck?"

"Nothing shall be concealed from thee, worthy and trusty Nelly; but are you certain that Ishmael will not awake?"

"No fear of him; he will sleep until the sun scorches his eyelids. The danger is from my aunt."

"Esther sleepeth!" the doctor sententiously replied. "Ellen, you have been watching on this rock today?"

"I was ordered to do so."

"And you have seen the bison, and the antelope, and the wolf, and the deer, as usual; animals of the orders Pecora, Pelluae, and Ferae."

"I have seen the creatures you named in English, but I know nothing of the Indian languages."

"There is still an order that I have not named, which you have also seen. The Primates—is it not true?"

"I cannot say. I know no animal by that name."

"Nay, Ellen, you confer with a friend. Of the genus Homo, child?"

"Whatever else I may have had in view, I have not seen the *Vespertilio horribi*——"

"Hush, Nelly, thy vivacity will betray us! Tell me, girl, have you not seen certain bipeds, called men, wandering about the prairies?"

"Surely. My uncle and his sons have been hunting the buffalo since the sun began to fall."

"I must speak in the vernacular to be comprehended. Ellen, I would say of the species Kentucky."

Though Ellen reddened like the rose, her blushes were concealed by the darkness. She hesitated an instant, and then summoned sufficient spirit to say decidedly, "If you wish to speak in parables, Dr. Battius, you must find another listener. Put your questions plainly in English, and I will answer them honestly in the same tongue."

"I have been journeying in this desert, as thou knowest, Nelly, in quest of animals that have been hidden from the eyes of science until now. Among others, I have discovered a Primates of the genus Homo, species Kentucky, which I term Paul——"

"Hist, for the sake of mercy!" said Ellen. "Speak lower, doctor, or we shall be ruined."

"Hover: by profession a collector of the Apes, or bee," continued the other. "Do I use the vernacular now; am I understood?"

"Perfectly, perfectly," returned the girl, breathing with difficulty, in her surprise. "But what of him? Did he tell you to mount this rock? He knows nothing himself, for the oath I gave my uncle has shut my mouth."

"Aye, but there is one that has taken no oath, who has revealed all. I would that the mantle which is wrapped around the mysteries of nature were as effectually withdrawn from its hidden treasures! Ellen! Ellen! The man with whom I have unwittingly formed a compactum, or agreement, is sadly forgetful of the obligations of honesty! Thy uncle, child."

"You mean Ishmael Bush, my father's brother's widow's husband," returned the offended girl a little proudly. "Indeed, indeed, it is cruel to reproach me with a tie that chance has formed and which I would rejoice so much to break forever!"

The humbled Ellen could utter no more, but sinking on a projection of the rock, she began to sob in a manner that rendered their situation doubly critical. The doctor muttered a few words, which he intended as an apologetic explanation, but before he had time to complete his labored vindication, she arose and said with decision, "I did not come here to pass my time in foolish tears, nor you to try to stop them. What then has brought you hither?"

"I must see the inmate of that tent."

"You know what it contains?"

"I am taught to believe I do, and I bear a letter which I must deliver with my own hands. If the animal prove a quadruped, Ishmael is a true man; if a biped, fledged or unfledged, I care not, he is false, and our compactum at an end!"

Ellen made a sign for the doctor to remain where he was and to be silent. She then glided into the tent, where she continued many minutes, that proved exceedingly weary and anxious to the expectant without; but the instant she returned, she took him by the arm, and together they entered beneath the folds of the mysterious cloth.

CHAPTER 12

Pray God the Duke of York excuse himself!
KING HENRY VI

THE MUSTERING OF the borderers on the following morning was silent, sullen, and gloomy. The repast of that hour was wanting in the inharmonious accompaniment with which Esther ordinarily enlivened their meals, for the effects of the powerful opiate the doctor had administered still muddled her intellects. The young men brooded over the absence of their elder brother, and the brows of Ishmael himself were knit as he cast his scowling eyes from one to the other like a man preparing to meet and to repel an expected assault on his authority. In the midst of this family distrust, Ellen and her midnight confederate, the naturalist, took their usual places among the children without awakening suspicion or exciting comment. The only apparent fruits of the adventure in which they had been engaged were occasional upliftings of the eyes on the part of the doctor, which were mistaken by the observers for some of his scientific contemplations of the heavens but which in reality were no other than furtive glances at the fluttering walls of the proscribed tent.

At length the squatter, who had waited in vain for some more decided manifestation of the expected rising among his sons, resolved to make a demonstration of his own intentions.

"Asa shall account to me for this undutiful conduct," he observed. "Here has the livelong night gone by, and he outlying on the prairie when his hand and his rifle might both have been wanted in a brush with the Siouxes, for any right he had to know the contrary."

"Spare your breath, good man," retorted his wife; "be

saving of your breath, for you may have to call long enough for the boy before he will answer!"

"It are a fact that some men be so womanish as to let the young master the old! But you, old Esther, should know better than to think such will ever be the nature of things in the family of Ishmael Bush."

"Ah! You are a hectorer with the boys when need calls! I know it well, Ishmael; and one of your sons have you driven from you by your temper; and that, too, at a time when he is most wanted."

"Father," said Abner, whose sluggish nature had gradually been stimulating itself to the exertion of taking so bold a stand, "the boys and I have pretty generally concluded to go out on the search of Asa. We are disagreeable about his camping on the prairie instead of coming in to his own bed as we all know he would like to do."

"Pshaw!" muttered Abiram. "The boy has killed a buck, or perhaps a buffalo, and he is sleeping by the carcass to keep off the wolves till day; we shall soon see him or hear him bawling for help to bring in his load."

" 'Tis little help that a son of mine will call for to shoulder a buck or to quarter your wild beef," returned the mother. "And you, Abiram, to say so uncertain a thing! You who said yourself that the redskins had been prowling around this place no later than yesterday——"

"I!" exclaimed her brother hastily, as if anxious to retract an error. "I said it then, and I say it now; and so you will find it to be. The Tetons are in our neighborhood, and happy will it prove for the boy if he is well shut of them."

"It seems to me," said Dr. Battius, speaking with the sort of deliberation and dignity one is apt to use after having thoroughly ripened his opinions by sufficient reflection, "it seems to me—a man but little skilled in the signs and tokens of Indian warfare, especially as practiced in these remote plains, but one who, I may say without vanity, has some insight into the mysteries of nature—it seems, then, to me, thus humbly qualified, that when doubts exist in a matter of moment, it would always be the wisest course to appease them."

"No more of your doctoring for me!" cried the grum Esther; "no more of your quiddities in a healthy family, say I! Here was I doing well, only a little out of sorts with over-instructing the young, and you dosed me with a drug that hangs about my tongue like a pound weight on a humming-bird's wing!"

"Is the medicine out?" drily demanded Ishmael. "It must be a rare dose that gives a heavy feel to the tongue of old Eester!"

"Friend," continued the doctor, waving his hand for the angry wife to maintain the peace, "that it cannot perform all that is said of it the very charge of good Mrs. Bush is a sufficient proof. But to speak of the absent Asa. There is doubt as to his fate, and there is a proposition to solve it. Now, in the natural sciences truth is always a desideratum; and I confess it would seem to be equally so in the present case of domestic uncertainty, which may be called a vacuum where, according to the laws of physic, there should exist some pretty palpable proofs of materiality."

"Don't mind him, don't mind him," cried Esther, observing that the rest of his auditors listened with an attention which might proceed equally from acquiescence in his proposal or ignorance of its meaning. "There is a drug in every word he utters."

"Dr. Battius wishes to say," Ellen modestly interposed, "that as some of us think Asa is in danger, and some think otherwise, the whole family might pass an hour or two in looking for him."

"Does he?" interrupted the woman. "Then Dr. Battius has more sense in him than I believed! She is right, Ishmael; and what she says shall be done. I will shoulder a rifle myself; and woe betide the redskin that crosses my path! I have pulled a trigger before today; aye, and heard an Indian yell too, to my sorrow."

The spirit of Esther diffused itself, like the stimulus which attends a war cry, among her sons. They arose in a body and declared their determination to second so bold a resolution. Ishmael prudently yielded to an impulse he could not resist, and in a few minutes the woman appeared, shouldering her arms, prepared to lead forth in person such of her descend-ants as chose to follow.

"Let them stay with the children that please," she said, "and them follow me who are not chickenhearted!"

"Abiram, it will not do to leave the huts without some guard," Ishmael whispered, glancing his eye upwards.

The man whom he addressed started and betrayed extraordinary eagerness in his reply.

"I will tarry and watch the camp."

A dozen voices were instantly raised in objection to this proposal. He was wanted to point out the places where the hostile tracks had been seen, and his termagant sister openly scouted at the idea as unworthy of his manhood. The reluctant Abiram was compelled to yield, and Ishmael made a new disposition for the defense of the place, which was admitted by everyone to be all-important to their security and comfort.

He offered the post of commandant to Dr. Battius, who, however, peremptorily and somewhat haughtily declined the doubtful honor, exchanging looks of intelligence with Ellen as he did so. In this dilemma the squatter was obliged to constitute the girl herself castellan, taking care, however, in deputing this important trust to omit no words of caution and instruction. When this preliminary point was settled, the young men proceeded to arrange certain means of defense and signals of alarm that were adapted to the weakness and character of the garrison. Several masses of rock were drawn to the edge of the upper level and so placed as to leave it at the discretion of the feeble Ellen and her associates to cast them or not, as they might choose, on the heads of any invaders, who would of necessity be obliged to mount the eminence by the difficult and narrow passage already so often mentioned. In addition to this formidable obstruction, the barriers were strengthened and rendered nearly impassable. Smaller missiles, that might be hurled even by the hands of the younger children but which would prove, from the elevation of the place, exceedingly dangerous, were provided in profusion. A pile of dried leaves and splinters was placed as a beacon on the upper rock, and then, even in the jealous judgment of the squatter, the post was deemed competent to maintain a creditable siege.

The moment the rock was thought to be in a state of sufficient security, the party who composed what might be called the sortie sallied forth on their anxious expedition. The advance was led by Esther in person, who, attired in a dress half masculine and bearing a weapon like the rest, seemed no unfit leader for the group of wildly clad frontiermen that followed in her rear.

"Now, Abiram!" cried the Amazon in a voice that was cracked and harsh for the simple reason of being used too often on a strained and unnatural key. "Now, Abiram, run with your nose low; show yourself a hound of the true breed, and do some credit to your training. You it was that saw the prints of the Indian moccasin, and it behoves you to let others be as wise as yourself. Come; come to the front, man, and give us a bold lead."

The brother, who appeared at all times to stand in awe of his sister's authority, complied, though it was with a reluctance so evident as to excite sneers even among the unobservant and indolent sons of the squatter. Ishmael himself moved among his tall children like one who expected nothing from the search and who was indifferent alike to its success or failure. In this manner the party proceeded until their distant fortress had sunk so low as to present an object no larger nor more distinct than a hazy point on the margin of the prairie. Hitherto their progress had been silent and somewhat rapid, for as swell after swell was mounted and passed without varying or discovering a living object to enliven the monotony of the view, even the tongue of Esther was hushed to increasing anxiety. Here, however, Ishmael chose to pause, and casting the butt of his rifle from his shoulder to the ground, he observed, "This is enough. Buffalo signs and deer signs are plenty, but where are thy Indian footsteps, Abiram?"

"Still further west," returned the other, pointing in the direction he named. "This was the spot where I struck the tracks of the buck; it was after I took the deer that I fell upon the Teton trail."

"And a bloody piece of work you made of it, man," cried the squatter, pointing tauntingly to the soiled garments of his kinsman and then directing the attention of the spectators to his own by the way of a triumphant contrast. "Here have I cut the throats of two lively does and a scampering fawn without spot or stain, while you, blundering dog as you are, have made as much work for Eester and her girls as though butchering was your regular calling. Come, boys; it is enough. I am too old not to know the signs of the frontiers; no Indian has been here since the last fall of water. Follow me, and I will make a turn that shall give us at least the beef of a fallow cow for our trouble."

"Follow *me!*" echoed Esther, stepping undauntedly forward. "I am leader today, and I *will* be followed. Who so proper, let me know, as a mother to head a search for her own lost child?"

Ishmael regarded his intractable mate with a smile of indulgent pity. Observing that she had already struck out a path for herself different both from that of Abiram and the one he had seen fit to choose, and being unwilling to draw the cord of authority too tight just at that moment, he submitted to her will. But Dr. Battius, who had hitherto been a silent and thoughtful attendant on the woman, now saw fit to raise his feeble voice in the way of remonstrance.

"I agree with thy partner in life, worthy and gentle Mrs. Bush," he said, "in believing that some *ignis fatuus* of the imagination has deceived Abiram in the signs or symptoms of which he has spoken."

"Symptoms yourself!" interrupted the termagant. "This is no time for bookish words, nor is this a place to stop and swallow medicines. If you are a-leg-weary, say so, as a plain-speaking man should; then seat yourself on the prairie like a hound that is footsore and take your natural rest."

"I accord in the opinion," the naturalist calmly replied, complying literally with the opinion of the deriding Esther by taking his seat very coolly by the side of an indigenous shrub, the examination of which he commenced on the instant in order that science might not lose any of its just and important dues. "I honor your excellent advice, Mistress Esther, as you may perceive. Go thou in quest of thy offspring, while I tarry here in pursuit of that which is better, viz., an insight into the arcana of Nature's volume."

The woman answered with a hollow, unnatural, and scornful laugh; and even her heavy sons, as they slowly passed the seat of the already abstracted naturalist, did not disdain to manifest their contempt in smiles. In a few minutes the train mounted the nearest eminence, and as it turned the rounded acclivity, the doctor was left to pursue his profitable investigations in entire solitude.

Another half hour passed, during which Esther continued to advance on her seemingly fruitless search. Her pauses, however, were becoming frequent, and her looks wandering and uncertain, when footsteps were heard clattering through the bottom, and at the next instant a buck was seen to bound up the ascent and to dart from before their eyes in the direction of the naturalist. So sudden and unlooked for had been the passage of the animal, and so much had he been favored by the shape of the ground, that before any one of the foresters had time to bring his rifle to his shoulder, it was already beyond the range of a bullet.

"Look out for the wolf!" shouted Abner, shaking his head in vexation at being a single moment too late. "A wolf's skin will be no bad gift in a winter's night; aye, yonder the hungry devil comes!"

"Hold!" cried Ishmael, knocking up the leveled weapon of his too eager son. " 'Tis not a wolf, but a hound of thorough blood and bottom. Ha! We have hunters nigh; there are two of them!"

He was still speaking when the animals in question came leaping on the track of the deer, striving with noble ardor to outdo each other. One was an aged dog whose strength seemed to be sustained purely by generous emulation, and the other a pup that gamboled even while he pressed most warmly on the chase. They both ran, however, with clean and powerful leaps, carrying their noses high, like animals of the most keen and subtle scent. They had passed, and in another minute they would have been running openmouthed with the deer in view had not the younger dog suddenly bounded from the course and uttered a cry of surprise. His aged companion stopped also and returned panting and exhausted to the place where the other was whirling around in swift and apparently in mad evolutions, circling the spot in his own footsteps and continuing his outcry in a short, snappish barking. But when the elder hound had reached the spot, he seated himself, and lifting his nose high into the air, he raised a long, loud, and wailing howl.

"It must be a strong scent," said Abner, who had been, with the rest of the family, an admiring observer of the movements of the dogs, "that can break off two such creatur's so suddenly from their trail."

"Murder them!" cried Abiram. "I'll swear to the old hound; 'tis the dog of the trapper, whom we now know to be our mortal enemy."

Though the brother of Esther gave so hostile advice, he appeared in no way ready to put it in execution himself. The surprise which had taken possession of the whole party exhibited itself in his own vacant, wondering stare as strongly as in any of the admiring visages by whom he was surrounded. His denunciation, therefore, notwithstanding its dire import, was disregarded; and the dogs were left to obey the impulses of their mysterious instinct without let or hindrance.

It was long before any of the spectators broke the silence, but the squatter at length so far recollected his authority as to take on himself the right to control the movements of his children.

"Come away, boys; come away and leave the hounds to sing their tunes for their own amusement," Ishmael said in his coldest manner. "I scorn to take the life of a beast because its master has pitched himself too nigh my clearing; come away, boys, come away; we have enough of our own work before us without turning aside to do that of the whole neighborhood."

"Come *not* away!" cried Esther in tones that sounded like the admonitions of some sibyl. "I say, come *not* away, my children. There is a meaning and a warning in this; and as I am a woman and a mother, will I know the truth of it all!"

So saying, the awakened wife brandished her weapon with an air that was not without its wild and secret influence and led the way towards the spot where the dogs still remained, filling the air with their long-drawn and piteous complaints. The whole party followed in her steps, some too indolent to oppose, others obedient to her will, and all more or less excited by the uncommon character of the scene.

"Tell me, you Abner—Abiram—Ishmael!" the woman cried, standing over a spot where the earth was trampled and beaten and plainly sprinkled with blood. "Tell me, you who are hunters! What sort of animal has here met his death? Speak! Ye are men, and used to the signs of the plains; is it the blood of wolf or panther?"

"A buffalo, and a noble and powerful creatur' has it been!" returned the squatter, who looked down calmly on the fatal signs which so strangely affected his wife. "Here are the marks of the spot where he has struck his hoofs into the earth in the death struggle; and yonder he has plunged and torn the ground with his horns. Aye, a buffalo bull of wonderful strength and courage has he been!"

"And who has slain him?" continued Esther. "Man! Where are the offals? Wolves! They devour not the hide! Tell me, ye men and hunters, is this the blood of a beast?"

"The creatur' has plunged over the hillock," said Abner, who had proceeded a short distance beyond the rest of the party. "Ah! There you will find it, in yon swale of alders. Look! A thousand carrion birds are hovering above the carcass."

"The animal has still life in him," returned the squatter, "or the buzzards would settle upon their prey! By the action of the dogs it must be something ravenous; I reckon it is the white bear from the upper falls. They are said to cling desperately to life!"

"Let us go back," said Abiram; "there may be danger, and there can be no good in attacking a ravenous beast. Remember, Ishmael, 'twill be a risky job, and one of small profit!"

The young men smiled at this new proof of the well-known pusillanimity of their uncle. The oldest even proceeded so far as to express his contempt by bluntly saying, "It will do to cage with the other animal we carry; then we may go back doublehanded into the settlements and set up for showmen around the courthouses and jails of Kentucky."

The threatening frown which gathered on the brow of his father admonished the young man to forbear. Exchanging looks that were half rebellious with his brethren, he saw fit to be silent. But instead of observing the caution recommended by Abiram, they proceeded in a body until they again came to a halt within a few yards of the matted cover of the thicket.

The scene had now, indeed, become wild and striking enough to have produced a powerful effect on minds better prepared than those of the unnurtured family of the squatter to resist the impressions of so exciting a spectacle. The heavens were, as usual at the season, covered with dark, driving clouds, beneath which interminable flocks of aquatic birds were again on the wing, holding their toilsome and heavy way towards the distant waters of the south. The wind had risen and was once more sweeping over the prairie in gusts, which it was often vain to oppose; and then again the blasts would seem to mount into the upper air, as if to sport with the drifting vapor, whirling and rolling vast masses of the dusky and ragged volumes over each other in a terrific and yet grand disorder. Above the little brake, the flocks of birds still held their flight, circling with heavy wings about the spot, struggling at times against the torrent of wind, and then, favored by their position and height, making bold swoops upon the thicket, away from which, however, they never failed to sail screaming in terror, as if apprised either by sight or instinct that the hour of their voracious dominion had not yet fully arrived.

Ishmael stood for many minutes with his wife and children clustered together in an amazement with which awe was singularly mingled, gazing in deathlike stillness on the sight. The voice of Esther at length broke the charm and reminded the spectators of the necessity of resolving their doubts in some manner more worthy of their manhood than by dull and inactive observation.

"Call in the dogs!" she said. "Call in the hounds and put them into the thicket; there are men enough of ye, if ye have not lost the spirit with which I know ye were born, to tame the tempers of all the bears west of the big river. Call in the dogs, I say, you Enoch! Abner! Gabriel! Has wonder made ye deaf?"

One of the young men complied, and having succeeded in detaching the hounds from the place around which until then they had not ceased to hover, he led them down to the margin of the thicket.

"Put them in, boy; put them in," continued the woman; "and you, Ishmael and Abiram, if anything wicked or hurtful comes forth, show them the use of your rifles like frontiermen. If ye are wanting in spirit, before the eyes of my children will I put ye both to shame!"

The youths who until now had detained the hounds let slip the thongs of skin by which they had been held and urged them to the attack with their voices. But it would seem that the elder dog was restrained by some extraordinary sensation or that he was much too experienced to attempt the rash adventure. After proceeding a few yards to the verge of the brake, he made a sudden pause and stood trembling in all his aged limbs, apparently as unable to recede as to advance. The encouraging calls of the young men were disregarded or only answered by a low and plaintive whining. For a minute the pup also was similarly affected; but less sage, or more easily excited, he was induced at length to leap forward and finally to dash into the cover. An alarmed and startling howl was heard, and at the next minute he broke out of the thicket and commenced circling the spot in the same wild and unsteady manner as before.

"Have I a man among my children?" demanded Esther. "Give me a truer piece than a childish shotgun, and I will show ye what the courage of a frontierwoman can do!"

"Stay, Mother," exclaimed Abner and Enoch; "if you *will* see the creatur' let *us* drive it into view."

This was quite as much as the youths were accustomed to

utter, even on more important occasions; but having given a pledge of their intentions, they were far from being backward in redeeming it. Preparing their arms with the utmost care, they advanced with steadiness to the brake. Nerves less often tried than those of the young borderers might have shrunk before the dangers of so uncertain an undertaking. As they proceeded, the howls of the dogs became more shrill and plaintive. The vultures and buzzards settled so low as to flap the bushes with their heavy wings, and the wind came hoarsely sweeping along the naked prairie, as if the spirits of the air had also descended to witness the approaching development.

There was a breathless moment when the blood of the undaunted Esther flowed backwards to her heart as she saw her sons push aside the matted branches of the thicket and bury themselves in its labyrinth. A deep and solemn pause succeeded. Then arose two loud and piercing cries in quick succession, which were followed by a quiet still more awful and appalling.

"Come back, come back, my children!" cried the woman, the feelings of a mother getting the ascendancy.

But her voice was hushed, and every faculty seemed frozen with horror, as at that instant the bushes once more parted, and the two adventurers reappeared, pale and nearly insensible themselves, and laid at her feet the stiff and motionless body of the lost Asa, with the marks of a violent death but too plainly stamped on every pallid lineament.

The dogs uttered a long and closing howl, and then breaking off together, they disappeared on the forsaken trail of the deer. The flight of birds wheeled upwards into the heavens, filling the air with their complaints at having been robbed of a victim which, frightful and disgusting as it was, still bore too much of the impression of humanity to become the prey of their obscene appetites.

CHAPTER 13

A pickax, and a spade, a spade,
For—and a shrouding sheet:
O, a pit of clay for to be made
For such a guest is meet.

SONG IN HAMLET

"STAND BACK! STAND off, the whole of ye!" said Esther hoarsely to the crowd, which pressed too closely on the corpse. "I am his mother, and my right is better than that of ye all! Who has done this? Tell me, Ishmael, Abiram, Abner! Open your mouths and your hearts, and let God's truth and no other issue from them. Who has done this bloody deed?"

Her husband made no reply, but stood leaning on his rifle, looking sadly, but with an unaltered eye, at the mangled remains of his son. Not so the mother; she threw herself on the earth, and receiving the cold and ghastly head into her lap, she sat contemplating those muscular features on which the death agony was still horridly impressed, in a silence far more expressive than any language of lamentation could have proved.

The voice of the woman was frozen in grief. In vain Ishmael attempted a few words of rude consolation; she neither listened nor answered. Her sons gathered about her in a circle and expressed after their uncouth manner their sympathy in her sorrow, as well as their sense of their own loss; but she motioned them away impatiently with her hand. At times her fingers played in the matted hair of the dead, and at others they lightly attempted to smooth the painfully expressive muscles of its ghastly visage, as the hand of the mother is seen lingering fondly about the features of her sleeping child. Then starting from their revolting office, her hands would flutter around her and seem to seek some fruitless remedy against the violent blow which had thus suddenly destroyed the child in whom she had not only placed her greatest hopes, but so much of her maternal pride. While engaged in the latter incomprehensible manner, the lethargic Abner turned aside, and swallowing the unwonted emotions which were rising in his own throat, he observed, "Mother means that we should look for the signs, that we may know in what manner Asa has come by his end."

"We owe it to the accursed Siouxes!" answered Ishmael; "twice have they put me deeply in their debt! The third time the score shall be cleared!"

But, not content with this plausible explanation, and perhaps secretly glad to avert their eyes from a spectacle which awakened so extraordinary and unusual sensations in their sluggish bosoms, the sons of the squatter turned away in a body from their mother and the corpse and proceeded to make the inquiries which they fancied the former had so repeatedly demanded. Ishmael made no objections, but though he accompanied his children while they proceeded in the investigation, it was more with the appearance of complying with their wishes, at a time when resistance might not be seemly, than with any visible interest in the result. As the borderers, notwithstanding their usual dullness, were well instructed in most things connected with their habits of life, an inquiry the success of which depended so much on signs and evidences that bore so strong a resemblance to a forest trail was likely to be conducted with skill and acuteness. Accordingly, they proceeded to the melancholy task with great readiness and intelligence.

Abner and Enoch agreed in their accounts as to the position in which they had found the body. It was seated nearly upright, the back supported by a mass of matted brush, and one hand still grasping a broken twig of the alders. It was most probably owing to the former circumstance that the body had escaped the rapacity of the carrion birds which had been seen hovering above the thicket, and the latter proved that life had not yet entirely abandoned the hapless victim when he entered the brake. The opinion now became general that the youth had received his death wound in the open prairie and had dragged his enfeebled form into the cover of the thicket for the purpose of concealment. A trail through the bushes confirmed this opinion. It also appeared on examination that a desperate struggle had taken place on the very margin of the thicket. This was sufficiently apparent by the trodden branches, the deep impressions on the moist ground, and the lavish flow of blood.

"He has been shot in the open ground and come here for a cover," said Abiram; "these marks would clearly prove it. The boy has been set upon by the savages in a body and has fought like a hero as he was until they have mastered his strength and then drawn him to the bushes."

To this probable opinion there was now but one dissenting voice, that of the slow-minded Ishmael, who demanded that the corpse itself should be examined in order to obtain a more accurate knowledge of its injuries. On examination it appeared that a rifle bullet had passed directly through the body of the deceased, entering beneath one of his brawny shoulders and making its exit by the breast. It required some knowledge in gunshot wounds to decide this delicate point, but the experience of the borderers was quite equal to the scrutiny; and a smile of wild and certainly of singular satisfaction passed among the sons of Ishmael when Abner confidently announced that the enemies of Asa had assailed him in the rear.

"It must be so," said the gloomy but attentive squatter. "He was of too good a stock and too well trained knowingly to turn the weak side to man or beast! Remember, boys, that while the front of manhood is to your enemy, let him be who or what he may, you are safe from cowardly surprise. Why, Eester, woman! You are getting beside yourself with picking at the hair and the garments of the child! Little good can you do him now, old girl."

"See!" interrupted Enoch, extricating from the fragments of cloth the morsel of lead which had prostrated the strength of one so powerful; "here is the very bullet!"

Ishmael took it in his hand and eyed it long and closely.

"There's no mistake," at length he muttered through his compressed teeth. "It is from the pouch of that accursed trapper. Like many of the hunters, he has a mark in his mold in order to know the work his rifle performs; and here you see it plainly—six little holes laid crossways."

"I'll swear to it," cried Abiram triumphantly. "He showed me his private mark himself and boasted of the number of deer he had laid upon the prairies with these very bullets. Now, Ishmael, will you believe me when I tell you the old knave is a spy of the redskins?"

The lead passed from the hand of one to that of another; and unfortunately for the reputation of the old man, several among them remembered also to have seen the aforesaid private bullet marks during the curious examination which all had made of his accouterments. In addition to this wound, however, were many others of a less dangerous nature, all of which were deemed to confirm the supposed guilt of the trapper.

The traces of many different struggles were to be seen between the spot where the first blood was spilt and the thicket to which it was now generally believed Asa had retreated as a place of refuge. These were interpreted into so many proofs of the weakness of the murderer, who would have sooner dispatched his victim had not even the dying strength of the youth rendered him formidable to the infirmities of one so old. The danger of drawing some others of the hunters to the spot by repeated firing was deemed a sufficient reason for not again resorting to the rifle after it had performed the important duty of disabling the victim. The weapon of the dead man was not to be found and had doubtless, together with many other less valuable and lighter articles that he was accustomed to carry about his person, become a prize to his destroyer.

But what, in addition to the telltale bullet, appeared to fix the ruthless deed with peculiar certainty on the trapper was the accumulated evidence furnished by the trail, which proved, notwithstanding his deadly hurt, that the wounded man had still been able to make a long and desperate resistance to the subsequent efforts of his murderer. Ishmael seemed to press this proof with a singular mixture of sorrow and pride: sorrow at the loss of a son whom, in their moments of amity, he highly valued; and pride at the courage and power he had manifested to his last and weakest breath.

"He died as a son of mine should die," said the squatter, gleaning a hollow consolation from so unnatural an exultation; "a dread to his enemy to the last, and without help from the law! Come, children; we have the grave to make, and then to hunt his murderer."

The sons of the squatter set about their melancholy office in silence and in sadness. An excavation was made in the hard earth at a great expense of toil and time, and the body was wrapped in such spare vestments as could be collected among the laborers. When these arrangements were completed, Ishmael approached the seemingly unconscious Esther and announced his intention to inter the dead. She heard him and quietly relinquished her grasp of the corpse, rising in silence to follow it to its narrow resting-place. Here she seated herself again at the head of the grave, watching each movement of the youths with eager and jealous eyes. When a sufficiency of earth was laid upon the senseless clay of Asa to protect it from injury, Enoch and Abner entered the cavity and trod it into a solid mass by the weight of their huge frames, with an appearance of a strange, not to say savage, mixture of care and indifference. This well-known precaution was adopted to prevent the speedy exhumation of the body by some of the carnivorous beasts of the prairie, whose instinct was sure to guide them to the spot. Even the rapacious birds appeared to comprehend the nature of the ceremony, for, mysteriously apprised that the miserable victim was now about to be abandoned by the human race, they once more began to make their airy circuits above the place, screaming as if to frighten the kinsmen from their labor of caution and love.

Ishmael stood with folded arms, steadily watching the manner in which this necessary duty was performed, and when the whole was completed, he lifted his cap to his sons to thank them for their services with a dignity that would have become one much better nurtured. Throughout the whole of a ceremony which is ever solemn and admonitory, the squatter had maintained a grave and serious deportment. His vast features were visibly stamped with an expression of deep concern; but at no time did they falter until he turned his back, as he believed forever, on the grave of his firstborn. Nature was then stirring powerfully within him, and the muscles of his stern visage began to work perceptibly. His children fastened their eyes on his as if to seek a direction to the strange emotions which were moving their own heavy natures, when the struggle in the bosom of the squatter suddenly ceased, and, taking his wife by the arm, he raised her to her feet as if she had been an infant, saying in a voice that was perfectly steady, though a nice observer would have discovered that it was kinder than usual, "Eester, we have now done all that man and woman can do. We raised the boy and made him such as few others were like on the frontiers of America, and we have given him a grave. Let us go our way."

The woman turned her eyes slowly from the fresh earth, and laying her hands on the shoulders of her husband, stood looking him anxiously in the eyes.

"Ishmael! Ishmael!" she said. "You parted from the boy in your wrath!"

"May the Lord pardon his sins freely as I have forgiven his worst misdeeds!" calmly returned the squatter. "Woman, go you back to the rock and read your Bible; a chapter in that book always does you good. You *can* read, Eester, which is a privilege I never did enjoy."

"Yes, yes," muttered the woman, yielding to his strength and suffering herself to be led, though with strong reluctance, from the spot. "I *can* read; and how have I used the knowledge! But he, Ishmael, he has not the sin of wasted larning to answer for. We have spared him *that,* at least! Whether it be in mercy or in cruelty, I know not."

Her husband made no reply, but continued steadily to lead her in the direction of their temporary abode. When they reached the summit of the swell of land which they knew was the last spot from which the situation of the grave of Asa could be seen, they all turned, as by common concurrence, to take a farewell view of the place. The little mound itself was not visible, but it was frightfully indicated by the flock of screaming birds which hovered above. In the opposite direction a low, blue hillock in the skirts of the horizon pointed out the place where Esther had left the rest of her young, and served as an attraction to draw her reluctant steps from the last abode of her eldest born. Nature quickened in the bosom of the mother at the sight, and she finally yielded the rights of the dead to the more urgent claims of the living.

The foregoing occurrences had struck a spark from the stern tempers of a set of beings so singularly molded in the habits of their uncultivated lives, which served to keep alive among them the dying embers of family affection. United to their parents by ties no stronger than those which use had created, there had been great danger, as Ishmael had foreseen, that the overloaded hive would swarm and leave him saddled with the difficulties of a young and helpless brood, unsupported by the exertions of those whom he had already brought to a state of maturity. The spirit of insubordination which emanated from the unfortunate Asa had spread among his juniors, and the squatter had been made painfully to remember the time when, in the wantonness of his youth and vigor, he had, reversing the order of the brutes, cast off his own aged and failing parents to enter into the world unshackled and free. But the danger had now abated, for a time at least; and if his authority was not restored with all its former influence, it was admitted to exist and to maintain its ascendancy a little longer.

It is true that his slow-minded sons, even while they submitted to the impressions of the recent event, had glimmerings of terrible distrust as to the manner in which their elder brother had met with his death. There were faint and indistinct images in the minds of two or three of the oldest, which portrayed the father himself as ready to imitate the example of Abraham, without the justification of the sacred authority which commanded the holy man to attempt the revolting office. But then these images were so transient and so much obscured in intellectual mists as to leave no very strong impressions; and the tendency of the whole transaction, as we have already said, was rather to strengthen than to weaken the authority of Ishmael.

In this disposition of mind the party continued their route towards the place whence they had that morning issued on a search which had been crowned with so melancholy a success.

The long and fruitless march which they had made under the direction of Abiram, the discovery of the body and its subsequent interment, had so far consumed the day that by the time their steps were retraced across the broad tract of waste which lay between the grave of Asa and the rock, the sun had fallen far below his meridian altitude. The hill had gradually risen as they approached, like some tower emerging from the bosom of the sea, and when within a mile, the minuter objects that crowned its height came dimly into view.

"It will be a sad meeting for the girls!" said Ishmael, who, from time to time, did not cease to utter something which he intended should be consolatory to the bruised spirit of his partner. "Asa was much regarded by all the young and seldom failed to bring in from his hunts something that they loved."

"He did, he did," murmured Esther; "the boy was the pride of the family. My other children are as nothing to him!"

"Say not so, good woman," returned the father, glancing his eye a little proudly at the athletic train which followed at no great distance in the rear. "Say not so, old Eester, for few fathers and mothers have greater reason to be boastful than ourselves."

"Thankful, thankful," muttered the humbled woman; "ye mean thankful, Ishmael!"

"Then thankful let it be, if you like the word better, my good girl; but what has become of Nelly and the young? The child has forgotten the charge I gave her and has not only suffered the children to sleep, but I warrant you is dreaming of the fields of Tennessee at this very moment. The mind of your niece is mainly fixed on the settlements, I reckon."

"Aye, she is not for us; I said it, and thought it, when I took her, because death had stripped her of all other friends. Death is a sad worker in the bosom of families, Ishmael! Asa had a kind feeling to the child, and they might have come one day into our places had things been so ordered."

"Nay, she is not gifted for a frontier wife if this is the manner she is to keep house while the husband is on the hunt. Abner, let off your rifle, that they may know we are coming. I fear Nelly and the young are asleep."

The young man complied with an alacrity that manifested how gladly he would see the rounded, active figure of Ellen enlivening the ragged summit of the rock. But the report was succeeded by neither signal nor answer of any sort. For a moment the whole party stood in suspense, awaiting the result, and then a simultaneous impulse caused the whole to let off their pieces at the same instant, producing a noise which might not fail to reach the ears of all within so short a distance.

"Ah! There they come at last!" cried Abiram, who was usually among the first to seize on any circumstance which promised relief from disagreeable apprehensions.

"It is a petticoat fluttering on the line," said Esther; "I put it there myself."

"You are right; but now she comes; the jade has been taking her comfort in the tent!"

"It is not so," said Ishmael, whose usually inflexible features were beginning to manifest the uneasiness he felt. "It is the tent itself blowing about loosely in the wind. They have loosened the bottom, like silly children as they are, and unless care is had, the whole will come down!"

The words were scarcely uttered before a rushing blast of wind swept by the spot where they stood, raising the dust in little eddies in its progress; and then, as if guided by a master hand, it quitted the earth and mounted to the precise spot on which all eyes were just then riveted. The loosened linen felt its influence and tottered, but regained its poise and for a moment it became tranquil. The cloud of leaves next played in circling revolutions around the place, and then descended with the velocity of a swooping hawk and sailed away into the prairie in long straight lines like a flight of swallows resting on their expanded wings. They were followed for some distance by the snow-white tent, which, however, soon fell behind the rock, leaving its highest peak as naked as when it lay in the entire solitude of the desert.

"The murderers have been here!" moaned Esther. "My babes! My babes!"

For a moment even Ishmael faltered before the weight of so unexpected a blow. But shaking himself like an awakened lion, he sprang forward, and pushing aside the impediments of the barrier as if they had been feathers, he rushed up the ascent with an impetuosity which proved how formidable a sluggish nature may become when thoroughly aroused.

CHAPTER 14

Whose party do the townsmen yet admit?

KING JOHN

IN ORDER TO preserve an even pace between the incidents of the tale, it becomes necessary to revert to such events as occurred during the ward of Ellen Wade.

For the first few hours the cares of the honest and warm-hearted girl were confined to the simple offices of satisfying the often repeated demands which her younger associates made on her time and patience under the pretenses of hunger, thirst, and all the other ceaseless wants of captious and inconsiderate childhood. She had seized a moment from their importunities to steal into the tent, where she was administering to the comforts of one far more deserving of her tenderness when an outcry among the children recalled her to the duties she had momentarily forgotten.

"See, Nelly, see!" exclaimed half a dozen eager voices. "Yonder are men; and Phoebe says that they are Sioux Indians!"

Ellen turned her eyes in the direction in which so many arms were already extended, and to her consternation beheld several men advancing manifestly and swiftly in a straight line towards the rock. She counted four, but was unable to make out anything concerning their characters except that they were not any of those who of right were entitled to admission into the fortress. It was a fearful moment for Ellen.

Looking around at the juvenile and frightened flock that pressed upon the skirts of her garments, she endeavored to recall to her confused faculties some one of the many tales of female heroism with which the history of the Western frontier abounded. In one a stockade had been successfully defended by a single man, supported by three or four women, for days against the assaults of a hundred enemies. In another the women alone had been able to protect the children and the less valuable effects of their absent husbands; and a third was not wanting, in which a solitary female had destroyed her sleeping captors and given liberty not only to herself, but to a brood of helpless young. This was the case most nearly assimilated to the situation in which Ellen now found herself; and with flushing cheeks and kindling eyes, the girl began to consider and to prepare her slender means of defense.

She posted the larger girls at the little levers that were to cast the rocks on the assailants; the smaller were to be used more for show than any positive service they could perform; while like any other leader she reserved her own person as a superintendent and encourager of the whole. When these dispositions were made she endeavored to await the issue with an air of composure that she intended should inspire her assistants with the confidence necessary to ensure success.

Although Ellen was vastly their superior in that spirit which emanates from moral qualities, she was by no means the equal of the two eldest daughters of Esther in the important military property of insensibility to danger. Reared in the hardihood of a migrating life on the skirts of society, where they had become familiarized to the sights and dangers of the wilderness, these girls promised fairly to become at some future day no less distinguished than their mother for daring and for that singular mixture of good and evil which in a wider sphere of action would probably have enabled the wife of the squatter to enroll her name among the remarkable females of her time. Esther had already on one occasion made good the log tenement of Ishmael against an inroad of savages; and on another she had been left for dead by her enemies after a defense that with a more civilized foe would have entitled her to the honors of a liberal capitulation. These facts and sundry others of a similar nature had often been recapitulated with suitable exultation in the presence of her daughters, and the bosoms of the young

Amazons were now strangly fluctuating between natural
terror and the ambitious wish to do something that might render them worthy of being the children of such a mother. It
appeared that the opportunity for distinction of this wild
character was no longer to be denied them.

The party of strangers was already within a hundred rods
of the rock. Either consulting their usual wary method of
advancing, or admonished by the threatening attitudes of two
figures who had thrust forth the barrels of as many old
muskets from behind the stone entrenchment, the newcomers
halted, under favor of an inequality in the ground, where a
growth of grass thicker than common offered the advantage
of concealment. From this spot they reconnoitered the
fortress for several anxious, and to Ellen, interminable minutes. Then one advanced singly, and apparently more in
the character of a herald than of an assailant.

"Phoebe, *do you* fire," and "No, Hetty, *you*," were beginning to be heard between the half-frightened and yet eager
daughters of the squatter, when Ellen probably saved the
advancing stranger from some imminent alarm, if from no
greater danger, by exclaiming, "Lay down the muskets; it is
Dr. Battius!"

Her subordinates so far complied as to withdraw their
hands from the locks, though the threatening barrels still
maintained the portentous levels. The naturalist, who had
advanced with sufficient deliberation to note the smallest
hostile demonstration of the garrison, now raised a white
handkerchief on the end of his fusee and came within
speaking distance of the fortress. Then assuming what he intended should be an imposing and dignified semblance of
authority, he blustered forth in a voice that might have been
heard at a much greater distance, "What, ho! I summon ye
all, in the name of the Confederacy of the United Sovereign
States of North America, to submit yourselves to the laws."

"Doctor or no doctor, he is an enemy, Nelly; hear him!
Hear him! He talks of the law."

"Stop! Stay till I hear his answer!" said the nearly breathless Ellen, pushing aside the dangerous weapons which were
again pointed in the direction of the shrinking person of the
herald.

"I admonish and forewarn ye all," continued the startled
doctor, "that I am a peaceful citizen of the before-named
Confederacy, or to speak with greater accuracy, Union, a

supporter of the Social Compact, and a lover of good order and amity." Then, perceiving that the danger was at least temporarily removed, he once more raised his voice to the hostile pitch, "I charge ye all, therefore, to submit to the laws."

"I thought you were a friend," Ellen replied, "and that you traveled with my uncle in virtue of an agreement——"

"It is void! I have been deceived in the very premises, and I hereby pronounce a certain compactum, entered into and concluded between Ishmael Bush, squatter, and Obed Battius, M.D., to be incontinently null and of noneffect. Nay, children, to be null is merely a negative property, and is fraught with no evil to your worthy parent; so lay aside the firearms and listen to the admonitions of reason. I declare it vicious—null—abrogated. As for thee, Nelly, my feelings towards thee are not at all given to hostility; therefore listen to that which I have to utter, nor turn away thine ears in the wantonness of security. Thou knowest the character of the man with whom thou dwellest, young woman, and thou also knowest the danger of being found in evil company. Abandon, then, the trifling advantages of thy situation and yield the rock peaceably to the will of those who accompany me— a legion, young woman—I do assure you an invincible and powerful legion! Render, therefore, the effects of this lawless and wicked squatter; nay, children, such disregard of human life is frightful in those who have so recently received the gift in their own persons! Point those dangerous weapons aside, I entreat of you, more for your own sakes than for mine. Hetty, hast thou forgotten who appeased thine anguish when thy auricular nerves were tortured by the colds and damps of the naked earth! And thou, Phoebe, ungrateful and forgetful Phoebe! But for this very arm, which you would prostrate with an endless paralysis, thy incisors would still be giving thee pain and sorrow! Lay then aside thy weapons and hearken to the advice of one who has always been thy friend. And now, young woman"—still keeping a jealous eye on the muskets which the girl had suffered to be diverted a little from their aim—"and now, young woman, for the last, and therefore the most solemn asking: I demand of thee the surrender of this rock, without delay or resistance, in the joint names of power, of justice, and of the——" "Law" he would have added, but recollecting that this ominous word would again provoke the hostility of the squatter's children, he succeeded in swallowing it in good season and concluded with the less dangerous and more convertible term of "reason."

This extraordinary summons failed, however, of producing the desired effect. It proved utterly unintelligible to his younger listeners, with the exception of the few offensive terms, already sufficiently distinguished; and though Ellen better comprehended the meaning of the herald, she appeared as little moved by his rhetoric as her companions. At those passages which he intended should be tender and affecting, the intelligent girl, though tortured by painful feelings, had even manifested a disposition to laugh, while to the threats she turned an utterly insensible ear.

"I know not the meaning of all you wish to say, Dr. Battius," she quietly replied when he had ended, "but I am sure if it would teach me to betray my trust, it is what I ought not to hear. I caution you to attempt no violence, for let my wishes be what they may, you see I am surrounded by a force that can easily put me down, and you know, or ought to know, too well the temper of this family to trifle in such a matter with any of its members, let them be of what sex or age they may."

"I am not entirely ignorant of human character," returned the naturalist, prudently receding a little from the position which he had until now stoutly maintained at the very base of the hill. "But here comes one who may know its secret windings still better than I."

"Ellen! Ellen Wade," cried Paul Hover, who had advanced to his elbow without betraying any of that sensitiveness which had so manifestly discomposed the doctor; "I didn't expect to find an enemy in you!"

"Nor shall you when you ask that which I can grant without treachery. You know that my uncle has trusted his family to my care, and shall I so far betray the trust as to let in his bitterest enemies to murder his children, perhaps, and to rob him of the little which the Indians have left?"

"Am I a murderer—is this old man—this officer of the States"—pointing to the trapper and his newly discovered friend, both of whom by this time stood at his side—"is either of these likely to do the things you name?"

"What is it then you ask of me?" said Ellen, wringing her hands in excessive doubt.

"The beast! Nothing more nor less than the squatter's hidden, ravenous, dangerous beast!"

"Excellent young woman," commenced the young stranger who had so lately joined himself to the party on the prairie, but his mouth was immediately stopped by a significant sign from the trapper, who whispered in his ear: "Let the lad be our spokesman. Natur' *will* work in the bosom of the child, and we shall gain our object in good time."

"The whole truth is out, Ellen," Paul continued, "and we have lined the squatter into his most secret misdoings. We have come to right the wronged and to free the imprisoned; now, if you are the girl of a true heart, as I have always believed, so far from throwing straws in our way, you will join in the general swarming and leave old Ishmael and his hive to the bees of his own breed."

"I have sworn a solemn oath——"

"A compactum which is entered into through ignorance or in duress is null in the sight of all good moralists," cried the doctor.

"Hush, hush," again the trapper whispered; "leave it all to natur' and the lad!"

"I have sworn in the sight and by the name of Him who is the founder and ruler of all that is good, whether it be in morals or in religion," Ellen continued, "neither to reveal the contents of that tent nor to help its prisoner to escape. We are both solemnly, terribly sworn; our lives perhaps have been the gift we received for the promises. It is true you are masters of the secret, but not through any means of ours; nor do I know that I can justify myself for even being neutral while you attempt to invade the dwelling of my uncle in this hostile manner."

"I can prove beyond the power of refutation," the naturalist eagerly exclaimed, "by Paley, Berkeley, aye, even by the immortal Binkershoeck, that a compactum concluded while one of the parties, be it a state or be it an individual, is in durance——"

"You will ruffle the temper of the child with your abusive language," said the cautious trapper, "while the lad, if left to human feelings, will bring her down to the meekness of a fawn. Ah! You are like myself, little knowing in the natur' of hidden kindnesses!"

"Is this the only vow you have taken, Ellen?" Paul continued in a tone which for the gay, lighthearted bee hunter sounded dolorous and reproachful. "Have you sworn only to this? Are the words which the squatter says to be as honey in your mouth, and all other promises like so much useless comb?"

The paleness which had taken possession of the usually cheerful countenance of Ellen was hid in a bright glow that was plainly visible even at the distance at which she stood. She hesitated a moment, as if struggling to repress something very like resentment, before she answered with all her native spirit, "I know not what right anyone has to question me about oaths and promises, which can only concern her who has made them, if, indeed, any of the sort you mention have ever been made at all. I shall hold no further discourse with one who thinks so much of himself and takes advice merely of his own feelings."

"Now, old trapper, do you hear that!" said the unsophisticated bee hunter, turning abruptly to his aged friend. "The meanest insect that skims the heavens, when it has got its load, flies straight and honestly to its nest or hive, according to its kind; but the ways of a woman's mind are as knotty as a gnarled oak and more crooked than the windings of the Mississippi!"

"Nay, nay, child," said the trapper, good-naturedly interfering in behalf of the offending Paul, "you are to consider that youth is hasty and not overgiven to thought. But then a promise is a promise, and not to be thrown aside and forgotten like the hoofs and horns of a buffalo."

"I thank you for reminding me of my oath," said the still resentful Ellen, biting her pretty nether lip with vexation; "I might else have proved forgetful!"

"Ah! Female natur' is awakened in her," said the old man, shaking his head in a manner to show how much he was disappointed in the result; "but it manifests itself against the true spirit!"

"Ellen!" cried the young stranger, who until now had been an attentive listener to the parley. "Since Ellen is the name by which you are known——"

"They often add it to another. I am sometimes called by the name of my father."

"Call her Nelly Wade at once," muttered Paul; "it is her rightful name, and I care not if she keeps it forever!"

"Wade, I should have added," continued the youth. "You will acknowledge that though bound by no oath myself, I at least have known how to respect those of others. You are a witness yourself that I have forborne to utter a single call, while I am certain it could reach those ears it would gladden so much. Permit me then to ascend the rock singly; I promise a perfect indemnity to your kinsman against any injury his effects may sustain."

Ellen seemed to hesitate, but catching a glimpse of Paul, who stood leaning proudly on his rifle, whistling with an appearance of the utmost indifference the air of a boating song, she recovered her recollection in time to answer, "I have been left the captain of the rock while my uncle and his sons hunt, and captain will I remain till he returns to receive back the charge."

"This is wasting moments that will not soon return and neglecting an opportunity that may never occur again," the young soldier gravely remarked. "The sun is beginning to fall already, and many minutes cannot elapse before the squatter and his savage brood will be returning to their huts."

Dr. Battius cast a glance behind him and took up the discourse by saying, "Perfection is always found in maturity, whether it be in the animal or in the intellectual world. Reflection is the mother of wisdom, and wisdom the parent of success. I propose that we retire to a discreet distance from this impregnable position and there hold a convocation, or council, to deliberate on what manner we may sit down regularly before the place, or perhaps by postponing the siege to another season, gain the aid of auxiliaries from the inhabited countries and thus secure the dignity of the laws from any danger of a repulse."

"A storm would be better," the soldier smilingly answered, measuring the height and scanning all its difficulties with a deliberate eye; " 'twould be but a broken arm or a bruised head at the worst."

"Then have at it!" shouted the impetuous bee hunter, making a spring that at once put him out of danger from shot by carrying him beneath the projecting ledge on which the garrison was posted; "now do your worst, young devils of a wicked breed; you have but a moment to work your mischief!"

"Paul! Rash Paul!" shrieked Ellen. "Another step and the rocks will crush you! They hang but by a thread, and these girls are ready and willing to let them fall!"

"Then drive the accursed swarm from the hive, for scale

the rock I will, though I find it covered with hornets."

"Let her if she dare!" tauntingly cried the eldest of the girls, brandishing a musket with a mien and resolution that would have done credit to her Amazonian dam. "I know you, Nelly Wade; you are with the lawyers in your heart, and if you come a foot nigher, you shall have frontier punishment. Put in another pry, girls; in with it! I should like to see the man of them all that dare come up into the camp of Ishmael Bush without asking leave of his children!"

"Stir not, Paul; for your life, keep beneath the rock!"

Ellen was interrupted by the same bright vision which on the preceding day had stayed another scarcely less portentous tumult by exhibiting itself on the same giddy height where it was now seen.

"In the name of Him who commandeth all, I implore you to pause—both you who so madly incur the risk, and you who so rashly offer to take that which you never can return!" said a voice in a slightly foreign accent that instantly drew all eyes upwards.

"Inez!" cried the officer. "Do I again see you! Mine shall you now be, though a million devils were posted on this rock. Push up, brave woodsman, and give room for another!"

The sudden appearance of the figure from the tent had created a momentary stupor among the defenders of the rock, which might, with suitable forbearance, have been happily improved; but startled by the voice of Middleton, the surprised Phoebe discharged her musket at the female, scarcely knowing whether she aimed at the life of a mortal or at some being which belonged to another world. Ellen uttered a cry of horror and then sprang after her alarmed or wounded friend, she new not which, into the tent.

During this moment of dangerous byplay the sounds of a serious attack were very distinctly audible beneath. Paul had profited by the commotion over his head to change his place so far as to make room for Middleton. The latter was followed by the naturalist, who, in a state of mental aberration, produced by the report of the musket, had instinctively rushed towards the rocks for cover. The trapper remained where he was last seen, an unmoved but close observer of the several proceedings. Though averse to enter into actual hostilities, the old man was, however, far from being useless. Favored by his position, he was enabled to apprise his friends of the movements of those who plotted their destruction above and to advise and control their advance accordingly.

In the meantime the children of Esther were true to the spirit they had inherited from their redoubtable mother. The instant they found themselves delivered from the presence of Ellen and her unknown companion, they bestowed an undivided attention on their more masculine and certainly more dangerous assailants, who by this time had made a complete lodgment among the crags of the citadel. The repeated summons to surrender, which Paul uttered in a voice that he intended should strike terror into their young bosoms, were as little heeded as were the calls of the trapper to abandon a resistance which might prove fatal to some among them without offering the smallest probability of eventual success. Encouraging each other to persevere, they poised the fragments of rocks, prepared the lighter missiles for immediate service, and thrust forward the barrels of the muskets with a businesslike air and a coolness that would have done credit to men practiced in warfare.

"Keep under the ledge," said the trapper, pointing out to Paul the manner in which he should proceed; "keep in your foot more, lad—ah! You see the warning was not amiss! Had the stone struck it, the bees would have had the prairies to themselves. Now, namesake of my friend; Uncas, in name and spirit! Now, if you have the activity of Le Cerf Agile, you may make a fair leap to the right and gain twenty feet without danger. Beware the bush—beware the bush! 'Twill prove a treacherous hold! Ah! He has done it; safely and bravely has he done it! Your turn comes next, friend, that follows the fruits of natur'. Push you to the left and divide the attention of the children. Nay, girls, fire—my old ears are used to the whistling of lead; and little reason have I to prove a doe-heart, with fourscore years on my back." He shook his head with a melancholy smile but without flinching in a muscle as the bullet, which the exasperated Hetty fired, passed innocently at no great distance from the spot where he stood. "It is safer keeping in your track than dodging when a weak finger pulls the trigger," he continued; "but it is a solemn sight to witness how much human natur' is inclined to evil in one so young! Well done, my man of beasts and plants! Another such leap, and you may laugh at all the squatter's bars and walls. The doctor has got his temper up! I see it in his eye, and something good will come of him! Keep closer, man—keep closer."

The trapper, though he was not deceived as to the state of Dr. Battius' mind, was, however, greatly in error as to the exciting cause. While imitating the movements of his companions and toiling his way upwards with the utmost caution, and not without great inward tribulation, the eye of the naturalist had caught a glimpse of an unknown plant a few yards above his head and in a situation more than commonly exposed to the missiles which the girls were unceasingly hurling in the direction of the assailants. Forgetting in an instant everything but the glory of being the first to give this jewel to the catalogs of science, he sprang upwards at the prize with the avidity with which the sparrow darts upon the butterfly. The rocks which instantly came thundering down announced that he was seen, and for a moment, while his form was concealed in the cloud of dust and fragments which followed the furious descent, the trapper gave him up for lost; but the next instant he was seen safely seated in a cavity formed by some of the projecting stones which had yielded to the shock, holding triumphantly in his hand the captured stem, which he was already devouring with delighted and certainly not unskillful eyes. Paul profited by the opportunity. Turning his course, with the quickness of thought he sprang to the post which Obed thus securely occupied, and unceremoniously making a footstool of his shoulder as the latter stooped over his treasure, he bounded through the breach left by the fallen rock and gained the level. He was followed by Middleton, who joined him in seizing and disarming the girls. In this manner a bloodless and complete victory was obtained over that citadel which Ishmael had vainly flattered himself might prove impregnable.

CHAPTER 15

So smile the heavens upon this holy act,
That after hours with sorrow chide us not!
SHAKESPEARE

IT IS PROPER that the course of the narrative should be stayed while we revert to those causes which have brought in their train of consequences the singular contest just related. The interruption must necessarily be as brief as we hope it may prove satisfactory to that class of readers who require that no gap should be left by those who assume the office of historians for their own fertile imaginations to fill.

Among the troops sent by the government of the United States to take possession of its newly acquired territory in the West was a detachment led by the young soldier who has become so busy an actor in the scenes of our legend. The mild and indolent descendants of the ancient colonists received their new compatriots without distrust, well knowing that the transfer raised them from the condition of subjects to the more enviable distinction of citizens in a government of laws. The new rulers exercised their functions with discretion and wielded their delegated authority without offense. In such a novel intermixture, however, of men born and nurtured in freedom and the compliant minions of absolute power, the Catholic and the Protestant, the active and the indolent, some little time was necessary to blend the discrepant elements of society. In attaining so desirable an end, woman was made to perform her accustomed and grateful office. The barriers of prejudice and religion were broken through by the irresistible power of the master passion, and family unions erelong began to cement the political tie which had made a forced conjunction between people so opposite in their habits, their educations, and their opinions.

Middleton was among the first of the new possessors of the soil who became captive charms of a Louisianian lady. In the immediate vicinity of the post he had been directed to occupy dwelt the chief of one of those ancient colonial families which had been content to slumber for ages amid the ease, indolence, and wealth of the Spanish provinces. He was an officer of the crown and had been induced to remove from the Floridas among the French of the adjoining province, by a rich succession of which he had become the inheritor. The name of Don Augustin de Certavallos was scarcely known beyond the limits of the little town in which he resided, though he found a secret pleasure himself in pointing it out, in large scrolls of musty documents, to an only child, as enrolled among the former heroes and grandees of Old and of New Spain. This fact, so important to himself and of so little moment to anybody else, was the principal reason that while his more vivacious Gallic neighbors were not slow to open a frank communion with their visitors, he chose to keep aloof, seemingly content with the society of his daughter, who was a girl just emerging from the condition of childhood into that of a woman.

The curiosity of the youthful Inez, however, was not so inactive. She had not heard the martial music of the garrison melting on the evening air, nor seen the strange banner which fluttered over the heights that rose at no great distance from her father's extensive grounds, without experiencing some of those secret impulses which are thought to distinguish the sex. Natural timidity and that retiring and perhaps peculiar lassitude which forms the very groundwork of female fascination in the tropical provinces of Spain held her in their seemingly indissoluble bonds; and it is more than probable that had not an accident occurred, in which Middleton was of some personal service to her father, so long a time would have elapsed before they met that another direction might have been given to the wishes of one who was just of an age to be alive to all the power of youth and beauty.

Providence—or if that imposing word is too just to be classical, fate—had otherwise decreed. The haughty and reserved Don Augustin was by far too observant of the forms of that station on which he so much valued himself to forget the duties of a gentleman. Gratitude for the kindness of Middleton induced him to open his doors to the officers of the garrison and to admit of a guarded but polite intercourse. Reserve gradually gave way before the propriety and candor of their spirited young leader, and it was not long ere the affluent planter rejoiced as much as his daughter whenever the well-known signal at the gate announced one of these agreeable visits from the commander of the post.

It is unnecessary to dwell on the impression which the charms of Inez produced on the soldier or to delay the tale in order to write a wire-drawn account of the progressive influence that elegance of deportment, manly beauty, and undivided assiduity and intelligence were likely to produce on the sensitive mind of a romantic, warmhearted, and secluded girl of sixteen. It is sufficient for our purpose to say that they loved, that the youth was not backward to declare his feelings, that he prevailed with some facility over the scruples of the maiden and with no little difficulty over the objections of her father, and that before the province of Louisiana had been six months in the possession of the

States, the officer of the latter was the affianced husband of the richest heiress on the banks of the Mississippi.

Although we have presumed the reader to be acquainted with the manner in which such results are commonly attained, it is not to be supposed that the triumph of Middleton, either over the prejudices of the father or over those of the daughter, was achieved without difficulty. Religion formed a stubborn and nearly irremovable obstacle with both. The devoted young man patiently submitted to a formidable essay which Father Ignatius was deputed to make in order to convert him to the true faith. The effort on the part of the worthy priest was systematic, vigorous, and long sustained. A dozen times (it was at those moments when glimpses of the light, sylphlike form of Inez flitted like some fairy being past the scene of their conferences) the good father fancied he was on the eve of a glorious triumph over infidelity, but all his hopes were frustrated by some unlooked-for opposition on the part of the subject of his pious labors. So long as the assault on his faith was distant and feeble, Middleton, who was no great proficient in polemics, submitted to its effects with the patience and humility of a martyr; but the moment the good father who felt such concern in his future happiness was tempted to improve his vantage ground by calling in the aid of some of the peculiar subtilties of his own creed, the young man was too good a soldier not to make head against the hot attack. He came to the contest, it is true, with no weapons more formidable than common sense and some little knowledge of the habits of his country as contrasted with that of his adversary; but with these home-bred implements he never failed to repulse the father with something of the power with which a nervous cudgel player would deal with a skillful master of the infidelity, but all his hopes were frustrated by some unanswerable arguments of a broken head and a shivered weapon.

Before the controversy was terminated, an inroad of Protestants had come to aid the soldier. The reckless freedom of such among them as thought only of this life, and the consistent and tempered piety of others, caused the honest priest to look about him in concern. The influence of example on the one hand and the contamination of too free an intercourse on the other began to manifest themselves even in that portion of his own flock which he had supposed to be too thoroughly folded in spiritual government ever to stray. It was time to turn his thoughts from the offensive and to prepare his followers to resist the lawless deluge of opinion which threatened to break down the barriers of their faith. Like a wise commander who finds he has occupied too much ground for the amount of his force, he began to curtail his outworks. The relics were concealed from profane eyes; his people were admonished not to speak of miracles before a race that not only denied their existence, but who had even the desperate hardihood to challenge their proofs; and even the Bible itself was prohibited with terrible denunciations for the triumphant reason that it was liable to be misinterpreted.

In the meantime it became necessary to report to Don Augustin the effects his arguments and prayers had produced on the heretical disposition of the young soldier. No man is prone to confess his weakness at the very moment when circumstances demand the utmost efforts of his strength. By a species of pious fraud, for which no doubt the worthy priest found his absolution in the purity of his motives, he declared that while no positive change was actually wrought in the mind of Middleton, there was every reason to hope the entering wedge of argument had been driven to its head and that in consequence an opening was left through which it might rationally be hoped the blessed seeds of a religious fructification would find their way, especially if the subject was left uninterruptedly to enjoy the advantage of Catholic communion.

Don Augustin himself was now seized with the desire of proselyting. Even the soft and amiable Inez thought it would be a glorious consummation of her wishes to be a humble instrument of bringing her lover into the bosom of the true church. The offers of Middleton were promptly accepted, and while the father looked forward impatiently to the day assigned for the nuptials as to the pledge of his own success, the daughter thought of it with feelings in which the holy emotions of her faith were blended with the softer sensations of her years and situation.

The sun rose, the morning of her nuptials, on a day so bright and cloudless that Inez hailed it as a harbinger of future happiness. Father Ignatius performed the offices of the church in a little chapel attached to the estate of Don Augustin; and long ere the sun had begun to fall, Middleton pressed the blushing and timid young Creole to his bosom, his acknowledged and unalienable wife. It had pleased the parties to pass the day of the wedding in retirement, dedicating it solely to the best and purest affections, aloof from the noisy and heartless rejoicings of a compelled festivity.

Middleton was returning through the grounds of Don Augustin, from a visit of duty to his encampment, at that hour in which the light of the sun begins to melt into the shadows of evening, when a glimpse of a robe similar to that in which Inez had accompanied him to the altar caught his eye through the foliage of a retired arbor. He approached the spot with a delicacy that was rather increased than diminished by the claim she had perhaps given him to intrude on her private moments, but the sounds of her soft voice, which was offering up prayers in which he heard himself named by the dearest of all appellations, overcame his scruples and induced him to take a position where he might listen without the fear of detection. It was certainly grateful to the feelings of a husband to be able in this manner to lay bare the spotless soul of his wife and to find that his own image lay enshrined amid its purest and holiest aspirations. His self-esteem was too much flattered not to induce him to overlook the immediate object of the petitioner. While she prayed that she might become the humble instrument of bringing him into the flock of the faithful, she petitioned for forgiveness on her own behalf if presumption or indifference to the counsel of the church had caused her to set too high a value on her influence and led her into the dangerous error of hazarding her own soul by espousing a heretic. There was so much of fervent piety mingled with so strong a burst of natural feeling, so much of the woman blended with the angel in her prayers, that Middleton could have forgiven her had she termed him a pagan for the sweetness and interest with which she petitioned in his favor.

The young man waited until his bride arose from her knees, and then he joined her, as if entirely ignorant of what had occurred.

"It is getting late, my Inez," he said, "and Don Augustin would be apt to reproach you with inattention to your health in being abroad at such an hour. What then am I to do, who am charged with all his authority, and twice his love?"

"Be like him in *every*thing," she answered, looking up in his face with tears in her eyes and speaking with emphasis;

"in *every*thing. Imitate my father, Middleton, and I can ask no more of you."

"Nor *for* me, Inez? I doubt not that I should be all you can wish were I to become as good as the worthy and respectable Don Augustin. But you are to make some allowances for the infirmities and habits of a soldier. Now let us go and join this excellent father."

"Not yet," said his bride, gently extricating herself from the arm that he had thrown around her slight form while he urged her from the place. "I have still another duty to perform before I can submit so implicitly to your orders, soldier though you are. I promised the worthy Inesella, my faithful nurse, she who, as you heard, has so long been a mother to me, Middleton—I promised her a visit at this hour. It is the last, as she thinks, that she can receive from her own child, and I cannot disappoint her. Go you then to Don Augustin; in one short hour I will rejoin you."

"Remember, it is but an hour!"

"One hour," repeated Inez as she kissed her hand to him; and then blushing, ashamed at her own boldness, she darted from the arbor, and was seen for an instant gliding towards the cottage of her nurse, in which at the next moment she disappeared.

Middleton returned slowly and thoughtfully to the house, often bending his eyes in the direction in which he had last seen his wife, as if he would fain trace her lovely form, in the gloom of the evening, still floating through the vacant space. Don Augustin received him with warmth, and for many minutes his mind was amused by relating to his new kinsman plans for the future. The exclusive old Spaniard listened to his glowing but true account of the prosperity and happiness of those states of which he had been an ignorant neighbor half his life, partly in wonder and partly with that sort of incredulity with which one attends to what he fancies are the exaggerated descriptions of a too partial friendship.

In this manner the hour for which Inez had conditioned passed away much sooner than her husband could have thought possible, in her absence. At length his looks began to wander to the clock, and then the minutes were counted as one rolled by after another and Inez did not appear. The hand had already made half of another circuit around the face of the dial when Middleton arose and announced his determination to go and offer himself as an escort to the absentee. He found the night dark and the heavens charged with threatening vapor, which in that climate was the infallible forerunner of a gust. Stimulated no less by the unpropitious aspect of the skies than by his secret uneasiness, he quickened his pace, making long and rapid strides in the direction of the cottage of Inesella. Twenty times he stopped, fancying that he caught glimpses of the fairy form of Inez tripping across the grounds on her return to the mansion-house, and as often he was obliged to resume his course in disappointment. He reached the gate of the cottage, knocked, opened the door, entered, and even stood in the presence of the aged nurse without meeting the person of her he sought. She had already left the place on her return to her father's house! Believing that he must have passed her in the darkness, Middleton retraced his steps to meet with another disappointment. Inez had not been seen. Without communicating his intention to anyone, the bridegroom proceeded with a palpitating heart to the little sequestered arbor where he had overheard his bride offering up those petitions for his happiness and conversion. Here too he was disappointed, and then all was afloat in the painful incertitude of doubt and conjecture.

For many hours a secret distrust of the motives of his wife caused Middleton to proceed in the search with delicacy and caution. But as day dawned without restoring her to the arms of her father or her husband, reserve was thrown aside, and her unaccountable absence was loudly proclaimed. The inquiries after the lost Inez were now direct and open, but they proved equally fruitless. No one had seen her or heard of her from the moment that she left the cottage of her nurse.

Day succeeded day, and still no tidings rewarded the search that was immediately instituted, until she was finally given over by most of her relations and friends as irretrievably lost.

An event of so extraordinary a character was not likely to be soon forgotten. It excited speculation, gave rise to an infinity of rumors and not a few inventions. The prevalent opinion among such of those emigrants who were overrunning the country as had time in the multitude of their employments to think of any foreign concerns was the simple and direct conclusion that the absent bride was no more nor less than a *felo de se*. Father Ignatius had many doubts and much secret compunction of conscience, but like a wise chief, he endeavored to turn the sad event to some account in the impending warfare of faith. Changing his battery, he whispered in the ears of a few of his oldest parishioners that he had been deceived in the state of Middleton's mind, which he was now compelled to believe was completely stranded on the quicksands of heresy. He began to show his relics again and was even heard to allude once more to the delicate and nearly forgotten subject of modern miracles. In consequence of these demonstrations on the part of the venerable priest, it came to be whispered among the faithful, and finally it was adopted as part of the parish creed, that Inez had been translated to heaven.

Don Augustin had all the feelings of a father, but they were smothered in the lassitude of a Creole. Like his spiritual governor, he began to think that they had been wrong in consigning one so pure, so young, so lovely, and above all so pious to the arms of a heretic; and he was fain to believe that the calamity which had befallen his age was a judgment on his presumption and want of adherence to established forms. It is true that as the whispers of the congregation came to his ears he found present consolation in their belief, but then nature was too powerful and had too strong a hold of the old man's heart not to give rise to the rebellious thought that the succession of his daughter to the heavenly inheritance was a little premature.

But Middleton, the lover, the husband, the bridegroom—Middleton was nearly crushed by the weight of the unexpected and terrible blow. Educated himself under the dominion of a simple and rational faith in which nothing is attempted to be concealed from the believers, he could have no other apprehensions for the fate of Inez than such as grew out of his knowledge of the superstitious opinions she entertained of his own church. It is needless to dwell on the mental tortures that he endured or all the various surmises, hopes, and disappointments that he was fated to experience in the first few weeks of his misery. A jealous distrust of the motives of Inez and a secret, lingering hope that he should yet find her had tempered his inquiries, without, however, causing him to abandon them entirely. But time was beginning to deprive him even of the mortifying reflection that he was intentionally though perhaps temporarily deserted, and he was gradually yielding to the more painful conviction that she was dead when his hopes were suddenly revived in a new and singular manner.

The young commander was slowly and sorrowfully returning from an evening parade of his troops to his own quarters, which stood at some little distance from the place of the encampment, and on the same high bluff of land, when his vacant eyes fell on the figure of a man who by the regulations of the place was not entitled to be there at that forbidden hour. The stranger was meanly dressed, with every appearance about his person and countenance of squalid poverty and of the most dissolute habits. Sorrow had softened the military pride of Middleton, and as he passed the crouching form of the intruder, he said in tones of great mildness, or rather of kindness, "You will be given a night in the guardhouse, friend, should the patrol find you here; there is a dollar, go and get a better place to sleep in and something to eat!"

"I swallow all my food, captain, without chewing," returned the vagabond with the low exultation of an accomplished villain, as he eagerly seized the silver. "Make this Mexican twenty, and I will sell you a secret."

"Go, go," said the other with a little of a soldier's severity returning to his manner. "Go before I order the guard to seize you."

"Well, go I will; but if I do go, captain, I shall take my knowledge with me; and then you may live a widower bewitched till the tattoo of life is beat off."

"What mean you, fellow?" exclaimed Middleton, turning quickly towards the wretch, who was already dragging his diseased limbs from the place.

"I mean to have the value of this dollar in Spanish brandy, and then come back and sell you my secret for enough to buy a barrel."

"If you have anything to say, speak now," continued Middleton, restraining with difficulty the impatience that urged him to betray his feelings.

"I am a-dry, and I can never talk with elegance when my throat is husky, captain. How much will you give to know what I can tell you; let it be something handsome, such as one gentleman can offer to another."

"I believe it would be better justice to order the drummer

to pay you a visit, fellow. To what does your boasted secret relate?"

"Matrimony; a wife and no wife; a pretty face and a rich bride; do I speak plain now, captain?"

"If you know anything relating to my wife, say it at once; you need not fear for your reward."

"Aye, captain, I have drove many a bargain in my time, and sometimes I have been paid in money, and sometimes I have been paid in promises; now the last are what I call pinching food."

"Name your price."

"Twenty—no, damn it, it's worth thirty dollars if it's worth a cent!"

"Here, then, is your money; but remember, if you tell me nothing worth knowing, I have a force that can easily deprive you of it again and punish your insolence into the bargain."

The fellow examined the bank bills he received with a jealous eye, and then pocketed them, apparently well satisfied of their being genuine.

"I like a northern note," he said very coolly; "they have a character to lose like myself. No fear of me, captain; I am a man of honor, and I shall not tell you a word more nor a word less than I know of my own knowledge to be true."

"Proceed then without further delay, or I may repent and order you to be deprived of all your gains, the silver as well as the notes."

"Honor, if you die for it!" returned the miscreant, holding up a hand in affected horror at so treacherous a threat. "Well, captain, you must know that gentlemen don't all live by the same calling; some keep what they've got, and some get what they can."

"You have been a thief."

"I scorn the word. I have been a humanity hunter. Do you know what that means? Aye, it has many interpretations. Some people think the woolly-heads are miserable, working on hot plantations under a broiling sun, and all such sorts of inconveniences. Well, captain, I have been, in my time, a man who has been willing to give them the pleasures of variety, at least, by changing the scene for them. You understand me?"

"You are, in plain language, a kidnapper."

"Have been, my worthy captain—have been; but just now a little reduced, like a merchant who leaves off selling tobacco by the hogshead to deal in it by the yard. I have been a soldier too in my day. What is said to be the great secret of our trade, can you tell me that?"

"I know not," said Middleton, beginning to tire of the fellow's trifling: "courage?"

"No, legs—legs to fight with, and legs to run away with —and therein you see my two callings agreed. My legs are none of the best just now, and without legs a kidnapper would carry on a losing trade; but then there are men enough left, better provided than I am."

"Stolen!" groaned the horror-struck husband.

"On her travels, as sure as you are standing still!"

"Villain, what reason have you for believing a thing so shocking?"

"Hands off—hands off—do you think my tongue can do its work the better for a little squeezing of the throat! Have patience, and you shall know it all; but if you treat me so ungenteelly again, I shall be obliged to call in the assistance of the lawyers."

"Say on; but if you utter a single word more or less than the truth, expect instant vengeance!"

"Are you fool enough to believe what such a scoundrel as I am tells you, captain, unless it has probability to back it? I know you are not; therefore I will give my facts and my opinions, and then leave you to chew on them while I go and drink of your generosity. I know a man who is called Abiram White. I believe the knave took that name to show his enmity to the race of blacks! But this gentleman is now and has been for years to my certain knowledge a regular translator of the human body from one state to another. I have dealt with him in my time, and a cheating dog he is! No more honor in him than meat in my stomach. I saw him here in this very town the day of your wedding. He was in company with his wife's brother and pretended to be a settler on the hunt for new land. A noble set they were to carry on business—seven sons, each of them as tall as your sergeant with his cap on. Well, the moment I heard that your wife was lost, I saw at once that Abiram had laid his hands on her."

"Do you know this—can this be true? What reason have you to fancy a thing so wild?"

"Reason enough; I know Abiram White. Now, will you add a trifle just to keep my throat from parching?"

"Go, go; you are stupefied with drink already, miserable man, and know not what you say. Go; go, and beware the drummer."

"Experience is a good guide," the fellow called after the retiring Middleton; and then turning with a chuckling laugh, like one well satisfied with himself, he made the best of his way towards the shop of the sutler.

A hundred times in the course of that night did Middleton fancy that the communication of the miscreant was entitled to some attention, and as often did he reject the idea as too wild and visionary for another thought. He was awakened early on the following morning, after passing a restless and nearly sleepless night, by his orderly, who came to report that a man was found dead on the parade at no great distance from his quarters. Throwing on his clothes he proceeded to the spot and beheld the individual with whom he had held the preceding conference, in the precise situation in which he had first been found.

The miserable wretch had fallen a victim to his intemperance. This revolting fact was sufficiently proclaimed by his obtruding eyeballs, his bloated countenance, and the nearly insufferable odors that were even then exhaling from his carcass. Disgusted with the odious spectacle, the youth was turning from the sight after ordering the corpse to be removed when the position of one of the dead men's hands struck him. On examination, he found the forefinger extended, as if in the act of writing in the sand, with the following incomplete sentence, nearly illegible, but yet in a state to be deciphered. "Captain, it is true, as I am a gentle—" He had either died or fallen into a sleep, the forerunner of his death, before the latter word was finished.

Concealing this fact from the others, Middleton repeated his orders and departed. The pertinacity of the deceased, and all the circumstances united, induced him to set on foot some secret inquiries. He found that a family answering the description which had been given him had in fact passed the place the day of his nuptials. They were traced along the margin of the Mississippi for some distance, until they took boat and ascended the river to its confluence with the Missouri. Here they had disappeared like hundreds of others in pursuit of the hidden wealth of the interior.

Furnished with these facts, Middleton detailed a small guard of his most trusty men, took leave of Don Augustin without declaring his hopes or his fears, and having arrived at the indicated point, he pushed into the wilderness in pursuit. It was not difficult to trace a train like that of Ishmael, until he was assured its object lay far beyond the usual limits of the settlements. This circumstance in itself quickened his suspicions and gave additional force to his hopes of final success.

After getting beyond the assistance of verbal directions, the anxious husband had recourse to the usual signs of a trail in order to follow the fugitives. This he also found a task of no difficulty, until he reached the hard and unyielding soil of the rolling prairies. Here, indeed, he was completely at fault. He found himself at length compelled to divide his followers, appointing a place of rendezvous at a distant day, and to endeavor to find the lost trail by multiplying, as much as possible, the number of his eyes. He had been alone a week when accident brought him in contact with the trapper and the bee hunter. Part of their interview has been related, and the reader can readily imagine the explanations that succeeded the tale he recounted and which led, as has already been seen, to the recovery of his bride.

CHAPTER 16

These likelihoods confirm her flight from hence.
Therefore, I pray you, stay not to discourse,
But mount you presently.

SHAKESPEARE

AN HOUR HAD slid by in hasty and nearly incoherent questions and answers before Middleton, hanging over his recovered treasure with that sort of jealous watchfulness with which a miser would regard his hoards, closed the disjointed narrative of his own proceedings by demanding, "And you, my Inez; in what manner were you treated?"

"In everything but the great injustice they did in separating me so forcibly from my friends, as well perhaps as the circumstances of my captors would allow. I think the man who is certainly the master here is but a new beginner in wickedness. He quarreled frightfully in my presence with the wretch who seized me, and then they made an impious bargain, to which I was compelled to acquiesce and to which they bound me, as well as themselves, by oaths. Ah! Middleton, I fear the heretics are not so heedful of their vows as we who are nurtured in the bosom of the true church!"

"Believe it not; these villains are of no religion! Did they forswear themselves?"

"No, not perjured; but was it not awful to call upon the good God to witness so sinful a compact?"

"And so we think, Inez, as truly as the most virtuous cardinal of Rome. But how did they observe their oath, and what was its purport?"

"They conditioned to leave me unmolested and free from their odious presence provided I would give a pledge to make no effort to escape, and that I would not even show myself until a time that my masters saw fit to name."

"And that time?" demanded the impatient Middleton, who so well knew the religious scruples of his wife. "That time?"

"It is already passed. I was sworn by my patron saint, and faithfully did I keep the vow until the man they call Ishmael forgot the terms by offering violence. I then made my appearance on the rock, for the time too was passed, though I even think Father Ignatius would have absolved me from the vow on account of the treachery of my keepers."

"If he had not," muttered the youth between his compressed teeth, "I would have absolved him forever from his spiritual care of your conscience!"

"You, Middleton!" returned his wife, looking up into his flushed face, while a bright flush suffused her own sweet countenance. "You may *receive* my vows, but surely you can have no power to *absolve* me from their observance!"

"No, no, no. Inez, you are right. I know but little of these conscientious subtilties, and I am anything but a priest; yet tell me, what has induced these monsters to play this desperate game—to trifle thus with my happiness?"

"You know my ignorance of the world and how ill I am qualified to furnish reasons for the conduct of beings so different from any I have ever seen before. But does not love of money drive men to acts even worse than this? I believe they thought that an aged and wealthy father could be tempted to pay them a rich ransom for his child; and perhaps," she added, stealing an inquiring glance through her tears at the attentive Middleton, "they counted something on the fresh affections of a bridegroom."

"They might have extracted the blood from my heart drop by drop!"

"Yes," resumed his young and timid wife, instantly with-drawing the stolen look she had hazarded and hurriedly pursuing the train of the discourse, as if glad to make him forget the liberty she had just taken, "I have been told there are men so base as to perjure themselves at the altar in order to command the gold of ignorant and confiding girls; and if love of money will lead to such baseness, we may surely expect it will hurry those who devote themselves to gain into acts of lesser fraud."

"It must be so; and now, Inez, though I am here to guard you with my life, and we are in possession of this rock, our difficulties, perhaps our dangers, are not ended. You will summon all your courage to meet the trial and prove your-self a soldier's wife, my Inez?"

"I am ready to depart this instant. The letter you sent by the physician had prepared me to hope for the best, and I have everything arranged for flight at the shortest warning."

"Let us then leave this place and join our friends."

"Friends!" interrupted Inez, glancing her eyes around the little tent in quest of the form of Ellen. "I too have a friend who must not be forgotten, but who is pledged to pass the remainder of her life with us. She is gone!"

Middleton gently led her from the spot, as he smilingly answered, "She may have had, like myself, her own private communications for some favored ear."

The young man had not, however, done justice to the motives of Ellen Wade. The sensitive and intelligent girl had readily perceived how little her presence was necessary in the interview that has just been related, and had retired with that intuitive delicacy of feeling which seems to belong more properly to her sex. She was now to be seen seated on a point of the rock, with her person so entirely enveloped in her dress as to conceal her features. Here she had re-mained for near an hour, no one approaching to address her, and as it appeared to her own quick and jealous eyes, totally unobserved. In the latter particular, however, even the vigilance of the quick-sighted Ellen was deceived.

The first act of Paul Hover on finding himself the master of Ishmael's citadel had been to sound the note of victory after the quaint and ludicrous manner that is so often prac-ticed among the borderers of the West. Flapping his sides with his hands as the conquering gamecock is wont to do with his wings, he raised a loud and laughable imitation of the exultation of this bird, a cry which might have proved a dangerous challenge had any one of the athletic sons of the squatter been within hearing.

"This has been a regular knock-down and drag-out," he cried, "and no bones broke! How now, old trapper; you have been one of your training, platoon, rank-and-file soldiers in your day and have seen forts taken and batteries stormed before this—am I right?"

"Aye, aye, that have I," answered the old man, who still maintained his post at the foot of the rock, so little disturbed by what he had just witnessed as to return the grin of Paul with a hearty indulgence in his own silent and peculiar laughter; "you have gone through the exploit like men!"

"Now tell me, is it not in rule to call over the names of the living and to bury the dead after every bloody battle?"

"Some did and other some didn't. When Sir William pushed the German Dieskau through the defiles at the foot of the Hori——"

"Your Sir William was a drone to Sir Paul and knew nothing of regularity. So here begins the roll call; by the by, old man, what between bee hunting and buffalo humps and certain other matters, I have been too busy to ask your name, for I intend to begin with my rear guard, well knowing that my man in front is too busy to answer."

"Lord, lad, I've been called in my time by as many names as there are people among whom I've dwelt. Now the Delawares named me for my eyes, and I was called after the farsighted hawk. Then ag'in, the settlers in the Otsego hills christened me anew from the fashion of my leggings; and various have been the names by which I have gone through life; but little will it matter when the time shall come that all are to be mustered, face to face, by what titles a mortal has played his part! I humbly trust I shall be able to answer to any of mine in a loud and manly voice."

Paul paid little or no attention to this reply, more than half of which was lost in the distance, but pursuing the humor of the moment, he called out in a stentorian voice to the naturalist to answer to his name. Dr. Battius had not thought it necessary to push his success beyond the comfortable niche which accident had so opportunely formed for his protection and in which he now reposed from his labors with a pleasing consciousness of security, added to great exultation at the possession of the botanical treasure already mentioned.

"Mount, mount, my worthy mole catcher! Come and behold the prospect of skirting Ishmael; come and look nature boldly in the face and not go sneaking any longer among the prairie grass and mullin tops like a gobbler nibbling for grasshoppers."

The mouth of the lighthearted and reckless bee hunter was instantly closed, and he was rendered as mute as he had just been boisterous and talkative by the appearance of Ellen Wade. When the melancholy maiden took her seat on the point of the rock as mentioned, Paul affected to employ himself in conducting a close inspection of the household effects of the squatter. He rummaged the drawers of Esther with no delicate hands, scattered the rustic finery of her girls on the ground without the least deference to its quality or elegance, and tossed her pots and kettles here and there as though they had been vessels of wood instead of iron. All this industry was, however, manifestly without an object. He reserved nothing for himself, not even appearing conscious of the nature of the articles which suffered by his familiarity. When he had examined the inside of every cabin, taken a fresh survey of the spot where he had confined the children and where he had thoroughly secured them with cords, and kicked one of the pails of the woman like a football fifty feet into the air in sheer wantonness, he returned to the edge of the rock, and thrusting both his hands through his wampum belt, he began to whistle the "Kentucky Hunters" as diligently as if he had been hired to supply his auditors with music by the hour. In this manner passed the remainder of the time until Middleton, as has been related, led Inez forth from the tent and gave a new direction to the thoughts of the whole party. He summoned Paul from his flourish of music, tore the doctor from the study of his plant, and, as acknowledged leader, gave the necessary orders for immediate departure.

In the bustle and confusion that were likely to succeed such a mandate, there was little opportunity to indulge in complaints or reflections. As the adventurers had not come unprepared for victory, each individual employed himself in such offices as were best adapted to his strength and situation. The trapper had already made himself master of the patient *Asinus,* who was quietly feeding at no great distance from the rock, and he was now busy in fitting his back with the complicated machinery that Dr. Battius saw fit to term a saddle of his own invention. The naturalist himself seized upon his portfolios, herbals, and collection of insects, which he quickly transferred from the encampment of the squatter to certain pockets in the aforesaid ingenious invention and which the trapper as uniformly cast away the moment his back was turned. Paul showed his dexterity in removing such light articles as Inez and Ellen had prepared for their flight to the foot of the citadel, while Middleton, after mingling threats and promises in order to induce the children to remain quietly in their bondage, assisted the females to descend. As time began to press upon them and there was great danger of Ishmael's returning, these several movements were made with singular industry and dispatch.

The trapper bestowed such articles as he conceived were necessary to the comfort of the weaker and more delicate members of the party in those pockets from which he had so unceremoniously expelled the treasures of the unconscious naturalist, and then gave way for Middleton to place Inez in one of those seats which he had prepared on the back of the animal for her and her companion.

"Go, child," the old man said, motioning to Ellen to follow the example of the lady and turning his head a little anxiously to examine the waste behind him. "It cannot be long afore the owner of this place will be coming to look after his household, and he is not a man to give up his property, however obtained, without complaint!"

"It is true," cried Middleton; "we have wasted moments that are precious, and have the utmost need of industry."

"Aye, aye, I thought it and would have said it, captain, but I remembered how your grand'ther used to love to look upon the face of her he led away for a wife in the days of his youth and his happiness. 'Tis natur', 'tis natur', and 'tis wiser to give way a little before its feelings than to try to stop a current that will have its course."

Ellen advanced to the side of the beast, and seizing Inez by the hand, she said with heartfelt warmth after struggling to suppress an emotion that nearly choked her, "God bless you, sweet lady! I hope you will forget and forgive the wrongs you have received from my uncle—"

The humbled and sorrowful girl could say no more, her

voice becoming entirely inaudible in an ungovernable burst of grief.

"How is this?" cried Middleton. "Did you not say, Inez, that this excellent young woman was to accompany us and to live with us for the remainder of her life, or at least until she found some more agreeable residence for herself?"

"I did, and I still hope it. She has always given me reason to believe that after having shown so much commiseration and friendship in my misery, she would not desert me should happier times return."

"I cannot—I ought not," continued Ellen, getting the better of her momentary weakness. "It has pleased God to cast my lot among these people, and I ought not to quit them. It would be adding the appearance of treachery to what will already seem bad enough with one of his opinions. He has been kind to me, an orphan, after his rough customs, and I cannot steal from him at such a moment."

"She is just as much a relation of skirting Ishmael as I am a bishop!" said Paul with a loud hem, as if his throat wanted clearing. "If the old fellow has done the honest thing by her in giving her a morsel of venison now and then or a spoon around his hominy dish, hasn't she paid him in teaching the young devils to read their Bible or in helping old Esther to put her finery in shape and fashion. Tell me that a drone has a sting, and I'll believe you as easily as I will that this young woman is a debtor to any of the tribe of Bush!"

"It is but little matter who owes me or where I am in debt. There are none to care for a girl who is fatherless and motherless and whose nearest kin are the offcasts of all honest people. No, no; go, lady, and heaven forever bless you! I am better here in this desert, where there are none to know my shame."

"Now, old trapper," retorted Paul, "this is what I call knowing which way the wind blows! You are a man that has seen life, and you know something of fashions; I put it to your judgment plainly, isn't it in the nature of things for the hive to swarm when the young get their growth, and if children will quit their parents, ought one who is of no kith or kin——"

"Hist!" interrupted the man he addressed. "Hector is discontented. Say it out plainly, pup; what is it, dog; what is it?"

The venerable hound had risen and was scenting the fresh breeze which continued to sweep heavily over the prairie. At the words of his master he growled and contracted the muscles of his lips, as if half disposed to threaten with the remnants of his teeth. The younger dog, who was resting after the chase of the morning, also made some signs that his nose detected a taint in the air, and then the two resumed their slumbers, as if they had done enough.

The trapper seized the bridle of the ass, and cried, urging the beast onward, "There is no time for words. The squatter and his brood are within a mile or two of this blessed spot!"

Middleton lost all recollection of Ellen in the danger which now so imminently beset his recovered bride; nor is it necessary to add that Dr. Battius did not wait for a second admonition to commence his retreat.

Following the route indicated by the old man, they turned the rock in a body and pursued their way as fast as possible across the prairie under the favor of the cover it afforded.

Paul Hover, however, remained in his tracks, sullenly leaning on his rifle. Near a minute had elapsed before he was observed by Ellen, who had buried her face in her hands to conceal her fancied desolation from herself.

"Why do you not fly?" the weeping girl exclaimed the instant she perceived she was not alone.

"I'm not used to it."

"My uncle will soon be here! You have nothing to hope from his pity."

"Nor from that of his niece, I reckon. Let him come; he can only knock me on the head!"

"Paul, Paul, if you love me, fly."

"Alone! If I do, may I be——"

"If you value your life, fly!"

"I value it not compared to you."

"Paul!"

"Ellen!"

She extended both her hands and burst into another and a still more violent flood of tears. The bee hunter put one of his sturdy arms around her waist, and in another moment he was urging her over the plain in rapid pursuit of their flying friends.

CHAPTER 17

Approach the chamber, and destroy your sight
With a new Gorgon. Do not bid me speak;
See, and then speak yourselves.

SHAKESPEARE

THE LITTLE RUN which supplied the family of the squatter with water and nourished the trees and bushes that grew near the base of the rocky eminence took its rise at no great distance from the latter in a small thicket of cottonwood and vines. Hither, then, the trapper directed the flight, as to the place affording the only available cover in so pressing an emergency. It will be remembered that the sagacity of the old man, which, from long practice in similar scenes, amounted nearly to an instinct in all cases of sudden danger, had first induced him to take this course, as it placed the hill between them and the approaching party. Favored by this circumstance, he succeeded in reaching the bushes in sufficient time, and Paul Hover had just hurried the breathless Ellen into the tangled brush as Ishmael gained the summit of the rock in the manner already described, where he stood like a man momentarily bereft of sense, gazing at the confusion which had been created among his chattels or at his gagged and bound children who had been safely bestowed, by the forethought of the bee hunter, under the cover of a bark roof in a sort of irregular pile. A long rifle would have thrown a bullet from the height on which the squatter now stood into the very cover where the fugitives who had wrought all this mischief were clustered.

The trapper was the first to speak, as the man on whose intelligence and experience they all depended for counsel, after running his eye over the different individuals who gathered about him in order to see that none were missing.

"Ah! Natur' is natur' and has done its work!" he said, nodding to the exulting Paul with a smile of approbation. "I thought it would be hard for those who had so often met in fair and foul, by starlight and under the clouded moon, to part at last in anger. Now is there little time to lose in talk, and everything to gain by industry! It cannot be long afore some of yonder brood will be nosing along the 'arth for our trail, and should they find it, as find it they surely will, and should they push us to stand on our courage, the dispute must be settled with the rifle, which may He in heaven forbid! Captain, can you lead us to the place where any of your warriors lie? For the stout sons of the squatter will make a manly brush of it, or I am but little of a judge in warlike dispositions!"

"The place of rendezvous is many leagues from this, on the banks of La Platte."

"It is bad—it is bad. If fighting is to be done it is always wise to enter on it on equal terms. But what has one so near his time to do with ill blood and hot blood at his heart! Listen to what a gray head and some experience have to offer, and then if any among you can point out a wiser fashion for a retreat, we can just follow his design and forget that I have spoken. This thicket stretches for near a mile as it may be slanting from the rock, and leads towards the sunset instead of the settlements."

"Enough, enough," cried Middleton, too impatient to wait until the deliberative and perhaps loquacious old man could end his minute explanation. "Time is too precious for words. Let us fly."

The trapper made a gesture of compliance, and turning in his tracks, he led *Asinus* across the trembling earth of the swale and quickly emerged on the hard ground on the side opposite to the encampment of the squatter.

"If old Ishmael gets a squint at that highway through the brush," cried Paul, casting as he left the place a hasty glance at the broad trail the party had made through the thicket, "he'll need no fingerboard to tell him which way his road lies. But let him follow! I know the vagabond would gladly cross his breed with a little honest blood, but if any son of his ever gets to be the husband of——"

"Hush, Paul, hush," said the terrified young woman, who leaned on his arm for support; "your voice might be heard."

The bee hunter was silent, though he did not cease to cast ominous looks behind him, as they flew along the edge of the run, which sufficiently betrayed the belligerent condition of his mind. As each one was busy for himself, but a few minutes elapsed before the party rose a swell of the prairie, and descending without a moment's delay on the opposite side, they were at once removed from every danger of being seen by the sons of Ishmael unless the pursuers should happen to fall upon their trail. The old man now profited by the formation of the land to take another direction with a view to elude pursuit, as a vessel changes her course in fogs and darkness to escape from the vigilance of her enemies.

Two hours passed in the utmost diligence enabled them to make a half circuit around the rock and to reach a point that was exactly opposite to the original direction of their flight. To most of the fugitives their situation was as entirely unknown as is that of a ship in the middle of the ocean to the uninstructed voyager, but the old man proceeded at every turn and through every bottom with a decision that inspired his followers with confidence, as it spoke favorably of his own knowledge of the localities. His hound, stopping now and then to catch the expression of his eye, had preceded the trapper throughout the whole distance with as much certainty as though a previous and intelligible communion between them had established the route by which they were to proceed. But at the expiration of the time just named, the dog suddenly came to a stand, and then seating himself on the prairie, he snuffed the air a moment and began a low and piteous whining.

"Aye, pup, aye. I know the spot—I know the spot, and reason there is to remember it well!" said the old man, stopping by the side of his uneasy associate until those who followed had time to come up. "Now, yonder is a thicket before us," he continued, pointing forward, "where we may lie till tall trees grow on these naked fields afore any of the squatter's kin will venture to molest us."

"This is the spot where the body of the dead man lay!" cried Middleton, examining the place with an eye that revolted at the recollection.

"The very same. But whether his friends have put him in the bosom of the ground or not remains to be seen. The hound knows the scent but seems to be a little at a loss too. It is therefore necessary that you advance, friend bee hunter. to examine, while I tarry to keep the dogs from complaining in too loud a voice."

"I!" exclaimed Paul, thrusting his hand into his shaggy locks like one who thought it prudent to hesitate before he undertook so formidable an adventure. "Now, harkee, old trapper; I've stood in my thinnest cottons in the midst of many a swarm that has lost its queen bee without winking, and let me tell you the man who can do that is not likely to fear any living son of skirting Ishmael; but as to meddling with dead men's bones, why it is neither my calling nor my inclination; so, after thanking you for the favor of your choice, as they say when they make a man a corporal in Kentucky, I decline serving."

The old man turned a disappointed look towards Middleton, who was too much occupied in solacing Inez to observe his embarrassment, which was, however, suddenly relieved from a quarter whence, from previous circumstances, there was little reason to expect such a demonstration of fortitude.

Dr. Battius had rendered himself a little remarkable throughout the whole of the preceding retreat, for the exceeding diligence with which he had labored to effect that desirable object. So very conspicuous was his zeal, indeed, as to have entirely got the better of all his ordinary predilections. The worthy naturalist belonged to that species of discoverers who make the worst possible traveling companions to a man who has reason to be in a hurry. No stone, no bush, no plant, is ever suffered to escape the examination of their vigilant eyes, and thunder may mutter and rain fall without disturbing the abstraction of their reveries. Not so, however, with the disciple of Linnaeus during the momentous period that it remained a mooted point at the tribunal of his better judgment whether the stout descendants of the squatter were not likely to dispute his right to traverse the prairie in freedom. The highest blooded and best trained hound with his game in view could not have run with an eye more riveted than that with which the doctor had pursued his curvilinear course. It was perhaps lucky for his fortitude that he was ignorant of the artifice of the trapper in leading them around the citadel of Ishmael and that he had imbibed the soothing impression that every inch of prairie he traversed was just so much added to the distance between his own person and the detested rock. Notwithstanding the momentary shock he certainly experienced when he discovered this error, he now boldly volunteered to enter the thicket in which there was some reason to believe the body of the murdered Asa still lay. Perhaps the naturalist was urged to show his spirit on this occasion by some secret consciousness that his excessive industry in the retreat might be liable to misconstruction; and it is certain that whatever might be his peculiar notions of danger from the quick, his habits and his knowledge had placed him far above the apprehension of suffering harm from any communication with the dead.

"If there is any service to be performed which requires the perfect command of the nervous system," said the man of science with a look that was slightly blustering, "you have only to give a direction to his intellectual faculties, and here stands one on whose physical powers you may depend."

"The man is given to speak in parables," muttered the single-minded trapper; "but I conclude there is always some meaning hidden in his words, though it is as hard to find sense in his speeches as to discover three eagles on the same tree. It will be wise, friend, to make a cover lest the sons of the squatter should be out skirting on our trail, and as you well know, there is some reason to fear yonder thicket contains a sight that may horrify a woman's mind. Are you man enough to look death in the face, or shall I run the risk of the hounds raising an outcry and go in myself? You see the pup is willing to run in with an open mouth already."

"Am I man enough! Venerable trapper, our communications have a recent origin, or thy interrogatory might have a tendency to embroil us in angry disputation. Am I man enough! I claim to be of the class Mammalia, order Primates, genus Homo! Such are my physical attributes; of my moral properties let posterity speak! It becomes me to be mute."

"Physic may do for such as relish it; to my taste and judgment it is neither palatable nor healthy; but morals never did harm to any living mortal, be it that he was a sojourner in the forest or a dweller in the midst of glazed windows and smoking chimneys. It is only a few hard words that divide us, friend, for I am of opinion that with use and freedom we should come to understand one another and mainly settle down into the same judgments of mankind, and of the ways of the world. Quiet, Hector, quiet; what ruffles your temper, pup; is it not used to the scent of human blood?"

The doctor bestowed a gracious but commiserating smile on the philosopher of nature as he retrograded a step or two from the place whither he had been impelled by his excess of spirit in order to reply with less expenditure of breath and with a greater freedom of air and attitude.

"A Homo is certainly a Homo," he said, stretching forth an arm in an argumentative manner; "so far as the animal functions extend, there are the connecting links of harmony, order, conformity, and design between the whole genus; but there the resemblance ends. Man may be degraded to the very margin of the line which separates him from the brute, by ignorance; or he may be elevated to a communion with the great Master Spirit of all, by knowledge; nay, I know not, if time and opportunity were given him, but he might become the master of all learning, and consequently equal to the great moving principle."

The old man, who stood leaning on his rifle in a thoughtful attitude, shook his head as he answered with a native steadiness that entirely eclipsed the imposing air which his antagonist had seen fit to assume, "This is neither more nor less than mortal wickedness! Here have I been a dweller on the earth for fourscore and six changes of the seasons, and all that time have I looked at the growing and the dying trees, and yet do I not know the reasons why the bud starts under the summer sun or the leaf falls when it is pinched by the frosts. Your larning, though it is man's boast, is folly in the eyes of Him who sits in the clouds and looks down in sorrow at the pride and vanity of his creatur's. Many is the hour that I've passed lying in the shades of the woods or stretched upon the hills of these open fields, looking up into the blue skies, where I could fancy the Great One had taken his stand and was solemnizing on the waywardness of man and brute below, as I myself had often looked at the ants tumbling over each other in their eagerness, though in a way and a fashion more suited to His mightiness and power. Knowledge! It is his plaything. Say, you who think it so easy to climb into the judgment seat above, can you tell me anything of the beginning and the end? Nay, you're a dealer in ailings and cures; what is life, and what is death? Why does the eagle live so long, and why is the time of the butterfly so short? Tell me a simpler thing; why is this hound so uneasy, while you who have passed your days in looking into books can see no reason to be disturbed?"

The doctor, who had been a little astounded by the dignity and energy of the old man, drew a long breath, like a sullen wrestler who is just released from the throttling grasp of his antagonist, and seized on the opportunity of the pause to reply, "It is his instinct."

"And what is the gift of instinct?"

"An inferior gradation of reason. A sort of mysterious combination of thought and matter."

"And what is that which you call thought?"

"Venerable venator, this is a method of reasoning which sets at naught the uses of definitions, and such as I do assure you is not at all tolerated in the schools."

"Then is there more cunning in your schools than I had thought, for it is a certain method of showing them their vanity," returned the trapper, suddenly abandoning a discussion from which the naturalist was just beginning to anticipate great delight by turning to his dog, whose restlessness he attempted to appease by playing with his ears. "This is foolish, Hector; more like an untrained pup than a sensible hound; one who has got his education by hard experience, and not by nosing over the trails of other dogs, as a boy in the settlements follows on the track of his masters, be it right or be it wrong. Well, friend; you who can do so much, are you equal to looking into the thicket; or must I go in myself?"

The doctor again assumed his air of resolution, and without further parlance, proceeded to do as desired. The dogs were so far restrained by the remonstrances of the old man as to confine their noise to low but often-repeated whinings. When they saw the naturalist advance, the pup, however, broke through all restraint and made a swift circuit around his person, scenting the earth as he proceeded; and then returning to his companion, he howled aloud.

"The squatter and his brood have left a strong scent on the earth," said the old man, watching as he spoke for some signal from his learned pioneer to follow; "I hope yonder school-bred man knows enough to remember the errand on which I have sent him."

Dr. Battius had already disappeared in the bushes, and the trapper was beginning to betray additional evidences of impatience when the person of the former was seen retiring from the thicket backwards, with his face fastened on the place he had just left, as if his look was bound in the thraldom of some charm.

"Here is something skeary, by the wildness of the creatur's countenance!" exclaimed the old man, relinquishing his hold of Hector and moving stoutly to the side of the totally unconscious naturalist. "How is it, friend; have you found a new leaf in your book of wisdom?"

"It is a basilisk!" muttered the doctor, whose altered visage betrayed the utter confusion which beset his faculties. "An animal of the order Serpens. I had thought its attributes were fabulous, but mighty nature is equal to all that man can imagine!"

"What is't? What is't? The snakes of the prairies are harmless unless it be now and then an angered rattler, and he always gives you notice with his tail afore he works his mischief with his fangs. Lord, Lord, what a humbling thing is fear! Here is one who in common delivers words too big for a humble mouth to hold, so much beside himself that his voice is as shrill as the whistle of the whippoorwill! Courage! What is it, man? What is it?"

"A prodigy! A *Lusus naturae*! A monster that nature has delighted to form in order to exhibit her power! Never before have I witnessed such an utter confusion in her laws or a specimen that so completely bids defiance to the distinctions of class and genera. Let me record its appearance"—fumbling for his tablets with hands that trembled too much to perform their office—"while time and opportunity are allowed: eyes, enthralling; color, various, complex, and profound——"

"One would think the man was crazed with his enthralling looks and piebald colors!" interrupted the discontented trapper, who began to grow a little uneasy that his party was all this time neglecting to seek the protection of some cover. "If there is a reptile in the brush, show me the creatur', and should it refuse to depart peaceably, why there must be a quarrel for the possession of the place."

"There!" said the doctor, pointing into a dense mass of the thicket to a spot within fifty feet of that where they both stood. The trapper turned his look with perfect composure in the required direction, but the instant his practiced glance met the object which had so utterly upset the philosophy of the naturalist, he gave a start himself, threw his rifle rapidly forward, and as instantly recovered it, as if a second flash of thought convinced him he was wrong. Neither the instinctive movement nor the sudden recollection was without a sufficient object. At the very margin of the thicket and in absolute contact with the earth lay an animate ball that might easily, by the singularity and fierceness of its aspect, have justified the disturbed condition of the naturalist's mind. It were difficult to describe the shape or colors of this extraordinary substance, except to say in general terms that it was nearly spherical and exhibited all the hues of the rainbow, intermingled without reference to harmony and without any very ostensible design. The predominant hues were a black and bright vermilion. With these, however, the several tints of white, yellow, and crimson were strangely and wildly blended. Had this been all it would have been difficult to have pronounced that the object was possessed of life, for it lay motionless as any stone; but a pair of dark, glaring, and moving eyeballs, which watched with jealousy the smallest movements of the trapper and his companion, sufficiently established the important fact of its possessing vitality.

"Your reptile is a scouter, or I'm no judge of Indian paints and Indian deviltries!" muttered the old man, dropping the butt of his weapon to the ground and gazing with a steady eye at the frightful object as he leaned on its barrel in an attitude of great composure. "He wants to face us out of sight and reason and make us think the head of a redskin is a stone covered with the autumn leaf; or he has some other devilish artifice in his mind!"

"Is the animal human?" demanded the doctor. "Of the genus Homo? I had fancied it a nondescript."

"It's as human and as mortal too as a warrior of these prairies is ever known to be. I have seen the time when a redskin would have shown a foolish daring to peep out of his ambushment in that fashion on a hunter I could name, but who is too old now and too near his time to be anything better than a miserable trapper. It will be well to speak to the imp and to let him know he deals with men whose beards are grown. Come forth from your cover, friend," he continued in the language of the extensive tribes of the Dakotas; "there is room on the prairie for another warrior."

The eyes appeared to glare more fiercely than before, but the mass which, according to the trapper's opinion, was neither more nor less than a human head, shorn, as usual among the warriors of the West, of its hair, still continued without motion or any other sign of life.

"It is a mistake!" exclaimed the doctor. "The animal is not even of the class Mammalia, much less a man."

"So much for your knowledge!" returned the trapper, laughing with great exultation. "So much for the larning of one who has looked into so many books that his eyes are not able to tell a moose from a wildcat! Now my Hector here is a dog of education after his fashion, and though the meanest primer in the settlements would puzzle his information, you could not cheat the hound in a matter like this. As you think the object no man, you shall see his whole formation and then let an ignorant old trapper who never willingly passed a day within reach of a spelling book in his life know by what name to call it. Mind, I mean no violence, but just to start the devil from his ambushment."

The trapper very deliberately examined the priming of his rifle, taking care to make as great a parade as possible of his hostile intentions in going through the necessary evolutions with the weapon. When he thought the stranger began to apprehend some danger, he very deliberately presented the piece and called aloud, "Now, friend, I am all for peace, or all for war, as you may say. No! Well it *is* no man, as the wiser one here says, and there can be no harm in just firing into a bunch of leaves."

The muzzle of the rifle fell as he concluded, and the weapon was gradually settling into a steady and what would easily have proved a fatal aim when a tall Indian sprang from beneath that bed of leaves and brush, which he had collected about his person at the approach of the party, and stood upright, uttering the exclamation, "Wagh!"

CHAPTER 18

My visor is Philemon's roof; within the house is Jove.
                                                SHAKESPEARE

THE TRAPPER, WHO had meditated no violence, dropped his rifle again, and laughing at the success of his experiment with great seeming self-complacency, he drew the astounded gaze of the naturalist from the person of the savage to himself by saying, "The imps will lie for hours, like sleeping alligators, brooding their deviltries in dreams and other craftiness until such time as they see some real danger is at hand, and then they look to themselves the same as other mortals. But this is a scouter in his war paint! There should be more of his tribe at no great distance. Let us draw the truth out of him, for an unlucky war party may prove more dangerous to us than a visit from the whole family of the squatter."

"It is truly a desperate and a dangerous species!" said the doctor, relieving his amazement by a breath that seemed to exhaust his lungs of air; "a violent race, and one that it is difficult to define or class within the usual boundaries of definitions. Speak to him, therefore; but let thy words be strong in amity."

The old man cast a keen eye on every side of him to ascertain the important particular whether the stranger was supported by any associates, and then making the usual signs of peace by exhibiting the palm of his naked hand, he boldly advanced. In the meantime the Indian betrayed no evidence of uneasiness. He suffered the trapper to draw nigh, maintaining by his own mien and attitude a striking air of dignity and fearlessness. Perhaps the wary warrior also knew that owing to the difference in their weapons, he should be placed more on an equality by being brought nearer to the strangers.

As a description of this individual may furnish some idea of the personal appearance of a whole race, it may be well to detain the narrative in order to present it to the reader in our hasty and imperfect manner. Would the truant eyes of Allston or Greenough turn but for a time from their gaze at the models of antiquity to contemplate this wronged and humbled people, little would be left for such inferior artists as ourselves to delineate.

The Indian in question was in every particular a warrior of fine stature and admirable proportions. As he cast aside his mask, composed of such parti-colored leaves as he had hurriedly collected, his countenance appeared in all the gravity, the dignity, and, it may be added, in the terror of his profession. The outlines of his lineaments were strikingly noble and nearly approaching to Roman, though the secondary features of his face were slightly marked with the well-known traces of his Asiatic origin. The peculiar tint of the skin, which in itself is so well designed to aid the effect of a martial expression, had received an additional aspect of wild ferocity from the colors of the war paint. But as if he disdained the usual artifices of his people, he bore none of those strange and horrid devices with which the children of the forest are accustomed, like the more civilized heroes of the moustache, to back their reputation for courage, contenting himself with a broad and deep shadowing of black that served as a sufficient and an admirable foil to the brighter gleamings of his native swarthiness. His head was, as usual, shaved to the crown, where a large and gallant scalp lock seemed to challenge the grasp of his enemies. The ornaments that were ordinarily pendent from the cartilages of his ears had been removed on account of his present pursuit. His body, notwithstanding the lateness of the season, was nearly naked, and the portion which was clad bore a vestment no warmer than a light robe of the finest dressed deerskin, beautifully stained with the rude design of some daring exploit, and which was carelessly worn, as if more in pride than from any unmanly regard to comfort. His leggings were of bright-scarlet cloth, the only evidence about his person that he had held communion with the traders of the palefaces. But as if to furnish some offset to this solitary submission to a womanish vanity, they were fearfully fringed, from the gartered knee to the bottom of the moccasin, with the hair of human scalps. He leaned lightly with one hand on a short hickory bow, while the other rather touched than sought support from the long, delicate handle of an ashen lance. A quiver made of the cougar skin, from which the tail of an animal depended as a characteristic ornament, was slung at his back; and a shield of hides, quaintly emblazoned with another of his warlike deeds, was suspended from his neck by a thong of sinews.

As the trapper approached, this warrior maintained his calm, upright attitude, discovering neither an eagerness to ascertain the character of those who advanced upon him nor the smallest wish to avoid a scrutiny in his own person. An eye that was darker and more shining than that of the stag was incessantly glancing, however, from one to another of the stranger party, seemingly never knowing rest for an instant.

"Is my brother far from his village?" demanded the old man in the Pawnee language after examining the paint and those other little signs by which a practiced eye knows the tribe of the warrior he encounters in the American deserts, with the same readiness and by the same sort of mysterious observation as that by which the seaman knows the distant sail.

"It is further to the towns of the Big Knives," was the laconic reply.

"Why is a Pawnee Loup so far from the fork of his own river without a horse to journey on, and in a spot empty as this?"

"Can the women and children of a paleface live without the meat of the bison? There was hunger in my lodge."

"My brother is very young to be already the master of a lodge," returned the trapper, looking steadily into the unmoved countenance of the youthful warrior; "but I dare say he is brave and that many a chief has offered him his daughters for wives. But he has been mistaken," pointing to the arrow which was dangling from the hand that held the bow, "in bringing a loose and barbed arrowhead to kill the buffalo. Do the Pawnees wish the wounds they give their game to rankle?"

"It is good to be ready for the Sioux. Though not in sight, a bush may hide him."

"The man is a living proof of the truth of his words," muttered the trapper in English, "and a close-jointed and gallant-looking lad he is, but far too young for a chief of any importance. It is wise, however, to speak him fair, for a single arm thrown into either party if we come to blows with the squatter and his brood may turn the day. You see, my children are weary," he continued in the dialect of the prairies, pointing as he spoke to the rest of the party, who by this time were also approaching. "We wish to camp and eat. Does my brother claim this spot?"

"The runners from the people on the big river tell us that your nation have traded with the tawny-faces who live beyond the salt lake and that the prairies are now the hunting grounds of the Big Knives!"

"It is true, as I hear also from the hunters and trappers on La Platte. Though it is with the Frenchers, and not with the men who claim to own the Mexicos, that my people have bargained."

"And warriors are going up the long river to see that they have not been cheated in what they have bought?"

"Aye, that is partly true too, I fear; and it will not be long before an accursed band of choppers and loggers will be following on their heels to humble the wilderness which lies so broad and rich on the western banks of the Mississippi, and then the land will be a peopled desert from the shores of the main sea to the foot of the Rocky Mountains, filled with all the abominations and craft of man and stripped of the comforts and loveliness it received from the hands of the Lord!"

"And where were the chiefs of the Pawnee Loups when this bargain was made?" suddenly demanded the youthful warrior, a look of startling fierceness gleaming, at the same instant, athwart his dark visage. "Is a nation to be sold like the skin of a beaver?"

"Right enough—right enough, and where were truth and honesty also? But might is right, according to the fashions of the 'arth; and what the strong choose to do, the weak must call justice. If the law of the Wahcondah was as much hearkened to, Pawnee, as the laws of the Long Knives, your right to the prairies would be as good as that of the greatest chief in the settlements to the house which covers his head."

"The skin of the traveler is white," said the young native, laying a finger impressively on the hard and wrinkled hand of the trapper. "Does his heart say one thing and his tongue another?"

"The Wahcondah of a white man has ears, and he shuts them to a lie. Look at my head; it is like a frosted pine, and must soon be laid in the ground. Why then should I wish to meet the Great Spirit face to face while his countenance is dark upon me."

The Pawnee gracefully threw his shield over one shoulder, and placing a hand on his chest, he bent his head, in deference to the gray locks exhibited by the trapper, after which his eye became more steady and his countenance less fierce. Still he maintained every appearance of a distrust and watchfulness that were rather tempered and subdued than forgotten. When this equivocal species of amity was established between the warrior of the prairies and the experienced old trapper, the latter proceeded to give his directions to Paul concerning the arrangements of the contemplated halt. While Inez and Ellen were dismounting and Middleton and the bee hunter were attending to their comforts, the discourse was continued, sometimes in the language of the natives, but often, as Paul and the doctor mingled their opinions with the two principal speakers, in the English tongue. There was a keen and subtle trial of skill between the Pawnee and the trapper, in which each endeavored to discover the objects of the other without betraying his own interest in the investigation. As might be expected, when the struggle was between adversaries so equal, the result of the encounter answered the expectations of neither. The latter had put all the interrogatories his ingenuity and practice could suggest concerning the state of the tribe of the Loups, their crops, their store of provisions for the ensuing winter, and their relations with their different warlike neighbors without extorting any answer which in the slightest degree elucidated the cause of his finding a solitary warrior so far from his people. On the other hand, while the questions of the Indian were far more dignified and delicate, they were equally ingenious. He commented on the state of the trade in peltries, spoke of the good or ill success of many white hunters whom he had either encountered or heard named, and even alluded to the steady march which the nation of his great father, as he cautiously termed the government of the States, was making towards the hunting grounds of his tribe. It was apparent, however, by the singular mixture of interest, contempt, and indignation that were occasionally gleaming through the reserved manner of this warrior that he knew the strange people who were thus trespassing on his native rights much more by report than by any actual intercourse. This personal ignorance of the whites was as much betrayed by the manner in which he regarded the females as by the brief but energetic expressions which occasionally escaped him.

While speaking to the trapper, he suffered his wandering glances to stray towards the intellectual and nearly infantile beauty of Inez as one might be supposed to gaze upon the loveliness of an ethereal being. It was very evident that he now saw for the first time one of those females of whom the fathers of his tribe so often spoke and who were considered of such rare excellence as to equal all that savage ingenuity could imagine in the way of loveliness. His observation of Ellen was less marked, but notwithstanding the warlike and chastened expression of his eye, there was much of the homage which man is made to pay to woman even in the more cursory look he sometimes turned on her maturer and perhaps more animated beauty. This admiration, however, was so tempered by his habits and so smothered in the pride of a warrior as completely to elude every eye but that of the trapper, who was too well skilled in Indian customs and was too well instructed in the importance of rightly conceiving the character of the stranger to let the smallest trait or the most trifling of his movements escape him. In the meantime the unconscious Ellen herself moved about the feeble and less resolute Inez with her accustomed assiduity and tenderness, exhibiting in her frank features those changing emotions of joy and regret which occasionally beset her as her active mind dwelt on the decided step she had just taken with the contending doubts and hopes, and possibly with some of the mental vacillation, that was natural to her situation and sex.

Not so Paul; conceiving himself to have obtained the two things dearest to his heart, the possession of Ellen and a triumph over the sons of Ishmael, he now enacted his part in the business of the moment with as much coolness as though he was already leading his willing bride from solemnizing their nuptials before a border magistrate to the security of his own dwelling. He had hovered around the moving family during the tedious period of their weary march, concealing himself by day and seeking interviews with his betrothed as opportunities offered, in the manner already described, until fortune and his own intrepidity had united to render him successful at the very moment when he was beginning to despair, and he now cared neither for distance, nor violence, nor hardships. To his sanguine fancy and determined resolution, all the rest was easily to be achieved. Such were his feelings, and such in truth they seemed to be. With his cap cast on one side, and whistling a low air, he thrashed among the bushes in order to make a place suitable for the females to repose on, while from time to time he cast an approving glance at the agile form of Ellen as she tripped past him, engaged in her own share of the duty.

"And so the Wolf tribe of the Pawnees have buried the hatchet with their neighbors the Konzas?" said the trapper, pursuing a discourse which he had scarcely permitted to flag, though it had been occasionally interrupted by the different directions with which he occasionally saw fit to interrupt it. (The reader will remember that while he spoke to the native warrior in his own tongue, he necessarily addressed his white companions in English.) "The Loups and the light-faced redskins are again friends. Doctor, that is a tribe of which I'll engage you've often read and of which many a round lie has been whispered in the ears of the ignorant people who live in the settlements. There was a story of a nation of Welshers that lived hereaway in the prairies, and how they came into the land afore the uneasy-minded man who first let in the Christians to rob the heathens of their inheritance had ever dreamt that the sun set on a country as big as that it rose from. And how they knew the white ways and spoke with white tongues, and a thousand other follies and idle conceits."

"Have I not heard of them?" exclaimed the naturalist, dropping a piece of jerked bison's meat which he was rather roughly discussing at the moment. "I should be greatly ignorant not to have often dwelt with delight on so beautiful a theory, and one which so triumphantly establishes two positions, which I have often maintained are unanswerable, even without such living testimony in their favor, viz., that this continent can claim a more remote affinity with civilization than the time of Columbus, and that color is the fruit of climate and condition and not a regulation of nature. Propound the latter question to this Indian gentleman, venerable hunter; he is of a reddish tint himself, and his opinion may be said to make us masters of the two sides of the disputed point."

"Do you think a Pawnee is a reader of books and a believer of printed lies, like the idlers in the towns?" retorted the old man, laughing. "But it may be as well to humor the likings of the man, which, after all, it is quite possible are neither more nor less than his natural gift, and therefore to be followed, although they may be pitied. What does my brother think? All whom he sees here have pale skins, but the Pawnee warriors are red; does he believe that man changes with the season and that the son is not like his father?"

The young warrior regarded his interrogator for a moment with a steady and deliberating eye; then raising his finger upwards, he answered with dignity, "The Wahcondah pours the rain from his clouds; when he speaks, he shakes the hills; and the fire which scorches the trees is the anger of his eye; but he fashioned his children with care and thought. What he has thus made never alters!"

"Aye, 'tis in the reason of natur' that it should be so, doctor," continued the trapper when he had interpreted this answer to the disappointed naturalist. "The Pawnees are a wise and a great people, and I'll engage they abound in many a wholesome and honest tradition. The hunters and trappers that I sometimes see speak of a great warrior of your race."

"My tribe are not women. A brave is no stranger in my village."

"Aye, but he they speak of most is a chief far beyond the renown of common warriors, and one that might have done credit to that once mighty but now fallen people, the Delawares of the hills."

"Such a warrior should have a name?"

"They call him Hard Heart from the stoutness of his resolution; and well is he named if all I have heard of his deeds be true."

The stranger cast a glance which seemed to read the guileless soul of the old man as he demanded, "Has the paleface seen the partisan of my people?"

"Never. It is not with me now as it used to be some forty years ago, when warfare and bloodshed were my calling and my gifts!"

A loud shout from the reckless Paul interrupted his speech, and at the next moment the bee hunter appeared, leading an Indian war-horse from the side of the thicket opposite to the one occupied by the party.

"Here is a beast for a redskin to straddle!" he cried, as he made the animal go through some of its wild paces. "There's not a brigadier in all Kentucky that can call himself master of so sleek and well-jointed a nag! A Spanish saddle too, like a grandee of the Mexicos! And look at the mane and tail braided and plaited down with little silver balls, as if it were Ellen herself getting her shining hair ready for a dance or a husking frolic! Isn't this a real trotter, old trapper, to eat out of the manger of a savage?"

"Softly, lad, softly. The Loups are famous for their horses, and it is often that you see a warrior on the prairies far better mounted than a congressman in the settlements. But this, indeed, is a beast that none but a powerful chief should ride! The saddle, as you rightly think, has been sat upon in its day by a great Spanish captain, who has lost it and his life together in some of the battles which this people often fight against the southern provinces. I warrant me, I warrant me the youngster is the son of a great chief, maybe of the mighty Hard Heart himself!"

During this rude interruption to the discourse the young Pawnee manifested neither impatience nor displeasure, but when he thought his beast had been the subject of sufficient comment, he very coolly and with the air of one accustomed to have his will respected relieved Paul of the bridle, and throwing the reins on the neck of the animal, he sprang upon his back with the activity of a professor of the equestrian art. Nothing could be finer or firmer than the seat of the savage. The highly wrought and cumbrous saddle was evidently more for show than use. Indeed it impeded rather than aided the action of limbs which disdained to seek assistance or admit of restraint from so womanish inventions as stirrups. The horse, which immediately began to prance, was, like its rider, wild and untutored in all its motions, but while there was so little of art there was all the freedom and grace of nature in the movements of both. The animal was probably indebted to the blood of Araby for its excellence, through a long pedigree that embraced the steed of Mexico, the Spanish barb, and the Moorish charger. The rider, in obtaining his steed from the provinces of Central America, had also obtained that spirit and grace in controlling him which unite to form the most intrepid and perhaps the most skillful horseman in the world.

Notwithstanding this sudden occupation of his animal, the Pawnee discovered no hasty wish to depart. More at his ease, and possibly more independent now he found himself secure of the means of retreat, he rode back and forth eyeing the different individuals of the party with far greater freedom than before. But at each extremity of his ride, just as the sagacious trapper expected to see him profit by his advantage and fly, he would turn his horse and pass over the same ground, sometimes with the rapidity of the flying deer, and at others more slowly and with greater dignity of mien and attitude. Anxious to ascertain such facts as might have an influence on his future movements, the old man determined to invite him to a renewal of their conference. He therefore made a gesture expressive at the same time of his wish to resume the interrupted discourse and of his own pacific intentions. The quick eye of the stranger was not slow to note the action, but it was not until a sufficient time had passed to allow him to debate the prudence of the measure in his own mind that he seemed willing to trust himself again so near a party that was so much superior to himself in physical power, and consequently one that was able at any instant to command his life or control his personal liberty. When he did approach nigh enough to converse with facility, it was with a singular mixture of haughtiness and of distrust.

"It is far to the village of the Loups," he said, stretching his arm in a direction contrary to that in which the trapper well knew the tribe dwelt, "and the road is crooked. What has the Big Knife to say?"

"Aye, crooked enough," muttered the old man in English, "if you are to set out on your journey by that path, but not half so winding as the cunning of an Indian's mind. Say, my brother, do the chiefs of the Pawnees love to see strange faces in their lodges?"

The young warrior bent his body gracefully, though but slightly, over the saddlebow as he replied, "When have my people forgotten to give food to the stranger?"

"If I lead my daughters to the doors of the Loups, will the women take them by the hand, and will the warriors smoke with my young men?"

"The country of the palefaces is behind them. Why do they journey so far towards the setting sun? Have they lost the path, or are these the women of the white warriors that I hear are wading up the river of 'the troubled waters'?"

"Neither. They who wade the Missouri are the warriors of my great father, who has sent them on his message; but we are peace-runners. The white men and the red are neighbors, and they wish to be friends. Do not the Omahas visit the Loups when the tomahawk is buried in the path between the two nations?"

"The Omahas are welcome."

"And the Yanktons, and the burnt-wood Tetons who live in the elbow of the river 'with muddy water'; do they not come into the lodges of the Loups and smoke?"

"The Tetons are liars!" exclaimed the other. "They dare not shut their eyes in the night. No; they sleep in the sun. See," he added, pointing with fierce triumph to the frightful ornaments of his leggings, "their scalps are so plenty that the Pawnees tread on them! Go; let a Sioux live in banks of snow; the plains and buffaloes are for men!"

"Ah! The secret is out," said the trapper to Middleton, who was an attentive because a deeply interested observer of what was passing. "This good-looking young Indian is scouting on the track of the Siouxes—you may see it by his arrowheads and his paint, aye, and by his eye too, for a redskin lets his natur' follow the business he is on, be it for peace or be it for war; quiet, Hector, quiet. Have you never scented a Pawnee afore, pup? Keep down, dog—keep down —my brother is right. The Siouxes are thieves. Men of all colors and nations say it of them, and say it truly. But the people from the rising sun are not Siouxes, and they wish to visit the lodges of the Loups."

"The head of my brother is white," returned the Pawnee, throwing one of those glances at the trapper which were so remarkably expressive of distrust, intelligence, and pride; and then pointing, as he continued, towards the eastern horizon, "and his eyes have looked on many things—can he tell me the name of what he sees yonder—is it a buffalo?"

"It looks more like a cloud peeping above the skirt of the plain with the sunshine lighting its edges. It is the smoke of the heavens."

"It is a hill of the earth, and on its top are the lodges of palefaces! Let the women of my brother wash their feet among the people of their own color."

"The eyes of a Pawnee are good if he can see a whiteskin so far."

The Indian turned slowly towards the speaker, and after a pause of a moment he sternly demanded, "Can my brother hunt?"

"Alas! I claim to be no better than a miserable trapper!"

"When the plain is covered with the buffaloes, can he see them?"

"No doubt, no doubt—it is far easier to see than to take a scampering bull."

"And when the birds are flying from the cold, and the clouds are black with their feathers, can he see *them* too?"

"Aye, aye, it is not hard to find a duck or a goose when millions are darkening the heavens."

"When the snow falls and covers the lodges of the Long Knives, can the stranger see flakes in the air?"

"My eyes are none of the best now," returned the old man a little resentfully, "but the time has been when I had a name for my sight!"

"The redskins find the Big Knives as easily as the strangers see the buffalo, or the traveling birds, or the falling snow. Your warriors think the Master of Life has made the whole earth white. They are mistaken. They are pale, and it is their own faces that they see. Go! A Pawnee is not blind that he need look long for your people!"

The warrior suddenly paused and bent his face aside, like one who listened with all his faculties absorbed in the act. Then turning the head of his horse, he rode to the nearest angle of the thicket and looked intently across the bleak prairie in a direction opposite to the side on which the party stood. Returning slowly from this unaccountable and to his observers startling procedure, he riveted his eyes on Inez and paced back and forth several times with the air of one who maintained a warm struggle on some difficult point in the recesses of his own thoughts. He had drawn the reins of his impatient steed and was seemingly about to speak when his head again sank on his chest and he resumed his former attitude of attention. Galloping like a deer to the place of his former observations, he rode for a moment swiftly in short and rapid circles, as if still uncertain of his course, and then darted away like a bird that had been fluttering around its nest before it takes a distant flight. After scouring the plain for a minute he was lost to the eye behind a swell of the land.

The hounds, who had also manifested great uneasiness for some time, followed him for a little distance and then terminated their chase by seating themselves on the ground and raising their usual low, whining, and warning howls.

CHAPTER 19

How if he will not stand?

SHAKESPEARE

THE SEVERAL MOVEMENTS related in the close of the preceding chapter had passed in so short a space of time that the old man, while he neglected not to note the smallest incident, had no opportunity of expressing his opinion concerning the stranger's motives. After the Pawnee had disappeared, however, he shook his head and muttered while he walked slowly to the angle of the thicket that the Indian had just quitted, "There are both scents and sounds in the air, though my miserable senses are not good enough to hear the one or to catch the taint of the other."

"There is nothing to be seen," cried Middleton, who kept close at his side. "My eyes and my ears are good, and yet I can assure you that I neither hear nor see anything."

"Your eyes are good! And you are not deaf!" returned the other with a slight air of contempt; "no, lad, no; they may be good to see across a church or to hear a town-bell, but afore you had passed a year in these prairies you would find yourself taking a turkey for a buffalo or conceiting fifty times that the roar of a buffalo bull was the thunder of the Lord! There is a deception of natur' in these naked plains in which the air throws up the images like water, and then it is hard to tell the prairies from a sea. But yonder is a sign that a hunter never fails to know!"

The trapper pointed to a flight of vultures that were sailing over the plain at no great distance, and apparently in the direction in which the Pawnee had riveted his eyes. At first Middleton could not distinguish the small dark objects that were dotting the dusky clouds; but as they came swiftly onward, first their forms and then their heavy, waving wings became distinctly visible.

"Listen," said the trapper when he had succeeded in making Middleton see the moving column of birds. "Now you hear the buffaloes, or bisons as your knowing doctor sees fit to call them, though buffaloes is their name among all the hunters of these regions. And I conclude that a hunter is a better judge of a beast and of its name," he added, winking to the young soldier, "than any man who has turned over the leaves of a book instead of traveling over the face of the 'arth in order to find out the natur's of its inhabitants."

"Of their habits, I will grant you," cried the naturalist, who rarely missed an opportunity to agitate any disputed point in his favorite studies. "That is, provided always deference is had to the proper use of definitions and that they are contemplated with scientific eyes."

"Eyes of a mole! As if any man's eyes were not as good for names as the eyes of any other creatur'! Who named the works of His hand? Can you tell me that with your books and college wisdom? Was it not the first man in the garden, and is it not a plain consequence that his children inherit his gifts?"

"That is certainly the Mosaic account of the event," said the doctor, "though your reading is by far too literal!"

"My reading! Nay, if you suppose that I have wasted my time in schools, you do such a wrong to my knowledge as one mortal should never lay to the door of another without sufficient reason. If I have ever craved the art of reading, it has been that I might better know the sayings of the book you name, for it is a book which speaks in every line according to human feelings, and therein according to reason."

"And do you then believe," said the doctor, a little provoked by the dogmatism of his stubborn adversary and perhaps secretly too confident in his own more liberal though scarcely as profitable attainments, "do you then believe that all these beasts were literally collected in a garden to be enrolled in the nomenclature of the first man?"

"Why not? I understand your meaning, for it is not needful to live in towns to hear all the devilish devices that the conceit of man can invent to upset his own happiness. What does it prove, except indeed it may be said to prove that the garden He made was not after the miserable fashions of our times, thereby directly giving the lie to what the world calls its civilizing? No, no, the garden of the Lord was the forest then, and is the forest now, where the fruits do grow and the birds do sing according to his own wise ordering. Now, lady, you may see the mystery of the vultures! There come the buffaloes themselves, and a noble herd it is! I warrant me that Pawnee has a troop of his people in some of the hollows nigh by; and as he has gone scampering after them, you are about to see a glorious chase. It will serve to keep the squatter and his brood under cover, and for ourselves there is little reason to fear. A Pawnee is not apt to be a malicious savage."

Every eye was now drawn to the striking spectacle that succeeded. Even the timid Inez hastened to the side of Middleton to gaze at the sight, and Paul summoned Ellen from her culinary labors to become a witness of the lively scene.

Throughout the whole of those moving events which it has been our duty to record, the prairies had lain in the majesty of perfect solitude. The heavens had been blackened with the passage of the migratory birds, it is true; but the dogs of the party and the ass of the doctor were the only quadrupeds that had enlivened the broad surface of the waste beneath. There was now a sudden exhibition of animal life which changed the scene, as it were, by magic, to the very opposite extreme.

A few enormous bison bulls were first observed scouring along the most distant roll of the prairie, and then succeeded long files of single beasts, which, in their turns, were followed by a dark mass of bodies, until the dun-colored herbage of the plain was entirely lost in the deeper hue of their shaggy coats. The herd, as the column spread and thickened, was like the endless flocks of the smaller birds, whose extended flanks are so often seen to heave up out of the abyss of the heavens, until they appear as countless as the leaves in those forests over which they wing their endless flight. Clouds of dust shot up in little columns from the center of the mass as some animal, more furious than the rest, plowed the plain with his horns, and from time to time a deep hollow bellowing was borne along on the wind, as if a thousand throats vented their plaints in a discordant murmuring.

A long and musing silence reigned in the party as they gazed on this spectacle of wild and peculiar grandeur. It was at length broken by the trapper, who, having been long accustomed to similar sights, felt less of its influence, or rather felt it in a less thrilling and absorbing manner, than those to whom the scene was more novel.

"There go ten thousand oxen in one drove, without keeper or master, except Him who made them and gave them these open plains for their pasture! Ay, it is here that man may see the proofs of his wantonness and folly! Can the proudest governor in all the States go into his fields and slaughter a nobler bullock than is here offered to the meanest hand; and when he has gotten his sirloin or his steak, can he eat it with as good a relish as he who has sweetened his food with wholesome toil and earned it according to the law of natur' by honestly mastering that which the Lord hath put before him?"

"If the prairie platter is smoking with a buffalo's hump, I answer no," interrupted the luxurious bee hunter.

"Aye, boy, you have tasted, and you feel the genuine reasoning of the thing! But the herd is heading a little thisaway, and it behoves us to make ready for their visit. If we hide ourselves altogether, the horned brutes will break through the place and trample us beneath their feet like so many creeping worms; so we will just put the weak ones apart and take post, as becomes men and hunters, in the van."

As there was but little time to make the necessary arrangements, the whole party set about them in good earnest. Inez and Ellen were placed in the edge of the thicket on the side furthest from the approaching herd. *Asinus* was posted in the center, in consideration of his nerves; and then the old man, with his three male companions, divided themselves in such a manner as they thought would enable them to turn the head of the rushing column should it chance to approach too nigh their position. By the vacillating movements of some fifty or a hundred bulls that led the advance, it remained questionable for many moments what course they intended to pursue. But a tremendous and painful roar, which came from behind the cloud of dust that rose in the center of the herd and which was horridly answered by the screams of the carrion birds that were greedily sailing directly above the flying drove, appeared to give a new impulse to their flight and at once to remove every symptom of indecision. As if glad to seek the smallest signs of the forest, the whole of the affrighted herd became steady in its direction, rushing in a straight line towards the little cover of bushes which has already been so often named.

The appearance of danger was now in reality of a character to try the stoutest nerves. The flanks of the dark, moving mass were advanced in such a manner as to make a concave line of the front, and every fierce eye that was glaring from the shaggy wilderness of hair in which the entire heads of the males were enveloped was riveted with mad anxiety on the thicket. It seemed as if each beast strove to outstrip his neighbor in gaining this desired cover, and as thousands in the rear pressed blindly on those in front, there was the appearance of an imminent risk that the leaders of the herd should be precipitated on the concealed party, in which case the destruction of every one of them was certain. Each of our adventurers felt the danger of his situation in a manner peculiar to his individual character and circumstances.

Middleton wavered. At times he felt inclined to rush through the bushes, and seizing Inez, attempt to fly. Then recollecting the impossibility of outstripping the furious speed of an alarmed bison, he felt for his arms, determined to make head against the countless drove. The faculties of Dr. Battius were quickly wrought up to the very summit of mental delusion. The dark forms of the herd lost their distinctness, and then the naturalist began to fancy he beheld a wild collection of all the creatures of the world rushing upon him in a body, as if to revenge the various injuries which in the course of a life of indefatigable labor in behalf of the natural sciences he had inflicted on their several genera. The paralysis it occasioned in his system was like the effect of the incubus. Equally unable to fly or to advance, he stood riveted to the spot until the infatuation became so complete that the worthy naturalist was beginning, by a desperate effort of scientific resolution, even to class the different specimens. On the other hand, Paul shouted and called on Ellen to come and assist him in shouting, but his voice was lost in the bellowings and trampling of the herd. Furious, and yet strangely excited by the obstinacy of the brutes and the wildness of the sight, and nearly maddened by sympathy and a species of unconscious apprehension in which the claims of nature were singularly mingled with concern for his mistress, he nearly split his throat in exhorting his aged friend to interfere.

"Come forth, old trapper," he shouted, "with your prairie inventions! Or we shall be all smothered under a mountain of buffalo humps!"

The old man, who had stood all this while leaning on his rifle and regarding the movements of the herd with a steady eye, now deemed it time to strike his blow. Leveling his piece at the foremost bull with an agility that would have done credit to his youth, he fired. The animal received the bullet on the matted hair between his horns and fell to his knees; but shaking his head, he instantly arose, the very shock seeming to increase his exertions. There was now no longer time to hesitate. Throwing down his rifle, the trapper stretched forth his arms and advanced from the cover with naked hands directly towards the rushing column of the beasts.

The figure of a man, when sustained by the firmness and steadiness that intellect can only impart, rarely fails of commanding respect from all the inferior animals of the creation. The leading bulls recoiled, and for a single instant there was a sudden stop to their speed, a dense mass of bodies rolling up in front, until hundreds were seen floundering and tumbling on the plain. Then came another of those hollow bellowings from the rear, and set the herd again in motion. The head of the column, however, divided, the immovable form of the trapper cutting it, as it were, into two gliding streams of life. Middleton and Paul instantly profited by his example and extended the feeble barrier by a similar exhibition of their own persons.

For a few moments the new impulse given to the animals in

front served to protect the thicket. But as the body of the herd pressed more and more upon the open line of its defenders and the dust thickened so as to obscure their persons, there was at each instant a renewed danger of the beasts breaking through. It became necessary for the trapper and his companions to become still more and more alert, and they were gradually yielding before the headlong multitude when a furious bull darted by Middleton so near as to brush his person, and, at the next instant, swept through the thicket with the velocity of the wind.

"Close, and die for the ground," shouted the old man, "or a thousand of the devils will be at his heels!"

All their efforts would have proved fruitless, however, against the living torrent had not *Asinus,* whose domains had just been so rudely entered, lifted his voice in the midst of the uproar. The most sturdy and furious of the bulls trembled at the alarming and unknown cry, and then each individual brute was seen madly pressing from that very thicket which the moment before he had endeavored to reach, with the eagerness with which the murderer seeks the sanctuary.

As the stream divided, the place became clear, the two dark columns moving obliquely from the copse to unite again at the distance of a mile on its opposite side. The instant the old man saw the sudden effect which the voice of *Asinus* had produced, he coolly commenced reloading his rifle, indulging at the same time in a heartfelt fit of his silent and peculiar merriment.

"There they go, like dogs with so many half-filled shot pouches dangling at their tails, and no fear of their breaking their order; for what the brutes in the rear didn't hear with their own ears, they'll conceit they did; besides, if they change their minds, it may be no hard matter to get the jack to sing the rest of his tune!"

"The ass has spoken, but Balaam is silent!" cried the bee hunter, catching his breath after a repeated burst of noisy mirth that might possibly have added to the panic of the buffaloes by its vociferation. "The man is as completely dumbfoundered as if a swarm of young bees had settled on the end of his tongue, and he not willing to speak for fear of their answer."

"How now, friend," continued the trapper, addressing the still motionless and entranced naturalist; "how now, friend;

are you, who make your livelihood by booking the names and natur's of the beasts of the field and the fowls of the air, frightened at a herd of scampering buffaloes? Though perhaps you are ready to dispute my right to call them by a word that is in the mouth of every hunter and trader on the frontier!"

The old man was, however, mistaken in supposing he could excite the benumbed faculties of the doctor by provoking a discussion. From that time henceforth he was never known, except on one occasion, to utter a word that indicated either the species or the genus of the animal. He obstinately refused the nutritious food of the whole ox family; and even to the present hour, now that he is established in all the scientific dignity and security of a savant in one of the maritime towns, he turns his back with a shudder on those delicious and unrivaled viands that are so often seen at the suppers of the craft and which are unequaled by anything that is served under the same name at the boasted chophouses of London or at the most renowned of the Parisian restaurants. In short, the distaste of the worthy naturalist for beef was not unlike that which the shepherd sometimes produces by first muzzling and fettering his delinquent dog and then leaving him as a stepping-stone for the whole flock to use in its transit over a wall or through the opening of a sheepfold, a process which is said to produce in the culprit a species of surfeit on the subject of mutton forever after. By the time Paul and the trapper saw fit to terminate the fresh bursts of merriment which the continued abstraction of their learned companion did not fail to excite, he commenced breathing again as if the suspended action of his lungs had been renewed by the application of a pair of artificial bellows, and was heard to make use of the ever afterwards proscribed term on that solitary occasion to which we have just alluded.

"*Boves americani horridi!*" exclaimed the doctor, laying great stress on the latter word, after which he continued mute, like one who pondered on strange and unaccountable events.

"Aye, horrid eyes enough, I will willingly allow," returned the trapper; "and altogether the creatur' has a frightful look to one unused to the sights and bustle of a natural life; but then the courage of the beast is in no way equal to its countenance. Lord, man, if you should once get fairly beset by a brood of grizzly bears, as happened to Hector and

I at the great falls of the Miss— Ah, here comes the tail of the herd, and yonder goes a pack of hungry wolves, ready to pick up the sick or such as get a disjointed neck by a tumble. Ha! There are mounted men on their trail, or I'm no sinner! Here, lad; you may see them hereaway, just where the dust is scattering afore the wind. They are hovering around a wounded buffalo, making an end of the surly devil with their arrows!"

Middleton and Paul soon caught a glimpse of the dark group that the quick eye of the old man had so readily detected. Some fifteen or twenty horsemen were, in truth, to be seen riding in quick circuits about a noble bull which stood at bay, too grievously hurt to fly, and yet seeming to disdain to fall, notwithstanding his hardy body had already been the target for a hundred arrows. A thrust from the lance of a powerful Indian, however, completed his conquest, and the brute gave up his obstinate hold of life with a roar that passed bellowing over the place where our adventurers stood, and reaching the ears of the affrighted herd, added a new impulse to their flight.

"How well the Pawnee knew the philosophy of a buffalo hunt!" said the old man after he had stood regarding the animated scene for a few moments with evident satisfaction. "You saw how he went off like the wind before the drove. It was in order that he might not taint the air and that he might turn the flank and join— Ha! How is this! Yonder redskins are no Pawnees! The feathers in their heads are from the wings and tails of owls. Ah! As I am but a miserable half-sighted trapper, it is a band of the accursed Siouxes! To cover, lads, to cover. A single cast of an eye thisaway would strip us of every rag of clothes, as surely as the lightning scorches the bush, and it might be that our very lives would be far from safe."

Middleton had already turned from the spectacle to seek that which pleased him better—the sight of his young and beautiful bride. Paul seized the doctor by the arm; and as the trapper followed with the smallest possible delay, the whole party was quickly collected within the cover of the thicket. After a few short explanations concerning the character of this new danger, the old man, on whom the whole duty of directing their movements was devolved in deference to his great experience, continued his discourse as follows, "This is a region, as you must all know, where a strong arm

is far better than the right, and where the white law is as
little known as needed. Therefore does everything now depend on judgment and power. If," he continued, laying his
finger on his cheek like one who considered deeply all sides
of the embarrassing situation in which he found himself, "if
an invention could be framed which would set these
Siouxes and the brood of the squatter by the ears, then might
we come in, like the buzzards after a fight atween the beasts,
and pick up the gleanings of the ground—there are Pawnees
nigh us too! It is a certain matter, for yonder lad is not so
far from his village without an errand. Here are therefore
four parties within sound of a cannon, not one of whom can
trust the other. All which makes movement a little difficult
in a district where covers are far from plenty. But we are
three well armed, and I think I may see three stouthearted
men——"

"Four," interrupted Paul.

"Anan," said the old man, looking up simply at his companion.

"Four," repeated the bee hunter, pointing to the naturalist.

"Every army has its hangers-on and idlers," rejoined the
blunt borderman. "Friend, it will be necessary to slaughter
this ass."

"To slay *Asinus!* Such a deed would be an act of supere-
rogatory cruelty."

"I know nothing of your words, which hide their meaning in sound; but that is cruel which sacrifices a Christian
to a brute. This is what I call the reason of mercy. It would
be just as safe to blow a trumpet as to let the animal raise
his voice again, inasmuch as it would prove a manifest
challenge to the Siouxes."

"I will answer for the discretion of *Asinus,* who seldom
speaks without a reason."

"They say a man can be known by the company he keeps,"
retorted the old man, "and why not a brute? I once made a
forced march and went through a great deal of jeopardy
with a companion who never opened his mouth but to sing;
and trouble enough and great concern of mind did the fellow give me. It was in that very business with your grand'ther,
captain. But then he had a human throat, and well did he
know how to use it on occasion, though he didn't always stop
to regard the time and seasons fit for such outcries. Ah's me!
If I was now as I was then, it wouldn't be a band of thieving

Siouxes that should easily drive me from such a lodgment as this! But what signifies boasting when sight and strength are both failing. The warrior that the Delawares once saw fit to call after the hawk for the goodness of his eyes would now be better termed the mole! In my judgment, therefore, it will be well to slay the brute."

"There's argument and good logic in it," said Paul; "music is music, and it's always noisy, whether it comes from a fiddle or a jackass. Therefore I agree with the old man and say kill the beast."

"Friends," said the naturalist, looking with a sorrowful eye from one to another of his bloodily disposed companions, "slay not *Asinus;* he is a specimen of his kind of whom much good and little evil can be said. Hardy and docile for his genus, abstemious and patient even for his humble species. We have journeyed much together, and his death would grieve me. How would it trouble thy spirit, venerable venator, to separate in such an untimely manner from your faithful hound?"

"The animal shall not die," said the old man, suddenly clearing his throat in a manner that proved he felt the force of the appeal; "but his voice must be smothered. Bind his jaws with the halter, and then I think we may trust the rest to Providence."

With this double security for the discretion of *Asinus,* for Paul instantly bound the muzzle of the ass in the manner required, the trapper seemed content. After which he proceeded to the margin of the thicket to reconnoiter.

The uproar which attended the passage of the herd was now gone, or rather it was heard rolling along the prairie at the distance of a mile. The clouds of dust were already blown away by the wind, and a clear range was left to the eye in that place where ten minutes before there existed a scene of so much wildness and confusion.

The Siouxes had completed their conquest, and apparently satisfied with this addition to the numerous previous captures they had made, they now seemed content to let the remainder of the herd escape. A dozen remained around the carcass, over which a few buzzards were balancing themselves with steady wings and greedy eyes, while the rest were riding about in quest of such further booty as might come in their way on the trail of so vast a drove. The trapper measured the proportions and scanned the equipments of such indi-

viduals as drew nearer to the side of the thicket with careful
eyes. At length he pointed out one among them to Middleton
as Weucha.

"Now know we not only who they are, but their errand,"
the old man continued, deliberately shaking his head. "They
have lost the trail of the squatter and are on its hunt. These
buffaloes have crossed their path, and in chasing the animals,
bad luck has led them in open sight of the hill on which the
brood of Ishmael have harbored. Do you see yon birds
watching for the offals of the beast they have killed? Therein
is a moral which teaches the manner of a prairie life. A band
of Pawnees are outlying for these very Siouxes, as you see the
buzzards looking down for their food; and it behoves us, as
Christian men who have so much at stake, to look down
upon them both. Ha! What brings yonder two skirting reptiles to a stand? As you live, they have found the place where
the miserable son of the squatter met his death!"

The old man was not mistaken. Weucha and a savage who
accompanied him had reached that spot which has already
been mentioned as furnishing the frightful evidences of violence and bloodshed. There they sat on their horses, examining the well-known signs with the intelligence that dis-
tinguishes the habits of Indians. Their scrutiny was long, and
apparently not without distrust. At length they raised a cry
that was scarcely less piteous and startling than that which
the hounds had before made over the same fatal signs, and
which did not fail to draw the whole band immediately
around them as the fell bark of the jackal is said to gather
his comrades to the chase.

CHAPTER 20

Welcome, ancient Pistol.

SHAKESPEARE

IT WAS NOT long before the trapper pointed out the commanding person of Mahtoree as the leader of the Siouxes.
This chief, who had been among the last to obey the vociferous summons of Weucha, no sooner reached the spot where
his whole party was now gathered than he threw himself
from his horse and proceeded to examine the marks of the
extraordinary trail with that degree of dignity and attention

which became his high and responsible station. The warriors, for it was but too evident that they were to a man of that fearless and ruthless class, awaited the result of his investigation with patient reserve, none but a few of the principal braves presuming even to speak while their leader was thus gravely occupied. It was several minutes before Mahtoree seemed satisfied. He then directed his eyes along the ground to those several places where Ishmael had found the same revolting evidences of the passage of some bloody struggle, and motioned to his people to follow.

The whole band advanced in a body towards the thicket, until they came to a halt within a few yards of the precise spot where Esther had stimulated her sluggish sons to break into the cover. The reader will readily imagine that the trapper and his companions were not indifferent observers of so threatening a movement. The old man summoned all who were capable of bearing arms to his side and demanded in very unequivocal terms, though in a voice that was suitably lowered in order to escape the ears of their dangerous neighbors, whether they were disposed to make battle for their liberty or whether they should try the milder expedient of conciliation. As it was a subject in which all had an equal interest, he put the question as to a council of war, and not without some slight exhibition of the lingering vestiges of a nearly extinct military pride. Paul and the doctor were diametrically opposed to each other in opinion, the former declaring for an immediate appeal to arms, and the latter was warmly espousing the policy of pacific measures. Middleton, who saw that there was great danger of a hot verbal dispute between two men who were governed by feelings so diametrically opposed, saw fit to assume the office of arbiter, or rather to decide the question, his situation making him a sort of umpire. He also leaned to the side of peace, for he evidently saw that in consequence of the vast superiority of their enemies, violence would irretrievably lead to their destruction.

The trapper listened to the reasons of the young soldier with great attention; and as they were given with the steadiness of one who did not suffer apprehension to blind his judgment, they did not fail to produce a suitable impression.

"It is rational," rejoined the trapper when the other had delivered his reasons; "it is very rational, for what man cannot move with his strength he must circumvent with his wits. It is reason that makes him stronger than the buffalo and swifter than the moose. Now stay you here and keep yourselves close. My life and my traps are but of little value when the welfare of so many human souls is concerned; and moreover, I may say that I know the windings of Indian cunning. Therefore will I go alone upon the prairie. It may so happen that I can yet draw the eyes of a Sioux from this spot and give you time and room to fly."

As if resolved to listen to no remonstrance, the old man quietly shouldered his rifle, and moving leisurely through the thicket, he issued on the plain at a point whence he might first appear before the eyes of the Siouxes without exciting their suspicions that he came from its cover.

The instant that the figure of a man dressed in the garb of a hunter and bearing the well-known and much-dreaded rifle appeared before the eyes of the Siouxes, there was a sensible though a suppressed sensation in the band. The artifice of the trapper had so far succeeded as to render it extremely doubtful whether he came from some point on the open prairie or from the thicket, though the Indians still continued to cast frequent and suspicious glances at the cover. They had made their halt at the distance of an arrow flight from the bushes; but when the stranger came sufficiently nigh to show that the deep coating of red and brown which time and exposure had given to his features was laid upon the original color of a paleface, they slowly receded from the spot until they reached a distance that might defeat the aim of firearms.

In the meantime the old man continued to advance until he had got nigh enough to make himself heard without difficulty. Here he stopped, and dropping his rifle to the earth, he raised his hand with the palm outward in token of peace. After uttering a few words of reproach to his hound, who watched the savage group with eyes that seemed to recognize them, he spoke in the Sioux tongue, "My brothers are welcome," he said, cunningly constituting himself the master of the region in which they had met and assuming the offices of hospitality. "They are far from their villages and are hungry. Will they follow to my lodge to eat and sleep?"

No sooner was his voice heard than the yell of pleasure which burst from a dozen mouths convinced the sagacious trapper that he also was recognized. Feeling that it was too late to retreat, he profited by the confusion which prevailed among them, while Weucha was explaining his character, to advance until he was again face to face with the redoubtable Mahtoree. The second interview between these two men, each of whom was extraordinary in his way, was marked by the usual caution of the frontiers. They stood for nearly a minute examining each other without speaking.

"Where are your young men?" sternly demanded the Teton chieftain after he found that the immovable features of the trapper refused to betray any of their master's secrets under his intimidating look.

"The Long Knives do not come in bands to trap the beaver. I am alone."

"Your head is white, but you have a forked tongue. Mahtoree has been in your camp. He knows that you are not alone. Where is your young wife, and the warrior that I found upon the prairie?"

"I have no wife. I have told my brother that the woman and her friend were strangers. The words of a gray head should be heard and not forgotten. The Dakotas found travelers asleep, and they thought they had no need of horses. The women and children of a paleface are not used to go far on foot. Let them be sought where you left them."

The eyes of the Teton flashed fire as he answered, "They are gone; but Mahtoree is a wise chief, and his eyes can see a great distance!"

"Does the partisan of the Tetons see men on these naked fields?" retorted the trapper with great steadiness of mien. "I am very old, and my eyes grow dim. Where do they stand?"

The chief remained silent a moment, as if he disdained to contest any further the truth of a fact concerning which he was already satisfied. Then pointing to the traces on the earth, he said with a sudden transition to mildness in his eye and manner, "My father has learnt wisdom in many winters; can he tell me whose moccasin has left this trail?"

"There have been wolves and buffaloes on the prairies, and there may have been cougars too."

Mahtoree glanced his eye at the thicket as if he thought the latter suggestion not impossible. Pointing to the place, he ordered his young men to reconnoiter it more closely, cautioning them at the same time, with a stern look at the trapper, to beware of treachery from the Big Knives. Three or four half-naked, eager-looking youths lashed their horses at the word and darted away to obey the mandate. The old man trembled a little for the discretion of Paul when he saw this demonstration. The Tetons encircled the place two or three times, approaching nigher and nigher at each circuit, and then galloped back to their leader to report that the copse seemed empty. Notwithstanding the trapper watched the eye of Mahtoree to detect the inward movements of his mind and if possible to anticipate, in order to direct his suspicions, the utmost sagacity of one so long accustomed to study the cold habits of the Indian race, could however detect no symptom or expression that denoted how far he credited or distrusted this intelligence. Instead of replying to the information of his scouts, he spoke kindly to his horse, and motioning to a youth to receive the bridle, or rather halter, by which he governed the animal, he took the trapper by the arm and led him a little apart from the rest of the band.

"Has my brother been a warrior?" said the wily Teton in a tone that he intended should be conciliating.

"Do the leaves cover the trees in the season of fruits? Go. The Dakotas have not seen as many warriors living as I have looked on in their blood! But what signifies idle remembrancing," he added in English, "when limbs grow stiff and sight is failing!"

The chief regarded him a moment with a severe look, as if he would lay bare the falsehood he had heard; but meeting in the calm eye and steady mien of the trapper a confirmation of the truth of what he said, he took the hand of the old man and laid it gently on his head in token of the respect that was due to the other's years and experience.

"Why then do the Big Knives tell their red brethren to bury the tomahawk," he said, "when their own young men never forget that they are braves, and meet each other so often with bloody hands?"

"My nation is more numerous than the buffaloes on the prairies or the pigeons in the air. Their quarrels are frequent, yet their warriors are few. None go out on the warpath but they who are gifted with the qualities of a brave, and therefore such see many battles."

"It is not so—my father is mistaken," returned Mahtoree, indulging in a smile of exulting penetration at the very instant he corrected the force of his denial in deference to the years and services of one so aged. "The Big Knives are very wise, and they are men; all of them would be warriors. They would leave the redskins to dig roots and hoe the corn. But a Dakota is not born to live like a woman; he must strike the Pawnee and the Omaha or he will lose the name of his fathers."

"The Master of Life looks with an open eye on his children who die in a battle that is fought for the right, but he is blind and his ears are shut to the cries of an Indian who is killed when plundering or doing evil to his neighbor."

"My father is old," said Mahtoree, looking at his aged companion with an expression of irony that sufficiently denoted he was one of those who overstep the trammels of education and who are perhaps a little given to abuse the mental liberty they thus obtain. "He is *very* old; has he made a journey to the far country, and has he been at the trouble to come back to tell the young men what he has seen?"

"Teton," returned the trapper, throwing the breech of his rifle to the earth with startling vehemence and regarding his companion with steady serenity, "I have heard that there are men among my people who study their great medicines until they believe themselves to be gods and who laugh at all faith except in their own vanities. It may be true. It *is* true, for I have seen them. When man is shut up in towns and schools with his own follies, it may be easy to believe himself greater than the Master of Life; but a warrior who lives in a house with the clouds for its roof, where he can at any moment look both at the heavens and at the earth, and who daily sees the power of the Great Spirit should be more humble. A Dakota chieftain ought to be too wise to laugh at justice."

The crafty Mahtoree, who saw that his freethinking was not likely to produce a favorable impression on the old man, instantly changed his ground by alluding to the more immediate subject of their interview. Laying his hand gently on the shoulder of the trapper, he led him forward until they both stood within fifty feet of the margin of the thicket. Here he fastened his penetrating eyes on the other's honest countenance and continued the discourse, "If my father has hid his young men in the bush, let him tell them to come forth. You see that a Dakota is not afraid. Mahtoree is a great chief! A warrior whose head is white and who is about to go to the Land of Spirits cannot have a tongue with two ends like a serpent."

"Dakota, I have told no lie. Since the Great Spirit made me a man I have lived in the wilderness or on these naked plains without lodge or family. I am a hunter and go on my path alone."

"My father has a good carbine. Let him point it in the bush and fire."

The old man hesitated a moment and then slowly prepared himself to give this delicate assurance of the truth of what he said, without which he plainly perceived the suspicions of his crafty companion could not be lulled. As he lowered his rifle, his eye, although greatly dimmed and weakened by age, ran over the confused collection of objects that lay embedded amid the parti-colored foliage of the thicket, until it succeeded in catching a glimpse of the brown covering of the stem of a small tree. With this object in view, he raised the piece to a level and fired. The bullet had no sooner glided from the barrel than a tremor seized the hands of the trapper, which, had it occurred a moment sooner, would have utterly disqualified him for so hazardous an experiment. A frightful silence succeeded the report, during which he expected to hear the shrieks of the females; and then, as the smoke whirled away in the wind, he caught a view of the fluttering bark and felt assured that all his former skill was not entirely departed from him. Dropping the piece to the earth, he turned again to his companion with an air of the utmost composure and demanded, "Is my brother satisfied?"

"Mahtoree is a chief of the Dakotas," returned the cunning Teton, laying his hand on his chest in acknowledgment of the other's sincerity. "He knows that a warrior who has smoked at so many council fires, until his head has grown white, would not be found in wicked company. But did not my father once ride on a horse, like a rich chief of the pale-faces, instead of traveling on foot like a hungry Konza?"

"Never! The Wahcondah has given me legs, and he has given me resolution to use them. For sixty summers and winters did I journey in the woods of America, and ten tiresome years have I dwelt on these open fields without finding need to call often upon the gifts of the other creatur's of the Lord to carry me from place to place."

"If my father has so long lived in the shade, why has he come upon the prairies? The sun will scorch him."

The old man looked sorrowfully about for a moment, and then turning with a confidential air to the other, he replied,

"I passed the spring, summer, and autumn of life among the trees. The winter of my days had come and found me where I loved to be, in the quiet, aye, and in the honesty of the woods! Teton, then I slept happily, where my eyes could look up through the branches of the pines and the beeches to the very dwelling of the Good Spirit of my people. If I had need to open my heart to him while his fires were burning above my head, the door was open and before my eyes. But the axes of the choppers awoke me. For a long time my ears heard nothing but the uproar of clearings. I bore it like a warrior and a man; there was reason that I should bear it, but when that reason was ended, I bethought me to get beyond the accursed sounds. It was trying to the courage and to the habits, but I had heard of these vast and naked fields, and I come hither to escape the wasteful temper of my people. Tell me, Dakota, have I not done well?"

The trapper laid his long lean finger on the naked shoulder of the Indian as he ended, and seemed to demand his felicitations on his ingenuity and success with a ghastly smile in which triumph was singularly blended with regret. His companion listened intently and replied to the question by saying in the sententious manner of his race, "The head of my father is very gray; he has always lived with men and he has seen everything. What he does is good; what he speaks is wise. Now let him say is he sure that he is a stranger to the Big Knives, who are looking for their beasts on every side of the prairies and cannot find them."

"Dakota, what I have said is true. I live alone, and never do I mingle with men whose skins are white if——"

His mouth was suddenly closed by an interruption that was as mortifying as it was unexpected. The words were still on his tongue when the bushes on the side of the thicket where they stood opened, and the whole of the party whom he had just left, and in whose behalf he was endeavoring to reconcile his love of truth to the necessity of prevaricating, came openly into view. A pause of mute astonishment succeeded this unlooked-for spectacle. Then Mahtoree, who did not suffer a muscle or a joint to betray the wonder and surprise he actually experienced, motioned towards the advancing friends of the trapper with an air of assumed civility and a smile that lighted his fierce, dark visage as the glare of the setting sun reveals the volume and load of the cloud that is charged to bursting with the electric fluid. He however disdained to speak or to give any other evidence of his intentions than by calling to his side the distant band, who sprang forward at his beck with the alacrity of willing subordinates.

In the meantime the friends of the old man continued to advance. Middleton himself was foremost, supporting the light and aerial-looking figure of Inez, on whose anxious countenance he cast such occasional glances of tender interest as in similar circumstances a father would have given to his child. Paul led Ellen close in their rear. But while the eye of the bee hunter did not neglect his blooming companion, it scowled angrily, resembling more the aspect of the sullen and retreating bear than the soft intelligence of a favored suitor. Obed and *Asinus* came last, the former leading his companion with a degree of fondness that could hardly be said to be exceeded by any other of the party. The approach of the naturalist was far less rapid than that of those who preceded him. His feet seemed equally reluctant to advance or to remain stationary, his position bearing a great anology to that of Mahomet's coffin, with the exception that the quality of repulsion rather than that of attraction held him in a state of rest. The repulsive power in his rear, however, appeared to predominate; and by a singular exception, as he would have said himself, to all philosophical principles, it rather increased than diminished by distance. As the eyes of the naturalist steadily maintained a position that was the opposite of his route, they served to give a direction to those of the observers of all these movements, and at once furnished a sufficient clue by which to unravel the mystery of so sudden a debouchment from the cover.

Another cluster of stout and armed men was seen at no great distance, just rounding a point of the thicket and moving directly though cautiously towards the place where the band of the Siouxes was posted, as a squadron of cruisers is often seen to steer across the waste of waters towards the rich but well-protected convoy. In short, the family of the squatter, or at least such among them as were capable of bearing arms, appeared in view on the broad prairie, evidently bent on revenging their wrongs.

Mahtoree and his party slowly retired from the thicket the moment they caught a view of the strangers, until they halted on a swell that commanded a wide and unobstructed view of the naked fields on which they stood. Here the Dakota appeared disposed to make his stand and to bring matters to an issue. Notwithstanding this retreat, in which he compelled the trapper to accompany him, Middleton still advanced until he too halted on the same elevation and within speaking distance of the warlike Siouxes. The borderers in their turn took a favorable position, though at a much greater distance. The three groups now resembled so many fleets at sea lying with their topsails to the masts, with the commendable precaution of reconnoitering before each could ascertain who among the strangers might be considered as friends and who as foes.

During this moment of suspense the dark, threatening eye of Mahtoree rolled from one of the strange parties to the other in keen and hasty examination, and then it turned its withering look on the old man, as the chief said in a tone of high and bitter scorn, "The Big Knives are fools! It is easier to catch the cougar asleep than to find a blind Dakota. Did the white head think to ride on the horse of a Sioux?"

The trapper, who had found time to recollect his perplexed faculties, saw at once that Middleton, having perceived Ishmael on the trail by which they had fled, preferred trusting to the hospitality of the savages than to the treatment he would be likely to receive from the hands of the squatter. He therefore disposed himself to clear the way for the favorable reception of his friends, since he found that the unnatural coalition became necessary to secure the liberty, if not the lives, of the party.

"Did my brother ever go on a warpath to strike my people?" he calmly demanded of the indignant chief, who still awaited his reply.

The lowering aspect of the Teton warrior so far lost its severity as to suffer a gleam of pleasure and triumph to lighten its ferocity, as sweeping his arm in an entire circle around his person he answered, "What tribe or nation has not felt the blows of the Dakotas? Mahtoree is their partisan."

"And has he found the Big Knives women, or has he found them men?"

A multitude of fierce passions were struggling in the tawny countenance of the Indian. For a moment inextinguishable hatred seemed to hold the mastery; and then a nobler expression, and one that better became the character of a brave, got possession of his features and maintained itself until, first throwing aside his light robe of pictured deerskin and pointing to the scar of a bayonet in his breast, he replied, "It was given as it was taken, face to face."

"It is enough. My brother is a brave chief, and he should be wise. Let him look; is that a warrior of the palefaces? Was it one such as that who gave the great Dakota his hurt?"

The eyes of Mahtoree followed the direction of the old man's extended arm until they rested on the drooping form of Inez. The look of the Teton was long, riveted, and admiring. Like that of the young Pawnee, it resembled more the gaze of a mortal on some heavenly image than the admiration with which man is wont to contemplate even the loveliness of woman. Starting as if suddenly self-convicted of forgetfulness, the chief next turned his eyes on Ellen, where they lingered an instant with a much more intelligible expression of admiration, and then pursued their course until they had taken another glance at each individual of the party.

"My brother sees that my tongue is not forked," continued the trapper, watching the emotions the other betrayed with a readiness of comprehension little inferior to that of the Teton himself. "The Big Knives do not send their women to war. I know that the Dakotas will smoke with the strangers."

"Mahtoree is a great chief! The Big Knives are welcome," said the Teton, laying his hand on his breast with an air of lofty politeness that would have done credit to any state of society. "The arrows of my young men are in their quivers."

The trapper motioned to Middleton to approach, and in a few moments the two parties were blended in one, each of the males having exchanged friendly greetings after the fashions of the prairie warriors. But even while engaged in this hospitable manner, the Dakota did not fail to keep a strict watch on the more distant party of white men, as if he still distrusted an artifice or sought further explanation. The old man, in his turn, perceived the necessity of being more explicit and of securing the slight and equivocal advantage he had already obtained. While affecting to examine the group which still lingered at the spot where it had first halted, as if to discover the characters of those who composed it, he plainly saw that Ishmael contemplated immediate hostilities. The result of a conflict on the open prairie between a dozen resolute bordermen and the half-armed natives, even though seconded by their white allies, was, in his experienced judgment, a point of great uncertainty; and though far from reluctant to engage in the struggle on account of himself, the aged trapper thought it far more worthy of his years and his character to avoid than to court the contest. His feelings were, for obvious reasons, in accordance with those of Paul and Middleton, who had lives still more precious than their own to watch over and protect. In this dilemma the three consulted on the means of escaping the frightful consequences which might immediately follow a single act of hostility on the part of the borderers, the old man taking care that their communication should, in the eyes of those who noted the expression of their countenances with jealous watchfulness, bear the appearance of explanations as to the reason why such a party of travelers was met so far in the deserts.

"I know that the Dakotas are a wise and great people," at length the trapper commenced, again addressing himself to the chief, "but does not their partisan know a single brother who is base?"

The eye of Mahtoree wandered proudly around his band, but rested a moment reluctantly on Weucha as he answered, "The Master of Life has made chiefs, and warriors, and women," conceiving that he thus embraced all the gradations of human excellence from the highest to the lowest.

"And he has also made palefaces who are wicked. Such are they whom my brother sees yonder."

"Do they go on foot to do wrong?" demanded the Teton with a wild gleam from his eyes that sufficiently betrayed how well he knew the reason why they were reduced to so humble an expedient.

"Their beasts are gone. But their powder, and their lead, and their blankets remain."

"Do they carry their riches in their hands like miserable Konzas? Or are they brave, and leave them with the women, as men should do, who know where to find what they lose?"

"My brother sees the spot of blue across the prairie; look, the sun has touched it for the last time today."

"Mahtoree is not a mole."

"It is a rock; on it are the goods of the Big Knives."

An expression of savage joy shot into the dark countenance of the Teton as he listened; turning to the old man he seemed to read his soul, as if to assure himself he was not deceived. Then he bent his look on the party of Ishmael and counted its number.

"One warrior is wanting," he said.

"Does my brother see the buzzards? There is his grave. Did he find blood on the prairie? It was his."

"Enough! Mahtoree is a wise chief. Put your women on the horses of the Dakotas; we shall see, for our eyes are open very wide."

The trapper wasted no unnecessary words in explanation. Familiar with the brevity and promptitude of the natives, he immediately communicated the result to his companions. Paul was mounted in an instant, with Ellen at his back. A few more moments were necessary to assure Middleton of the security and ease of Inez. While he was thus engaged, Mahtoree advanced to the side of the beast he had allotted to this service, which was his own, and manifested an intention to occupy his customary place on its back. The young soldier seized the reins of the animal, and glances of sudden anger and lofty pride were exchanged between them.

"No man takes this seat but myself," said Middleton sternly in English.

"Mahtoree is a great chief!" retorted the savage, neither comprehending the meaning of the other's words.

"The Dakota will be too late," whispered the old man at his elbow; "see; the Big Knives are afraid, and they will soon run."

The Teton chief instantly abandoned his claim and threw himself on another horse, directing one of his young men to furnish a similar accommodation for the trapper. The warriors who were dismounted got up behind as many of their companions. Dr. Battius bestrode *Asinus;* and notwithstanding the brief interruption, in half the time we have taken to relate it the whole party was prepared to move.

When he saw that all were ready, Mahtoree gave the signal to advance. A few of the best mounted of the warriors, the chief himself included, moved a little in front and made a threatening demonstration, as if they intended to attack the strangers. The squatter, who was in truth slowly retiring, instantly halted his party and showed a willing front. Instead, however, of coming within reach of the dangerous aim of the western rifle, the subtle savages kept wheeling about the strangers until they had made a half circuit, keeping the latter in constant expectation of an assault. Then, perfectly secure of their object, the Tetons raised a loud shout and darted across the prairie in a line for the distant rock, with the directness and nearly with the velocity of the arrow that has just been shot from its bow.

CHAPTER 21

Dally not with the gods, but get thee gone.
                                        SHAKESPEARE

MAHTOREE HAD SCARCELY given the first intimation of his real design before a general discharge from the borderers proved how well they understood it. The distance and the rapidity of the flight, however, rendered the fire harmless. As a proof how little he regarded the hostility of their party, the Dakota chieftain answered the report with a yell, and flourishing his carbine above his head, he made a circuit on the plain, followed by his chosen warriors, in scorn of the impotent attempt of his enemies. As the main body continued the direct course, this little band of the elite, in returning from its wild exhibition of savage contempt, took its place in the rear with a dexterity and a concert of action that showed the maneuver had been contemplated.

Volley swiftly succeeded volley, until the enraged squatter was reluctantly compelled to abandon the idea of injuring his enemies by means so feeble. Relinquishing his fruitless attempt, he commenced a rapid pursuit, occasionally discharging a rifle in order to give the alarm to the garrison, which he had prudently left under the command of the redoubtable Esther herself. In this manner the chase was continued for many minutes, the horsemen gradually gaining on their pursuers, who maintained the race, however, with an incredible power of foot.

As the little speck of blue rose against the heavens, like an island issuing from the deep, the savages occasionally raised a yell of triumph. But the mists of evening were already gathering along the whole of the eastern margin of the prairie, and before the band had made half of the necessary distance, the dim outline of the rock had melted into the haze of the background. Indifferent to this circumstance, which rather favored than disconcerted his plans, Mahtoree, who had again ridden in front, held on his course with the accuracy of a hound of the truest scent, merely slackening his speed a little, as the horses of his party were by this time thoroughly blown. It was at this stage of the enterprise that the old man rode up to the side of Middleton and addressed him as follows in English, "Here is likely to be a thieving business, and one in which I must say I have but little wish to be a partner."

"What would you do? It would be fatal to trust ourselves in the hands of the miscreants in our rear."

"Tut for miscreants, be they red or be they white. Look ahead, lad, as if ye were talking of our medicines, or perhaps praising the Teton beasts. For the knaves love to hear their horses commended, the same as a foolish mother in the settlements is fond of hearing the praises of her willful child. So pat the animal and lay your hand on the gewgaws with which the redskins have ornamented his mane, giving your eye, as it were, to one thing and your mind to another. Listen; if matters are managed with judgment, we may leave these Tetons as the night sets in."

"A blessed thought!" exclaimed Middleton, who retained a painful remembrance of the look of admiration with which Mahtoree had contemplated the loveliness of Inez, as well as of his subsequent presumption in daring to wish to take the office of her protector on himself.

"Lord, Lord! What a weak creatur' is man when the gifts of natur' are smothered in bookish knowledge and womanly manners! Such another start would tell these imps at our elbows that we were plotting against them, just as plainly as if it were whispered in their ears by a Sioux tongue. Aye, aye, I know the devils; they look as innocent as so many frisky fawns, but there is not one among them all that has not an eye on our smallest motions. Therefore, what is to be done is to be done in wisdom, in order to circumvent their cunning. That is right; pat his neck and smile as if you praised the horse, and keep the ear on my side open to my words. Be careful not to worry your beast, for though but little skilled in horses, reason teaches that breath is needful in a hard push and that a weary leg makes a dull race. Be ready to mind the signal when you hear a whine from old Hector. The first will be to make ready, the second to edge out of the crowd, and the third to go; am I understood?"

"Perfectly, perfectly," said Middleton, trembling in his excessive eagerness to put the plan in instant execution and pressing the little arm, which encircled his body, to his heart. "Perfectly. Hasten, hasten."

"Aye, the beast is no sloth," continued the trapper in the Teton language, as if he continued the discourse, edging cautiously through the dusky throng at the same time until he found himself riding at the side of Paul. He communicated his intentions in the same guarded manner as before. The high-spirited and fearless bee hunter received the intelligence with delight, declaring his readiness to engage the whole of the savage band should it become necessary to effect their object. When the old man drew off from the side of this pair also, he cast his eyes about him to discover the situation occupied by the naturalist.

The doctor, with infinite labor to himself and *Asinus,* had maintained a position in the very center of the Siouxes so long as there existed the smallest reason for believing that any of the missiles of Ishmael might arrive in contact with his person. After this danger had diminished, or rather disappeared entirely, his own courage revived, while that of his steed began to droop. To this mutual but very material change was owing the fact that the rider and the ass were now to be sought among that portion of the band who formed a sort of rear guard. Hither, then, the trapper contrived to turn his steed without exciting the suspicions of any of his subtle companions.

"Friend," commenced the old man when he found himself in a situation favorable to discourse, "should you like to pass a dozen years among the savages with a shaved head and a painted countenance, with, perhaps, a couple of wives and five or six children of the half-breed to call you father?"

"Impossible!" exclaimed the startled naturalist. "I am indisposed to matrimony in general, and more especially to all admixture of the varieties of species, which only tend to tarnish the beauty and to interrupt the harmony of nature. Moreover, it is a painful innovation on the order of all nomenclatures."

"Aye, aye, you have reason enough for your distaste to such a life; but should these Siouxes get you fairly into their village, such would be your luck, as certain as that the sun rises and sets at the pleasure of the Lord."

"Marry me to a woman who is not adorned with the comeliness of the species!" responded the doctor. "Of what crime have I been guilty that so grievous a punishment should await the offense? To marry a man against the movements of his will is to do a violence to human nature!"

"Now that you speak of natur', I have hopes that the gift of reason has not altogether deserted your brain," returned the old man with a covert expression playing about the angles of his deep-set eyes which betrayed he was not entirely destitute of humor. "Nay, they may conceive you a remarkable subject for their kindness, and for that matter marry you to five or six. I have known, in my days, favored chiefs who had numberless wives."

"But why should they meditate this vengeance?" demanded the doctor, whose hair began to rise as if each fiber was possessed of sensibility; "what evil have I done?"

"It is the fashion of their kindness. When they come to learn that you are a great medicine, they will adopt you into the tribe, and some mighty chief will give you his name, and perhaps his daughter, or it may be a wife or two of his own who have dwelt long in his lodge and of whose value he is a judge by experience."

"The Governor and Founder of natural harmony protect me!" ejaculated the doctor. "I have no affinity to a single consort, much less to duplicates and triplicates of the class! I shall certainly essay a flight from their abodes before I mingle in so violent a conjunction."

"There is reason in your words, but why not attempt the race you speak of now?"

The naturalist looked fearfully around, as if he had an inclination to make an instant exhibition of his desperate intention; but the dusky figures who were riding on every side of him seemed suddenly tripled in number, and the darkness that was already thickening on the prairie appeared in his eyes to possess the glare of high noon.

"It would be premature, and reason forbids it," he answered. "Leave me, venerable venator, to the council of my own thoughts, and when my plans are properly classed, I will advise you of my resolutions."

"Resolutions!" repeated the old man, shaking his head a little contemptuously as he gave the rein to his horse and allowed him to mingle with the steeds of the savages. "Resolution is a word that is talked of in the settlements and felt on the borders. Does my brother know the beast on which the paleface rides?" he continued, addressing a gloomy-looking warrior in his own tongue and making a motion with his arm that at the same time directed his attention to the naturalist and the meek *Asinus*.

The Teton turned his eyes for a minute on the animal but disdained to manifest the smallest portion of that wonder he had felt, in common with all his companions, on first viewing so rare a quadruped. The trapper was not ignorant that while asses and mules were beginning to be known to those tribes who dwelt nearest the Mexicos, they were not usually encountered so far north as the waters of La Platte. He therefore managed to read the mute astonishment that lay so deeply concealed in the tawny visage of the savage, and took his measures accordingly.

"Does my brother think that the rider is a warrior of the palefaces?" he demanded when he believed that sufficient time had elapsed for a full examination of the pacific mien of the naturalist.

The flash of scorn which shot across the features of the Teton was visible even by the dim light of the stars.

"Is a Dakota a fool?" was the answer.

"They are a wise nation, whose eyes are never shut; much do I wonder that they have not seen the great medicine of the Big Knives!"

"Wagh!" exclaimed his companion, suffering the whole of his amazement to burst out of his dark rigid countenance at the surprise, like a flash of lightning illuminating the gloom of midnight.

"The Dakota knows that my tongue is not forked. Let him open his eyes wider. Does he not see a very great medicine?"

The light was not necessary to recall to the savage each feature in the really remarkable costume and equipage of Dr. Battius. In common with the rest of the band, and in conformity with the universal practice of the Indians, this warrior, while he had suffered no gaze of idle curiosity to disgrace his manhood, had not permitted a single distinctive mark which might characterize any one of the strangers to escape his vigilance. He knew the air, the stature, the dress, and the features, even to the color of the eyes and of the hair, of every one of the Big Knives whom he had thus strangely encountered, and deeply had he ruminated on the causes which could have led a party so singularly constituted into the haunts of the rude inhabitants of his native wastes. He had already considered the several physical powers of the whole party and had duly compared their abilities with what he supposed might have been their intentions. Warriors they were not, for the Big Knives, like the Siouxes, left their women in their villages when they went out on the bloody path. The same objections applied to them as hunters, and even as traders, the two characters under which the white men commonly appeared in their villages. He had heard of a great council at which the Menahashah, or Long Knives, and the Washsheomantiqua, or Spaniards, had smoked together when the latter had sold to the former their incomprehensible rights over those vast regions through which his nation had roamed in freedom for so many ages. His simple mind had not been able to embrace the reasons why one people should thus assume a superiority over the possessions of another, and it will readily be perceived that at the hint just received from the trapper, he was not indisposed to fancy that some of the hidden subtlety of that magical influence of which he was so firm a believer was about to be practiced by the unsuspecting subject of their conversation in furtherance of these mysterious claims. Abandoning, therefore, all the reserve and dignity of his manner under the conscious helplessness of ignorance, he turned to the old man, and stretching forth his arms as if to denote how much he lay at his mercy, he said, "Let my father look at me. I am a wild man of the prairies; my body is naked, my hands empty, my skin red. I have struck the Pawnees, the Konzas, the Omahas, the Osages, and even the Long Knives. I am a man amid warriors, but a woman among the conjurers. Let my father speak; the ears of the Teton are open. He listens like a deer to the step of the cougar."

"Such are the wise and uns'archable ways of One who alone knows good from evil!" exclaimed the trapper in English. "To some He grants cunning, and on others He bestows the gift of manhood! It is humbling and it is afflicting to see so noble a creatur' as this, who has fought in many a bloody fray, truckling before his superstition like a beggar asking for the bones you would throw to the dogs. The Lord will forgive me for playing with the ignorance of the savage, for He knows I do it in no mockery of His state or in idle vaunting of my own, but in order to save mortal life and to give justice to the wronged while I defeat the deviltries of the wicked! Teton," speaking again in the language of the listener, "I ask you, is not that a wonderful medicine? If the

Dakotas are wise, they will not breathe the air he breathes, nor touch his robes. They know that the Wahconshecheh (bad spirit) loves his own children and will not turn his back on him that does them harm."

The old man delivered this opinion in an ominous and sententious manner and then rode apart as if he had said enough. The result justified his expectations. The warrior to whom he had addressed himself was not slow to communicate his important knowledge to the rest of the rear guard, and in a very few moments the naturalist was the object of general observation and reverence. The trapper, who understood that the natives often worshiped, with a view to propitiate, the evil spirit, awaited the workings of his artifice with the coolness of one who had not the smallest interest in its effects. It was not long before he saw one dark figure after another lashing his horse and galloping ahead into the center of the band, until Weucha alone remained nigh the persons of himself and Obed. The very dullness of this groveling-minded savage, who continued gazing at the supposed conjurer with a sort of stupid admiration, opposed now the only obstacle to the complete success of his artifice.

Thoroughly understanding the character of this Indian, the old man lost no time in getting rid of him also. Riding to his side, he said in an affected whisper, "Has Weucha drunk of the milk of the Big Knives today?"

"Hugh!" exclaimed the savage, every dull thought instantly recalled from heaven to earth by the question.

"Because the great captain of my people, who rides in front, has a cow that is never empty. I know it will not be long before he will say, 'Are any of my red brethren dry?'"

The words were scarcely uttered before Weucha, in his turn, quickened the gait of his beast, and was soon blended with the rest of the dark group, who were riding at a more moderate pace a few rods in advance. The trapper, who knew how fickle and sudden were the changes of a savage mind, did not lose a moment in profiting by this advantage. He loosened the reins of his own impatient steed, and in an instant he was again at the side of Obed.

"Do you see the twinkling star that is, may be, the length of four rifles above the prairie; hereaway to the north I mean."

"Aye, it is of the constellation——"

"A tut for your constellations, man; do you see the star I mean? Tell me in the English of the land, yes or no."

"Yes."

"The moment my back is turned, pull upon the rein of your ass until you lose sight of the savages. Then take the Lord for your dependence and yonder star for your guide. Turn neither to the right hand nor to the left, but make diligent use of your time, for your beast is not quick of foot, and every inch of prairie you gain is a day added to your liberty or to your life."

Without waiting to listen to the queries which the naturalist was about to put, the old man again loosened the reins of his horse, and presently he too was blended with the group in front.

Obed was now alone. *Asinus* willingly obeyed the hint which his master soon gave, rather in desperation than with any very collected understanding of the orders he had received, and checked his pace accordingly. As the Tetons, however, rode at a hand gallop, but a moment of time was necessary, after the ass began to walk, to remove them effectually from before the vision of his rider. Without plan, expectation, or hope of any sort, except that of escaping from his dangerous neighbors, the doctor, first feeling to assure himself that the package which contained the miserable remnants of his specimens and notes was safe at his crupper, turned the head of the beast in the required direction, and kicking him with a species of fury, he soon succeeded in exciting the speed of the patient animal into a smart run. He had barely time to descend into a hollow and ascend the adjoining swell of the prairie before he heard, or fancied he heard, his name shouted in good English from the throats of twenty Tetons. The delusion gave a new impulse to his ardor, and no professor of the saltant art ever applied himself with greater industry than the naturalist now used his heels on the ribs of *Asinus*. The conflict endured for several minutes without interruption, and to all appearances it might have continued to the present moment had not the meek temper of the beast become unduly excited. Borrowing an idea from the manner in which his master exhibited his agitation, *Asinus* so far changed the application of his own heels as to raise them simultaneously with a certain indignant flourish into the air, a measure that instantly decided the controversy in his favor. Obed took leave of his seat as of a position no longer tenable, continuing, however, the direction of his flight, while the ass, like a conqueror, took possession of the field of battle, beginning to crop the dry herbage as the fruits of victory.

When Dr. Battius had recovered his feet and rallied his faculties, which were in a good deal of disorder from the hurried manner in which he had abandoned his former situation, he returned in quest of his specimens and of his ass. *Asinus* displayed enough of magnanimity to render the interview amicable, and thenceforth the naturalist continued the required route with very commendable industry but with a much more tempered discretion.

In the meantime the old trapper had not lost sight of the important movements that he had undertaken to control. Obed had not been mistaken in supposing that he was already missed and sought, though his imagination had corrupted certain savage cries into the well-known sounds that composed his own latinized name. The truth was simply this. The warriors of the rear guard had not failed to apprise those in front of the mysterious character with which it had pleased the trapper to invest the unsuspecting naturalist. The same untutored admiration which on the receipt of this intelligence had driven those in the rear to the front now drove many of the front to the rear. The doctor was of course absent, and the outcry was no more than the wild yells which were raised in the first burst of savage disappointment.

But the authority of Mahtoree was prompt to aid the ingenuity of the trapper in suppressing these dangerous sounds. When order was restored and the former was made acquainted with the reason why his young men had betrayed so strong a mark of indiscretion, the old man, who had taken a post at his elbow, saw with alarm the gleam of keen distrust that flashed in his swarthy visage.

"Where is your conjurer?" demanded the chief, turning suddenly to the trapper as if he meant to make him responsible for the reappearance of Obed.

"Can I tell my brother the number of the stars? The ways of a great medicine are not like the ways of other men."

"Listen to me, gray head, and count my words," continued the other, bending on his rude saddlebow like some chevalier of a more civilized race and speaking in the haughty tones of absolute power; "the Dakotas have not chosen a woman for their chief; when Mahtoree feels the power of a great medicine, he will tremble; until then he will look with his own eyes without borrowing sight from a paleface. If your conjurer is not with his friends in the morning, my young men shall look for him. Your ears are open. Enough."

The trapper was not sorry to find that so long a respite was granted. He had before found reason to believe that the Teton partisan was one of those bold spirits who overstep the limits which use and education fix to the opinions of man in every state of society, and he now saw plainly that he must adopt some artifice to deceive him, different from that which had succeeded so well with his followers. The sudden appearance of the rock, however, which hove up, a bleak and ragged mass, out of the darkness ahead, put an end for the present to the discourse, Mahtoree giving all his thoughts to the execution of his designs on the rest of the squatter's movables. A murmur ran through the band as each dark warrior caught a glimpse of the desired haven, after which the nicest ear might have listened in vain to catch a sound louder than the rustling of feet among the tall grass of the prairie.

But the vigilance of Esther was not easily deceived. She had long listened anxiously to the suspicious sounds which approached the rock across the naked waste, nor had the sudden outcry been unheard by the unwearied sentinels of the rock. The savages, who had dismounted at some little distance, had not time to draw around the base of the hill in their customary silent and insidious manner before the voice of the Amazon was raised, demanding, "Who is beneath? Answer for your lives! Siouxes or devils, I fear ye not!"

No answer was given to this challenge, every warrior halting where he stood, confident that his dusky form was blended with the shadows of the plain. It was at this moment that the trapper determined to escape. He had been left with the rest of his friends under the surveillance of those who were assigned to the duty of watching the horses, and as they all continued mounted, the moment appeared favorable to his project. The attention of the guards was drawn to the rock, and a heavy cloud driving above them at that instant obscured even the feeble light which fell from the stars. Leaning on the neck of his horse, the old man muttered, "Where is my pup? Where is it—Hector—where is it, dog?"

The hound caught the well-known sounds and answered by a whine of friendship which threatened to break out into one of his piercing howls. The trapper was in the act of raising himself from this successful exploit when he felt the hand of Weucha grasping his throat, as if determined to suppress his voice by the very unequivocal process of strangulation. Profiting by the circumstance, he raised another low sound, as in the natural effort of breathing, which drew a second responsive cry from the faithful hound. Weucha instantly abandoned his hold of the master in order to wreak his vengeance on the dog. But the voice of Esther was again heard, and every other design was abandoned in order to listen.

"Aye, whine and deform your throats as you may, ye imps of darkness," she said with a cracked but scornful laugh; "I know ye; tarry, and ye shall have light for your misdeeds. Put in the coal, Phoebe; put in the coal; your father and the boys shall see that they are wanted at home to welcome their guests."

As she spoke, a strong light like that of a brilliant star was seen on the very pinnacle of the rock; then followed a forked flame, which curled for a moment amid the windings of an enormous pile of brush, and flashing upwards in an united sheet, it wavered to and fro in the passing air, shedding a bright glare on every object within its influence. A taunting laugh was heard from the height, in which the voices of all ages mingled, as though they triumphed at having so successfully exposed the treacherous intentions of the Tetons.

The trapper looked about him to ascertain in what situations he might find his friends. True to the signals, Middleton and Paul had drawn a little apart and now stood ready, by every appearance, to commence their flight at the third repetition of the cry. Hector had escaped his savage pursuer and was again crouching at the heels of his master's horse. But the broad circle of light was gradually increasing in extent and power, and the old man, whose eye and judgment so rarely failed him, patiently awaited a more propitious moment for his enterprise.

"Now, Ishmael, my man, if sight and hand are true as ever, now is the time to work upon these redskins, who claim to own all your property, even to your wife and children! Now, my good man, prove both breed and character!"

A distant shout was heard in the direction of the approaching party of the squatter, assuring the female garrison that succor was not far distant. Esther answered to the grateful sounds by a cracked cry of her own, lifting her form, in the first burst of exultation, above the rock in a manner to be visible to all below. Not content with this dangerous exposure of her person, she was in the act of tossing her arms in triumph when the dark figure of Mahtoree shot into the light and pinioned them to her side. The forms of three other warriors glided across the top of the rock, looking like naked demons flitting among the clouds. The air was filled with the brands of the beacon, and a heavy darkness succeeded, not unlike that of the appalling instant when the last rays of the sun are excluded by the intervening mass of the moon. A yell of triumph burst from the savages in their turn, and was rather accompanied than followed by a long, loud whine from Hector.

In an instant the old man was between the horses of Middleton and Paul, extending a hand to the bridle of each in order to check the impatience of their riders.

"Softly, softly," he whispered; "their eyes are as marvelously shut for the minute as if the Lord had stricken them blind; but their ears are open. Softly, softly; for fifty rods at least, we must move no faster than a walk."

The five minutes of doubt that succeeded appeared like an age to all but the trapper. As their sight was gradually restored, it seemed to each that the momentary gloom which followed the extinction of the beacon was to be replaced by as broad a light as that of noonday. Gradually the old man, however, suffered the animals to quicken their steps until they had gained the center of one of the prairie bottoms. Then laughing in his quiet manner, he released the reins and said, "Now let them give play to their legs, but keep on the old fog to deaden the sounds."

It is needless to say how cheerfully he was obeyed. In a few more minutes they ascended and crossed a swell of the land, after which the flight was continued at the top of their horses' speed, keeping the indicated star in view, as the laboring bark steers for the light which points the way to a haven and security.

CHAPTER 22

The clouds and sunbeams o'er his eye,
That once their shades and glories threw,
Have left, in yonder silent sky,
No vestige where they flew.

MONTGOMERY

A STILLNESS AS deep as that which marked the gloomy wastes
in their front was observed by the fugitives to distinguish
the spot they had just abandoned. Even the trapper lent his
practiced faculties, in vain, to detect any of the well-known
signs which might establish the important fact that hostilities
had actually commenced between the parties of Mahtoree
and Ishmael; but their horses carried them out of the reach
of sounds without the occurrence of the smallest evidence of
the sort. The old man from time to time muttered his discontent, but manifested the uneasiness he actually entertained in no other manner, unless it might be in exhibiting
a growing anxiety to urge the animals to increase their
speed. He pointed out, in passing, the deserted swale where
the family of the squatter had encamped the night they were
introduced to the reader, and afterwards he maintained an
ominous silence, ominous because his companions had already seen enough of his character to be convinced that
the circumstances must be critical indeed which possessed
the power to disturb the well-regulated tranquillity of the
old man's mind.

"Have we not done enough?" Middleton demanded, in tenderness to the inability of Inez and Ellen to endure so much
fatigue, at the end of some hours; "we have ridden hard and
have crossed a wide tract of plain. It is time to seek a place
of rest."

"You must seek it then in heaven if you find yourselves
unequal to a longer march," murmured the old trapper.
"Had the Tetons and the squatter come to blows, as anyone
might see in the natur' of things they were bound to do,
there would be time to look about us and to calculate not
only the chances but the comforts of the journey; but as the
case actually is, I should consider it certain death or endless
captivity to trust our eyes with sleep until our heads are
fairly hid in some uncommon cover."

"I know not," returned the youth, who reflected more on the sufferings of the fragile being he supported than on the experience of his companion; "I know not; we have ridden leagues, and I can see no extraordinary signs of danger; if you fear for yourself, my good friend, believe me you are wrong, for——"

"Your gran'ther, were he living and here," interrupted the old man, stretching forth a hand and laying a finger impressively on the arm of Middleton, "would have spared those words. He had some reason to think that in the prime of my days, when my eye was quicker than the hawk's and my limbs were as active as the legs of the fallow deer, I never clung too eagerly and fondly to life; then why should I now feel such a childish affection for a thing that I know to be vain, and the companion of pain and sorrow? Let the Tetons do their worst; they will not find a miserable and worn-out trapper the loudest in his complaints or his prayers."

"Pardon me, my worthy, my inestimable friend," exclaimed the repentant young man, warmly grasping the hand which the other was in the act of withdrawing; "I knew not what I said, or rather I thought only of those whose tenderness we are most bound to consider."

"Enough. It's natur', and it is right. Therein your gran'ther would have done the very same. Ah's me! What a number of seasons, hot and cold, wet and dry, have rolled over my poor head since the time we worried it out together among the Red Hurons of the Lakes, back in those rugged mountains of Old York! And many a noble buck has since that day fallen by my hand; aye, and many a thieving Mingo too! Tell me, lad, did the general, for general I know he got to be, did he ever tell you of the deer we took, that night the outliers of the accursed tribe drove us to the caves on the island, and how we feasted and drunk in security?"

"I have often heard him mention the smallest circumstance of the night you mean; but——"

"And the singer, and his open throat, and his shoutings in the fights!" continued the old man, laughing joyously at the strength of his own recollections.

"All—all—he forgot nothing, even to the most trifling incident. Do you not——"

"What! Did he tell you of the imp behind the log—and

of the miserable devil who went over the fall—or of the wretch in the tree?"

"Of each and all, with everything that concerned them.* I should think——"

"Aye," continued the old man in a voice which betrayed how powerfully his own faculties retained the impression of the spectacle, "I have been a dweller in forests and in the wilderness for threescore and ten years, and if any can pretend to know the world or to have seen scary sights, it is myself! But never, before nor since, have I seen human man in such a state of mortal despair as that very savage; and yet he scorned to speak, or to cry out, or to own his forlorn condition! It is their gift, and nobly did he maintain it!"

"Harkee, old trapper," interrupted Paul, who, content with the knowledge that his waist was grasped by one of the arms of Ellen, had hitherto ridden in unusual silence; "my eyes are as true and as delicate as a hummingbird's in the day, but they are nothing worth boasting of by starlight. Is that a sick buffalo crawling along in the bottom there, or is it one of the stray cattle of the savages!"

The whole party drew up in order to examine the object which Paul had pointed out. During most of the time they had ridden in the little vales in order to seek the protection of the shadows, but just at that moment they had ascended a roll of the prairie in order to cross into the very bottom where this unknown animal was now seen.

"Let us descend," said Middleton; "be it beast or man, we are too strong to have any cause of fear."

"Now, if the thing was not morally impossible," cried the trapper, who the reader must have already discovered was not always exact in the use of qualifying words, "if the thing was not morally impossible, I should say that was the man who journeys in search of reptiles and insects—our fellow traveler the doctor."

"Why impossible? Did you not direct him to pursue this course in order to rejoin us?"

"Aye, but I did not tell him to make an ass outdo the speed of a horse; you are right—you are right," said the trapper, interrupting himself, as by gradually lessening the distance between them his eyes assured him it was Obed

* They who have read the preceding books, in which the trapper appears as a hunter and a scout, will readily understand the allusions.

and *Asinus* whom he saw; "you are right, as certainly as the thing is a miracle. Lord, what a thing is fear! How now, friend; you have been industrious to have got so far ahead in so short a time. I marvel at the speed of the ass!"

"*Asinus* is overcome," returned the naturalist mournfully. "The animal has certainly not been idle since we separated, but he declines all my admonitions and invitations to proceed. I hope there is no instant fear from the savages?"

"I cannot say that; I cannot say that; matters are not as they should be atween the squatter and the Tetons, nor will I answer as yet for the safety of any scalp among us. The beast is broken down! You have urged him beyond his natural gifts, and he is like a worried hound. There is pity and discretion in all things, even though a man be riding for his life."

"You indicated the star," returned the doctor, "and I deemed it expedient to use great diligence in pursuing the direction."

"Did you expect to reach it by such haste? Go, go; you talk boldly of the creatur's of the Lord, though I plainly see you are but a child in matters that concern their gifts and instincts. What a plight would you now be in if there was need for a long and a quick push with our heels?"

"The fault exists in the formation of the quadruped," said Obed, whose placid temper began to revolt under so many scandalous imputations. "Had there been rotary levers for two of the members, a moiety of the fatigue would have been saved, for one item——"

"That, for your moieties and rotaries and items, man; a jaded ass is a jaded ass, and he who denies it is but a brother of the beast itself. Now, captain, are we driven to choose one of two evils. We must either abandon this man, who has been too much with us through good and bad to be easily cast away, or we must seek a cover to let the animal rest."

"Venerable venator!" exclaimed the alarmed Obed. "I conjure you by all the secret sympathies of our common nature, by all the hidden——"

"Ah, fear has brought him to talk a little rational sense! It is not natur', truly, to abandon a brother in distress; and the Lord he knows that I have never yet done the shameful deed. You are right, friend, you are right; we must all be hidden, and that speedily. But what to do with the ass!

Friend doctor, do you truly value the life of the creatur'?"

"He is an ancient and faithful servant," returned the disconsolate Obed, "and with pain should I see him come to any harm. Fetter his lower limbs and leave him to repose in this bed of herbage. I will engage he shall be found where he is left in the morning."

"And the Siouxes? What would become of the beast should any of the red imps catch a peep at his ears growing up out of the grass like two mullein-tops?" cried the bee hunter. "They would stick him as full of arrows as a woman's cushion is full of pins, and then believe they had done the job for the father of all rabbits! My word for it but they would find out their blunder at the first mouthful!"

Middleton, who began to grow impatient under the protracted discussion, interposed, and, as a good deal of deference was paid to his rank, he quickly prevailed in his efforts to effect a sort of compromise. The humble *Asinus,* too meek and too weary to make any resistance, was soon tethered and deposited in his bed of dying grass, where he was left with a perfect confidence on the part of his master of finding him again at the expiration of a few hours. The old man strongly remonstrated against this arrangement and more than once hinted that the knife was much more certain than the tether; but the petitions of Obed, aided perhaps by the secret reluctance of the trapper to destroy the beast, were the means of saving its life. When *Asinus* was thus secured, and as his master believed, secreted, the whole party proceeded to find someplace where they might rest themselves during the time required for the repose of the animal.

According to the calculations of the trapper, they had ridden twenty miles since the commencement of their flight. The delicate frame of Inez began to droop under the excessive fatigue, nor was the more robust but still feminine person of Ellen insensible to the extraordinary effort she had made. Middleton himself was not sorry to repose, nor did the vigorous and high-spirited Paul hesitate to confess that he should be all the better for a little rest. The old man alone seemed indifferent to the usual claims of nature. Although but little accustomed to the unusual description of exercise he had just been taking, he appeared to bid defiance to all the usual attacks of human infirmities. Though evidently so near its dissolution, his attenuated frame still stood like the shaft of seasoned oak, dry, naked, and tempest-riven, but unbending and apparently indurated to the consistency of stone. On the present occasion he conducted the search for a resting-place, which was immediately commenced with all the energy of youth tempered by the discretion and experience of his great age.

The bed of grass in which the doctor had been met and in which his ass had just been left was followed a little distance until it was found that the rolling swells of the prairie were melting away into one vast level plain that was covered, for miles on miles, with the same species of herbage.

"Ah, this may do, this may do," said the old man when they arrived on the borders of this sea of withered grass. "I know the spot, and often have I lain in its secret holes for days at a time while the savages have been hunting the buffaloes on the open ground. We must enter it with great care, for a broad trail might be seen, and Indian curiosity is a dangerous neighbor."

Leading the way himself, he selected a spot where the tall coarse herbage stood most erect, growing not unlike a bed of reeds both in height and density. Here he entered singly, directing the others to follow as nearly as possible in his own footsteps. When they had passed for some hundred or two feet into the wilderness of weeds, he gave his directions to Paul and Middleton, who continued a direct route deeper into the place, while he dismounted and returned on his tracks to the margin of the meadow. Here he passed many minutes in replacing the trodden grass and in effacing, as far as possible, every evidence of their passage.

In the meantime the rest of the party continued their progress, not without toil, and consequently at a very moderate gait, until they had penetrated a mile into the place. Here they found a spot suited to their circumstances, and dismounting, they began to make their dispositions to pass the remainder of the night. By this time the trapper had rejoined the party and again resumed the direction of their proceedings.

The weeds and grass were soon plucked and cut from an area of sufficient extent, and a bed for Inez and Ellen was speedily made a little apart, which for sweetness and ease might have rivaled one of down. The exhausted females, after receiving some light refreshments from the provident stores of Paul and the old man, now sought their repose, leaving their more stout companions at liberty to provide for their own necessities. Middleton and Paul were not long in following the example of their betrothed, leaving the trapper and the naturalist still seated around a savory dish of bison's meat which had been cooked at a previous halt and which was, as usual, eaten cold.

A certain lingering sensation which had so long been uppermost in the mind of Obed temporarily banished sleep; and as for the old man, his wants were rendered, by habit and necessity, as seemingly subject to his will as if they altogether depended on the pleasure of the moment. Like his companion, he chose therefore to watch instead of sleeping.

"If the children of ease and security knew the hardships and dangers the students of nature encounter in their behalf," said Obed after a moment of silence when Middleton took his leave for the night, "pillars of silver and statues of brass would be reared as the everlasting monuments of their glory!"

"I know not, I know not," returned his companion; "silver is far from plenty, at least in the wilderness, and your brazen idols are forbidden in the commandments of the Lord."

"Such indeed was the opinion of the great lawgiver of the Jews, but the Egyptians and the Chaldeans, the Greeks and the Romans, were wont to manifest their gratitude, in these types of the human form. Indeed many of the illustrious masters of antiquity have, by the aid of science and skill, even outdone the works of nature and exhibited a beauty and perfection in the human form that are difficult to be found in the rarest living specimens of any of the species, genus Homo."

"Can your idols walk or speak, or have they the glorious gift of reason?" demanded the trapper with some indignation in his voice. "Though but little given to run into the noise and chatter of the settlements, yet have I been into the towns in my day to barter the peltry for lead and powder, and often have I seen your waxen dolls with their tawdry clothes and glass eyes——"

"Waxen dolls!" interrupted Obed. "It is profanation in the view of the arts to liken the miserable handiwork of the dealers in wax to the pure models of antiquity!"

"It is profanation in the eyes of the Lord," retorted the old man, "to liken the works of his creatures to the power of his own hand."

"Venerable venator," resumed the naturalist, clearing his throat like one who was much in earnest, "let us discuss understandingly and in amity. You speak of the dross of ignorance, whereas my memory dwells on those precious jewels which it was my happy fortune formerly to witness among the treasured glories of the Old World."

"*Old* World!" retorted the trapper. "That is the miserable cry of all the half-starved miscreants that have come into this blessed land since the days of my boyhood! They tell you of the *Old* World, as if the Lord had not the power and the will to create the universe in a day, or as if he had not bestowed his gifts with an equal hand, though not with an equal mind or equal wisdom, have they been received and used. Were they to say a *worn-out,* and an *abused,* and a *sacrilegious* world, they might not be so far from the truth!"

Dr. Battius, who found it quite as arduous a task to maintain any of his favorite positions with so irregular an antagonist, as he would have found it difficult to keep his feet within the hug of a western wrestler, hemmed aloud and profited by the new opening the trapper had made to shift the grounds of the discussion, "By Old and New World, my excellent associate," he said, "it is not to be understood that the hills and the valleys, the rocks and the rivers, of our own moiety of the earth do not, physically speaking, bear a date as ancient as the spot on which the bricks of Babylon are found; it merely signifies that its moral existence is not coequal with its physical or geological formation."

"Anan!" said the old man, looking up inquiringly into the face of the philosopher.

"Merely that it has not been so long known in morals as the other countries of Christendom."

"So much the better, so much the better. I am no great admirer of your old morals, as you call them, for I have ever found, and I have lived long as it were in the very heart of natur', that your old morals are none of the best. Mankind twist and turn the rules of the Lord to suit their own wickedness when their devilish cunning has had too much time to trifle with his commands."

"Nay, venerable hunter, still am I not comprehended. By morals I do not mean the limited and literal signification of the term, such as is conveyed in its synonym, morality, but the practices of men as connected with their daily intercourse, their institutions, and their laws."

"And such I call barefaced and downright wantonness and waste," interrupted his sturdy disputant.

"Well, be it so," returned the doctor, abandoning the explanation in despair. "Perhaps I have conceded too much," he then instantly added, fancying that he still saw the glimmerings of an argument through another chink in the discourse. "Perhaps I have conceded too much in saying that this hemisphere is literally as old in its formation as that which embraces the venerable quarters of Europe, Asia, and Africa."

"It is easy to say a pine is not so tall as an alder, but it would be hard to prove. Can you give a reason for such a belief?"

"The reasons are numerous and powerful," returned the doctor, delighted by this encouraging opening. "Look into the plains of Egypt and Arabia; their sandy deserts teem with the monuments of their antiquity; and then we have also recorded documents of their glory, doubling the proofs of their former greatness, now that they lie stripped of their fertility, while we look in vain for similar evidences that man has ever reached the summit of civilization on this continent, or search, without our reward, for the path by which he has made the downward journey to his present condition of second childhood."

"And what see you in all this?" demanded the trapper, who, though a little confused by the terms of his companion, seized the thread of his ideas.

"A demonstration of my problem, that nature did not make so vast a region to lie an uninhabited waste so many ages. This is merely the moral view of the subject; as to the more exact and geological——"

"Your morals are exact enough for me," returned the old man, "for I think I see in them the very *pride* of *folly*. I am but little gifted in the fables of what you call the *Old* World, seeing that my time has been mainly passed looking natur' steadily in the face and in reasoning on what I've seen rather than on what I've heard in traditions. But I have never shut my ears to the words of the good book, and many is the long winter evening that I have passed in the wigwams of the Delawares listening to the good Moravians as they dealt forth the history and doctrines of the elder times to the people of the Lenape! It was pleasant to hearken to such wisdom after a weary hunt! Right pleasant did I find it, and often have I talked the matter over with the Great Serpent of the Delawares in the more peaceful hours of our outlyings, whether it might be on the trail of a war party of the Mingoes or on the watch for a York deer. I remember to have heard it then and there said that the Blessed Land was once fertile as the bottoms of the Mississippi and groaning with its stores of grain and fruits, but that the judgment has since fallen upon it and that it is now more remarkable for its barrenness than any qualities to boast of."

"It is true; but Egypt, nay, much of Africa furnishes still more striking proofs of this exhaustion of nature."

"Tell me," interrupted the old man, "is it a certain truth that buildings are still standing in that land of Pharaoh which may be likened in their stature to the hills of the 'arth?"

"It is as true as that nature never refuses to bestow her incisors on the animals Mammalia, genus Homo———"

"It is very marvelous, and it proves how great He must be, when his miserable creatur's can accomplish such wonders! Many men must have been needed to finish such an edifice, aye, and men gifted with strength and skill too! Does the land abound with such a race to this hour?"

"Far from it. Most of the country is a desert, and but for a mighty river all would be so."

"Yes, rivers are rare gifts to such as till the ground, as anyone may see who journeys far atween the Rocky Mountains and the Mississippi. But how do you account for these changes on the face of the 'arth itself and for this downfall of nations, you men of the schools?"

"It is to be ascribed to moral cau———"

"You're right; it is their morals, their wickedness and their pride, and chiefly their waste that has done it all! Now listen to what the experience of an old man teaches him. I have lived long, as these gray hairs and wrinkled hands will show, even though my tongue should fail in the wisdom of my years. And I have seen much of the folly of man, for his natur' is the same, be he born in the wilderness or be he born in the towns. To my weak judgment it hath ever seemed that his gifts are not equal to his wishes. That he would mount into the heavens with all his deformities about him if he only knew the road, no one will gainsay that witnesses his bitter strivings upon 'arth. If his power is not equal to his will, it is because the wisdom of the Lord hath set bounds to his evil workings."

"It is much too certain that certain facts will warrant a theory, which teaches the natural depravity of the genus; but if science could be fairly brought to bear on a whole species at once, for instance, education might eradicate the evil principle."

"That, for your education! The time has been when I have thought it possible to make a companion of a beast. Many are the cubs and many are the speckled fawns that I have reared with these old hands, until I have even fancied them rational and altered beings; but what did it amount to? The bear would bite, and the deer would run, notwithstanding my wicked conceit in fancying that I could change a temper that the Lord himself had seen fit to bestow. Now if man is so blinded in his folly as to go on, ages on ages, doing harm chiefly to himself, there is the same reason to think that he has wrought his evil here as in the countries you call so old. Look about you, man; where are the multitudes that once peopled these prairies, the kings and the palaces, the riches and the mightinesses of this desert?"

"Where are the monuments that would prove the truth of so vague a theory?"

"I know not what you call a monument."

"The works of man! The glories of Thebes, and Balbec— columns, catacombs, and pyramids standing amid the sands of the East like wrecks on a rocky shore to testify to the storms of ages!"

"They are gone. Time has lasted too long for them. For why? Time was made by the Lord, and they were made by man. This very spot of reeds and grass on which you now sit may once have been the garden of some mighty king. It is the fate of all things to ripen and then to decay. The tree blossoms and bears its fruit, which falls, rots, withers, and even the seed is lost! Go, count the rings of the oak and of the sycamore; they lie in circles, one about another, until the eye is blinded in striving to make out their numbers; and yet a full change of the seasons comes round while the stem is winding one of these little lines about itself, like the buffalo changing his coat or the buck his horns; and what does it all amount to? There does the noble tree fill its place in the forest, loftier, and grander, and richer, and more difficult to imitate than any of your pitiful pillars, for a thousand years, until the time which the Lord hath given it is full. Then come the winds that you cannot see to rive its bark, and the waters from the heavens to soften its pores, and the rot, which all can feel and none can understand, to humble its pride and bring it to the ground. From that moment its beauty begins to perish. It lies another hundred years, a moldering log, and then a mound of moss and 'arth, a sad effigy of a human grave. This is one of your genuine monuments, though made by a very different power than such as belongs to your chiseling masonry! And after all, the cunningest scout of the whole Dakota nation might pass his life in searching for the spot where it fell, and be no wiser when his eyes grew dim than when they were first opened. As if that was not enough to convince man of his ignorance, and as though it were put there in mockery of his conceit, a pine shoots up from the roots of the oak, just as barrenness comes after fertility or as these wastes have been spread where a garden may have been created. Tell me not of your worlds that are old! It is blasphemous to set bounds and seasons, in this manner, to the works of the Almighty, like a woman counting the ages of her young."

"Friend hunter, or trapper," returned the naturalist, clearing his throat in some intellectual confusion at the vigorous attack of his companion, "your deductions, if admitted by the world, would sadly circumscribe the efforts of reason and much abridge the boundaries of knowledge."

"So much the better, so much the better, for I have always found that a conceited man never knows content. All things prove it. Why have we not the wings of the pigeon, the eyes of the eagle, and the legs of the moose if it had been intended that man should be equal to all his wishes?"

"There are certain physical defects, venerable trapper, in which I am always ready to admit great and happy alterations might be suggested. For example, in my own order of Phalangacru——"

"Cruel enough would be the order that should come from miserable hands like thine! A touch from such a finger would destroy the mocking deformity of a monkey! Go, go; human folly is not needed to fill up the great design of God. There is no stature, no beauty, no proportions, nor any colors in which man himself can well be fashioned that is not already done to his hands."

"That is touching another great and much disputed question," exclaimed the doctor, who seized upon every distinct idea that the ardent and somewhat dogmatic old man left exposed to his mental grasp, with the vain hope of inducing a logical discussion, in which he might bring his battery of syllogisms to annihilate the unscientific defenses of his antagonist.

It is, however, unnecessary to our narrative to relate the erratic discourse that ensued. The old man eluded the annihilating blows of his adversary as the light-armed soldier is wont to escape the efforts of the more regular warrior, even while he annoys him most; and an hour passed away without bringing any of the numerous subjects on which they touched to a satisfactory conclusion. The arguments acted, however, on the nervous system of the doctor like so many soothing soporifics; and by the time his aged companion was disposed to lay his head on his pack, Obed, refreshed by his recent mental joust, was in a condition to seek his natural rest without enduring the torments of the incubus in the shapes of Teton warriors and bloody tomahawks.

CHAPTER 23

——Save you, sir.   SHAKESPEARE

THE SLEEP OF the fugitives lasted for several hours. The trapper was the first to shake off its influence, as he had been the last to court its refreshment. Rising just as the gray light of day began to brighten that portion of the studded vault which rested on the eastern margin of the plain, he summoned his companions from their warm lairs and pointed out the necessity of their being once more on the alert. While Middleton attended to the arrangements necessary to the comforts of Inez and Ellen in the long and painful journey which lay before them, the old man and Paul prepared the meal, which the former had advised them to take before they proceeded to horse. These several dispositions were not long in making, and the little group was soon seated about a repast which, though it might want the elegances to which the bride of Middleton had been accustomed, was not deficient in the more important requisites of savor and nutriment.

"When we get lower into the hunting grounds of the Pawnees," said the trapper, laying a morsel of delicate venison before Inez on a little trencher neatly made of horn and expressly for his own use, "we shall find the buffaloes fatter and sweeter, the deer in more abundance, and all the gifts of the Lord abounding to satisfy our wants. Perhaps we may even strike a beaver and get a morsel from his tail * by way of a rare mouthful."

"What course do you mean to pursue when you have once thrown these bloodhounds from the chase?" demanded Middleton.

"If I might advise," said Paul, "it would be to strike a watercourse and get upon its downward current as soon as may be. Give me a cottonwood, and I will turn you out a canoe that shall carry us all, the jackass excepted, in perhaps the work of a day and a night. Ellen, here, is a lively girl enough, but then she is no great race rider; and it would be far more comfortable to boat six or eight hundred miles than to go loping along like so many elks measuring the prairies; besides, water leaves no trail."

"I will not swear to that," returned the trapper; "I have often thought the eyes of a redskin would find a trail in air."

"See, Middleton," exclaimed Inez in a sudden burst of youthful pleasure that caused her for a moment to forget her situation, "how lovely is that sky; surely it contains a promise of happier times!"

"It is glorious!" returned her husband. "Glorious and heavenly is that streak of vivid red, and here is a still brighter crimson; rarely have I seen a richer rising of the sun."

"Rising of the sun!" slowly repeated the old man, lifting his tall person from its seat with a deliberate and abstracted air, while he kept his eye riveted on the changing and certainly beautiful tints that were garnishing the vault of heaven. "rising of the sun! I like not such risings of the sun. Ah's me! The imps have circumvented us with a vengeance. The prairie is on fire!"

"God in heaven protect us!" cried Middleton, catching Inez to his bosom under the instant impression of the imminence of their danger. "There is no time to lose, old man; each instant is a day; let us fly."

---

* The American hunters consider the tail of the beaver the most nourishing of all food.

"Whither?" demanded the trapper, motioning him with calmness and dignity to arrest his steps. "In this wilderness of grass and reeds, you are like a vessel in the broad lakes without a compass. A single step on the wrong course might prove the destruction of us all. It is seldom danger is so pressing that there is not time enough for reason to do its work, young officer; therefore let us await its biddings."

"For my own part," said Paul Hover, looking about him with no equivocal expression of concern, "I acknowledge that should this dry bed of weeds get fairly in a flame, a bee would have to make a flight higher than common to prevent his wings from scorching. Therefore, old trapper, I agree with the captain, and say mount and run."

"Ye are wrong—ye are wrong; man is not a beast to follow the gift of instinct and to snuff up his knowledge by a taint in the air or a rumbling in the sound; but he must see and reason, and then conclude. So follow me a little to the left, where there is a rise in the ground, whence we may make our reconnoiterings."

The old man waved his hand with authority and led the way without further parlance to the spot he had indicated, followed by the whole of his alarmed companions. An eye less practiced than that of the trapper might have failed in discovering the gentle elevation to which he alluded and which looked on the surface of the meadow like a growth a little taller than common. When they reached the place, however, the stinted grass itself announced the absence of that moisture which had fed the rank weeds of most of the plain, and furnished a clue to the evidence by which he had judged of the formation of the ground hidden beneath. Here a few minutes were lost in breaking down the tops of the surrounding herbage, which, notwithstanding the advantage of their position, rose even above the heads of Middleton and Paul, and in obtaining a lookout that might command a view of the surrounding sea of fire.

The frightful prospect added nothing to the hopes of those who had so fearful a stake in the result. Although the day was beginning to dawn, the vivid colors of the sky continued to deepen, as if the fierce element were bent on an impious rivalry of the light of the sun. Bright flashes of flame shot up here and there along the margin of the waste like the nimble coruscations of the North, but far more angry and threatening in their color and changes. The anxiety on the rigid features of the trapper sensibly deepened as he leisurely traced these evidences of a conflagration which spread in a broad belt about their place of refuge, until he had encircled the whole horizon.

Shaking his head as he again turned his face to the point where the danger seemed nighest and most rapidly approaching, the old man said, "Now have we been cheating ourselves with the belief that we had thrown these Tetons from our trail, while here is proof enough that they not only know where we lie, but that they intend to smoke us out like so many skulking beasts of prey. See; they have lighted the fire around the whole bottom at the same moment, and we are as completely hemmed in by the devils as an island by its waters."

"Let us mount and ride," cried Middleton; "is life not worth a struggle?"

"Whither would ye go? Is a Teton horse a salamander that can walk amid fiery flames unhurt, or do you think the Lord will show his might in your behalf, as in the days of old, and carry you harmless through such a furnace as you may see glowing beneath yonder red sky? There are Siouxes, too, hemming the fire with their arrows and knives on every side of us, or I am no judge of their murderous deviltries."

"We will ride into the center of the whole tribe," returned the youth fiercely, "and put their manhood to the test."

"Aye, it's well in words, but what would it prove in deeds? Here is a dealer in bees, who can teach you wisdom in a matter like this."

"Now for that matter, old trapper," said Paul, stretching his athletic form like a mastiff conscious of his strength, "I am on the side of the captain and am clearly for a race against the fire, though it line me into a Teton wigwam. Here is Ellen, who will——"

"Of what use, of what use are your stout hearts when the element of the Lord is to be conquered as well as human men. Look about you, friends; the wreath of smoke that is rising from the bottoms plainly says that there is no outlet from the spot without crossing a belt of fire. Look for yourselves, my men; look for yourselves; if you can find a single opening, I will engage to follow."

The examination which his companions so instantly and so intently made rather served to assure them of their desperate situation than to appease their fears. Huge columns of smoke were rolling up from the plain and thickening in gloomy masses around the horizon, the red glow which gleamed upon their enormous folds now lighting their volumes with the glare of the conflagration, and now flashing to another point as the flame beneath glided ahead, leaving all behind enveloped in awful darkness and proclaiming louder than words the character of the imminent and approaching danger.

"This is terrible!" exclaimed Middleton, folding the trembling Inez to his heart. "At such a time as this, and in such a manner?"

"The gates of heaven are open to all who truly believe," murmured the pious devotee in his bosom.

"This resignation is maddening! But we are men and will make a struggle for our lives! How now, my brave and spirited friend, shall we yet mount and push across the flames, or shall we stand here and see those we must love perish in this frightful manner without an effort?"

"I am for a swarming time and a flight before the hive is too hot to hold us," said the bee hunter, to whom it will be at once seen that Middleton addressed himself. "Come, old trapper, you must acknowledge this is but a slow way of getting out of danger. If we tarry here much longer, it will be in the fashion that the bees lie around the straw after the hive has been smoked for its honey. You may hear the fire begin to roar already, and I know by experience that when the flame once gets fairly into the prairie grass, it is no sloth that can outrun it."

"Think you," returned the old man, pointing scornfully at the mazes of the dry and matted grass which environed them, "that mortal feet can outstrip the speed of fire on such a path! If I only knew now on which side these miscreants lay!"

"What say you, friend doctor," cried the bewildered Paul, turning to the naturalist with that sort of helplessness with which the strong are often apt to seek aid of the weak when human power is baffled by the hand of a mightier being, "what say you; have you no advice to give away in a case of life and death?"

The naturalist stood, tablets in hand, looking at the awful spectacle with as much composure as if the conflagration had been lighted in order to solve the difficulties of some scientific problem. Aroused by the question of his companion, he turned to his equally calm though differently occupied associate, the trapper, demanding with the most provoking insensibility to the urgent nature of their situation, "Venerable hunter, you have often witnessed similar prismatic experiments——"

He was rudely interrupted by Paul, who struck the tablets from his hands with a violence that betrayed the utter intellectual confusion which had overset the equanimity of his mind. Before time was allowed for remonstrance, the old man, who had continued during the whole scene like one much at a loss how to proceed, though also like one who was rather perplexed than alarmed, suddenly assumed a decided air, as if he no longer doubted on the course it was most advisable to pursue.

"It is time to be doing," he said, interrupting the controversy that was about to ensue between the naturalist and the bee hunter; "it is time to leave off books and moanings and to be doing."

"You have come to your recollections too late, miserable old man," cried Middleton; "the flames are within a quarter of a mile of us, and the wind is bringing them down in this quarter with dreadful rapidity."

"Anan! The flames! I care but little for the flames. If I only knew how to circumvent the cunning of the Tetons as I know how to cheat the fire of its prey, there would be nothing needed but thanks to the Lord for our deliverance. Do you call this a fire? If you had seen what I have witnessed in the eastern hills, when mighty mountains were like the furnace of a smith, you would have known what it was to fear the flames and to be thankful that you were spared! Come, lads, come; 'tis time to be doing now and to cease talking, for yonder curling flame is truly coming on like a trotting moose. Put hands upon this short and withered grass where we stand, and lay bare the 'arth."

"Would you think to deprive the fire of its victims in this childish manner?" exclaimed Middleton.

A faint but solemn smile passed over the features of the old man as he answered, "Your gran'ther would have said that when the enemy was nigh, a soldier could do no better than to obey."

The captain felt the reproof and instantly began to imitate the industry of Paul, who was tearing the decayed herbage from the ground in a sort of desperate compliance with the trapper's direction. Even Ellen lent her hands to the labor, nor was it long before Inez was seen similarly employed, though none amongst them knew why or wherefore. When life is thought to be the reward of labor, men are wont to be industrous. A very few moments sufficed to lay bare a spot of some twenty feet in diameter. Into one edge of this little area the trapper brought the females, directing Middleton and Paul to cover their light and inflammable dresses with the blankets of the party. So soon as this precaution was observed, the old man approached the opposite margin of the grass which still environed them in a tall and dangerous circle, and selecting a handful of the driest of the herbage, he placed it over the pan of his rifle. The light combustible kindled at the flash. Then he placed the little flame in a bed of the standing fog, and withdrawing from the spot to the center of the ring, he patiently awaited the result.

The subtle element seized with avidity upon its new fuel, and in a moment forked flames were gliding among the grass as the tongues of ruminating animals are seen rolling among their food, apparently in quest of its sweetest portions.

"Now," said the old man, holding up a finger and laughing in his peculiarly silent manner, "you shall see fire fight fire! Ah's me! Many is the time I have burnt a smooty path, from wanton laziness to pick my way across a tangled bottom."

"But is this not fatal?" cried the amazed Middleton. "Are you not bringing the enemy nigher to us instead of avoiding it?"

"Do you scorch so easily? Your gran'ther had a tougher skin. But we shall live to see; we shall all live to see."

The experience of the trapper was in the right. As the fire gained strength and heat, it began to spread on three sides, dying of itself on the fourth for want of aliment. As it increased and the sullen roaring announced its power, it cleared everything before it, leaving the black and smoking soil far more naked than if the scythe had swept the place. The situation of the fugitives would have still been hazardous had not the area enlarged as the flame encircled them. But by advancing to the spot where the trapper had kindled the grass, they avoided the heat, and in a very few moments the flames began to recede in every quarter, leaving them enveloped in a cloud of smoke, but perfectly safe from the torrent of fire that was still furiously rolling onwards.

The spectators regarded the simple expedient of the trapper with that species of wonder with which the courtiers of Ferdinand are said to have viewed the manner in which Columbus made his egg stand on its end, though with feelings that were filled with gratitude instead of envy.

"Most wonderful!" said Middleton when he saw the complete success of the means by which they had been rescued from a danger that he had conceived to be unavoidable. "The thought was a gift from heaven, and the hand that executed it should be immortal!"

"Old trapper," cried Paul, thrusting his fingers through his shaggy locks, "I have lined many a loaded bee into his hole, and know something of the nature of the woods, but this is robbing a hornet of his sting without touching the insect!"

"It will do—it will do," returned the old man, who after the first moment of his success seemed to think no more of the exploit; "now get the horses in readiness. Let the flames do their work for a short half hour, and then we will mount. That time is needed to cool the meadow, for these unshod Teton beasts are as tender on the hoof as a barefooted girl."

Middleton and Paul, who considered this unlooked-for escape as a species of resurrection, patiently awaited the time the trapper mentioned with renewed confidence in the infallibility of his judgment. The doctor regained his tablets, a little the worse from having fallen among the grass which had been subject to the action of the flames, and was consoling himself for this slight misfortune by recording uninterruptedly such different vacillations in light and shadow as he chose to consider phenomena.

In the meantime the veteran on whose experience they all so implicitly relied for protection employed himself in reconnoitering objects in the distance through the openings which the air occasionally made in the immense bodies of smoke, that by this time lay in enormous piles on every part of the plain.

"Look you here, lads," the trapper said after a long and anxious examination, "your eyes are young and may prove better than my worthless sight—though the time has been, when a wise and brave people saw reason to think me quick on a lookout; but those times are gone, and many a true and tried friend has passed away with them. Ah's me! If I could choose a change in the orderings of Providence—which I cannot, and which it would be blasphemy to attempt, seeing that all things are governed by a wiser mind than belongs to mortal weakness—but if I were to choose a change, it would be to say that such as they who have lived long together in friendship and kindness, and who have proved their fitness to go in company by many acts of suffering and daring in each other's behalf, should be permitted to give up life at such times as when the death of one leaves the other but little reason to live."

"Is it an Indian that you see?" demanded the impatient Middleton.

"Redskin or whiteskin, it is much the same. Friendship and use can tie men as strongly together in the woods as in the towns—aye, and for that matter, stronger. Here are the young warriors of the prairies. Often do they sort themselves in pairs and set apart their lives for deeds of friendship, and well and truly do they act up to their promises. The death blow to one is commonly mortal to the other! I have been a solitary man much of my time, if he can be called solitary who has lived for seventy years in the very bosom of natur' and where he could at any instant open his heart to God without having to strip it of the cares and wickednesses of the settlements—but making that allowance, have I been a solitary man; and yet have I always found that intercourse with my kind was pleasant and painful to break off, provided that the companion was brave and honest. Brave, because a skeary comrade in the woods"—suffering his eyes inadvertently to rest a moment on the person of the abstracted naturalist—"is apt to make a short path long; and honest, inasmuch as craftiness is rather an instinct of the brutes than a gift becoming the reason of a human man."

"But the object that you saw—was it a Sioux?"

"What the world of America is coming to and where the machinations and inventions of its people are to have an end, the Lord, he only knows. I have seen in my day the chief who, in his time, had beheld the first Christian that placed his wicked foot in the regions of York! How much has the beauty of the wilderness been deformed in two short lives! My own eyes were first opened on the shores of the eastern sea, and well do I remember that I tried the virtues of the first rifle I ever bore after such a march, from the door of my father to the forest, as a stripling could make between sun and sun, and that without offense to the rights or prejudices of any man who set himself up to be the owner of the beasts of the fields. Natur' then lay in its glory along the whole coast, giving a narrow stripe between the woods and the ocean to the greediness of the settlers. And where am I now? Had I the wings of an eagle, they would tire before a tenth of the distance which separates me from that sea could be passed; and towns and villages, farms and highways, churches and schools, in short, all the inventions and deviltries of man, are spread across the region. I have known the time when a few redskins, shouting along the borders, could set the provinces in a fever; and men were to be armed, and troops were to be called to aid from a distant land, and prayers were said, and the women frighted, and few slept in quiet because the Iroquois were on the warpath or the accursed Mingo had the tomahawk in hand. How is it now? The country sends out her ships to foreign lands to wage their battles, cannon are plentier than the rifle used to be, and trained soldiers are never wanting in tens of thousands when need calls for their services. Such is the difference atween a province and a state, my men; and I, miserable and worn out as I seem, have lived to see it all!"

"That you must have seen many a chopper skimming the cream from the face of the earth, and many a settler getting the very honey of nature, old trapper," said Paul, "no reasonable man can, or for that matter shall, doubt. But here is Ellen getting uneasy about the Siouxes, and now you have opened your mind so freely concerning these matters, if you will just put us on the line of our flight, the swarm will make another move."

"Anan!"

"I say that Ellen is getting uneasy; and as the smoke is lifting from the plain, it may be prudent to take another flight."

"The boy is reasonable. I had forgotten we were in the midst of a raging fire and that Siouxes were round about us like hungry wolves watching a drove of buffaloes. But when memory is at work in my old brain on times long past, it is apt to overlook the matters of the day. You say right, my children; it is time to be moving, and now comes the real nicety of our case. It is easy to outwit a furnace, for it is nothing but a raging element; and it is not always difficult to throw a grizzly bear from his scent, for the creatur' is both enlightened and blinded by his instinct; but to shut the eyes of a waking Teton is a matter of greater judgment, inasmuch as his deviltry is backed by reason."

Notwithstanding the old man appeared so conscious of the difficulty of the undertaking, he set about its achievement with great steadiness and alacrity. After completing the examination, which had been interrupted by the melancholy wanderings of his mind, he gave the signal to his companions to mount. The horses, which had continued passive and trembling amid the raging of the fire, received their burdens with a satisfaction so very evident as to furnish a favorable augury of their future industry. The trapper invited the doctor to take his own steed, declaring his intention to proceed on foot.

"I am but little used to journeying with the feet of others," he added as a reason for the measure, "and my legs are a-weary of doing nothing. Besides, should we light suddenly on an ambushment, which is a thing far from impossible, the horse will be in a better condition for a hard run with one man on his back than with two. As for me, what matters it whether my time is to be a day shorter or a day longer! Let the Tetons take my scalp if it be God's pleasure: they will find it covered with gray hairs; and it is beyond the craft of man to cheat me of the knowledge and experience by which they have been whitened."

As no one among the impatient listeners seemed disposed to dispute the arrangement, it was acceded to in silence. The doctor, though he muttered a few mourning exclamations on behalf of the lost *Asinus,* was by far too well pleased in finding that his speed was likely to be sustained by four legs instead of two to be long in complying; and consequently, in a very few moments the bee hunter, who was never last to speak on such occasions, vociferously announced that they were ready to proceed.

"Now look off yonder to the east," said the old man as he began to lead the way across the murky and still-smoking plain; "little fear of cold feet in journeying such a path as this; but look you off to the east, and if you see a sheet of shining white glistening like a plate of beaten silver through the openings of the smoke, why that is water. A noble stream is running thereaway, and I thought I got a glimpse of it a while since; but other thoughts came, and I lost it. It is a broad and swift river, such as the Lord has made many of its fellows in this desert. For here may natur' be seen in all its richness, trees alone excepted. Trees, which are to the 'arth as fruits are to a garden; without them nothing can be pleasant or thoroughly useful. Now watch, all of you, with open eyes, for that stripe of glittering water; we shall not be safe until it is flowing between our trail and these sharp-sighted Tetons."

The latter declaration was enough to ensure a vigilant lookout for the desired stream on the part of all the trapper's followers. With this object in view, the party proceeded in profound silence, the old man having admonished them of the necessity of caution as they entered the clouds of smoke, which were rolling like masses of fog along the plain, more particularly over those spots where the fire had encountered occasional pools of stagnant water.

They traveled near a league in this manner without obtaining the desired glimpse of the river. The fire was still raging in the distance, and as the air swept away the first vapor of the conflagration, fresh volumes rolled along the place, limiting the view. At length the old man, who had begun to betray some little uneasiness, which caused his followers to apprehend that even his acute faculties were beginning to be confused in the mazes of the smoke, made a sudden pause, and dropping his rifle to the ground, he stood, apparently musing over some object at his feet. Middleton and the rest rode up to his side and demanded the reason of the halt.

"Look ye here," returned the trapper, pointing to the mutilated carcass of a horse that lay more than half consumed in a little hollow of the ground; "here may you see the power of a prairie conflagration. The 'arth is moist, hereaway, and the grass has been taller than usual. This miserable beast has been caught in his bed. You see the bones, the crackling and scorched hide, and the grinning teeth. A thousand winters could not wither an animal so thoroughly as the element has done it in a minute."

"And this might have been our fate," said Middleton, "had the flames come upon us in our sleep!"

"Nay, I do not say that, I do not say that. Not but that man will burn as well as tinder; but, that being more reasoning than a horse, he would better know how to avoid the danger."

"Perhaps this, then, has been but the carcass of an animal, or he too would have fled?"

"See you these marks in the damp soil? Here have been his hoofs, and there is a moccasin print, as I'm a sinner! The owner of the beast has tried hard to move him from the place, but it is in the instinct of the creatur' to be faint-hearted and obstinate in a fire."

"It is a well-known fact. But if the animal has had a rider, where is he?"

"Aye, therein lies the mystery," returned the trapper, stooping to examine the signs in the ground with a closer eye. "Yes, yes, it is plain there has been a long struggle atween the two. The master has tried hard to save his beast, and the flames must have been very greedy, or he would have had better success."

"Harkee, old trapper," interrupted Paul, pointing to a little distance, where the ground was drier and the herbage had, in consequence, been less luxuriant; "just call them two horses. Yonder lies another."

"The boy is right! Can it be that the Tetons have been caught in their own snares? Such things do happen, and here is an example to all evildoers. Aye, look you here, this is iron; there have been some white inventions about the trappings of the beast—it must be so—it must be so—a party of the knaves have been skirting in the grass after us while their friends have fired the prairie, and look you at the consequences: they have lost their beasts, and happy have they been if their own souls are not now skirting along the path which leads to the Indian heaven."

"They had the same expedient at command as yourself," rejoined Middleton as the party slowly proceeded, approaching the other carcass which lay directly on their route.

"I know not that. It is not every savage that carries his steel and flint or as good a rifle pan as this old friend of mine. It is slow making a fire with two sticks, and little time was given to consider or invent just at this spot, as you may see by yon streak of flame, which is flashing along afore the wind as if it were on a trail of powder. It is not many minutes since the fire has passed hereaway, and it may be well to look at our primings; not that I would willingly combat the Tetons, God forbid! But if a fight needs be, it is always wise to get the first shot."

"This has been a strange beast, old man," said Paul, who had pulled the bridle, or rather halter, of his steed over the second carcass while the rest of the party were already pass-

ing, in their eagerness to proceed; "a strange horse do I call
it; it had neither head nor hoofs!"

"The fire has not been idle," returned the trapper, keeping
his eye vigilantly employed in profiting by those glimpses of
the horizon which the whirling smoke offered to his examination. "It would soon bake you a buffalo whole, or for that
matter powder his hoofs and horns into white ashes. Shame,
shame, old Hector; as for the captain's pup, it is to be expected that he would show his want of years, and I may
say, I hope without offense, his want of education too; but
for a hound like you, who have lived so long in the
forest afore you came into these plains, it is very disgrace-
ful, Hector, to be showing your teeth and growling at the
carcass of a roasted horse, the same as if you were telling
your master that you had found the trail of a grizzly
bear."

"I tell you, old trapper, this is no horse, neither in hoofs,
head, nor hide."

"Anan! Not a horse? Your eyes are good for the bees
and for the hollow trees, my lad, but—bless me, the boy
is right! That I should mistake the hide of a buffalo, scorched
and crimpled as it is, for the carcass of a horse! Ah's me!
The time has been, my men, when I would tell you the
name of a beast as far as eye could reach, and that too with
most of the particulars of color, age, and sex."

"An inestimable advantage have you then enjoyed, venerable venator!" observed the attentive naturalist. "The man
who can make these distinctions in a desert is saved the pain
of many a weary walk, and often of an inquiry that in its
result proves useless. Pray tell me, did your exceeding excellence of vision extend so far as to enable you to decide on
their order or genus?"

"I know not what you mean by your orders of genius."

"No!" interrupted the bee hunter, a little disdainfully for
him when speaking to his aged friend. "Now, old trapper,
that is admitting your ignorance of the English language
in a way I should not expect from a man of your experience and understanding. By order our comrade means
whether they go in promiscuous droves, like a swarm that
is following its queen bee, or in single file, as you often
see the buffaloes trailing each other through a prairie. And
as for genius, I'm sure *that* is a word well understood
and in everybody's mouth. There is the congressman in our

district, and that tonguey little fellow who puts out the paper in our country—they are both so called for their smart-
ness; which is what the doctor means, as I take it, seeing
that he seldom speaks without some considerable meaning."

When Paul finished this very clever explanation he
looked behind him with an expression which, rightly interpreted, would have said, "You see, though I don't often
trouble myself in these matters, I am no fool."

Ellen admired Paul for anything but his learning. There
was enough in his frank, fearless, and manly character,
backed was it was by great personal attraction, to awaken
her sympathies without the necessity of prying into his mental attainments. The poor girl reddened like a rose, her
pretty fingers played with the belt by which she sustained
herself on the horse, and she hurriedly observed, as if
anxious to direct the attentions of the other listeners from a
weakness on which her own thoughts could not bear to
dwell, "And this is not a horse, after all?"

"It is nothing more nor less than the hide of a buffalo,"
continued the trapper, who had been no less puzzled by the
explanation of Paul than by the language of the doctor; "the
hair is beneath; the fire has run over it as you see, for being
fresh, the flames could take no hold. The beast has not
been long killed, and it may be that some of the beef is still
hereaway."

"Lift the corner of the skin, old trapper," said Paul with
the tone of one who felt as if he had now proved his right
to mingle his voice in any council; "if there is a morsel of the
hump left, it must be well cooked, and it shall be welcome."

The old man laughed heartily at the conceit of his companion. Thrusting his foot beneath the skin, it moved. Then it
was suddenly cast aside, and an Indian warrior sprang from
its cover to his feet with an agility that bespoke how urgent
he deemed the occasion.

CHAPTER 24

I would it were bedtime, Hal, and all well.

SHAKESPEARE

A SECOND GLANCE sufficed to convince the whole of the
startled party that the young Pawnee whom they had al-

ready encountered again stood before them. Surprise kept both sides mute, and more than a minute was passed in surveying each other with eyes of astonishment, if not of distrust. The wonder of the young warrior was, however, much more tempered and dignified than that of his Christian acquaintances. While Middleton and Paul felt the tremor which shook the persons of their dependent companions thrilling through their own quickened blood, the glowing eye of the Indian rolled from one to another as if it could never quail before the rudest assaults. His gaze, after making the circuit of every wondering countenance, finally settled in a steady look on the equally immovable features of the trapper. The silence was first broken by Dr. Battius, in the ejaculation of, "Order Primates, genus Homo, species Prairie!"

"Aye—aye—the secret is out," said the old trapper, shaking his head like one who congratulated himself on having mastered the mystery of some knotty difficulty. "The lad has been in the grass for a cover; the fire has come upon him in his sleep, and having lost his horse, he has been driven to save himself under that fresh hide of a buffalo. No bad invention when powder and flint were wanting to kindle a ring. I warrant me, now, this is a clever youth, and one that it would be safe to journey with! I will speak to him kindly, for anger can at least serve no turn of ours. My brother is welcome again"—using the language which the other understood; "the Tetons have been smoking him as they would a raccoon."

The young Pawnee rolled his eye over the place as if he were examining the terrific danger from which he had just escaped, but he disdained to betray the smallest emotion at its imminency. His brow contracted as he answered to the remark of the trapper by saying—"A Teton is a dog. When the Pawnee war whoop is in their ears, the whole nation howls."

"It is true. The imps are on our trail, and I am glad to meet a warrior with the tomahawk in his hand who does not love them. Will my brother lead my children to his village? If the Siouxes follow on our path, my young men shall help him to strike them."

The young Pawnee turned his eyes from one to another of the strangers in a keen scrutiny before he saw fit to answer so important an interrogatory. His examination of the males was short and apparently satisfactory. But his gaze was fastened long and admiringly, as in their former interview, on the surpassing and unwonted beauty of a being so fair and so unknown as Inez. Though his glance wandered, for moments, from her countenance to the more intelligible and yet extraordinary charms of Ellen, it did not fail to return promptly to the study of a creature who, in the view of his unpracticed eye and untutored imagination, was formed with all that perfection with which the youthful poet is apt to endow the glowing images of his brain. Nothing so fair, so ideal, so every way worthy to reward the courage and self-devotion of a warrior had ever before been encountered on the prairies, and the young brave appeared to be deeply and intuitively sensible to the influence of so rare a model of the loveliness of the sex. Perceiving, however, that his gaze gave uneasiness to the subject of his admiration, he withdrew his eyes, and laying his hand impressively on his chest, he modestly answered, "My father shall be welcome. The young men of my nation shall hunt with his sons; the chiefs shall smoke with the grayhead. The Pawnee girls will sing in the ears of his daughters."

"And if we meet the Tetons?" demanded the trapper, who wished to understand thoroughly the more important conditions of this new alliance.

"The enemy of the Big Knives shall feel the blow of the Pawnee."

"It is well. Now let my brother and I meet in council, that we may not go on a crooked path, but that our road to his village may be like the flight of the pigeons."

The young Pawnee made a significant gesture of assent and followed the other a little apart in order to be removed from all danger of interruption from the reckless Paul or the abstracted naturalist. Their conference was short, but, as it was conducted in the sententious manner of the natives, it served to make each of the parties acquainted with all the necessary information of the other. When they rejoined their associates, the old man saw fit to explain a portion of what had passed between them as follows, "Aye, I was not mistaken," he said; "this good-looking young warrior—for good-looking and noble-looking he is, though a little horrified perhaps with paint—this good-looking youth, then, tells me he is out on the scout for these very Tetons. His party was not strong enough to strike the devils, who are down from their towns in great numbers to hunt the buffalo, and runners have gone to the Pawnee villages for aid. It would seem that this lad is a fearless boy, for he has been hanging on their skirts alone until, like ourselves, he was driven to the grass for a cover. But he tells me more, my men, and what I am mainly sorry to hear, which is, that the cunning Mahtoree, instead of going to blows with the squatter, has become his friend and that both broods, red and white, are on our heels and outlying around this very burning plain to circumvent us to our destruction."

"How knows he all this to be true?" demanded Middleton.

"Anan!"

"In what manner does he know that these things are so?"

"In what manner! Do you think newspapers and town criers are needed to tell a scout what is doing on the prairies, as they are in the bosom of the States? No gossiping woman who hurries from house to house to spread evil of her neighbor can carry tidings with her tongue so fast as these people will spread their meaning by signs and warnings that they alone understand. 'Tis their larning, and what is better, it is got in the open air, and not within the walls of a school. I tell you, captain, that what he says is true."

"For that matter," said Paul, "I'm ready to swear to it. It is reasonable, and therefore it must be true."

"And well you might, lad; well you might. He furthermore declares that my old eyes for once were true to me and that the river lies, hereaway, at about the distance of half a league. You see the fire has done most of its work in that quarter, and our path is clouded in smoke. He also agrees that it is needful to wash our trail in water. Yes, we must put that river atween us and the Sioux eyes, and then, by the favor of the Lord, not forgetting our industry, we may gain the village of the Loups."

"Words will not forward us a foot," said Middleton; "let us move."

The old man assented, and the party once more prepared to renew its route. The Pawnee threw the skin of the buffalo over his shoulder and led the advance, casting many a stolen glance behind him as he proceeded in order to fix his gaze on the extraordinary and, to him, unaccountable loveliness of the unconscious Inez.

An hour sufficed to bring the fugitives to the bank of the

stream, which was one of the hundred rivers that serve to conduct, through the mighty arteries of the Missouri and Mississippi, the waters of that vast and still uninhabited region to the ocean. The river was not deep, but its current was troubled and rapid.

The flames had scorched the earth to its very margin, and as the warm streams of the fluid mingled, in the cooler air of the morning, with the smoke of the raging conflagration, most of its surface was wrapped in a mantle of moving vapor. The trapper pointed out the circumstance with pleasure, saying as he assisted Inez to dismount on the margin of the watercourse, "The knaves have outwitted themselves! I am far from certain that I should not have fired the prairie to have got the benefit of this very smoke to hide our movements had not the heartless imps saved us the trouble. I've known such things done in my day, and done with success. Come, lady, put your tender foot upon the ground—for a fearful time has it been to one of your breeding and skeary qualities. Ah's me! What have I not known the young, and the delicate, and the virtuous, and the modest, to undergo in my time among the horrifications and circumventions of Indian warfare! Come, it is a short quarter of a mile to the other bank, and then our trail at least will be broken."

Paul had by this time assisted Ellen to dismount, and he now stood looking with rueful eyes at the naked banks of the river. Neither tree nor shrub grew along its borders, with the exception of here and there a solitary thicket of low bushes, from among which it would not have been an easy matter to have found a dozen stems of a size sufficient to make an ordinary walking stick.

"Harkee, old trapper," the moody-looking bee hunter exclaimed; "it is very well to talk of the other side of this ripple of a river, or brook, or whatever you may call it, but in my judgment it would be a smart rifle that would throw its lead across it—that is, to any detriment to Indian or deer."

"That it would—that it would, though I carry a piece here that has done its work in time of need at as great a distance."

"And do you mean to shoot Ellen and the captain's lady across; or do you intend them to go, trout fashion, with their mouths under water?"

"Is this river too deep to be forded?" asked Middleton, who, like Paul, began to consider the impossibility of transporting her whose safety he valued more than his own to the opposite shore.

"When the mountains above feed it with their torrents, it is, as you see, a swift and powerful stream. Yet have I crossed its sandy bed in my time without wetting a knee. But we have the Sioux horses; I warrant me that the kicking imps will swim like so many deer."

"Old trapper," said Paul, thrusting his fingers into his mop of a head as was usual with him when any difficulty confounded his philosophy, "I have swum like a fish in my day, and I can do it again when there is need; nor do I much regard the weather; but I question if you get Nelly to sit a horse with this water whirling like a millrace before her eyes; besides, it is manifest the thing is not to be done dryshod."

"Ah, the lad is right. We must to our inventions, therefore, or the river cannot be crossed." Then cutting the discourse short, he turned to the Pawnee and explained to him the difficulty which existed in relation to the women. The young warrior listened gravely, and throwing the buffalo skin from his shoulder, he immediately commenced, assisted by the occasional aid of the understanding old man, the preparations necessary to effect this desirable object.

The hide was soon drawn into the shape of an umbrella top, or an inverted parachute, by thongs of deerskin, with which both the laborers were well provided. A few light sticks served to keep the parts from collapsing or falling in. When this simple and natural expedient was arranged, it was placed on the water, the Indian making a sign that it was ready to receive its freight. Both Inez and Ellen hesitated to trust themselves in a bark of so frail a construction, nor would Middleton or Paul consent that they should do so until each had assured himself by actual experiment that the vessel was capable of sustaining a load much heavier than it was destined to receive. Then indeed their scruples were reluctantly overcome, and the skin was made to receive its precious burden.

"Now leave the Pawnee to be the pilot," said the trapper; "my hand is not so steady as it used to be; but he has limbs like toughened hickory. Leave all to the wisdom of the Pawnee."

The husband and lover could not well do otherwise, and

they were fain to become deeply interested, it is true, but passive spectators of this primitive species of ferrying. The Pawnee selected the beast of Mahtoree from among the three horses, with a readiness that proved he was far from being ignorant of the properties of that noble animal, and throwing himself upon its back, he rode into the margin of the river. Thrusting an end of his lance into the hide, he bore the light vessel up against the stream, and giving his steed the rein, they pushed boldly into the current. Middleton and Paul followed, pressing as nigh the bark as prudence would at all warrant. In this manner the young warrior bore his precious cargo to the opposite bank in perfect safety, without the slightest inconvenience to the passengers, and with a steadiness and celerity which proved that both horse and rider were not unused to the operation. When the shore was gained, the young Indian undid his work, threw the skin over his shoulder, placed the sticks under his arm, and returned, without speaking, to transfer the remainder of the party in a similar manner to what was very justly considered the safer side of the river.

"Now, friend doctor," said the old man when he saw the Indian plunging into the river a second time, "do I know there is faith in yonder redskin. He is a good-looking, aye, and an honest-looking youth, but the winds of heaven are not more deceitful than these savages when the devil has fairly beset them. Had the Pawnee been a Teton or one of them heartless Mingoes that used to be prowling through the woods of York a time back, that is, some sixty years agone, we should have seen his back and not his face turned towards us. My heart had its misgivings when I saw the lad choose the better horse, for it would be as easy to leave us with that beast as it would for a nimble pigeon to part company from a flock of noisy and heavy-winged crows. But you see that truth is in the boy, and make a redskin once your friend, he is yours so long as you deal honestly by him."

"What may be the distance to the sources of this stream?" demanded Dr. Battius, whose eyes were rolling over the whirling eddies of the current with a very portentous expression of doubt. "At what distance may its secret springs be found?"

"That may be as the weather proves. I warrant me your legs would be a-weary before you had followed its bed into the Rocky Mountains; but then there are seasons when it might be done without wetting a foot."

"And in what particular divisions of the year do these periodical seasons occur?"

"He that passes this spot a few months from this time will find that foaming watercourse a desert of drifting sand."

The naturalist pondered deeply. Like most others who are not endowed with a superfluity of physical fortitude, the worthy man had found the danger of passing the river in so simple a manner magnifying itself in his eyes so rapidly, as the moment of adventure approached, that he actually contemplated the desperate effort of going round the river in order to escape the hazard of crossing it. It may not be necessary to dwell on the incredible ingenuity with which terror will at any time prop a tottering argument. The worthy Obed had gone over the whole subject with commendable diligence and had just arrived at the consoling conclusion that there was nearly as much glory in discerning the hidden sources of so considerable a stream as in adding a plant or an insect to the lists of the learned, when the Pawnee reached the shore for the second time. The old man took his seat with the utmost deliberation in the vessel of skin (so soon as it had been duly arranged for his reception), and having carefully disposed of Hector between his legs, he beckoned to his companion to occupy the third place.

The naturalist placed a foot in the frail vessel as an elephant will try a bridge, or a horse is often seen to make a similar experiment before he will trust the whole of his corporeal treasure on the dreaded flat, and then withdrew just as the old man believed he was about to seat himself.

"Venerable venator," he said mournfully, "this is a most unscientific bark. There is an inward monitor which bids me distrust its security!"

"Anan!" said the old man, who was pinching the ears of the hound as a father would play with the same member in a favorite child.

"I incline not to this irregular mode of experimenting on fluids. The vessel has neither form nor proportions."

"It is not as handsomely turned as I have seen a canoe in birchen bark, but comfort may be taken in a wigwam as well as in a palace."

"It is impossible that any vessel constructed on principles

so repugnant to science can be safe. This tub, venerable hunter, will never reach the opposite shore in safety."

"You are a witness of what it has done."

"Aye; but it was an anomaly in prosperity. If exceptions were to be taken as rules in the government of things, the human race would speedily be plunged in the abysses of ignorance. Venerable trapper, this expedient in which you would repose your safety is, in the annals of regular inventions, what a *Lusus naturae* may be termed in the lists of natural history—a monster!"

How much longer Dr. Battius might have felt disposed to prolong the discourse it is difficult to say, for in addition to the powerful personal considerations which induced him to procrastinate an experiment which was certainly not without its dangers, the pride of reason was beginning to sustain him in the discussion. But, fortunately for the credit of the old man's forbearance, when the naturalist reached the word with which he terminated his last speech, a sound arose in the air that seemed a sort of supernatural echo to the idea itself. The young Pawnee, who had awaited the termination of the incomprehensible discussion with grave and characteristic patience, raised his head and listened to the unknown cry like a stag whose mysterious faculties had detected the footsteps of the distant hounds in the gale. The trapper and the doctor were not, however, entirely so uninstructed as to the nature of the extraordinary sounds. The latter recognized in them the well-known voice of his own beast, and he was about to rush up the little bank which confined the current, with all the longings of strong affection, when *Asinus* himself galloped into view at no great distance, urged to the unnatural gait by the impatient and brutal Weucha, who bestrode him.

The eyes of the Teton and those of the fugitives met. The former raised a long, loud, and piercing yell, in which the notes of exultation were fearfully blended with those of warning. The signal served for a finishing blow to the discussion on the merits of the bark, the doctor stepping as promptly to the side of the old man as if a mental mist had been miraculously removed from his eyes. In another instant the steed of the young Pawnee was struggling with the torrent.

The utmost strength of the horse was needed to urge the fugitives beyond the flight of arrows that came sailing through the air at the next moment. The cry of Weucha had brought fifty of his comrades to the shore, but fortunately, among them all, there was not one of a rank sufficient to entitle him to the privilege of bearing a fusee. One half the stream, however, was not passed before the form of Mahtoree himself was seen on its bank, and an ineffectual discharge of firearms announced the rage and disappointment of the chief. More than once the trapper had raised his rifle as if about to try its power on his enemies, but he as often lowered it without firing. The eyes of the Pawnee warrior glared like those of the cougar at the sight of so many of the hostile tribe, and he answered the impotent effort of their chief by tossing a hand into the air in contempt and raising the war cry of his nation. The challenge was too taunting to be endured. The Tetons dashed into the stream in a body, and the river became dotted with the dark forms of beasts and riders.

There was now a fearful struggle for the friendly bank. As the Dakotas advanced with beasts which had not, like that of the Pawnee, expended their strength in former efforts, and as they moved unencumbered by anything but their riders, the speed of the pursuers greatly outstripped that of the fugitives. The trapper, who clearly comprehended the whole danger of their situation, calmly turned his eyes from the Tetons to his young Indian associate in order to examine whether the resolution of the latter began to falter as the former lessened the distance between them. Instead of betraying fear, however, or any of that concern which might so readily have been excited by the peculiarity of his risk, the brow of the young warrior contracted to a look which indicated high and deadly hostility.

"Do you greatly value life, friend doctor?" demanded the old man with a sort of philosophical calmness, which made the question doubly appalling to his companion.

"Not for itself," returned the naturalist, sipping some of the water of the river from the hollow of his hand in order to clear his husky throat. "Not for itself, but exceedingly inasmuch as natural history has so deep a stake in my existence. Therefore—"

"Aye!" resumed the other, who mused too deeply to dissect the ideas of the doctor with his usual sagacity. " 'Tis in truth the history of natur', and a base and craven feeling it is! Now is life as precious to this young Pawnee as to any governor in the States, and he might save it, or at least stand some chance of saving it, by letting us go down the stream; and yet you see he keeps his faith manfully, and like an Indian warrior. For myself, I am old and willing to take the fortune that the Lord may see fit to give, nor do I conceit that you are of much benefit to mankind; and it is a crying shame, if not a sin, that so fine a youth as this should lose his scalp for two beings so worthless as ourselves. I am therefore disposed, provided that it shall prove agreeable to you, to tell the lad to make the best of his way and to leave us to the mercy of the Tetons."

"I repel the proposition as repugnant to nature and as treason to science!" exclaimed the alarmed naturalist. "Our progress is miraculous; and as this admirable invention moves with so wonderful a facility, a few more minutes will serve to bring us to land."

The old man regarded him intently for an instant, and shaking his head, he said, "Lord, what a thing is fear! It transforms the creatur's of the world and the craft of man, making that which is ugly seemly in our eyes, and that which is beautiful unsightly. Lord, Lord, what a thing is fear!"

A termination was, however, put to the discussion by the increasing interest of the chase. The horses of the Dakotas had by this time gained the middle of the current, and their riders were already filling the air with yells of triumph. At this moment Middleton and Paul, who had led the females to a little thicket, appeared again on the margin of the stream, menacing their enemies with the rifle.

"Mount, mount," shouted the trapper the instant he beheld them; "mount and fly if you value those who lean on you for help. Mount, and leave us in the hands of the Lord."

"Stoop your head, old trapper," returned the voice of Paul; "down with ye both into your nest. The Teton devil is in your line; down with your heads, and make way for a Kentucky bullet."

The old man turned his head and saw that the eager Mahtoree, who preceded his party some distance, had brought himself nearly in a line with the bark and the bee hunter, who stood perfectly ready to execute his hostile threat. Bending his body low, the rifle was discharged, and the swift lead whizzed harmlessly past him on its more distant errand. But the eye of the Teton chief was not less quick and certain than that of his enemy. He threw himself from his horse the moment preceding the report and sank into the water. The beast snorted with terror and anguish, throwing half his form out of the river in a desperate plunge. Then he was seen drifting away in the torrent, and dyeing the turbid waters with his blood.

The Teton chief soon reappeared on the surface, and understanding the nature of his loss, he swam with vigorous strokes to the nearest of the young men, who relinquished his steed as a matter of course to so renowned a warrior. The incident, however, created a confusion in the whole of the Dakota band, who appeared to await the intention of their leader before they renewed their efforts to reach the shore. In the meantime the vessel of skin had reached the land, and the fugitives were once more united on the margin of the river.

The savages were now swimming about in indecision, as a flock of pigeons is often seen to hover in confusion after receiving a heavy discharge into its leading column, apparently hesitating on the risk of storming a bank so formidably defended. The well-known precaution of Indian warfare prevailed, and Mahtoree, admonished by his recent adventure, led his warriors back to the shore from which they had come in order to relieve their beasts, which were already becoming unruly.

"Now, mount you with the tender ones and ride for yonder hillock," said the trapper; "beyond it you will find another stream, into which you must enter, and turning to the sun, follow its bed for a mile, until you reach a high and sandy plain; there will I meet you. Go; mount; this Pawnee youth and I, and my stout friend the physician, who is a desperate warrior, are men enough to keep the bank, seeing that show and not use is all that is needed."

Middleton and Paul saw no use in wasting their breath in remonstrances against this proposal. Glad to know that their rear was to be covered, even in this imperfect manner, they hastily got their horses in motion and soon disappeared on the required route. Some twenty or thirty minutes succeeded this movement before the Tetons on the opposite shore seemed inclined to enter on any new enterprise. Mahtoree was distinctly visible in the midst of his warriors, issuing his mandates and betraying his desire for vengeance by occasionally shaking an arm in the direction of the fugitives; but no step was taken which appeared to threaten any further act of immediate hostility. At length a yell arose among the savages, which announced the occurrence of some fresh event. Then Ishmael and his sluggish sons were seen in the distance, and soon the whole of the united force moved down to the very limits of the stream. The squatter proceeded to examine the position of his enemies with his usual coolness, and as if to try the power of his rifle, he sent a bullet among them with a force sufficient to do execution even at the distance at which he stood.

"Now let us depart!" exclaimed Obed, endeavoring to catch a furtive glimpse of the lead, which he fancied was whizzing at his very ear. "We have maintained the bank in a gallant manner for a sufficient length of time; quite as much military skill is to be displayed in a retreat as in an advance."

The old man cast a look behind him, and seeing that the equestrians had reached the cover of the hill, he made no objections to the proposal. The remaining horse was given to the doctor, with instructions to pursue the course just taken by Middleton and Paul. When the naturalist was mounted and in full retreat, the trapper and the young Pawnee stole from the spot in such a manner as to leave their enemies for some time in doubt as to their movements. Instead, however, of proceeding across the plain towards the hill, a route on which they must have been in open view, they took a shorter path, covered by the formation of the ground, and intersected the little watercourse at the point where Middleton had been directed to leave it, and just in season to join his party. The doctor had used so much diligence in the retreat as to have already overtaken his friends, and of course all the fugitives were again assembled.

The trapper now looked about him for some convenient spot where the whole party might halt, as he expressed it, for some five or six hours.

"Halt!" exclaimed the doctor when the alarming proposal reached his ears. "Venerable hunter, it would seem that on the contrary many days should be passed in industrious flight."

Middleton and Paul were both of this opinion, and each in his particular manner expressed as much.

The old man heard them with patience but shook his head like one who was unconvinced, and then answered all their arguments in one general and positive reply.

"Why should we fly?" he asked. "Can the legs of mortal men outstrip the speed of horses? Do you think the Tetons

will lie down and sleep; or will they cross the water and nose
for our trail? Thanks be to the Lord we have washed it well
in this stream, and if we leave the place with discretion and
wisdom we may yet throw them off its track. But a prairie
is not a wood. *There* a man may journey long, caring for
nothing but the prints his moccasin leaves, whereas on these
open plains a runner placed on yonder hill, for instance,
could see far on every side of him like a hovering hawk
looking down on his prey. No, no; night must come and
darkness be upon us afore we leave this spot. But listen to
the words of the Pawnee; he is a lad of spirit, and I warrant
me many is the hard race that he has run with the Sioux
bands. Does my brother think our trail is long enough?" he
demanded in the Indian tongue.

"Is a Teton a fish, that he can see it in the river?"

"But my young men think we should stretch it until it
reaches across the prairie."

"Mahtoree has eyes; he will see it."

"What does my brother counsel?"

The young warrior studied the heavens a moment and
appeared to hesitate. He mused some time with himself, and
then he replied, like one whose opinion was fixed: "The
Dakotas are not asleep," he said; "we must lie in the grass."

"Ah! This lad is of my mind," said the old man, briefly
explaining the opinion of his companion to his white friends.
Middleton was obliged to acquiesce, and as it was confessedly
dangerous to remain upon their feet, each one set about assisting in the means to be adopted for their security. Inez and
Ellen were quickly bestowed beneath the warm and not uncomfortable shelter of the buffalo skins, which formed a
thick covering; and tall grass was drawn over the place in
such a manner as to evade any examination from a common
eye. Paul and the Pawnee fettered the beasts and cast them
to the earth, where, after supplying them with food, they were
also left concealed in the fog of the prairie. No time was
lost when these several arrangements were completed before
each of the others sought a place of rest and concealment,
and then the plain appeared again deserted to its solitude.

The old man had advised his companions of the absolute
necessity of their continuing for hours in this concealment.
All their hopes of escape depended on the success of the
artifice. If they might elude the cunning of their pursuers by
this simple and therefore less suspected expedient, they could

renew their flight as the evening approached, and by changing their course, the chance of final success would be greatly increased. Influenced by these momentous considerations, the whole party lay musing on their situation until thoughts grew weary and sleep finally settled on them all, one after another.

The deepest silence had prevailed for hours when the quick ears of the trapper and the Pawnee were startled by a faint cry of surprise from Inez. Springing to their feet like men who were about to struggle for their lives, they found the vast plain, the rolling swells, the little hillock, and the scattered thickets covered alike in one white, dazzling sheet of snow.

"The Lord have mercy on ye all!" exclaimed the old man, regarding the prospect with a rueful eye. "Now, Pawnee, do I know the reason why you studied the clouds so closely; but it is too late; it is too late! A squirrel would leave his trail on this light coating of the 'arth. Ha! There come the imps to a certainty. Down with ye all, down with ye; your chance is but small, and yet it must not be willfully cast away."

The whole party was instantly concealed again, though many an anxious and stolen glance was directed through the tops of the grass on the movements of their enemies. At the distance of half a mile, the Teton band was seen riding in a circuit, which was gradually contracting itself, and evidently closing upon the very spot where the fugitives lay. There was but little difficulty in solving the mystery of this movement. The snow had fallen in time to assure them that those they sought were in their rear, and they were now employed, with the unwearied perseverance and patience of Indian warriors, in circling the certain boundaries of their place of concealment.

Each minute added to the jeopardy of the fugitives. Paul and Middleton deliberately prepared their rifles, and as the occupied Mahtoree came, at length, within fifty feet of them, keeping his eyes riveted on the grass through which he rode, they leveled them together and pulled the triggers. The effort was answered by the mere snapping of the locks.

"Enough," said the old man, rising with dignity; "I have cast away the priming, for certain death would follow your rashness. Now let us meet our fates like men. Cringing and complaining find no favor in Indian eyes."

His appearance was greeted by a yell that spread far and

wide over the plain, and in a moment a hundred savages were seen riding madly to the spot. Mahtoree received his prisoners with great self-restraint, though a single gleam of fierce joy broke through his clouded brow, and the heart of Middleton grew cold as he caught the expression of that eye, which the chief turned on the nearly insensible but still lovely Inez.

The exultation of receiving the white captives was so great as for a time to throw the dark and immovable form of their young Indian companion entirely out of view. He stood apart, disdaining to turn an eye on his enemies, as motionless as if he were frozen in that attitude of dignity and composure. But when a little time had passed, even this secondary object attracted the attention of the Tetons. Then it was that the trapper first learned, by the shout of triumph and the long-drawn yell of delight which burst at once from a hundred throats, as well as by the terrible name which filled the air, that his youthful friend was no other than that redoubtable and hitherto invincible warrior Hard Heart.

CHAPTER 25

What, are ancient Pistol and you friends, yet?
SHAKESPEARE

THE CURTAIN OF our imperfect drama must fall to rise upon another scene. The time is advanced several days, during which very material changes had occurred in the situation of the actors. The hour is noon, and the place an elevated plain that rose, at no great distance from the water, somewhat abruptly from a fertile bottom which stretched along the margin of one of the numberless watercourses of that region. The river took its rise near the base of the Rocky Mountains, and after washing a vast extent of plain, it mingled its waters with a still-larger stream to become finally lost in the turbid current of the Missouri.

The landscape was changed materially for the better, though the hand which had impressed so much of the desert on the surrounding region had laid a portion of its power on this spot. The appearance of vegetation was, however, less discouraging than in the more sterile wastes of the rolling prairies. Clusters of trees were scattered in greater profusion, and a long outline of ragged forest marked the northern boundary of the view. Here and there on the bottom were to be seen the evidences of a hasty and imperfect culture of such indigenous vegetables as were of a quick growth and which were known to flourish without the aid of art in deep and alluvial soils. On the very edge of what might be called the tableland were pitched the hundred lodges of a horde of wandering Siouxes. Their light tenements were arranged without the least attention to order. Proximity to the water seemed to be the only consideration which had been consulted in their disposition, nor had even this important convenience been always regarded. While most of the lodges stood along the brow of the plain, many were to be seen at greater distances, occupying such places as had first pleased the capricious eyes of their untutored owners. The encampment was not military nor in the slightest degree protected from surprise by its position or defenses. It was open on every side, and on every side as accessible as any other point in those wastes if the imperfect and natural obstruction offered by the river be excepted. In short, the place bore the appearance of having been tenanted longer than its occupants had originally intended, while it was not wanting in the signs of readiness for a hasty or even a compelled departure.

This was the temporary encampment of that portion of his people who had long been hunting under the direction of Mahtoree on those grounds which separated the stationary abodes of his nation from those of the warlike tribes of the Pawnees. The lodges were tents of skin, high, conical, and of the most simple and primitive construction. The shield, the quiver, the lance, and the bow of its master were to be seen suspended from a light post before the opening or door of each habitation. The different domestic implements of his one, two, or three wives, as the brave was of greater or lesser renown, were carelessly thrown at its side, and here and there the round, full, patient countenance of an infant might be found peeping from its comfortless wrappers of bark, as, suspended by a deerskin thong from the same post, it rocked in the passing air. Children of a larger growth were tumbling over each other in piles, the males, even at that early age, making themselves distinguished for that species of domination which, in afterlife, was to mark the vast distinction between the sexes. Youths were in the bottom, essaying their juvenile powers in curbing the wild steeds of their fathers, while here and there a truant girl was to be seen stealing from her labors to admire their fierce and impatient daring.

Thus far the picture was the daily exhibition of an encampment confident in its security. But immediately in front of the lodges was a gathering that seemed to forebode some movements of more than usual interest. A few of the withered and remorseless crones of the band were clustering together in readiness to lend their fell voices if needed to aid in exciting their descendants to an exhibition which their depraved tastes coveted, as the luxurious Roman dame witnessed the struggles and the agony of the gladiator. The men were subdivided into groups, assorted according to the deeds and reputations of the several individuals of whom they were composed.

They who were of that equivocal age which admitted them to the hunts, while their discretion was still too doubtful to permit them to be trusted on the warpath, hung around the skirts of the whole, catching from the fierce models before them that gravity of demeanor and restraint of manner which in time was to become so deeply ingrafted in their own characters. A few of the still older class, and who had heard the whoop in anger, were a little more presuming, pressing nigher to the chiefs, though far from presuming to mingle in their councils, sufficiently distinguished by being permitted to catch the wisdom which fell from lips so venerated. The ordinary warriors of the band were still less diffident, not hesitating to mingle among the chiefs of lesser note, though far from assuming the right to dispute the sentiments of any established brave or to call in question the prudence of measures that were recommended by the more gifted counselors of the nation.

Among the chiefs themselves there was a singular compound of exterior. They were divided into two classes, those who were mainly indebted for their influence to physical causes and to deeds in arms, and those who had become distinguished rather for their wisdom than for their services in the field. The former was by far the most numerous and the most important class. They were men of stature and mien whose stern countenances were often rendered doubly imposing by those evidences of their valor which had been roughly traced on their lineaments by the hands of their enemies. That class which had gained its influence by a moral ascendancy was extremely limited. They were uniformly to be distinguished by the quick and lively expression of their eyes, by the air of distrust that marked their movements, and occasionally by the vehemence of their utterance in those sudden outbreakings of the mind by which their present consultations were from time to time distinguished.

In the very center of a ring formed by these chosen counselors was to be seen the person of the disquieted but seemingly calm Mahtoree. There was a conjunction of all the several qualities of the others in his person and character. Mind as well as matter had contributed to establish his authority. His scars were as numerous and deep as those of the whitest head in his nation, his limbs were in their greatest vigor, his courage at its fullest height. Endowed with this rare combination of moral and physical influence, the keenest eye in all that assembly was wont to lower before his threatening glance. Courage and cunning had established his ascendancy, and it had been rendered in some degree sacred by time. He knew so well how to unite the powers of reason and force that in a state of society which admitted of a greater display of his energies, the Teton would in all probability have been both a conqueror and a despot.

A little apart from the gathering of the band was to be seen a set of beings of an entirely different origin. Taller and far more muscular in their persons, the lingering vestiges of their Saxon and Norman ancestry were yet to be found beneath the swarthy complexions which had been bestowed by an American sun. It would have been a curious investigation for one skilled in such an inquiry to have traced those points of difference by which the offspring of the most western European was still to be distinguished from the descendant of the most remote Asiatic, now that the two, in the revolutions of the world, were approximating in their habits, their residence, and not a little in their characters. The group of whom we write was composed of the family of the squatter. They stood indolent, lounging, and inert as usual when no immediate demand was made on their dormant energies, clustered in front of some four or five habitations of skin for which they were indebted to the hospitality of their Teton allies. The terms of their unexpected confederation were sufficiently explained by the presence of the horses and domestic cattle that were quietly grazing on the bottom beneath, under the jealous eyes of the spirited Hetty. Their wagons were drawn about the lodges in a sort of irregular barrier, which at once manifested that their confidence was not entirely restored, while, on the other hand, their policy or indolence prevented any very positive exhibition of distrust. There was a singular union of passive enjoyment and of dull curiosity slumbering in every dull countenance as each of the party stood leaning on his rifle regarding the movements of the Sioux conference. Still no sign of expectation or interest escaped from the youngest among them, the whole appearing to emulate the most phlegmatic of their savage allies in an exhibition of patience. They rarely spoke, and when they did it was in some short and contemptuous remark which served to put the physical superiority of a white man and that of an Indian in a sufficiently striking point of view. In short, the family of Ishmael appeared now to be in the plenitude of an enjoyment which depended on inactivity but which was not entirely free from certain confused glimmerings of a perspective in which their security stood in some little danger of a rude interruption from Teton treachery. Abiram alone formed a solitary exception to this state of equivocal repose.

After a life passed in the commission of a thousand mean and insignificant villainies, the mind of the kidnapper had become hardy enough to attempt the desperate adventure which has been laid before the reader in the course of the narrative. His influence over the bolder but less active spirit of Ishmael was far from great, and had not the latter been suddenly expelled a fertile bottom, of which he had taken possession with intent to keep it without much deference to the forms of law, he would never have succeeded in enlisting the husband of his sister in an enterprise that required so much decision and forethought. Their original success and subsequent disappointment have been seen; and Abiram now sat apart plotting the means by which he might secure to himself the advantages of his undertaking, which he perceived were each moment becoming more uncertain through the open admiration of Mahtoree for the innocent subject of his villainy. We shall leave him to his vacillating and confused expedients in order to pass to the description of certain other personages in the drama.

There was still another corner of the picture that was occupied. On a little bank at the extreme right of the encampment lay the forms of Middleton and Paul. Their limbs were painfully bound with thongs cut from the skin of a bison, while, by a sort of refinement in cruelty, they were so placed that each could see a reflection of his own misery in the case of his neighbor. Within a dozen yards of them a post was set firmly in the ground, and against it was bound the light and Apollo-like person of Hard Heart. Between the two stood the trapper, deprived of his rifle, his pouch, and his horn, but otherwise left in a sort of contemptuous liberty. Some five or six young warriors, however, with quivers at their backs and long tough bows dangling from their shoulders, who stood with grave watchfulness at no great distance from the spot, sufficiently proclaimed how fruitless any attempt to escape on the part of one so aged and so feeble might prove. Unlike the other spectators of the important conference, these individuals were engaged in a discourse that for them contained an interest of its own.

"Captain," said the bee hunter with an expression of comical concern that no misfortune could depress in one of his buoyant feelings, "do you really find that accursed strap of untanned leather cutting into your shoulder, or is it only the tickling in my own arm that I feel?"

"When the spirit suffers so deeply, the body is insensible to pain," returned the more refined, though scarcely so spirited Middleton; "would to heaven that some of my trusty artillerists might fall upon this accursed encampment!"

"You might as well wish that these Teton lodges were so many hives of hornets, and that the insects would come forth and battle with yonder tribe of half-naked savages." Then, chuckling with his own conceit, the bee hunter turned away from his companion and sought a momentary relief from his misery by imagining that so wild an idea might be realized and fancying the manner in which the attack would upset even the well-established patience of an Indian.

Middleton was glad to be silent; but the old man, who had listened to their words, drew a little nigher and continued the discourse.

"Here is likely to be a merciless and a hellish business!" he said, shaking his head in a manner to prove that even his experience was at a loss for a remedy in so trying a dilemma. "Our Pawnee friend is already staked for the torture, and I well know, by the eye and the countenance of the great Sioux, that he is leading on the temper of his people to further enormities."

"Harkee, old trapper," said Paul, writhing in his bonds to catch a glimpse of the other's melancholy face; "you are

skilled in Indian tongues and know somewhat of Indian deviltries. Go you to the council and tell their chiefs in my name,
that is to say, in the name of Paul Hover, of the state of
Kentucky, that provided they will guarantee the safe return
of one Ellen Wade into the States, they are welcome to take
his scalp when and in such manner as best suits their amuse-
ments; or, if so be they will not trade on these conditions, you
may throw in an hour or two of torture beforehand in order
to sweeten the bargain to their damnable appetites."

"Ah! Lad, it is little they would hearken to such an offer,
knowing, as they do, that you are already like a bear in a
trap, as little able to fight as to fly. But be not downhearted,
for the color of a white man is sometimes his death warrant
among these far tribes of savages, and sometimes his shield.
Though they love us not, cunning often ties their hands.
Could the red nations work their will, trees would shortly be
growing again on the plowed fields of America, and woods
would be whitened with Christian bones. No one can
doubt that, who knows the quality of the love which a redskin bears a paleface; but they have counted our numbers
until their memories fail them, and they are not without their
policy. Therefore is our fate unsettled, but I fear me there is
small hope left for the Pawnee!"

As the old man concluded, he walked slowly towards the
subject of his latter observation, taking his post at no great
distance from his side. Here he stood, observing such a silence
and mien as became him to manifest to a chief so renowned
and so situated as his captive associate. But the eye of
Hard Heart was fastened on the distance, and his whole air
was that of one whose thoughts were entirely removed from
the present scene.

"The Siouxes are in council on my brother," the trapper at
length observed, when he found he could only attract the
other's attention by speaking.

The young partisan turned his head with a calm smile as
he answered, "They are counting the scalps over the lodge of
Hard Heart!"

"No doubt, no doubt; their tempers begin to mount as
they remember the number of Tetons you have struck, and
better would it be for you now had more of your days been
spent in chasing the deer, and fewer on the warpath. Then
some childless mother of this tribe might take you in the

place of her lost son, and your time would be filled in peace."

"Does my father think that a warrior can ever die? The Master of Life does not open his hand to take away his gifts again. When he wants his young men he calls them, and they go. But the redskin he has once breathed on lives forever."

"Aye, this is a more comfortable and a more humble faith than that which yonder heartless Teton harbors! There is something in these Loups which opens my inmost heart to them; they seem to have the courage, aye, and the honesty too, of the Delawares of the hills. And this lad—it is wonderful, it is very wonderful; but the age, and the eye, and the limbs are as if they might have been brothers! Tell me, Pawnee, have you ever in your traditions heard of a mighty people who once lived on the shores of the salt lake, hard by the rising sun?"

"The earth is white, by people of the color of my father."

"Nay, nay, I speak not now of any strollers who have crept into the land to rob the lawful owners of their birthright, but of a people who are, or rather were, what with nature and what with paint, red as the berry on the bush."

"I have heard the old men say that there were bands who hid themselves in the woods under the rising sun because they dared not come upon the open prairies to fight with men."

"Do not your traditions tell you of the greatest, the bravest, and the wisest nation of redskins that the Wahcondah has ever breathed upon?"

Hard Heart raised his head with a loftiness and dignity that even his bonds could not repress as he answered, "Has age blinded my father, or does he see so many Siouxes that he believes there are no longer any Pawnees?"

"Ah! Such is mortal vanity and pride!" exclaimed the disappointed old man in English. "Natur' is as strong in a redskin as in the bosom of a man of white gifts. Now would a Delaware conceit himself far mightier than a Pawnee, just as a Pawnee boasts himself to be of the princes of the 'arth. And so it was atween the Frenchers of the Canadas and the red-coated English that the king did use to send into the States when states they were not, but outcrying and petitioning provinces; they fought and they fought, and what marvelous boastings did they give forth to the world of their own valor and victories, while both parties forgot to name the humble soldier of the land who did the real service, but who, as he was not privileged then to smoke at the great council fire of his nation, seldom heard of his deeds after they were once bravely done."

When the old man had thus given vent to the nearly dormant, but far from extinct, military pride that had so unconsciously led him into the very error he deprecated, his eye, which had begun to quicken and glimmer with some of the ardor of his youth, softened and turned its anxious look on the devoted captive, whose countenance was also restored to its former cold look of abstraction and thought.

"Young warrior," he continued in a voice that was growing tremulous, "I have never been father_ or brother. The Wahcondah made me to live alone. He never tied my heart to house or field by the cords with which the men of my race are bound to their lodges; if he had, I should not have journeyed so far and seen so much. But I have tarried long among a people who lived in those woods you mention, and much reason did I find to imitate their courage and love their honesty. The Master of Life has made us all, Pawnee, with a feeling for our kind. I never was a father, but well do I know what is the love of one. You are like a lad I valued, and I had even begun to fancy that some of his blood might be in your veins. But what matters that? You are a true man, as I know by the way in which you keep your faith; and honesty is a gift too rare to be forgotten. My heart yearns to you, boy, and gladly would I do you good."

The youthful warrior listened to the words which came from the lips of the other with a force and simplicity that established their truth, and he bowed his head on his naked bosom in testimony of the respect with which he met the proffer. Then lifting his dark eye to the level of the view, he seemed to be again considering of things removed from every personal consideration. The trapper, who well knew how high the pride of a warrior would sustain him in those moments he believed to be his last, awaited the pleasure of his young friend with a meekness and patience that he had acquired by his association with that remarkable race. At length the gaze of the Pawnee began to waver; and then quick, flashing glances were turned from the countenance of the old man to the air, and from the air to his deeply marked lineaments again, as if the spirit, which governed their movements, was beginning to be troubled.

"Father," the young brave finally answered in a voice of confidence and kindness, "I have heard your words. They have gone in at my ears and are now within me. The white-headed Long Knife has no son; the Hard Heart of the Pawnees is young, but he is already the oldest of his family. He found the bones of his father on the hunting ground of the Osages, and he has sent them to the prairies of the Good Spirits. No doubt the great chief, his father, has seen them and knows what is part of himself. But the Wahcondah will soon call to us both, you because you have seen all that is to be seen in this country, and Hard Heart because he has need of a warrior who is young. There is no time for the Pawnee to show the paleface the duty that a son owes to his father."

"Old as I am, and miserable and helpless as I now stand, to what I once was, I may live to see the sun go down in the prairie. Does my son expect to do as much?"

"The Tetons are counting the scalps on my lodge!" returned the young chief with a smile whose melancholy was singularly illuminated by a gleam of triumph.

"And they find them many. Too many for the safety of its owner while he is in their revengeful hands. My son is not a woman, and he looks on the path he is about to travel with a steady eye. Has he nothing to whisper in the ears of his people before he starts? These legs are old, but they may yet carry me to the forks of the Loup River."

"Tell them that Hard Heart has tied a knot in his wampum for every Teton!" burst from the lips of the captive with that vehemence with which sudden passion is known to break through the barriers of artificial restraint. "If he meets one of them all in the prairies of the Master of Life his heart will become Sioux!"

"Ah! That feeling would be a dangerous companion for a man with white gifts to start with on so solemn a journey," muttered the old man in English. "This is not what the good Moravians said to the councils of the Delawares, nor what is so often preached to the whiteskins in the settlements, though, to the shame of the color be it said, it is so little heeded. Pawnee, I love you; but being a Christian man, I cannot be the runner to bear such a message."

"If my father is afraid the Tetons will hear him, let him whisper it softly to our old men."

"As for fear, young warrior, it is no more the shame of a paleface than of a redskin. The Wahcondah teaches us to love the life he gives; but it is as men love their hunts, and their dogs, and their carbines, and not with the doting that a mother looks upon her infant. The Master of Life will not have to speak aloud twice when he calls my name. I am as ready to answer to it now as I shall be tomorrow or at any time it may please his mighty will. But what is a warrior without his traditions? Mine forbid me to carry your words."

The chief made a dignified motion of assent, and here there was great danger that those feelings of confidence which had been so singularly awakened would as suddenly subside. But the heart of the old man had been too sensibly touched, through long dormant but still living recollections, to break off the communication so rudely. He pondered for a minute, and then bending his look wistfully on his young associate, again continued, "Each warrior must be judged by his gifts. I have told my son what I cannot, but let him open his ears to what I can do. An elk shall not measure the prairie much swifter than these old legs if the Pawnee will give me a message that a white man may bear."

"Let the paleface listen," returned the other after hesitating a single instant longer, under a lingering sensation of his former disappointment. "He will stay here till the Siouxes have done counting the scalps of their dead warriors. He will wait until they have tried to cover the heads of eighteen Tetons with the skin of one Pawnee; he will open his eyes wide, that he may see the place where they bury the bones of a warrior."

"All this will I, and may I, do, noble boy."

"He will mark the spot, that he may know it."

"No fear, no fear that I shall forget the place," interrupted the other, whose fortitude began to give way under so trying an exhibition of calmness and resignation.

"Then I know that my father will go to my people. His head is gray, and his words will not be blown away with the smoke. Let him get on my lodge and call the name of Hard Heart aloud. No Pawnee will be deaf. Then let my father ask for the colt that has never been ridden, but which is sleeker than the buck and swifter than the elk."

"I understand you, boy, I understand you," interrupted

the attentive old man; "and what you say shall be done, aye, and well done too, or I'm but little skilled in the wishes of a dying Indian."

"And when my young men have given my father the halter of that colt, he will lead him by a crooked path to the grave of Hard Heart?"

"Will I! Aye, that I will, brave youth, though the winter covers these plains in banks of snow and the sun is hidden as much by day as by night. To the head of the holy spot will I lead the beast, and place him with his eyes looking towards the setting sun."

"And my father will speak to him, and tell him that the master who has fed him since he was foaled has now need of him."

"That too will I do; though the Lord, he knows that I shall hold discourse with a horse, not with any vain conceit that my words will be understood, but only to satisfy the cravings of Indian superstition. Hector, my pup, what think *you*, dog, of talking to a horse?"

"Let the graybeard speak to him with the tongue of a Pawnee," interrupted the young victim, perceiving that his companion had used an unknown language for the preceding speech.

"My son's will shall be done. And with these old hands, which I had hoped had nearly done with bloodshed, whether it be of man or beast, will I slay the animal on your grave!"

"It is good," returned the other, a gleam of satisfaction flitting across his features. "Hard Heart will ride his horse to the blessed prairies, and he will come before the Master of Life like a chief!"

The sudden and striking change which instantly occurred in the countenance of the Indian caused the trapper to look aside, when he perceived that the conference of the Siouxes had ended and that Mahtoree, attended by one or two of the principal warriors, was deliberately approaching his intended victim.

CHAPTER 26

I am not prone to weeping, as our sex
Commonly are.
　　　But I have that honorable
Grief lodged here, which burns worse than
Tears drown.

SHAKESPEARE

WHEN WITHIN TWENTY feet of the prisoners, the Tetons stopped, and their leader made a sign to the old man to draw nigh. The trapper obeyed, quitting the young Pawnee with a significant look, which was received, as it was meant, for an additional pledge that he would never forget his promise. So soon as Mahtoree found that the other had stopped within reach of him, he stretched forth his arm, and laying a hand upon the shoulder of the attentive old man, he stood regarding him a minute with eyes that seemed willing to penetrate the recesses of his most secret thoughts.

"Is a paleface always made with two tongues?" he demanded, when he found that, as usual with the subject of this examination, he was as little intimidated by his present frown as moved by any apprehensions of the future.

"Honesty lies deeper than the skin."

"It is so. Now let my father hear me. Mahtoree has but one tongue, the grayhead has many. They may be all straight, and none of them forked. A Sioux is no more than a Sioux, but a paleface is everything! He can talk to the Pawnee, and the Konza, and the Omaha, and he can talk to his own people."

"Aye, there are linguisters in the settlements that can do still more. But what profits it all? The Master of Life has an ear for every language!"

"The grayhead has done wrong. He has said one thing when he meant another. He has looked before him with his eyes, and behind him with his mind. He has ridden the horse of a Sioux too hard; he has been the friend of a Pawnee, and the enemy of my people."

"Teton, I am your prisoner. Though my words are white, they will not complain. Act your will."

"No. Mahtoree will not make a white hair red. My father is free. The prairie is open on every side of him. But before

293

the grayhead turns his back on the Siouxes, let him look well at them, that he may tell his own chief how great is a Dakota!"

"I am not in a hurry to go on my path. You see a man with a white head, and no woman, Teton; therefore shall I not run myself out of breath to tell the nations of the prairies what the Siouxes are doing."

"It is good. My father has smoked with the chiefs at many councils," returned Mahtoree, who now thought himself sufficiently sure of the other's favor to go more directly to his object. "Mahtoree will speak with the tongue of his very dear friend and father. A young paleface will listen when an old man of that nation opens his mouth. Go; my father will make what a poor Indian says fit for a white ear."

"Speak aloud!" said the trapper, who readily understood the metaphorical manner in which the Teton expressed a desire that he should become an interpreter of his words into the English language. "Speak; my young men listen. Now, captain, and you too, friend bee hunter, prepare yourselves to meet the deviltries of this savage with the stout hearts of white warriors. If you find yourselves giving way under his threats, just turn your eyes on that noble-looking Pawnee, whose time is measured with a hand as niggardly as that with which a trader in the towns gives forth the fruits of the Lord, inch by inch, in order to satisfy his covetousness. A single look at the boy will set you both up in resolution."

"My brother has turned his eyes on the wrong path," interrupted Mahtoree with a complacency that betrayed how unwilling he was to offend his intended interpreter.

"The Dakota will speak to my young men?"

"After he has sung in the ear of the flower of the palefaces."

"The Lord forgive the desperate villain!" exclaimed the old man in English. "There are none so tender, or so young, or so innocent as to escape his ravenous wishes. But hard words and cold looks will profit nothing; therefore it will be wise to speak him fair. Let Mahtoree open his mouth."

"Would my father cry out that the women and children should hear the wisdom of chiefs? We will go into the lodge and whisper."

As the Teton ended, he pointed significantly towards a tent, vividly emblazoned with the history of one of his own boldest and most commended exploits, and which stood a little apart from the rest, as if to denote it was the residence of some privileged individual of the band. The shield and quiver at its entrance were richer than common, and the high distinction of a fusee attested the importance of its proprietor. In every other particular it was rather distinguished by signs of poverty than of wealth. The domestic utensils were fewer in number and simpler in their forms than those to be seen about the openings of the meanest lodges, nor was there a single one of those highly prized articles of civilized life which were occasionally bought of the traders in bargains that bore so hard on the ignorant natives. All these had been bestowed, as they had been acquired, by the generous chief on his subordinates to purchase an influence that might render him the master of their lives and persons, a species of wealth that was certainly more noble in itself and far dearer to his ambition.

The old man well knew this to be the lodge of Mahtoree, and in obedience to the sign of the chief, he held his way towards it with slow and reluctant steps. But there were others present who were equally interested in the approaching conference, whose apprehensions were not to be so easily suppressed. The watchful eyes and jealous ears of Middleton had taught him enough to fill his soul with horrible forebodings. With an incredible effort he succeeded in gaining his feet, and called aloud to the retiring trapper, "I conjure you, old man, if the love you bore my parents was more than words, or if the love you bear your God is that of a Christian man, utter not a syllable that may wound the ear of that innocent—"

Exhausted in spirit and fettered in limbs, he then fell like an animate log to the earth, where he lay like one dead.

Paul had, however, caught the clue, and completed the exhortation in his peculiar manner.

"Harkee, old trapper," he shouted, vainly endeavoring at the same time to make a gesture of defiance with his hand; "if you are about to play the interpreter, speak such words to the ears of that damnable savage as becomes a white man to use and a heathen to hear. Tell him from me that if he does or says the thing that is uncivil to the girl called Nelly Wade, that I'll curse him with my dying breath, that I'll pray for all good Christians in Kentucky to curse him, sitting and standing, eating and drinking, fighting, praying, or at horse races, indoors and outdoors, in summer or winter or in the month of March; in short, I'll—aye, it are a fact, morally true—I'll haunt him if the ghost of a paleface can contrive to lift itself from a grave made by the hands of a redskin!"

Having thus ventured the most terrible denunciation he could devise, and the one which, in the eyes of the honest bee hunter, there seemed the greatest likelihood of his being able to put in execution, he was obliged to await the fruits of his threat with that resignation which would be apt to govern a western borderman who, in addition to the prospects just named, had the advantage of contemplating them in fetters and bondage. We shall not detain the narrative to relate the quaint morals with which he next endeavored to cheer the drooping spirits of his more sensitive companion, or the occasional pithy and peculiar benedictions that he pronounced on all the bands of the Dakotas, commencing with those whom he accused of stealing or murdering on the banks of the distant Mississippi and concluding, in terms of suitable energy, with the Teton tribe. The latter more than once received from his lips curses as sententious and as complicated as that celebrated anathema of the church, for a knowledge of which most unlettered Protestants are indebted to the pious researches of the worthy Tristram Shandy. But as Middleton recovered from his exhaustion he was fain to appease the boisterous temper of his associate by admonishing him of the uselessness of such denunciations and of the possibility of their hastening the very evil he deprecated by irritating the resentments of a race who were sufficiently fierce and lawless, even in their most pacific moods.

In the meantime the trapper and the Sioux chief pursued their way to the lodge. The former had watched with painful interest the expression of Mahtoree's eyes while the words of Middleton and Paul were pursuing their footsteps; but the mien of the Indian was far too much restrained and self-guarded to permit the smallest of his emotions to escape through any of those ordinary outlets by which the condition of the human volcano is commonly betrayed. His look was fastened on the little habitation they approached, and for the moment his thoughts appeared to brood alone on the purposes of this extraordinary visit.

The appearance of the interior of the lodge corresponded with its exterior. It was larger than most of the others, more finished in its form, and finer in its materials; but there its superiority ceased. Nothing could be more simple and republican than the form of living that the ambitious and powerful Teton chose to exhibit to the eyes of his people. A choice collection of weapons for the chase, and three or four medals, bestowed by the traders and political agents of the Canadas as a homage to, or rather as an acknowledgment of, his rank, with a few of the most indispensable articles of personal accommodation composed its furniture. It abounded in neither venison nor the wild beef of the prairies, its crafty owner having well understood that the liberality of a single individual would be abundantly rewarded by the daily contributions of a band. Although as preeminent in the chase as in war, a deer or a buffalo was never seen to enter whole into his lodge. In return, an animal was rarely brought into the encampment that did not contribute to support the family of Mahtoree. But the policy of the chief seldom permitted more to remain than sufficed for the wants of the day, perfectly assured that all must suffer before hunger, the bane of savage life, could lay its fell fangs on so important a victim.

Immediately beneath the favorite bow of the chief, and encircled in a sort of magical ring of spears, shields, lances, and arrows, all of which had in their time done good service, was suspended the mysterious and sacred medicine bag. It was highly wrought in wampum and profusely ornamented with beads and porcupines' quills, after the most cunning devices of Indian ingenuity. The peculiar freedom of Mahtoree's religious creed has been more than once intimated, and by a singular species of contradiction, he appeared to have lavished his attentions on this emblem of a supernatural agency in a degree that was precisely inverse to his faith. It was merely the manner in which the Sioux imitated the well-known expedient of the Pharisees, "in order that they might be seen of men."

The tent had not, however, been entered by its owner since his return from the recent expedition. As the reader has already anticipated, it had been made the prison of Inez and Ellen. The bride of Middleton was seated on a simple couch of sweet-scented herbs covered with skins. She had already suffered so much and witnessed so many wild and unlooked-for events within the short space of her captivity that every additional misfortune fell with a diminished force on her seemingly devoted head. Her cheeks were bloodless, her dark and usually animated eye was contracted in an expression of settled concern, and her form appeared shrinking and sensitive, nearly to extinction. But in the midst of these evidences of natural weakness, there were at times such an air of pious resignation, such gleams of meek but holy hope lighting her countenance, as might well have rendered it a question whether the hapless captive was most a subject of pity or of admiration. All the precepts of Father Ignatius were riveted in her faithful memory, and not a few of his pious visions were floating before her imagination. Sustained by so sacred resolutions, the mild, the patient, and the confiding girl was bowing her head to this new stroke of Providence with the same sort of meekness as she would have submitted to any other prescribed penitence for her sins, though nature, at moments, warred powerfully with so compelled a humility.

On the other hand, Ellen had exhibited far more of the woman, and consequently of the passions of the world. She had wept until her eyes were swollen and red. Her cheeks were flushed and angry, and her whole mien was distinguished by an air of spirit and resentment that was not a little, however, qualified by apprehensions for the future. In short, there was that about the eye and step of the betrothed of Paul which gave a warranty that should happier times arrive, and the constancy of the bee hunter finally meet with its reward, he would possess a partner every way worthy to cope with his own thoughtless and buoyant temperament.

There was still another and a third figure in that little knot of females. It was the youngest, the most highly gifted, and until now the most favored of the wives of the Teton. Her charms had not been without the most powerful attraction in the eyes of her husband until they had so unexpectedly opened on the surpassing loveliness of a woman of the pale-faces. From that hapless moment the graces, the attachment, the fidelity of the young Indian had lost their power to please. Still the complexion of Tachechana, though less dazzling than that of her rival, was, for her race, clear and healthy. Her hazel eye had the sweetness and playfulness of the antelope's, her voice was soft and joyous as the song of the wren, and her happy laugh was the very melody of the forest. Of all the Sioux girls, Tachechana (or the Fawn) was the lightest hearted and the most envied. Her father had been a distinguished brave, and her brothers had already left their bones on a distant and dreary warpath. Numberless were the warriors who had sent presents to the lodge of her parents, but none of them were listened to until a messenger from the great Mahtoree had come. She was his third wife, it is true, but she was confessedly the most favored of them all. Their union had existed but two short seasons, and its fruits now lay sleeping at her feet, wrapped in the customary ligatures of skin and bark which form the swaddlings of an Indian infant.

At the moment when Mahtoree and the trapper arrived at the opening of the lodge, the young Sioux wife was seated on a simple stool, turning her soft eyes with looks that varied, like her emotions, with love and wonder, from the unconscious child to those rare beings who had filled her youthful and uninstructed mind with so much admiration and astonishment. Though Inez and Ellen had passed an entire day in her sight, it seemed as if the longings of her curiosity were increasing with each new gaze. She regarded them as beings of an entirely different nature and condition from the females of the prairies. Even the mystery of their complicated attire had its secret influence on her simple mind, though it was the grace and charms of sex, to which nature has made every people so sensible, that most attracted her admiration. But while her ingenuous disposition freely admitted the superiority of the strangers over the less brilliant attractions of the Dakota maidens, she had seen no reason to deprecate their advantages. The visit that she was now about to receive was the first which her husband had made to the tent since his return from the recent inroad, and he was ever present to her thoughts as a successful warrior who was not ashamed in the moments of inaction to admit the softer feelings of a father and a husband.

We have everywhere endeavored to show that while Mahtoree was in all essentials a warrior of the prairies, he was much in advance of his people in those acquirements which announce the dawnings of civilization. He had held frequent communion with the traders and troops of the Canadas, and the intercourse had unsettled many of those wild opinions which were his birthright, without perhaps substituting any others of a nature sufficiently definite to be profitable. His reasoning was rather subtle than true, and his philosophy far more audacious than profound. Like thousands of more enlightened beings who fancy they are able to go through the trials of human existence without any other support than their own resolutions, his morals were accommodating and his motives selfish. These several characteristics will be understood always with reference to the situation of the Indian, though little apology is needed for finding resemblances between men who essentially possess the same nature, however it may be modified by circumstances.

Notwithstanding the presence of Inez and Ellen, the entrance of the Teton warrior into the lodge of his favorite wife was made with the tread and mien of a master. The step of his moccasin was noiseless, but the rattling of his bracelets and of the silver ornaments of his leggings sufficed to announce his approach as he pushed aside the skin covering of the opening of the tent and stood in the presence of its inmates. A faint cry of pleasure burst from the lips of Tachechana in the suddenness of her surprise, but the emotion was instantly suppressed in that subdued demeanor which should characterize a matron of her tribe. Instead of returning the stolen glance of his youthful and secretly rejoicing wife, Mahtoree moved to the couch occupied by his prisoners and placed himself in the haughty upright attitude of an Indian chief before their eyes. The old man had glided past him and already taken a position suited to the office he had been commanded to fill.

Surprise kept the females silent and nearly breathless. Though accustomed to the sight of savage warriors in the horrid panoply of their terrible profession, there was something so startling in the entrance and so audacious in the inexplicable look of their conqueror that the eyes of both sank to the earth under a feeling of terror and embarrassment. Then Inez recovered herself, and addressing the trapper, she demanded with the dignity of an offended gentlewoman, though with her accustomed grace, to what circumstance they owed this extraordinary and unexpected visit. The old man hesitated, but clearing his throat like one who was about to make an effort to which he was little used, he ventured on the following reply: "Lady," he said, "a savage is a savage, and you are not to look for the uses and formalities of the settlements on a bleak and windy prairie. As these Indians would say, fashions and courtesies are things so light that they would blow away. As for myself, though a man of the forest, I have seen the ways of the great in my time, and I am not to learn that they differ from the ways of the lowly. I was long a serving man in my youth, not one of your beck-and-nod runners about a household, but a man that went through the servitude of the forest with his officer, and well do I know in what manner to approach the wife of a captain. Now, had I the ordering of this visit, I would first have hemmed aloud at the door in order that you might hear that strangers were coming, and then I——"

"The manner is indifferent," interrupted Inez, too anxious to await the prolix explanations of the old man; "why is the visit made?"

"Therein shall the savage speak for himself. The daughters of the palefaces wish to know why the great Teton has come into his lodge."

Mahtoree regarded his interrogator with a surprise which showed how extraordinary he deemed the question. Then placing himself in a posture of condescension, after a moment's delay he answered, "Sing in the ears of the dark-eye. Tell her the lodge of Mahtoree is very large and that it is not full. She shall find room in it, and none shall be greater than she. Tell the light-hair that she too may stay in the lodge of a brave and eat of his venison. Mahtoree is a great chief. His hand is never shut."

"Teton," returned the trapper, shaking his head in evidence of the strong disapprobation with which he heard this language, "the tongue of a redskin must be colored white before it can make music in the ears of a paleface. Should your words be spoken, my daughters would shut their ears, and Mahtoree would seem a trader to their eyes. Now listen to what comes from a grayhead, and then speak accordingly. My people is a mighty people. The sun rises on their eastern and sets on their western border. The land is filled with bright-eyed and laughing girls, like these you see—aye, Teton, I tell no lie"—observing his auditor to start with an air of distrust—"bright-eyed and pleasant to behold, as these before you."

"Has my father a hundred wives?" interrupted the savage, laying his finger on the shoulder of the trapper with a look of curious interest in the reply.

"No, Dakota. The Master of Life has said to me, live alone; your lodge shall be the forest; the roof of your wigwam the clouds. But though never bound in the secret faith which in my nation ties one man to one woman, often have I seen the workings of that kindness which brings the two together. Go into the regions of my people; you will see the daughters of the land fluttering through the towns like many-colored

and joyful birds in the season of blossoms. You will meet
them singing and rejoicing along the great paths of the country, and you will hear the woods ringing with their laughter.
They are very excellent to behold, and the young men find
pleasure in looking at them."

"Hugh!" ejaculated the attentive Mahtoree.

"Aye, well may you put faith in what you hear, for it is no
lie. But when a youth has found a maiden to please him, he
speaks to her in a voice so soft that none else can hear. He
does not say, my lodge is empty and there is room for another; but shall I build, and will the virgin show me near
what spring she would dwell. His voice is sweeter than honey
from the locust, and goes into the ear thrilling like the song
of a wren. Therefore, if my brother wishes his words to be
heard, he must speak with a white tongue."

Mahtoree pondered deeply, and in a wonder that he did
not attempt to conceal. It was reversing all the order of
society, and according to his established opinions, endanger-
ing the dignity of a chief for a warrior thus to humble himself before a woman. But as Inez sat before him, reserved
and imposing in air, utterly unconscious of his object, and
least of all suspecting the true purport of so extraordinary a
visit, the savage felt the influence of a manner to which he
was unaccustomed. Bowing his head in acknowledgment of
his error, he stepped a little back, and placing himself in an
attitude of easy dignity, he began to speak with the confidence
of one who had been no less distinguished for eloquence than
for deeds in arms. Keeping his eyes riveted on the unconscious bride of Middleton, he proceeded in the following
words: "I am a man with a red skin, but my eyes are dark.
They have been open since many snows. They have seen
many things—they know a brave from a coward. When a boy,
I saw nothing but the bison and the deer. I went to the
hunts, and I saw the cougar and the bear. This made Mahtoree a man. He talked with his mother no more. His ears
were open to the wisdom of the old men. They told him
everything—they told him of the Big Knives. He went on
the warpath. He was then the last—now he is the first. What
Dakota dare say he will go before Mahtoree into the
hunting grounds of the Pawnees? The chiefs met him at
their doors, and they said my son is without a home. They
gave him their lodges, they gave him their riches, and they
gave him their daughters. Then Mahtoree became a chief, as

his fathers had been. He struck the warriors of all the nations, and he could have chosen wives from the Pawnees, the Omahas, and the Konzas; but he looked at the hunting grounds, and not at his village. He thought a horse was pleasanter than a Dakota girl. But he found a flower on the prairies, and he plucked it and brought it into his lodge. He forgets that he is the master of a single horse. He gives them all to the stranger, for Mahtoree is not a thief; he will only keep the flower he found on the prairie. Her feet are very tender. She cannot walk to the door of her father; she will stay in the lodge of a valiant warrior forever."

When he had finished this extraordinary address, the Teton awaited to have it translated, with the air of a suitor who entertained no very disheartening doubts of his success. The trapper had not lost a syllable of the speech, and he now prepared himself to render it into English in such a manner as should leave its principal idea even more obscure than in the original. But as his reluctant lips were in the act of parting, Ellen lifted a finger, and with a keen glance from her quick eye at the still attentive Inez, she interrupted him. "Spare your breath," she said; "all that a savage says is not to be repeated before a Christian lady."

Inez started, blushed, and bowed with an air of reserve as she coldly thanked the old man for his intentions, and observed that she could now wish to be alone.

"My daughters have no need of ears to understand what a great Dakota says," returned the trapper, addressing himself to the expecting Mahtoree. "The look he has given and the signs he has made are enough. They understand him; they wish to think of his words, for the children of great braves, such as their fathers are, do nothing without much thought."

With this explanation, so flattering to the energy of his eloquence and so promising to his future hopes, the Teton was every way content. He made the customary ejaculation of assent and prepared to retire. Saluting the females in the cold but dignified manner of his people, he drew his robe about him and moved from the spot where he had stood with an air of ill-concealed triumph.

But there had been a stricken though a motionless and unobserved auditor of the foregoing scene. Not a syllable had fallen from the lips of the long and anxiously expected husband that had not gone directly to the heart of his unoffend-

ing wife. In this manner had he wooed her from the lodge
of her father, and it was to listen to similar pictures of
the renown and deeds of the greatest brave in her tribe
that she had shut her ears to the tender tales of so many of
the Sioux youths.

As the Teton turned to leave his lodge in the manner just
mentioned, he found this unexpected and half-forgotten object before him. She stood in the humble guise and with the
shrinking air of an Indian girl, holding the pledge of their
former love in her arms, directly in his path. Starting, the
chief regained the marblelike indifference of countenance
which distinguished in so remarkable a degree the restrained
or more artificial expression of his features, and signed to
her with an air of authority to give place.

"Is not Tachechana the daughter of a chief?" demanded
a subdued voice, in which pride struggled with anguish.
"Were not her brothers braves?"

"Go; the men are calling their partisan. He has no ears
for a woman."

"No," replied the supplicant; "it is not the voice of
Tachechana that you hear, but this boy, speaking with the
tongue of his mother. He is the son of a chief, and his words
will go up to his father's ears. Listen to what he says.
When was Mahtoree hungry, and Tachechana had not food
for him? When did he go on the path of the Pawnees and find
it empty, that my mother did not weep? When did he come
back with the marks of their blows, that she did not sing?
What Sioux girl has given a brave a son like me? Look at
me well, that you may know me. My eyes are the eagle's.
I look at the sun and laugh. In a little time the Dakotas will
follow me to the hunts and on the warpath. Why does my
father turn his eyes from the woman that gives me milk? Why
has he so soon forgotten the daughter of a mighty Sioux?"

There was a single instant as the exulting father suffered
his cold eye to wander to the face of the laughing boy that
the stern nature of the Teton seemed touched. But shaking off
the grateful sentiment like one who would gladly be rid of
any painful, because reproachful, emotion, he laid his hand
calmly on the arm of his wife and led her directly in front
of Inez. Pointing to the sweet countenance that was beaming
on her own with a look of tenderness and commiseration, he
paused to allow his wife to contemplate a loveliness which
was quite as excellent to her ingenuous mind as it had proved

dangerous to the character of her faithless husband. When he thought abundant time had passed to make the contrast sufficiently striking, he suddenly raised a small mirror that dangled at her breast, an ornament he had himself bestowed in an hour of fondness as a compliment to her beauty, and placed her own dark image in its place. Wrapping his robe again about him, the Teton motioned to the trapper to follow, and stalked haughtily from the lodge, muttering as he went, "Mahtoree is very wise! What nation has so great a chief as the Dakotas?"

Tachechana stood frozen into a statue of humility. Her mild and usually joyous countenance worked as if the struggle within was about to dissolve the connection between her soul and that more material part, whose deformity was becoming so loathsome. Inez and Ellen were utterly ignorant of the nature of her interview with her husband, though the quick and sharpened wits of the latter led her to suspect a truth to which the entire innocence of the former furnished no clue. They were both, however, about to tender those sympathies which are so natural to, and so graceful in, the sex, when their necessity seemed suddenly to cease. The convulsions in the features of the young Sioux disappeared, and her countenance became cold and rigid like chiseled stone. A single expression of subdued anguish, which had made its impression on a brow that had rarely before contracted with sorrow, alone remained. It was never removed in all the changes of seasons, fortunes, and years which in the vicissitudes of a suffering, female, savage life she was subsequently doomed to endure. As in the case of a premature blight, let the plant quicken and revive as it may, the effects of that withering touch were always present.

Tachechana first stripped her person of every vestige of those rude but highly prized ornaments which the liberality of her husband had been wont to lavish on her, and she tendered them meekly, and without a murmur, as an offering to the superiority of Inez. The bracelets were forced from her wrists, the complicated mazes of beads from her leggings, and the broad silver band from her brow. Then she paused, long and painfully. But it would seem that the resolution she had once adopted was not to be conquered by the lingering emotions of any affection, however natural. The boy himself was next laid at the feet of her supposed rival, and well might the self-abased wife of the Teton believe that the burden of her sacrifice was now full.

While Inez and Ellen stood regarding these several strange movements with eyes of wonder, a low, soft, musical voice was heard saying in a language that to them was unintelligible: "A strange tongue will tell my boy the manner to become a man. He will hear sounds that are new, but he will learn them and forget the voice of his mother. It is the will of the Wahcondah, and a Sioux girl should not complain. Speak to him softly, for his ears are very little; when he is big, your words may be louder. Let him not be a girl, for very sad is the life of a woman. Teach him to keep his eyes on the men. Show him how to strike them that do him wrong, and let him never forget to return blow for blow. When he goes to hunt, the flower of the palefaces," she concluded, using in bitterness the metaphor which had been supplied by the imagination of her truant husband, "will whisper softly in his ears that the skin of his mother was red and that she was once the Fawn of the Dakotas."

Tachechana pressed a kiss on the lips of her son and withdrew to the further side of the lodge. Here she drew her light calico robe over her head and took her seat, in token of humility, on the naked earth. All efforts to attract her attention were fruitless. She neither heard remonstrances nor felt the touch. Once or twice her voice rose in a sort of wailing song from beneath her quivering mantle, but it never mounted into the wildness of savage music. In this manner she remained unseen for hours, while events were occurring without the lodge which not only materially changed the complexion of her own fortunes, but left a lasting and deep impression on the future movements of the wandering Sioux.

CHAPTER 27

> I'll no swaggerers. I am in good name and fame with the very best; shut the door; there come no swaggerers here: I have not lived all this while, to have swaggering now; shut the door, I pray you.
>
> SHAKESPEARE

MAHTOREE ENCOUNTERED, AT the door of his lodge, Ishmael, Abiram, and Esther. The first glance of his eye at the countenance of the heavy-molded squatter served to tell the cunning Teton that the treacherous truce he had made with these dupes of his superior sagacity was in some danger of a violent termination.

"Look you here, old graybeard," said Ishmael, seizing the trapper and whirling him round as if he had been a top; "that I am tired of carrying on a discourse with fingers and thumbs, instead of a tongue, are a natural fact; so you'll play linguister and put my words into Indian without much caring whether they suit the stomach of a redskin or not."

"Say on, friend," calmly returned the trapper; "they shall be given as plainly as you send them."

"Friend!" repeated the squatter, eyeing the other for an instant with an expression of indefinable meaning. "But it is no more than a word, and sounds break no bones and survey no farms. Tell this thieving Sioux, then, that I come to claim the conditions of our solemn bargain, made at the foot of the rock."

When the trapper had rendered his meaning into the Sioux language, Mahtoree demanded with an air of surprise, "Is my brother cold? Buffalo skins are plenty. Is he hungry? Let my young men carry venison into his lodges."

The squatter elevated his clenched fist in a menacing manner and struck it with violence on the palm of his open hand, by way of confirming his determination, as he answered, "Tell the deceitful liar I have not come like a beggar to pick his bones, but like a freeman asking for his own; and have it I will. And, moreover, tell him I claim that you too, miserable sinner as you are, should be given up to justice. There's no mistake. My prisoner, my niece, and you. I demand the three at his hands, according to a sworn agreement."

The immovable old man smiled with an expression of singular intelligence as he answered, "Friend squatter, you ask what few men would be willing to grant. You would first cut the tongue from the mouth of the Teton, and then the heart from his bosom."

"It is little that Ishmael Bush regards who or what is damaged in claiming his own. But put you the questions in straightgoing Indian, and when you speak of yourself, make such a sign as a white man will understand, in order that I may know there is no foul play."

The trapper laughed in his silent fashion and muttered a few words to himself before he addressed the chief, "Let the Dakota open his ears very wide," he said, "that big words may have room to enter. His friend the Big Knife comes with an empty hand, and he says that the Teton must fill it."

"Wagh! Mahtoree is a rich chief. He is master of the prairies."

"He must give the dark-hair."

The brow of the chief contracted in an ominous frown that threatened instant destruction to the audacious squatter, but as suddenly recollecting his policy, he craftily replied, "A girl is too light for the hand of such a brave. I will fill it with buffaloes."

"He says he has need of the light-hair too, who has his blood in her veins."

"She shall be the wife of Mahtoree; then the Long Knife will be the father of a chief."

"And me," continued the trapper, making one of those expressive signs by which the natives communicate with nearly the same facility as with their tongue, and turning to the squatter at the same time in order that the latter might see he dealt fairly by him; "he asks for a miserable and worn-out trapper."

The Dakota threw his arm over the shoulder of the old man with an air of great affection before he replied to this third and last demand.

"My friend is old," he said, "and cannot travel far. He will stay with the Tetons, that they may learn wisdom from his words. What Sioux has a tongue like my father! No; let his words be very soft, but let them be very clear. Mahtoree will give skins and buffaloes. He will give the young men of the palefaces wives, but he cannot give away any who live in his own lodge."

Perfectly satisfied himself with this laconic reply, the chief was moving towards his expecting counselors, when suddenly returning, he interrupted the translation of the trapper by adding, "Tell the Great Buffalo" (a name by which the Tetons had already christened Ishmael) "that Mahtoree has a hand which is always open. See," he added, pointing to the hard and wrinkled visage of the attentive Esther, "his wife is too old for so great a chief. Let him put her out of his lodge. Mahtoree loves him as a brother. He *is* his brother. He shall have the youngest wife of the Teton. Tachechana, the pride of the Sioux girls, shall cook his venison, and

many braves will look at him with longing minds. Go, a
Dakota is generous."

The singular coolness with which the Teton concluded this
audacious proposal confounded even the practiced trapper.
He stared after the retiring form of the Indian with an astonishment he did not care to conceal, nor did he renew his
attempt at interpretation until the person of Mahtoree was
blended with the cluster of warriors who had so long, and
with so characteristic patience, awaited his return.

"The Teton chief has spoken very plainly," the old man continued; "he will not give you the lady, to whom the Lord in
heaven knows you have no claim, unless it be such as the
wolf has to the lamb. He will not give you the child you call
your niece, and therein I acknowledge that I am far from
certain he has the same justice on his side. Moreover, neighbor
squatter, he flatly denies your demand for me, miserable
and worthless as I am; nor do I think he has been unwise in
so doing, seeing that I should have many reasons against
journeying far in your company. But he makes you an offer,
which it is right and convenient you should know. The Teton
says through me, who am no more than a mouthpiece and
therein not answerable for the sin of his words, but he says
as this good woman is getting past the comely age, it is
reasonable for you to tire of such a wife. He therefore tells
you to turn her out of your lodge, and when it is empty, he
will send his own favorite, or rather she that was his favorite, the Skipping Fawn, as the Siouxes call her, to fill her
place. You see, neighbor, though the redskin is minded to
keep your property, he is willing to give you wherewithal to
make yourself some return!"

Ishmael listened to these replies to his several demands
with that species of gathering indignation with which the
dullest tempers mount into the most violent paroxysms of
rage. He even affected to laugh at the conceit of exchanging
his long-tried partner for the more flexible support of the
youthful Tachechana, though his voice was hollow and unnatural in the effort. But Esther was far from giving the
proposal so facetious a reception. Lifting her voice to its
most audible key, she broke forth, after catching her breath
like one who had been in some imminent danger of strangulation, as follows: "Hoity-toity; who set an Indian up for a
maker and breaker of the rights of wedded wives! Does he
think a woman is a beast of the prairie, that she is to be

chased from a village by dog and gun? Let the bravest squaw of them all come forth and boast of her doings; can she show such a brood as mine? A wicked tyrant is that thieving redskin, and a bold rogue I warrant me. He would be captain indoors as well as out! An honest woman is no better in his eyes than one of your broomstick jumpers. And you, Ishmael Bush, the father of seven sons and so many comely daughters, to open *your* sinful mouth, except to curse him! Would ye disgrace color, and family, and nation by mixing white blood with red, and would ye be the parent of a race of mules! The devil has often tempted you, my man, but never before has he set so cunning a snare as this. Go back among your children, friend; go, and remember that you are not a prowling bear, but a Christian man, and thank God that you are a lawful husband!"

The clamor of Esther was anticipated by the judicious trapper. He had easily foreseen that her meek temper would overflow at so scandalous a proposal as repudiation, and he now profited by the tempest to retire to a place where he was at least safe from any immediate violence on the part of her less excited but certainly more dangerous husband. Ishmael, who had made his demands with a stout determination to enforce them, was diverted by the windy torrent, like many a more obstinate husband, from his purpose, and in order to appease a jealousy that resembled the fury with which the bear defends her cubs, was fain to retire to a distance from the lodge that was known to contain the unoffending object of the sudden uproar.

"Let your copper-colored minx come forth and show her tawny beauty before the face of a woman who has heard more than one church bell and seen a power of real quality," cried Esther, flourishing her hand in triumph as she drove Ishmael and Abiram before her, like two truant boys, towards their own encampment. "I warrant me, I warrant me, here is one who would shortly talk her down! Never think to tarry here, my men; never think to shut an eye in a camp through which the devil walks as openly as if he were a gentleman, and sure of his welcome. Here, you Abner, Enoch, Jesse, where are ye gotten to? Put to, put to; if that weak-minded, soft-feeling man, your father, eats or drinks again in this neighborhood, we shall see him poisoned with the craft of the redskins. Not that I care, I who comes into my place when it is once lawfully empty; but, Ishmael, I never thought that you, who have had one woman with a white skin, would find pleasure in looking on a brazen—aye, that she is copper are a fact; you can't deny it, and I warrant me, brazen enough is she too!"

Against this ebullition of wounded female pride, the experienced husband made no other head than by an occasional exclamation, which he intended to be the precursor of a simple asseveration of his own innocence. The fury of the woman would not be appeased. She listened to nothing but her own voice, and consequently nothing was heard but her mandates to depart.

The squatter had collected his beasts and loaded his wagons as a measure of precaution before proceeding to the extremity he contemplated. Esther consequently found everything favorable to her wishes. The young men stared at each other as they witnessed the extraordinary excitement of their mother, but took little interest in an event which, in the course of their experience, had found so many parallels. By command of their father, the tents were thrown into the vehicles as a sort of reprisal for the want of faith in their late ally, and then the train left the spot in its usual listless and sluggish order.

As a formidable division of well-armed borderers protected the rear of the retiring party, the Siouxes saw it depart without manifesting the smallest evidence of surprise or resentment. The savage, like the tiger, rarely makes his attack on an enemy who expects him; and if the warriors of the Tetons meditated any hostility, it was in the still and patient manner with which the feline beasts watch for the incautious moment in order to ensure the blow. The councils of Mahtoree, however, on whom so much of the policy of his people depended, lay deep in the depository of his own thoughts. Perhaps he rejoiced at so easy a manner of getting rid of claims so troublesome; perhaps he awaited a fitting time to exhibit his power; or it even might be that matters of so much greater importance were pressing on his mind that it had not leisure to devote any of its faculties to an event of so much indifference.

But it would seem that while Ishmael made such a concession to the awakened feelings of Esther, he was far from abandoning his original intentions. His train followed the course of the river for a mile, and then it came to a halt on the brow of the elevated land, and in a place which afforded the necessary facilities. Here he again pitched his tents, unharnessed his teams, sent his cattle on the bottom, and, in short, made all the customary preparations to pass the night, with the same coolness and deliberation as if he had not hurled an irritating defiance into the teeth of his dangerous neighbors.

In the meantime the Tetons proceeded to the more regular business of the hour. A fierce and savage joy had existed in the camp from the instant when it had been announced that their own chief was returning with the long-dreaded and hated partisan of their enemies. For many hours the crones of the tribe had been going from lodge to lodge in order to stimulate the tempers of the warriors to such a pass as might leave but little room for mercy. To one they spoke of a son whose scalp was drying in the smoke of a Pawnee lodge. To another they enumerated his own scars, his disgraces, and defeats; with a third they dwelt on his losses of skins and horses; and a fourth was reminded of vengeance by a significant question concerning some flagrant adventure in which he was known to have been a sufferer.

By these means the men had been so far excited as to have assembled in the manner already related, though it still remained a matter of doubt how far they intended to carry their revenge. A variety of opinions prevailed on the policy of executing their prisoners, and Mahtoree had suspended the discussions in order to ascertain how far the measure might propitiate or retard his own particular views. Hitherto the consultations had merely been preliminary, with a design that each chief might discover the number of supporters his particular views would be likely to obtain when the important subject should come before a more solemn council of the tribe. The moment for the latter had now arrived, and the preparations were made with a dignity and solemnity suited to the momentous interests of the occasion.

With a refinement in cruelty that none but an Indian would have imagined, the place selected for this grave deliberation was immediately about the post to which the most important of its subjects was attached. Middleton and Paul were brought in their bonds and laid at the feet of the Pawnee; then the men began to take their places, according to their several claims to distinction. As warrior after warrior approached, he seated himself in the wide circle with a mien as composed and thoughtful as if his mind were actually in a condition to deal out justice, tempered, as it should be, with the heavenly quality of mercy. A place was reserved for three or four of the principal chiefs; and a few of the oldest of the women, as withered as age, exposure, hardships, and lives of savage passions could make them, thrust themselves into the foremost circle with a temerity to which they were impelled by their insatiable desire for cruelty, and which nothing but their years and their long-tried fidelity to the nation could have excused.

All but the chiefs already named were now in their places. These had delayed their appearance in the vain hope that their own unanimity might smooth the way to that of their respective factions, for notwithstanding the superior influence of Mahtoree, his power was to be maintained only by constant appeals to the opinions of his inferiors. As these important personages at length entered the circle in a body, their sullen looks and clouded brows, notwithstanding the time given for consultation, sufficiently proclaimed the discontent which reigned among them. The eye of Mahtoree was varying in its expression, from sudden gleams that seemed to kindle with the burning impulses of his soul, to that cold and guarded steadiness which was thought more peculiarly to become a chief in council. He took his seat with the studied simplicity of a demagogue, though the keen and flashing glance that he immediately threw around the silent assembly betrayed the more predominant temper of a tyrant.

When all were present, an aged warrior lighted the great pipe of his people and blew the smoke towards the four quarters of the heavens. So soon as this propitiatory offering was made, he tendered it to Mahtoree, who, in affected humility, passed it to a gray-headed chief by his side. After the influence of the soothing weed had been courted by all, a grave silence succeeded, as if each was not only qualified to, but actually did, think more deeply on the matters before them. Then an old Indian arose, and spoke as follows: "The eagle at the falls of the endless river was in its egg many snows after my hand had struck a Pawnee. What my tongue says, my eyes have seen. Bohrecheena is very old. The hills have stood longer in their places than he has been in his tribe, and the rivers were full and empty before he was born; but where is the Sioux that knows it besides myself? What he says, they will hear. If any of his words fall to the ground, they will pick them up and hold them to their ears. If any blow away in the wind, my young men, who are very nimble, will catch them. Now listen. Since water ran and trees grew, the Sioux has found the Pawnee on his warpath. As the cougar loves the antelope, the Dakota loves his enemy. When the wolf finds the fawn, does he lie down and sleep? When the panther sees the doe at the spring, does he shut his eyes? You know that he does not. He drinks too, but it is of blood! A Sioux is a leaping panther, a Pawnee a trembling deer. Let my children hear me. They will find my words good. I have spoken."

A deep guttural exclamation of assent broke from the lips of all the partisans of Mahtoree as they listened to this sanguinary advice from one who was certainly among the most aged men of the nation. That deeply seated love of vengeance which formed so prominent a feature in their characters was gratified by his metaphorical allusions, and the chief himself augured favorably of the success of his own schemes by the number of supporters who manifested themselves to be in favor of the counsels of his friend. But still unanimity was far from prevailing. A long and decorous pause was suffered to succeed the words of the first speaker in order that all might duly deliberate on their wisdom before another chief took on himself the office of refutation. The second orator, though past the prime of his days, was far less aged than the one who had preceded him. He felt the disadvantage of this circumstance and endeavored to counteract it as far as possible by the excess of his humility.

"I am but an infant," he commenced, looking furtively around him in order to detect how far his well-established character for prudence and courage contradicted his assertion. "I have lived with the women since my father has been a man. If my head is getting gray, it is not because I am old. Some of the snow which fell on it while I have been sleeping on the warpaths has frozen there, and the hot sun near the Osage villages has not been strong enough to melt it." A low murmur was heard, expressive of admiration of the services to which he thus artfully alluded. The orator modestly awaited for the feeling to subside a little, and then he continued with increasing energy, encouraged by their commendations. "But the eyes of a young brave are good. He can see very far. He is a lynx. Look at me well. I will now turn my back, that you may see both sides of me. Now do you know I am your friend, for you look on a part that a Pawnee never yet saw. Now look at my face; not in this seam, for there your eyes can never see into my spirit. It is a hole cut by a Konza. But here is an opening made by the Wahcondah, through which you may look into the soul. What am I? A Dakota, within and without. You know it. Therefore hear me. The blood of every creature on the prairie is red. Who can tell the spot where a Pawnee was struck from the place where my young men took a bison? It is of the same color. The Master of Life made them for each other. He made them alike. But will the grass grow green where a paleface is killed? My young men must not think *that* nation so numerous that it will not miss a warrior. They call them over often, and say, 'Where are my sons?' If they miss one, they will send into the prairies to look for him. If they cannot find him, they will tell their runners to ask for him among the Siouxes. My brethren, the Big Knives are not fools. There is a mighty medicine of their nation now among us; who can tell how loud is his voice, or how long is his arm——"

The speech of the orator, who was beginning to enter into his subject with warmth, was cut short by the impatient Mahtoree, who suddenly arose and exclaimed in a voice in which authority was mingled with contempt, and at the close with a keen tone of irony also, "Let my young men lead the evil spirit of the palefaces to the council. My brother shall see his medicine face to face!"

A deathlike and solemn stillness succeeded this extraordinary interruption. It not only involved a deep offense against the sacred courtesy of debate, but the mandate was likely to brave the unknown power of one of those incomprehensible beings whom few Indians were enlightened enough at that day to regard without reverence, or few hardy enough to oppose. The subordinates, however, obeyed, and Obed was led forth from the lodge mounted on *Asinus* with a ceremony and state which was certainly intended for derision, but which nevertheless was greatly enhanced by fear. As they entered the ring, Mahtoree, who had foreseen and had endeavored to anticipate the influence of the doctor by bringing him into contempt, cast an eye around the assembly in order to gather his success in the various dark visages by which he was encircled.

Truly nature and art had combined to produce such an effect from the air and appointments of the naturalist as might have made him the subject of wonder in any place. His head had been industriously shaved, after the most approved fashion of Sioux taste. A gallant scalp lock, which would probably not have been spared had the doctor himself been consulted in the matter, was all that remained of an exuberant, and at that particular season of the year, far from uncomfortable head of hair. Thick coats of paint had been laid on the naked poll, and certain fanciful designs in the same material had even been extended into the neighborhood of the eyes and mouth, lending to the keen expression of the former a look of twinkling cunning, and to the dogmatism of the latter not a little of the grimness of necromancy. He had been despoiled of his upper garments, and in their stead his body was sufficiently protected from the cold by a fantastically painted robe of dressed deerskin. As if in mockery of his pursuit, sundry toads, frogs, lizards, butterflies, etc., all duly prepared to take their places at some future day in his own private cabinet, were attached to the solitary lock on his head, to his ears, and to various other conspicuous parts of his person. If, in addition to the effect produced by these quaint auxiliaries to his costume, we add the portentous and troubled gleamings of doubt, which rendered his visage doubly austere and proclaimed the misgivings of the worthy Obed's mind as he beheld his personal dignity thus prostrated, and what was of far greater moment in his eyes, himself led forth, as he firmly believed, to be the victim of some heathenish sacrifice, the reader will find no difficulty in giving credit to the sensation of awe that was already excited by his appearance in a band already more than half prepared to worship him as a powerful agent of the evil spirit.

Weucha led *Asinus* directly into the center of the circle, and leaving them together (for the legs of the naturalist were attached to the beast in such a manner that the two animals might be said to be incorporated, and to form a new order), he withdrew to his proper place, gazing at the conjurer as he retired with a wonder and admiration that were natural to the groveling dullness of his mind.

The astonishment seemed mutual between the spectators and the subject of this strange exhibition. If the Tetons contemplated the mysterious attributes of the medicine with awe and fear, the doctor gazed on every side of him with a mixture of quite as many extraordinary emotions, in which the latter sensation, however, formed no inconsiderable ingredient. Everywhere his eyes, which just at that moment possessed a secret magnifying quality, seemed to rest on several dark, savage, and obdurate countenances at once, from none of which could he extract a solitary gleam of sympathy or commiseration. At length his wandering gaze fell on the grave and decent features of the trapper, who, with Hector at his feet, stood in the edge of the circle leaning on that rifle which he had been permitted, as an acknowledged friend, to resume, and apparently musing on the events that were likely to succeed a council marked by so many and such striking ceremonies.

"Venerable venator, or hunter, or trapper," said the disconsolate Obed, "I rejoice greatly in meeting thee again. I fear that the precious time which had been allotted me in order to complete a mighty labor is drawing to a premature close, and I would gladly unburden my mind to one who, if not a pupil of science, has at least some of the knowledge which civilization imparts to its meanest subjects. Doubtless many and earnest inquiries will be made after my fate by the learned societies of the world, and perhaps expeditions will be sent into these regions to remove any doubt which may arise on so important a subject. I esteem myself happy that a man who speaks the vernacular is present to preserve the record of my end. You will say that after a well-spent and glorious life, I died a martyr to science, and a victim to mental darkness. As I expect to be particularly calm and abstracted in my last moments, if you add a few details concerning the fortitude and scholastic dignity with which I met my death, it may serve to encourage future aspirants for similar honors, and assuredly give offense to no one. And now, friend trapper, as a duty I owe to human nature, I will conclude by demanding if all hope has deserted me or if any means still exist by which so much valuable information may be rescued from the grasp of ignorance and preserved to the pages of natural history."

The old man lent an attentive ear to this melancholy appeal, and apparently he reflected on every side of the important question before he would presume to answer.

"I take it, friend physicianer," he at length gravely replied, "that the chances of life and death in your particular case depend altogether on the will of Providence as it may be pleased to manifest it through the accursed windings of In-

dian cunning. For my own part, I see no great difference
in the main end to be gained, inasmuch as it can matter no
one greatly, yourself excepted, whether you live or die."

"Would you account the fall of a cornerstone from the
foundations of the edifice of learning a matter of indifference to contemporaries or to posterity?" interrupted Obed.
"Besides, my aged associate," he reproachfully added, "the
interest that a man has in his own existence is by no means
trifling, however it may be eclipsed by his devotion to more
general and philanthropic feelings."

"What I would say is this," resumed the trapper, who
was far from understanding all the subtle distinctions with
which his more learned companion so often saw fit to embel-
lish his discourse; "there is but one birth and one death to
all things, be it hound or be it deer, be it redskin or be it
white. Both are in the hands of the Lord, it being as unlawful for man to strive to hasten the one as impossible to prevent the other. But I will not say that something may not
be done to put the last moment aside, for a while at least;
and therefore it is a question, that anyone has a right to put
to his own wisdom, how far he will go and how much pain he
will suffer to lengthen out a time that may have been too
long already. Many a dreary winter and scorching summer
has gone by since I have turned to the right hand or to the
left to add an hour to a life that has already stretched beyond fourscore years. I keep myself as ready to answer to
my name as a soldier at evening roll call. In my judgment,
if your cases are left to Indian tempers, the policy of the great
Sioux will lead his people to sacrifice you all; nor do I put
much dependence on his seeming love for me; therefore it
becomes a question whether you are ready for such a journey,
and if, being ready, whether this is not as good a time to
start as another. Should my opinion be asked, thus far will
I give it in your favor; that is to say, it is my belief your
life has been innocent enough, touching any great offenses
that you may have committed, though honesty compels me
to add that I think all you can lay claim to on the score of
activity in deeds will not amount to anything worth naming
in the great account."

Obed turned a rueful eye on the calm, philosophic countenance of the other as he answered with so discouraging a
statement of his case, clearing his throat as he did so in order
to conceal the desperate concern which began to beset his

faculties, with a vestige of that pride which rarely deserts poor human nature even in the greatest emergencies.

"I believe, venerable hunter," he replied, "considering the question in all its bearings, and assuming that your theory is just, it will be the safest to conclude that I am not prepared to make so hasty a departure and that measures of precaution should be forthwith resorted to."

"Being in that mind," returned the deliberate trapper, "I will act for you as I would for myself; though as time has begun to roll down the hill with you, I will just advise that you look to your case speedily, for it may so happen that your name will be heard when quite as little prepared to answer to it as now."

With this amicable understanding, the old man drew back again into the ring, where he stood musing on the course he should now adopt with the singular mixture of decision and resignation that proceeded from his habits and his humility, and which united to form a character in which excessive energy and the most meek submission to the will of Providence were oddly enough combined.

CHAPTER 28

The witch, in Smithfield, shall be burned to ashes,
And you three shall be strangled on the gallows.
                                        SHAKESPEARE

THE SIOUXES HAD awaited the issue of the foregoing dialogue with commendable patience. Most of the band were restrained by the secret awe with which they regarded the mysterious character of Obed, while a few of the more intelligent chiefs gladly profited by the opportunity to arrange their thoughts for the struggle that was plainly foreseen. Mahtoree, influenced by neither of these feelings, was content to show the trapper how much he conceded to his pleasure; and when the old man discontinued the discourse, he received from the chief a glance that was intended to remind him of the patience with which he had awaited his movements. A profound and motionless silence succeeded the short interruption. Then Mahtoree arose, evidently prepared to speak. First placing himself in an attitude of dignity, he turned a steady and severe look on the whole assembly. The expression of his eye, however, changed as it glanced across the different countenances of his supporters and of his opponents. To the former the look, though stern, was not threatening, while it seemed to tell the latter all the hazards they incurred in daring to brave the resentment of one so powerful.

Still, in the midst of so much hauteur and confidence, the sagacity and cunning of the Teton did not desert him. When he had thrown the gauntlet, as it were, to the whole tribe and sufficiently asserted his claim to superiority, his mien became more affable and his eye less angry. Then it was that he raised his voice, in the midst of a deathlike stillness, varying its tones to suit the changing character of his images and of his eloquence.

"What is a Sioux?" the chief sagaciously began. "He is ruler of the prairies and master of its beasts. The fishes in the 'river of troubled waters' know him and come at his call. He is a fox in counsel, an eagle in sight, a grizzly bear in combat. A Dakota is a man!" After waiting for the low murmur of approbation which followed this flattering portrait of his people to subside, the Teton continued, "What is a Pawnee? A thief who only steals from women, a redskin who is not brave, a hunter that begs for his venison. In counsel he is a squirrel, hopping from place to place; he is an owl that goes on the prairies at night; in battle he is an elk whose legs are long. A Pawnee is a woman." Another pause succeeded, during which a yell of delight broke from several mouths, and a demand was made that the taunting words should be translated to the unconscious subject of their biting contempt. The old man took his cue from the eyes of Mahtoree and complied. Hard Heart listened gravely, and then, as if apprised that his time to speak had not arrived, he once more bent his look on the vacant air. The orator watched his countenance with an expression that manifested how inextinguishable was the hatred he felt for the only chief, far and near, whose fame might advantageously be compared with his own. Though disappointed in not having touched the pride of one whom he regarded as a boy, he proceeded, what he considered as far more important, to quicken the tempers of the men of his own tribe in order that they might be prepared to work his savage purposes. "If the earth was covered with rats, which are good for nothing," he said, "there would be no room for buffaloes, which give food and clothes to an Indian. If the prairies were covered with Pawnees, there would be no room for the foot of a Dakota. A Loup is a rat, a Sioux a heavy buffalo; let the buffalos tread upon the rats and make room for themselves.

"My brothers, a little child has spoken to you. He tells you his hair is not gray, but frozen, that the grass will not grow where a paleface has died! Does he know the color of the blood of a Big Knife? No! I know he does not; he has never seen it. What Dakota besides Mahtoree has ever struck a paleface? Not one. But Mahtoree must be silent. Every Teton will shut his ears when he speaks. The scalps over his lodge were taken by the women. They were taken by Mahtoree and he is a woman. His mouth is shut; he waits for the feasts, to sing among the girls!"

Notwithstanding the exclamations of regret and resentment which followed so abasing a declaration, the chief took his seat, as if determined to speak no more. But the murmurs grew louder and more general, and there were threatening symptoms that the council would dissolve itself in confusion; and he arose and resumed his speech by changing his manner to the fierce and hurried enunciation of a warrior bent on revenge.

"Let my young men go look for Tetao!" he cried. "They will find his scalp drying in Pawnee smoke. Where is the son of Bohrecheena? His bones are whiter than the faces of his murderers. Is Mahhah asleep in his lodge? You know it is many moons since he started for the blessed prairies; would he were here, that he might say of what color was the hand that took his scalp!"

In this strain the artful chief continued for many minutes, calling those warriors by name who were known to have met their deaths in battle with the Pawnees or in some of those lawless frays which so often occurred between the Sioux bands and a class of white men who were but little removed from them in the qualities of civilization. Time was not given to reflect on the merits, or rather the demerits, of most of the different individuals to whom he alluded, in consequence of the rapid manner in which he ran over their names; but so cunningly did he time his events, and so thrillingly did he make his appeals, aided as they were by the power of his deep-toned and stirring voice, that each of them struck an answering chord in the breast of some one of his auditors.

It was in the midst of one of his highest flights of eloquence that a man so aged as to walk with the greatest difficulty entered the very center of the circle and took his stand directly in front of the speaker. An ear of great acuteness might possibly have detected that the tones of the orator faltered a little as his flashing look first fell on this unexpected object, though the change was so trifling that none but such as thoroughly knew the parties would have suspected it. The stranger had once been as distinguished for his beauty and proportions as had been his eagle eye for its irresistible and terrible glance. But his skin was now wrinkled and his features furrowed with so many scars as to have obtained for him half a century before, from the French of the Canadas, a title which has been borne by so many of the heroes of France and which had now been adopted into the language of the wild horde of whom we are writing as the one most expressive of the deeds of their own brave. The murmur of Le Balafré that ran through the assembly when he appeared announced not only his name and the high estimation of his character, but how extraordinary his visit was considered. As he neither spoke nor moved, however, the sensation created by his appearance soon subsided, and then every eye was again turned upon the speaker, and every ear once more drank in the intoxication of his maddening appeals.

It would have been easy to have traced the triumph of Mahtoree in the reflecting countenances of his auditors. It was not long before a look of ferocity and of revenge was to be seen seated on the grim visages of most of the warriors, and each new and crafty allusion to the policy of extinguishing their enemies was followed by fresh and less restrained bursts of approbation. In the height of this success the Teton closed his speech by a rapid appeal to the pride and hardihood of his native band and suddenly took his seat.

In the midst of the murmurs of applause which succeeded so remarkable an effort of eloquence, a low, feeble, and hollow voice was heard rising on the ear, as if it rolled from the inmost cavities of the human chest, and gathered strength and energy as it issued into the air. A solemn stillness followed the sounds, and then the lips of the aged man were first seen to move.

"The day of Le Balafré is near its end," were the first words that were distinctly audible. "He is like a buffalo on whom the hair will grow no longer. He will soon be ready to leave his lodge to go in search of another that is far from the villages of the Siouxes; therefore, what he has to say concerns not him, but those he leaves behind him. His words are like the fruit on the tree, ripe and fit to be given to chiefs.

"Many snows have fallen since Le Balafré has been found on the warpath. His blood has been very hot, but it has had time to cool. The Wahcondah gives him dreams of war no longer; he sees that it is better to live in peace.

"My brothers, one foot is turned to the happy hunting grounds, the other will soon follow, and then an old chief will be seen looking for the prints of his father's moccasins, that he may make no mistake, but be sure to come before the Master of Life by the same path as so many good Indians have already traveled. But who will follow? Le Balafré has no son. His oldest has ridden too many Pawnee horses; the bones of the youngest have been gnawed by Konza dogs. Le Balafré has come to look for a young arm on which he may lean and to find a son, that when he is gone his lodge may not be empty. Tachechana, the skipping fawn of the Tetons, is too weak to prop a warrior who is old. She looks before her, and not backwards. Her mind is in the lodge of her husband."

The enunciation of the veteran warrior had been calm, but distinct and decided. His declaration was received in silence; and though several of the chiefs who were in the counsels of Mahtoree turned their eyes on their leader, none presumed to oppose so aged and so venerated a brave in a resolution that was strictly in conformity to the usages of the nation. The Teton himself was content to await the result with seeming composure, though the gleams of ferocity that played about his eye occasionally betrayed the nature of those feelings with which he witnessed a procedure that was likely to rob him of that one of all his intended victims whom he most hated.

In the meantime Le Balafré moved with a slow and painful step towards the captives. He stopped before the person of Hard Heart, whose faultless form, unchanging eye, and lofty mien he contemplated long, with high and evident satisfaction. Then making a gesture of authority, he awaited until his order had been obeyed, and the youth was released from the post and his bonds by the same blow of the knife. When the young warrior was led nearer to his dimmed and failing sight, the examination was renewed with strictness of scrutiny and that admiration which physical excellence is so apt to excite in the breast of a savage.

"It is good," the wary veteran murmured when he found that all his skill in the requisites of a brave could detect no blemish; "this is a leaping panther! Does my son speak with the tongue of a Teton?"

The intelligence which lighted the eyes of the captive betrayed how well he understood the question, but still he was far too haughty to communicate his ideas through the medium of a language that belonged to a hostile people. Some of the surrounding warriors explained to the old chief that the captive was a Pawnee Loup.

"My son opened his eyes on the 'waters of the wolves,'" said Le Balafré in the language of that nation, "but he will shut them in the bend of the 'river with a troubled stream.' He was born a Pawnee, but he will die a Dakota. Look at me. I am a sycamore that once covered many with my shadow. The leaves are fallen and the branches begin to drop. But a single sucker is springing from my roots; it is a little vine, and it winds itself about a tree that is green. I have long looked for one fit to grow by my side. Now have I found him. Le Balafré is no longer without a son; his name will not be forgotten when he is gone! Men of the Tetons, I take this youth into my lodge."

No one was bold enough to dispute a right that had so often been exercised by warriors far inferior to the present speaker, and the adoption was listened to in grave and respectful silence. Le Balafré took his intended son by the arm, and leading him into the very center of the circle, he stepped aside with an air of triumph in order that the spectators might approve of his choice. Mahtoree betrayed no evidence of his intentions, but rather seemed to await a moment better suited to the crafty policy of his character. The more experienced and sagacious chiefs distinctly foresaw the utter impossibility of two partisans so renowned, so hostile, and who had so long been rivals in fame as their prisoner and their native leader existing amicably in the same tribe. Still the character of Le Balafré was so imposing and the custom to which he had resorted so sacred that none dared to lift a voice in opposition to the measure. They watched the result with increasing interest, but with a coldness of demeanor that concealed the nature of their inquietude. From this state of embarrassment, and as it might readily have proved of disorganization, the tribe was unexpectedly relieved by the decision of the one most interested in the success of the aged chief's designs.

During the whole of the foregoing scene it would have been difficult to have traced a single distinct emotion in the lineaments of the captive. He had heard his release proclaimed with the same indifference as the order to bind him to the stake. But now that the moment had arrived when it became necessary to make his election, he spoke in a way to prove that the fortitude which had brought him so distinguished a name had in no degree deserted him.

"My father is very old, but he has not yet looked upon everything," said Hard Heart in a voice so clear as to be heard by all in presence. "He has never seen a buffalo change to a bat; he will never see a Pawnee become a Sioux!"

There was a suddenness and yet a calmness in the manner of delivering this decision which assured most of the auditors that it was unalterable. The heart of Le Balafré, however, was yearning towards the youth, and the fondness of age was not so readily repulsed. Reproving the burst of admiration and triumph to which the boldness of the declaration and the freshened hopes of revenge had given rise, by turning his gleaming eye around the band, the veteran again addressed his adopted child, as if his purpose was not to be denied.

"It is well," he said; "such are the words a brave should use, that the warriors may see his heart. The day has been when the voice of Le Balafré was loudest among the lodges of the Konzas. But the root of a white hair is wisdom. My child will show the Tetons that he is brave by striking their enemies. Men of the Dakotas, this is my son!"

The Pawnee hesitated a moment, and then stepping in front of the chief, he took his hard and wrinkled hand and laid it with reverence on his head, as if to acknowledge the extent of his obligation. Then recoiling a step, he raised his person to its greatest elevation and looked upon the hostile band by whom he was environed with an air of loftiness and disdain, as he spoke aloud in the language of the Siouxes, "Hard Heart has looked at himself within and without. He has thought of all he has done in the hunts and in the wars. Everywhere he is the same. There is no change. He is in all things a Pawnee. He has struck so many Tetons that he could never eat in their lodges. His arrows would fly backwards, the point of his lance would be on the wrong end, their friends would weep at every whoop he gave, their enemies would laugh. Do the Tetons know a Loup? Let them look at him again. His head is painted, his arm is flesh, his heart is rock. When the Tetons see the sun come from the Rocky Mountains and move towards the land of the palefaces, the mind of Hard Heart will soften and his spirit will become Sioux. Until that day he will live and die a Pawnee."

A yell of delight, in which admiration and ferocity were strangely mingled, interrupted the speaker and but too clearly announced the character of his fate. The captive awaited a moment for the commotion to subside, and then turning again to Le Balafré, he continued in tones conciliating and kind, as if he felt the propriety of softening his refusal, in a manner not to wound the pride of one who would so gladly be his benefactor.

"Let my father lean heavier on the fawn of the Dakotas," he said; "she is weak now, but as her lodge fills with young, she will be stronger. See," he added, directing the eyes of the other to the earnest countenance of the attentive trapper; "Hard Heart is not without a grayhead to show him the path to the blessed prairies. If he ever has another father, it shall be that just warrior."

Le Balafré turned away in disappointment from the youth and approached the stranger who had thus anticipated his design. The examination between these two aged men was long, mutual, and curious. It was not easy to detect the real character of the trapper through the mask which the hardships of so many years had laid upon his features, especially when aided by his wild and peculiar attire. Some moments elapsed before the Teton spoke, and then it was in doubt whether he addressed one like himself or some wanderer of that race who, he had heard, were spreading themselves like hungry locusts throughout the land.

"The head of my brother is very white," he said, "but the eye of Le Balafré is no longer like the eagle's. Of what color is his skin?"

"The Wahcondah made me like these you see waiting for a Dakota judgment; but fair and foul has colored me darker than the skin of a fox. What of that! Though the bark is ragged and riven, the heart of the tree is sound."

"My brother is a Big Knife! Let him turn his face towards

the setting sun and open his eyes. Does he see the salt lake beyond the mountains?"

"The time has been, Teton, when few could see the white on an eagle's head further than I; but the glare of four-score and seven winters has dimmed my eyes, and but little can I boast of sight in my latter days. Does the Sioux think a paleface is a god, that he can look through hills!"

"Then let my brother look at me. I am nigh him, and he can see that I am a foolish red man. Why cannot his people see everything, since they crave all?"

"I understand you, chief, nor will I gainsay the justice of your words, seeing that they are too much founded in truth. But though born of the race you love so little, my worst enemy, not even a lying Mingo, would dare to say that I ever laid hands on the goods of another, except such as were taken in manful warfare, or that I ever coveted more ground than the Lord has intended each man to fill."

"And yet my brother has come among the redskins to find a son?"

The trapper laid a finger on the naked shoulder of Le Bala-fré and looked into his scarred countenance with a wistful and confidential expression as he answered, "Aye, but it was only that I might do good to the boy. If you think, Dakota, that I adopted the youth in order to prop my age, you do as much injustice to my good will as you seem to know little of the merciless intentions of your own people. I have made him my son that he may know that one is left behind him. Peace, Hector, peace! Is this decent, pup, when gray heads are counseling together, to break in upon their discourse with the whinings of a hound! The dog is old, Teton, and though well taught in respect to behavior, he is getting, like ourselves, I fancy, something forgetful of the fashions of his youth."

Further discourse between these veterans was interrupted by a discordant yell which burst at that moment from the lips of the dozen withered crones who have already been mentioned as having forced themselves into a conspicuous part of the circle. The outcry was excited by a sudden change in the air of Hard Heart. When the old men turned to-wards the youth, they saw him standing in the very center of the ring with his head erect, his eye fixed on vacancy, one leg advanced and an arm a little raised, as if all his faculties were absorbed in the act of listening. A smile lighted his countenance for a single moment, and then the whole man sank again into his former look of dignity and coldness, suddenly recalled to self-possession. The movement had been construed into contempt, and even the tempers of the chiefs began to be excited. Unable to restrain their fury, the women broke into the circle in a body and commenced their attack by loading the captive with the most bitter revilings. They boasted of the various exploits which their sons had achieved at the expense of the different tribes of the Pawnees. They undervalued his own reputation and told him to look at Mahtoree if he had never yet seen a warrior. They accused him of having been suckled by a doe and of having drunk in cowardice with his mother's milk. In short, they lavished upon their unmoved captive a torrent of that vindictive abuse in which the women of the savages are so well known to excel, but which has been too often described to need a repetition here.

The effect of this outbreaking was inevitable. Le Balafré turned away disappointed and hid himself in the crowd, while the trapper, whose honest features were working with inward emotion, pressed nigher to his young friend, as those who are linked to the criminal by ties so strong as to brave the opinions of men are often seen to stand about the place of execution to support his dying moments. The excitement soon spread among the inferior warriors, though the chiefs still forbore to make the signal which committed the victim to their mercy. Mahtoree, who had awaited such a movement among his fellows with the wary design of concealing his own jealous hatred, soon grew weary of delay and by a glance of his eye encouraged the tormentors to proceed.

Weucha, who, eager for this sanction, had long stood watching the countenance of the chief, bounded forward at the signal like a bloodhound loosened from the leash. Forcing his way into the center of the hags, who were already proceeding from abuse to violence, he reproved their impatience and bade them wait until a warrior had begun to torment, and then they should see their victim shed tears like a woman.

The heartless savage commenced his efforts by flourishing his tomahawk about the head of the captive in such a manner as to give reason to suppose that each blow would bury the weapon in the flesh, while it was so governed as not to touch the skin. To this customary expedient Hard Heart was perfectly insensible. His eye kept the same steady, riveted look on the air, though the glittering ax described in its evolutions a bright circle of light before his countenance. Frustrated in this attempt, the callous Sioux laid the cold edge on the naked head of his victim and began to describe the different manners in which a prisoner might be flayed. The women kept time to his cruelties with their taunts and endeavored to force some expression of the lingerings of nature from the insensible features of the Pawnee. But he evidently reserved himself for the chiefs and for those moments of extreme anguish when the loftiness of his spirit might evince itself in a manner better becoming his high and untarnished reputation.

The eyes of the trapper followed every movement of the tomahawk with the interest of a real father, until at length, unable to command his indignation, he exclaimed, "My son has forgotten his cunning. This is a low-minded Indian, and one easily hurried into folly. I cannot do the thing myself, for my traditions forbid a dying warrior to revile his persecutors, but the gifts of a redskin are different. Let the Pawnee say the bitter words and purchase an easy death. I will answer for his success, provided he speaks before the grave men set their wisdom to back the folly of this fool."

The savage Sioux, who heard his words without comprehending their meaning, turned to the speaker and menaced him with death for his temerity.

"Aye, work your will," said the unflinching old man; "I am as ready now as I shall be tomorrow. Though it would be a death that an honest man might not wish to die. Look at that noble Pawnee, Teton, and see what a redskin may become who fears the Master of Life and follows his laws. How many of your people has he sent to the distant prairies!" he continued in a sort of pious fraud, thinking that while the danger menaced himself, there could surely be no sin in extolling the merits of another. "How many howling Siouxes has he struck, like a warrior in open combat, while arrows were sailing in the air plentier than flakes of falling snow! Go! Will Weucha speak the name of one enemy he has ever struck?"

"Hard Heart!" shouted the Sioux, turning in his fury and aiming a deadly blow at the head of his victim. His arm fell into the hollow of the captive's hand. For a single moment the two stood as if entranced in that attitude, the one paralyzed by so unexpected a resistance and the other bending his head, not to meet his death, but in the act of the most intense attention. The women screamed with triumph, for they thought the nerves of the captive had at length failed him. The trapper trembled for the honor of his friend; and Hector, as if conscious of what was passing, raised his nose into the air and uttered a piteous howl.

But the Pawnee hesitated only for that moment. Raising the other hand like lightning, the tomahawk flashed in the air, and Weucha sank to his feet, brained to the eye. Then cutting a way with the bloody weapon, he darted through the opening left by the frightened women and seemed to descend the declivity at a single bound.

Had a bolt from heaven fallen in the midst of the Teton band it would not have occasioned greater consternation than this act of desperate hardihood. A shrill plaintive cry burst from the lips of all the women, and there was a moment that even the oldest warriors appeared to have lost their faculties. This stupor endured only for the instant. It was succeeded by a yell of revenge that burst from a hundred throats, while as many warriors started forward at the cry, bent on the most bloody retribution. But a powerful and authoritative call from Mahtoree arrested every foot. The chief, in whose countenance disappointment and rage were struggling with the affected composure of his station, extended an arm towards the river, and the whole mystery was explained.

Hard Heart had already crossed half the bottom which lay between the acclivity and the water. At this precise moment a band of armed and mounted Pawnees turned a swell and galloped to the margin of the stream, into which the plunge of the fugitive was distinctly heard. A few minutes sufficed for his vigorous arm to conquer the passage, and then the shout from the opposite shore told the humbled Tetons the whole extent of the triumph of their adversaries.

CHAPTER 29

If that shepherd be not in hand-fast, let him fly; the curses he shall have, the tortures he shall feel, will break the back of man, the heart of monster.

SHAKESPEARE

IT WILL READILY be seen that the event just related was attended by an extraordinary sensation among the Siouxes. In leading the hunters of the band back to the encampment, their chief had neglected none of the customary precautions of Indian prudence in order that his trail might escape the eyes of his enemies. It would seem, however, that the Pawnees had not only made the dangerous discovery, but had managed with great art to draw nigh the place by the only side on which it was thought unnecessary to guard the approaches with the usual line of sentinels. The latter, who were scattered along the different little eminences which lay in the rear of the lodges, were among the last to be apprised of the danger.

In such a crisis there was little time for deliberation. It was by exhibiting the force of his character in scenes of similar difficulty that Mahtoree had obtained and strengthened his ascendancy among his people, nor did he seem likely to lose it by the manifestation of any indecision on the present occasion. In the midst of the screams of the young, the shrieks of the women, and the wild howlings of the crones, which were sufficient of themselves to have created a chaos in the thoughts of one less accustomed to act in emergencies, he promptly asserted his authority, issuing his orders with the coolness of a veteran.

While the warriors were arming, the boys were dispatched to the bottom for the horses. The tents were hastily struck by the women and disposed of on such of the beasts as were not deemed fit to be trusted in combat. The infants were cast upon the backs of their mothers, and those children who were of a size to march were driven to the rear like a herd of less reasoning animals. Though these several movements were made amid outcries and a clamor that likened the place to another Babel, they were executed with incredible alacrity and intelligence.

In the meantime Mahtoree neglected no duty that belonged to his responsible station. From the elevation on which he stood he could command a perfect view of the force and evolutions of the hostile party. A grim smile lighted his visage when he found that, in point of numbers, his own band was greatly the superior. Notwithstanding this advantage, however, there were other points of inequality, which would probably have a tendency to render his success in the approaching conflict exceedingly doubtful. His people were the inhabitants of a more northern and less hospitable

region than their enemies and were far from being rich in
that species of property, horses and arms, which con-
stitutes the most highly prized wealth of a Western Indian.
The band in view was mounted to a man; and as it had come
so far to rescue or to revenge their greatest partisan, he had
no reason to doubt its being composed entirely of braves.
On the other hand, many of his followers were far better in
a hunt than in a combat, men who might serve to divert the
attention of his foes but from whom he could expect little
desperate service. Still, his flashing eye glanced over a body
of warriors on whom he had often relied and who had
never deceived him; and though, in the precise position in
which he found himself, he felt no disposition to precipi-
tate the conflict, he certainly would have had no intention to
avoid it had not the presence of his women and children
placed the option altogether in the power of his adversaries.

On the other hand, the Pawnees, so unexpectedly successful in their first and greatest object, manifested no intention
to drive matters to an issue. The river was a dangerous barrier to pass in the face of a determined foe, and it would now
have been in perfect accordance with their cautious policy to
have retired for a season in order that their onset might be
made in the hours of darkness and of seeming security. But
there was a spirit in their chief that elevated him for the
moment above the ordinary expedients of savage warfare.
His bosom burned with the desire to wipe out that disgrace of
which he had been the subject, and it is possible that he believed the retiring camp of the Siouxes contained a prize
that began to have a value in his eyes, far exceeding any that
could be found in fifty Teton scalps. Let that be as it might,
Hard Heart had no sooner received the brief congratula-
tions of his band and communicated to the chiefs such
facts as were important to be known than he prepared himself
to act such a part in the coming conflict as would at once
maintain his well-earned reputation and gratify his secret
wishes. A led horse, one that had been long trained in the
hunts, had been brought to receive his master, with but little
hope that his services would ever be needed again in this
life. With a delicacy and consideration that proved how much
the generous qualities of the youth had touched the feelings
of his people, a bow, a lance, and a quiver were thrown
across the animal, which it had been intended to immolate

on the grave of the young brave, a species of care that would have superseded the necessity for the pious duty that the trapper had pledged himself to perform.

Though Hard Heart was sensible of the kindness of his warriors and believed that a chief, furnished with such appointments, might depart with credit for the distant hunting grounds of the Master of Life, he seemed equally disposed to think that they might be rendered quite as useful in the actual state of things. His countenance lighted with stern pleasure as he tried the elasticity of the bow and poised the well-balanced spear. The glance he bestowed on the shield was more cursory and indifferent, but the exultation with which he threw himself on the back of his favored warhorse was so great as to break through the forms of Indian reserve. He rode to and fro among his scarcely less delighted warriors, managing the animal with a grace and address that no artificial rules can ever supply, at times flourishing his lance as if to assure himself of his seat, and at others examining critically into the condition of the fusee, with which he had also been furnished, with the fondness of one who was miraculously restored to the possession of treasures that constituted his pride and his happiness.

At this particular moment, Mahtoree, having completed the necessary arrangements, prepared to make a more decisive movement. The Teton had found no little embarrassment in disposing of his captives. The tents of the squatter were still in sight, and his wary cunning did not fail to apprise him that it was quite as necessary to guard against an attack from that quarter as to watch the motions of his more open and more active foes. His first impulse had been to make the tomahawk suffice for the men and to trust the females under the same protection as the women of his band, but the manner in which many of his braves continued to regard the imaginary medicine of the Long Knives forewarned him of the danger of so hazardous an experiment on the eve of a battle. It might be deemed the omen of defeat. In this dilemma he motioned to a superannuated warrior to whom he had confided the charge of the noncombatants, and leading him apart, he placed a finger significantly on his shoulder as he said in a tone in which authority was tempered by confidence, "When my young men are striking the Pawnees, give the women knives. Enough;

my father is very old; he does not want to hear wisdom from a boy."

The grim old savage returned a look of ferocious assent, and then the mind of the chief appeared to be at rest on this important subject. From that moment he bestowed all his care on the achievement of his revenge and the maintenance of his martial character. Throwing himself on his horse, he made a sign, with the air of a prince, to his followers to imitate his example, interrupting, without ceremony, the war songs and solemn rites by which many among them were stimulating their spirits to deeds of daring. When all were in order, the whole moved with great steadiness and silence towards the margin of the river.

The hostile bands were now separated by the water. The width of the stream was too great to admit of the use of the ordinary Indian missiles, but a few useless shots were exchanged from the fusees of the chiefs, more in bravado than with any expectation of doing execution. As some time was suffered to elapse in demonstrations and abortive efforts, we shall leave them for that period to return to such of our characters as remained in the hands of the savages.

We have shed much ink in vain and wasted quires that might possibly have been better employed, if it be necessary now to tell the reader that few of the foregoing movements escaped the observation of the experienced trapper. He had been, in common with the rest, astonished at the sudden act of Hard Heart, and there was a single moment when a feeling of regret and mortification got the better of his longings to save the life of the youth. The simple and well-intentioned old man would have felt, at witnessing any failure of firmness on the part of a warrior who had so strongly excited his sympathies, the same species of sorrow that a Christian parent would suffer in hanging over the dying moments of an impious child. But when, instead of an impotent and unmanly struggle for existence, he found that his friend had forborne, with the customary and dignified submission of an Indian warrior, until an opportunity had offered to escape, and that he had then manifested the spirit and decision of the most gifted brave, his gratification became nearly too powerful to be concealed. In the midst of the wailing and commotion which succeeded the death of Weucha and the escape of the captive, he placed himself nigh the persons of his white associates with a determination of interfering at every hazard should the fury of the savages take that direction. The appearance of the hostile band spared him, however, so desperate and probably so fruitless an effort and left him to pursue his observations and to mature his plans more at leisure.

He particularly remarked that while by far the greater part of the women and all the children, together with the effects of the party, were hurried to the rear, probably with an order to secrete themselves in some of the adjacent woods, the tent of Mahtoree himself was left standing and its contents undisturbed. Two chosen horses, however, stood nearby, held by a couple of youths who were too young to go into the conflict and yet of an age to understand the management of the beasts. The trapper perceived in this arrangement the reluctance of Mahtoree to trust his newly found "flowers" beyond the reach of his eye, and at the same time, his forethought in providing against a reverse of fortune. Neither had the manner of the Teton in giving his commission to the old savage nor the fierce pleasure with which the latter had received the bloody charge escaped his observation. From all these mysterious movements the old man was aware that a crisis was at hand, and he summoned the utmost knowledge he had acquired in so long a life to aid him in the desperate conjuncture. While musing on the means to be employed, the doctor again attracted his attention to himself by a piteous appeal for assistance.

"Venerable trapper, or, as I may now say, liberator," commenced the dolorous Obed, "it would seem that a fitting time has at length arrived to dissever the unnatural and altogether irregular connection which exists between my inferior members and the body of *Asinus*. Perhaps if such a portion of my limbs were released as might leave me master of the remainder, and this favorable opportunity were suitably improved by making a forced march towards the settlements, all hopes of preserving the treasures of knowledge of which I am the unworthy receptacle would not be lost. The importance of the results is surely worth the hazard of the experiment."

"I know not, I know not," returned the deliberate old man; "the vermin and reptiles which you bear about you were intended by the Lord for the prairies, and I see no good in sending them into regions that may not suit their natur's.

And, moreover, you may be of great and particular use as you now sit on the ass, though it creates no wonder in my mind to perceive that you are ignorant of it, seeing that usefulness is altogether a new calling to so bookish a man."

"Of what service can I be in this painful thralldom, in which the animal functions are in a manner suspended and the spiritual or intellectual blinded by the secret sympathy that unites mind to matter? There is likely to be blood spilt between yonder adverse hosts of heathens; and though but little desiring the office, it would be better that I should employ myself in surgical experiments than in thus wasting the precious moments mortifying both soul and body."

"It is little that a redskin would care to have a physician to his hurts while the whoop is ringing in his ears. Patience is a virtue in an Indian and can be no shame to a Christian white man. Look at these hags of squaws, friend doctor; I have no judgment in savage tempers if they are not bloody-minded and ready to work their accursed pleasures on us all. Now, so long as you keep upon the ass and maintain the fierce look which is far from being your natural gift, fear of so great a medicine may serve to keep down their courage. I am placed here like a general at the opening of the battle, and it has become my duty to make such use of all my force as, in my judgment, each is best fitted to perform. If I know these niceties, you will be more serviceable for your countenance just now than in any more stirring exploits."

"Harkee, old trapper," shouted Paul, whose patience could no longer maintain itself under the calculating and prolix explanations of the other, "suppose you cut two things I can name, short off. That is to say, your conversation, which is agreeable enough over a well-baked buffalo's hump, and these damnable thongs of hide, which, according to my experience, can be pleasant nowhere. A single stroke of your knife would be of more service just now than the longest speech that was ever made in a Kentucky courthouse."

"Aye, courthouses are the 'happy hunting grounds,' as a redskin would say, for them that are born with gifts no better than such as lie in the tongue. I was carried into one of the lawless holes myself once, and it was all about a thing of no more value than the skin of a deer. The Lord forgive them! The Lord forgive them! They knew no better, and they did according to their weak judgments, and therefore the more are they to be pitied; and yet it was a solemn sight to see an aged man who had always lived in the air laid neck and heels by the law and held up as a spectacle for the women and boys of a wasteful settlement to point their fingers at!"

"If such be your opinions of confinement, honest friend, you had better manifest the same by putting us at liberty with as little delay as possible," said Middleton, who, like his companion, began to find the tardiness of his often-tried companion quite as extraordinary as it was disagreeable.

"I should greatly like to do the same, especially in your behalf, captain, who, being a soldier, might find not only pleasure but profit in examining, more at your ease, into the circumventions and cunning of an Indian fight. As to our friend here, it is of but little matter how much of this affair he examines, or how little, seeing that a bee is not to be overcome in the same manner as an Indian."

"Old man, this trifling with our misery is inconsiderate, to give it a name no harsher——"

"Aye, your gran'ther was of a hot and hurrying mind, and one must not expect that the young of the panther will crawl the 'arth like the litter of a porcupine. Now keep you both silent, and what I say shall have the appearance of being spoken concerning the movements that are going on in the bottom, all of which will serve to put jealousy to sleep and to shut the eyes of such as rarely close them on wickedness and cruelty. In the first place, then, you must know that I have reason to think yonder treacherous Teton has left an order to put us all to death so soon as he thinks the deed may be done secretly and without tumult."

"Great heaven! Will you suffer us to be butchered like unresisting sheep?"

"Hist, captain, hist; a hot temper is none of the best when cunning is more needed than blows. Ah, the Pawnee is a noble boy! It would do your heart good to see how he draws off from the river in order to invite his enemies to cross; and yet, according to my failing sight, they count two warriors to his one! But as I was saying, little good comes of haste and thoughtlessness. The facts are so plain that any child may see their wisdom. The savages are of many minds as to the manner of our treatment. Some fear us for our color and would gladly let us go, and other some would show us the mercy that the doe receives from the hungry wolf. When opposition gets fairly into the councils of a tribe, it is rare that humanity is the gainer. Now see you these wrinkled and cruel-minded squaws—no, you cannot see them as you lie, but nevertheless they are here, ready and willing, like so many raging she-bears, to work their will upon us so soon as the proper time shall come."

"Harkee, old gentleman trapper," interrupted Paul with a little bitterness in his manner; "do you tell us these matters for our amusement or for your own? If for ours, you may keep your breath for the next race you run, as I am tickled nearly to suffocation already with my part of the fun."

"Hist!" said the trapper, cutting with great dexterity and rapidity the thong which bound one of the arms of Paul to his body, and dropping his knife at the same time within reach of the liberated hand. "Hist, boy, hist! That was a lucky moment! The yell from the bottom drew the eyes of these bloodsuckers in another quarter, and so far we are safe. Now make a proper use of your advantages, but be careful that what you do is done without being seen."

"Thank you for this small favor, old deliberation," muttered the bee hunter, "though it comes like a snow in May, somewhat out of season."

"Foolish boy!" reproachfully exclaimed the other, who had moved to a little distance from his friends and appeared to be attentively regarding the movements of the hostile parties. "Will you never learn to know the wisdom of patience? And you too, captain; though a man myself that seldom ruffles his temper by vain feelings, I see that you are silent because you scorn to ask favors any longer from one you think too slow to grant them. No doubt ye are both young and filled with the pride of your strength and manhood, and I dare say you thought it only needful to cut the thongs to leave you masters of the ground. But he that has seen much is apt to think much. Had I run like a bustling woman to have given you freedom, these hags of the Siouxes would have seen the same, and then where would you both have found yourselves? Under the tomahawk and the knife, like helpless and outcrying children, though gifted with the size and beards of men. Ask our friend the bee hunter in what condition he finds himself to struggle with a Teton boy after so many hours of bondage, much less with a dozen marciless and bloodthirsty squaws!"

"Truly, old trapper," returned Paul, stretching his limbs, which were by this time entirely released, and endeavoring

to restore the suspended circulation, "you have some judg-
matical notions in these matters. Now here am I, Paul Hover,
a man who will give in to few at wrestle or race, nearly as
helpless as the day I paid my first visit to the house of old
Paul, who is dead and gone—the Lord forgive him any little
blunders he may have made while he tarried in Kentucky!
Now there is my foot on the ground, so far as eyesight has
any virtue, and yet it would take no great temptation to make
me swear it didn't touch the earth by six inches. I say,
honest friend, since you have done so much, have the goodness to keep these damnable squaws, of whom you say so
many interesting things, at a little distance till I have got
the blood of this arm in motion and am ready to receive
them."

The trapper made a sign that he perfectly understood the
case, and he walked towards the superannuated savage, who
began to manifest an intention of commencing his assigned
task, leaving the bee hunter to recover the use of his limbs
as well as he could and to put Middleton in a similar
situation to defend himself.

Mahtoree had not mistaken his man in selecting the one
he did to execute his bloody purpose. He had chosen one of
those ruthless savages, more or less of whom are to be
found in every tribe, who had purchased a certain share of
military reputation by the exhibition of a hardihood that
found its impulses in an innate love of cruelty. Contrary to
the high and chivalrous sentiment which among the Indians
of the prairies renders it a deed of even greater merit to
bear off the trophy of victory from a fallen foe than to
slay him, he had been remarkable for preferring the pleasure
of destroying life to the glory of striking the dead. While
the more self-devoted and ambitious braves were intent on
personal honor, he had always been seen, established behind
some favorable cover, depriving the wounded of hope by
finishing that which a more gallant warrior had begun. In all
the cruelties of the tribe he had ever been foremost, and
no Sioux was so uniformly found on the side of merciless
counsels.

He had awaited with an impatience which his long-
practiced restraint could with difficulty subdue for the moment to arrive when he might proceed to execute the wishes
of the great chief, without whose approbation and powerful
protection he would not have dared to undertake a step that

had so many opposers in the nation. But events had been hastening to an issue between the hostile parties, and the time had now arrived, greatly to his secret and malignant joy, when he was free to act his will.

The trapper found him distributing knives to the ferocious hags, who received the presents chanting a low monotonous song that recalled the losses of their people in various conflicts with the whites and which extolled the pleasures and glory of revenge. The appearance of such a group was enough of itself to have deterred one less accustomed to such sights than the old man from trusting himself within the circle of their wild and repulsive rites.

Each of the crones, as she received the weapon, commenced a slow and measured but ungainly step around the savage until the whole were circling him in a sort of magic dance. The movements were timed, in some degree, by the words of their songs, as were their gestures by the ideas. When they spoke of their own losses, they tossed their long straight locks of gray into the air or suffered them to fall in confusion upon their withered necks; but as the sweetness of returning blow for blow was touched upon by any among them, it was answered by a common howl, as well as by gestures that were sufficiently expressive of the manner in which they were exciting themselves to the necessary state of fury.

Into the very center of this ring of seeming demons the trapper now stalked, with the same calmness and observation as he would have walked into a village church. No other change was made by his appearance than a renewal of the threatening gestures with, if possible, a still less equivocal display of their remorseless intentions. Making a sign for them to cease, the old man demanded, "Why do the mothers of the Tetons sing with bitter tongues? The Pawnee prisoners are not yet in their village; their young men have not come back loaded with scalps!"

He was answered by a general howl, and a few of the boldest of the furies even ventured to approach him, flourishing their knives within a dangerous proximity of his own steady eyeballs.

"It is a warrior you see, and no runner of the Long Knives, whose face grows pale at the sight of a tomahawk," returned the trapper without moving a muscle. "Let the

Sioux women think; if one whiteskin dies, a hundred spring up where he falls."

Still the hags made no other answer than by increasing their speed in the circle, and occasionally raising the threatening expressions of their chant into louder and more intelligible strains. Suddenly one of the oldest and the most ferocious of them all broke out of the ring and skirred away in the direction of her victims, like a rapacious bird that, having wheeled on poised wings for the time necessary to ensure its object, makes the final dart upon its prey. The others followed, a disorderly and screaming flock, fearful of being too late to reap their portion of the sanguinary pleasure.

"Mighty medicine of my people," shouted the old man in the Teton tongue, "lift your voice and speak, that the Sioux nation may hear."

Whether *Asinus* had aquired so much knowledge by his recent experience as to know the value of his sonorous properties, or the strange spectacle of a dozen hags flitting past him, filling the air with such sounds as were even grating to the ears of an ass, most moved his temper, it is certain that the animal did that which Obed was requested to do, and probably with far greater effect than if the naturalist had striven with his mightiest effort to be heard. It was the first time the strange beast had spoken since his arrival in the encampment. Admonished by so terrible a warning, the hags scattered themselves like vultures frightened from their prey, still screaming and but half diverted from their purpose.

In the meantime the sudden appearance and the imminency of the danger quickened the blood in the veins of Paul and Middleton more than all their laborious frictions and physical expedients. The former had actually risen to his feet and assumed an attitude which perhaps threatened more than the worthy bee hunter was able to perform, and even the latter had mounted to his knees and shown a disposition to do good service for his life. The unaccountable release of the captives from their bonds was attributed by the hags to the incantations of the medicine, and the mistake was probably of as much service as the miraculous and timely interposition of *Asinus* in their favor.

"Now is the time to come out of our ambushment," exclaimed the old man, hastening to join his friends, "and to make open and manful war. It would have been policy to have kept back the struggle until the captain was in better condition to join, but as we have unmasked our battery, why, we must maintain the ground——"

He was interrupted by feeling a gigantic hand on his shoulder. Turning, under a sort of confused impression that necromancy was actually abroad in the place, he found that he was in the hands of a sorcerer no less dangerous and powerful than Ishmael Bush. The file of the squatter's well-armed sons that was seen issuing from behind the still standing tent of Mahtoree explained at once not only the manner in which their rear had been turned while their attention had been so earnestly bestowed on matters in front, but the utter impossibility of resistance.

Neither Ishmael nor his sons deemed it necessary to enter into prolix explanations. Middleton and Paul were bound again, with extraordinary silence and dispatch, and this time not even the aged trapper was exempt from a similar fortune. The tent was struck, the females placed upon the horses, and the whole were on the way towards the squatter's encampment, with a celerity that might well have served to keep alive the idea of magic.

During this summary and brief disposition of things, the disappointed agent of Mahtoree and his callous associates were seen flying across the plain in the direction of the retiring families; and when Ishmael left the spot with his prisoners and his booty, the ground which had so lately been alive with the bustle and life of an extensive Indian encampment was as still and empty as any other spot in those extensive wastes.

CHAPTER 30

Is this proceeding just and honorable?

SHAKESPEARE

DURING THE OCCURRENCE of these events on the upland plain, the warriors on the bottom had not been idle. We left the adverse bands watching one another on the opposite banks of the stream, each endeavoring to excite its enemy to some act of indiscretion by the most reproachful taunts and revilings. But the Pawnee chief was not slow to discover that his crafty antagonist had no objection to waste the time so idly and, as they mutually proved, in expedients that were so entirely useless. He changed his plans accordingly and withdrew from the bank, as has been already explained through the mouth of the trapper, in order to invite the more numerous host of the Siouxes to cross. The challenge was not accepted, and the Loups were compelled to frame some other method to attain their end.

Instead of any longer throwing away the precious moments in fruitless endeavors to induce his foe to cross the stream, the young partisan of the Pawnees led his troops at a swift gallop along its margin in quest of some favorable spot where by a sudden push he might throw his own band without loss to the opposite shore. The instant his object was discovered, each mounted Teton received a footman behind him, and Mahtoree was still enabled to concentrate his whole force against the effort. Perceiving that his design was anticipated, and unwilling to blow his horses by a race that would disqualify them for service, even after they had succeeded in outstripping the more heavily burdened cattle of the Siouxes, Hard Heart drew up and came to a dead halt on the very margin of the watercourse.

As the country was too open for any of the usual devices of savage warfare, and time was so pressing, the chivalrous Pawnee resolved to bring on the result by one of those acts of personal daring for which the Indian braves are so remarkable and by which they often purchase their highest and dearest renown. The spot he had selected was favorable to such a project. The river, which throughout most of its course was deep and rapid, had expanded there to more than twice its customary width, and the rippling of its waters proved that it flowed over a shallow bottom. In the center of the current there was an extensive and naked bed of sand but a little raised above the level of the stream and of a color and consistency which warranted, to a practiced eye, that it afforded a firm and safe foundation for the foot. To this spot the partisan now turned his wistful gaze, nor was he long in making his decision. First speaking to his warriors and apprising them of his intentions, he dashed into the current, and partly by swimming, and more by the use of his horse's feet, he reached the island in safety.

The experience of Hard Heart had not deceived him. When his snorting steed issued from the water, he found himself on a tremendous but damp and compact bed of sand that was admirably adapted to the exhibition of the finest powers of the animal. The horse seemed conscious of the advantage and bore his warlike rider with an elasticity of step and a loftiness of air that would have done no discredit to the highest trained and most generous charger. The blood of the chief himself quickened with the excitement of his situation. He sat the beast as if conscious that the eyes of two tribes were on his movements; and as nothing could be more acceptable and grateful to his own band than this display of native grace and courage, so nothing could be more taunting and humiliating to their enemies.

The sudden appearance of the Pawnee on the sands was announced among the Tetons by a general yell of savage anger. A rush was made to the shore, followed by a discharge of fifty arrows and a few fusees, and on the part of several braves there was a plain manifestation of a desire to plunge into the water in order to punish the temerity of their insolent foe. But a call and a mandate from Mahtoree checked the rising and nearly ungovernable temper of his band. So far from allowing a single foot to be wet or a repetition of the fruitless efforts of his people to drive away their foe with missiles, the whole of the party was commanded to retire from the shore, while he himself communicated his intentions to one or two of his most favored followers.

When the Pawnees observed the rush of their enemies, twenty warriors rode into the stream; but so soon as they perceived that the Tetons had withdrawn, they fell back to a man, leaving the young chief to the support of his own often-tried skill and well-established courage. The instructions of Hard Heart on quitting his band had been worthy of the self-devotion and daring of his character. So long as single warriors came against him he was to be left to the keeping of the Wahcondah and his own arm, but should the Siouxes attack him in number, he was to be sustained man for man, even to the extent of his whole force. These generous orders were strictly obeyed, and though so many hearts in the troop panted to share in the glory and danger of their partisan, not a warrior was found among them all who did not know how to conceal his impatience under the usual mask of Indian self-restraint. They watched the issue with quick and jealous eyes, nor did a single exclamation of surprise escape them when they saw, as will soon be apparent, that the experiment of their chief was as likely to conduce to peace as to war.

Mahtoree was not long in communicating his plans to his confidants, whom he as quickly dismissed to join their fellows in the rear. The Teton entered a short distance into the stream and halted. Here he raised his hands several times, with the palm outwards, and made several of those other signs which are construed into a pledge of amicable intentions among the inhabitants of those regions. Then, as if to confirm the sincerity of his faith, he cast his fusee to the shore and entered deeper into the water, where he again came to a stand in order to see in what manner the Pawnee would receive his pledge of peace.

The crafty Sioux had not made his calculations on the noble and honest nature of his more youthful rival in vain. Hard Heart had continued galloping across the sands during the discharge of missiles and the appearance of a general onset with the same proud and confident mien as that with which he had first braved the danger. When he saw the well-known person of the Teton partisan enter the river, he waved his hand in triumph, and flourishing his lance, he raised the thrilling war cry of his people as a challenge for him to come on. But when he saw the signs of a truce, though deeply practiced in the treachery of savage combats, he disdained to show a less manly reliance on himself than that which his enemy had seen fit to exhibit. Riding to the furthest extremity of the sands, he cast his own fusee from him and returned to the point whence he had started.

The two chiefs were now armed alike. Each had his spear, his bow, his quiver, his little battle-ax, and his knife; and each had also a shield of hides, which might serve as a means of defense against a surprise from any of these weapons. The Sioux no longer hesitated, but advanced deeper into the stream, and soon landed on a point of the island which his courteous adversary had left free for that purpose. Had one been there to watch the countenance of Mahtoree as he crossed the water that separated him from the most formidable and the most hated of all his rivals, he might have fancied that he could trace the gleamings of a secret joy breaking through the cloud which deep cunning and heartless treachery had drawn before his swarthy visage; and yet there would have been moments when he might have believed that the flashings of the Teton's eye and the expansion of his nostrils had their origin in a nobler sentiment and one more worthy of an Indian chief.

The Pawnee awaited the time of his enemy with calmness and dignity. The Teton made a short turn or two to curb the impatience of his steed and to recover his seat after the effort of crossing, and then he rode into the center of the place and invited the other by a courteous gesture to approach. Hard Heart drew nigh until he found himself at a distance equally suited to advance or to retreat, and, in his turn, he came to a stand, keeping his glowing eye riveted on that of his enemy. A long and grave pause succeeded this movement, during which these two distinguished braves, who were now for the first time confronted with arms in their hands, sat regarding each other like warriors who knew how to value the merits of a gallant foe, however hated. But the mien of Mahtoree was far less stern and warlike than that of the partisan of the Loups. Throwing his shield over his shoulder, as if to invite the confidence of the other, he made a gesture of salutation and was the first to speak.

"Let the Pawnees go upon the hills," he said, "and look from the morning to the evening sun, from the country of snows to the land of many flowers, and they will see that the earth is very large. Why cannot the red men find room on it for all their villages?"

"Has the Teton ever known a warrior of the Loups come to his towns to beg a place for his lodge?" returned the young brave with a look in which pride and contempt were not attempted to be concealed. "When the Pawnees hunt, do they send runners to ask Mahtoree if there are no Siouxes on the prairies?"

"When there is hunger in the lodge of a warrior, he looks for the buffalo, which is given him for food," the Teton continued, struggling to keep down the ire excited by the other's scorn. "The Wahcondah has made more of them than he has made Indians. He has not said, 'This buffalo shall be for a Pawnee, and that for a Dakota; this beaver for a Konza, and that for an Omaha.' No; he said, 'There are enough. I love my red children, and I have given them great riches. The swiftest horse shall not go from the village of the Tetons to the village of the Loups in many suns. It is far from the towns of the Pawnees to the river of the Osages. There is room for all that I love.' Why then should a red man strike his brother?"

Hard Heart dropped one end of his lance to the earth, and having also cast his shield across his shoulder, he sat leaning lightly on the weapon as he answered with a smile of no doubtful expression, "Are the Tetons weary of the hunts and of the warpath? Do they wish to cook the venison, and not to kill it? Do they intend to let the hair cover their heads, that their enemies shall not know where to find their scalps? Go; a Pawnee warrior will never come among such Sioux squaws for a wife!"

A frightful gleam of ferocity broke out of the restraint of the Dakota's countenance as he listened to this biting insult, but he was quick in subduing the telltale feeling in an expression much better suited to his present purpose.

"This is the way a young chief should talk of war," he answered with singular composure; "but Mahtoree has seen the misery of more winters than his brother. When the nights have been long, and darkness has been in his lodge, while the young men slept, he has thought of the hardships of his people. He has said to himself, 'Teton, count the scalps in your smoke. They are all red but two! Does the wolf destroy the wolf, or the rattler strike his brother? You know they do not; therefore, Teton, are you wrong to go on a path that leads to the village of a redskin with a tomahawk in your hand.'"

"The Sioux would rob the warrior of his fame! He would say to his young men, 'Go, dig roots in the prairies and find holes to bury your tomahawks in; you are no longer braves!'"

"If the tongue of Mahtoree ever says thus," returned the crafty chief with an appearance of strong indignation, "let his women cut it out and burn it with the offals of the buffalo. No," he added, advancing a few feet nigher to the immovable Hard Heart, as if in the sincerity of confidence, "the red man can never want an enemy: they are plentier than the leaves on the trees, the birds in the heavens, or the buffaloes on the prairies. Let my brother open his eyes wide; does he nowhere see an enemy he would strike?"

"How long is it since the Teton counted the scalps of his warriors that were drying in the smoke of a Pawnee lodge? The hand that took them is here, and ready to make eighteen, twenty."

"Now, let not the mind of my brother go on a crooked path. If a redskin strikes a redskin forever, who will be masters of the prairies when no warriors are left to say,

'They are mine'? Hear the voices of the old men. They tell us that in their days many Indians have come out of the woods under the rising sun and that they have filled the prairies with their complaints of the robberies of the Long Knives. Where a paleface comes, a red man cannot stay. The land is too small. They are always hungry. See, they are here already!"

As the Teton spoke, he pointed towards the tents of Ishmael, which were in plain sight, and then he paused to await the effect of his words on the mind of his ingenuous foe. Hard Heart listened like one in whom a train of novel ideas had been excited by the reasoning of the other. He mused for a minute before he demanded, "What do the wise chiefs of the Sioux say must be done?"

"They think that the moccasin of every paleface should be followed, like the track of the bear. That the Long Knife who comes upon the prairie should never go back. That the path shall be open to those who come, and shut to those who go. Yonder are many. They have horses and guns. They are rich, but we are poor. Will the Pawnees meet the Tetons in council? And when the sun is gone behind the Rocky Mountains, they will say, 'This is for a Loup and this for a Sioux.' "

"Teton—no! Hard Heart has never struck the stranger. They come into his lodge and eat, and they go out in safety. A mighty chief is their friend! When my people call the young men to go on the warpath, the moccasin of Hard Heart is the last. But his village is no sooner hid by the trees than it is the first. No, Teton, his arm will never be lifted against the stranger."

"Fool, die with empty hands!" Mahtoree exclaimed, setting an arrow to his bow and sending it, with a sudden and deadly aim, full at the naked bosom of his generous and confiding enemy.

The action of the treacherous Teton was too quick and too well matured to admit of any of the ordinary means of defense on the part of the Pawnee. His shield was hanging at his shoulder, and even the arrow had been suffered to fall from its place and lay in the hollow of the hand which grasped his bow. But the quick eye of the brave had time to see the movement, and his ready thoughts did not desert him. Pulling hard and with a jerk upon the rein, his steed reared his forward legs into the air, and as the rider bent his body low, the horse served for a shield against the danger. So true, however, was the aim, and so powerful the force by which it was sent, that the arrow entered the neck of the animal and broke the skin on the opposite side.

Quicker than thought Hard Heart sent back an answering arrow. The shield of the Teton was transfixed, but his person was untouched. For a few moments the twang of the bow and the glancing of arrows were incessant, notwithstanding the combatants were compelled to give so large a portion of their care to the means of defense. The quivers were soon exhausted, and though blood had been drawn, it was not in sufficient quantities to impair the energy of the combat.

A series of masterly and rapid evolutions with the horses now commenced. The wheelings, the charges, the advances, and the circuitous retreats were like the flights of circling swallows. Blows were struck with the lance, the sand was scattered in the air, and the shocks often seemed to be unavoidably fatal; but still each party kept his seat, and still each rein was managed with a steady hand. At length the Teton was driven to the necessity of throwing himself from his horse to escape a thrust that would otherwise have proved fatal. The Pawnee passed his lance through the beast, uttering a shout of triumph as he galloped by. Turning in his tracks, he was about to push the advantage, when his own mettled steed staggered and fell under a burden that he could no longer sustain. Mahtoree answered his premature cry of victory and rushed upon the entangled youth with knife and tomahawk. The utmost agility of Hard Heart had not sufficed to extricate himself in season from the fallen beast. He saw that his case was desperate. Feeling for his knife, he took the blade between a finger and thumb and cast it with admirable coolness at his advancing foe. The keen weapon whirled a few times in the air, and its point meeting the naked breast of the impetuous Sioux, the blade was buried to the buckhorn haft.

Mahtoree laid his hand on the weapon and seemed to hesitate whether to withdraw it or not. For a moment his countenance darkened with the most inextinguishable hatred and ferocity, and then, as if inwardly admonished how little time he had to lose, he staggered to the edge of the sands and halted with his feet in the water. The cunning and duplicity which had so long obscured the brighter and nobler traits of his character were lost in the never-dying sentiment of pride which he had imbibed in youth.

"Boy of the Loups," he said with a smile of grim satisfaction, "the scalp of a mighty Dakota shall never dry in Pawnee smoke!"

Drawing the knife from the wound, he hurled it towards the enemy in disdain. Then shaking his arm at his successful foe, his swarthy countenance appearing to struggle with volumes of scorn and hatred that he could not utter with the tongue, he cast himself headlong into one of the most rapid veins of the current, his hand still waving in triumph above the fluid, even after his body had sunk into the tide forever. Hard Heart was by this time free. The silence which had hitherto reigned in the bands was suddenly broken by general and tumultuous shouts. Fifty of the adverse warriors were already in the river, hastening to destroy or to defend the conqueror, and the combat was rather on the eve of its commencement than near its termination. But to all these signs of danger and need, the young victor was insensible. He sprang for the knife and bounded with the foot of an antelope along the sands, looking for the receding fluid which concealed his prize. A dark, bloody spot indicated the place, and armed with the knife, he plunged into the stream, resolute to die in the flood or to return with his trophy.

In the meantime the sands became a scene of bloodshed and violence. Better mounted and perhaps more ardent, the Pawnees had, however, reached the spot in sufficient numbers to force their enemies to retire. The victors pushed their success to the opposite shore and gained the solid ground in the melee of the fight. Here they were met by all the unmounted Tetons, and, in their turn, they were forced to give way.

The combat now became more characteristic and circumspect. As the hot impulses which had driven both parties to mingle in so deadly a struggle began to cool, the chiefs were enabled to exercise their influence and to temper the assaults with prudence. In consequence of the admonitions of their leaders, the Siouxes sought such covers as the grass afforded, or here and there some bush or slight inequality of the ground, and the charges of the Pawnee warriors necessarily became more wary, and of course less fatal.

In this manner the contest continued with a varied success, and without much loss. The Siouxes had succeeded in forcing themselves into a thick growth of rank grass, where the horses of their enemies could not enter, or where, when entered, they were worse than useless. It became necessary to dislodge the Tetons from this cover, or the object of the combat must be abandoned. Several desperate efforts had been repulsed, and the disheartened Pawnees were beginning to think of a retreat when the well-known war cry of Hard Heart was heard at hand, and at the next instant the chief appeared in their center, flourishing the scalp of the great Sioux as a banner that would lead to victory.

He was greeted by a shout of delight and followed into the cover with an impetuosity that, for the moment, drove all before it. But the bloody trophy in the hand of the partisan served as an incentive to the attacked as well as to the assailants. Mahtoree had left many a daring brave behind him in his band, and the orator who in the debates of that day had manifested such pacific thoughts now exhibited the most generous self-devotion in order to wrest the memorial of a man he had never loved from the hands of the avowed enemies of his people.

The result was in favor of numbers. After a severe struggle, in which the finest displays of personal intrepidity were exhibited by all the chiefs, the Pawnees were compelled to retire upon the open bottom, closely pressed by the Siouxes, who failed not to seize each foot of ground ceded by their enemies. Had the Tetons stayed their efforts on the margin of the grass, it is probable that the honor of the day would have been theirs, notwithstanding the irretrievable loss they had sustained in the death of Mahtoree. But the more reckless braves of the band were guilty of an indiscretion that entirely changed the fortunes of the fight and suddenly stripped them of their hard-earned advantages.

A Pawnee chief had sunk under the numerous wounds he had received, and he fell, a target for a dozen arrows, in the very last group of his retiring party. Regardless alike of inflicting further injury on their foes and of the temerity of the act, the Sioux braves bounded forward with a whoop, each man burning with the wish to reap the high renown of striking the body of the dead. They were met by Hard Heart and a chosen knot of warriors, all of whom were just as stoutly bent on saving the honor of their nation from so foul a stain. The struggle was hand to hand, and blood began to flow more freely. As the Pawnees retired with the body, the Siouxes pressed upon their footsteps, and at length the whole of the latter broke out of the cover with a common yell and threatened to bear down all opposition by sheer physical superiority.

The fate of Hard Heart and his companions, all of whom would have died rather than relinquish their object, would have been quickly sealed but for a powerful and unlooked-for interposition in their favor. A shout was heard from a little brake on the left, and a volley from the fatal Western rifle immediately succeeded. Some five or six Siouxes leaped forward in the death agony, and every arm among them was as suddenly suspended as if the lightning had flashed from the clouds to aid the cause of the Loups. Then came Ishmael and his stout sons in open view, bearing down upon their late treacherous allies with looks and voices that proclaimed the character of the succor.

The shock was too much for the fortitude of the Tetons. Several of their bravest chiefs had already fallen, and those that remained were instantly abandoned by the whole of the inferior herd. A few of the most desperate braves still lingered nigh the fatal symbol of their honor and there nobly met their deaths under the blows of the reencouraged Pawnees. A second discharge from the rifles of the squatter and his party completed the victory.

The Siouxes were now to be seen flying to more distant covers, with the same eagerness and desperation as, a few moments before, they had been plunging into the fight. The triumphant Pawnees bounded forward in chase like so many high-blooded and well-trained hounds. On every side were heard the cries of victory or the yell of revenge. A few of the fugitives endeavored to bear away the bodies of their fallen warriors, but the hot pursuit quickly compelled them to abandon the slain in order to preserve the living. Among all the struggles which were made on that occasion to guard the honor of the Siouxes from the stain which their peculiar opinions attached to the possession of the scalp of a fallen brave, but one solitary instance of success occurred.

The opposition of a particular chief to the hostile proceedings in the councils of that morning has been already seen. But after having raised his voice in vain in support of peace, his arm was not backward in doing its duty in the war. His prowess has been mentioned, and it was chiefly by his courage and example that the Tetons sustained themselves in the heroic manner they did when the death of Mahtoree was known. This warrior, who, in the figurative language of his people, was called the Swooping Eagle, had been the last to abandon the hopes of victory. When he found that the support of the dreaded rifle had robbed his band of the hard-earned advantages, he sullenly retired amid a shower of missiles to the secret spot where he had hid his horse in the mazes of the highest grass. Here he found a new and an entirely unexpected competitor, ready to dispute with him for the possession of the beast. It was Bohrecheena, the aged friend of Mahtoree, he whose voice has been given in opposition to his own wiser opinions, transfixed with an arrow and evidently suffering under the pangs of approaching death.

"I have been on my last warpath," said the grim old warrior when he found that the real owner of the animal had come to claim his property; "shall a Pawnee carry the white hairs of a Sioux into his village to be a scorn to his women and children?"

The other grasped his hand, answering to the appeal with a stern look of inflexible resolution. With this silent pledge he assisted the wounded man to mount. So soon as he had led the horse to the margin of the cover, he threw himself also on its back, and securing his companion to his belt, he issued on the open plain, trusting entirely to the well-known speed of the beast for their mutual safety. The Pawnees were not long in catching a view of these new objects, and several turned their steeds to pursue. The race continued for a mile without a murmur from the sufferer, though, in addition to the agony of his body, he had the pain of seeing his enemies approach at every leap of their horses.

"Stop," he said, raising a feeble arm to check the speed of his companion; "the Eagle of my tribe must spread his wings wider. Let him carry the white hairs of an old warrior into the burnt-wood village!"

Few words were necessary between men who were governed by the same feelings of glory and who were so well trained in the principles of their romantic honor. The Swooping Eagle threw himself from the back of the horse and assisted the other to alight. The old man raised his tottering frame to its knees, and first casting a glance upwards at the countenance of his countryman, as if to bid him adieu, he stretched out his neck to the blow he himself invited. A few strokes of the tomahawk, with a circling gash of the knife, sufficed to sever the head from the less valued trunk. The Teton mounted

again, just in season to escape a flight of arrows which
came from his eager and disappointed pursuers. Flourishing
the grim and bloody visage, he darted away from the spot
with a shout of triumph, and was seen scouring the plains,
as if he were actually borne along on the wings of the powerful bird from whose qualities he had received his flattering
name. The Swooping Eagle reached his village in safety. He
was one of the few Siouxes who escaped from the massacre of
that fatal day, and for a long time he alone of the saved
was able to lift his voice in the councils of his nation with
undiminished confidence.

The knife and the lance cut short the retreat of the larger
portion of the vanquished. Even the retiring party of the
women and children were scattered by the conquerors, and
the sun had long sunk behind the rolling outline of the western horizon before the fell business of that disastrous
defeat was entirely ended.

CHAPTER 31

Which is the merchant here, and which the Jew?
SHAKESPEARE

THE DAY DAWNED the following morning on a more tranquil
scene. The work of blood had entirely ceased; and as the sun
arose, its light was shed on a broad expanse of quiet and
solitude. The tents of Ishmael were still standing where they
had been last seen, but not another vestige of human existence
could be traced in any other part of the waste. Here and
there little flocks of ravenous birds were sailing and screaming
above those spots where some heavy-footed Teton had met
his death, but every other sign of the recent combat had
passed away. The river was to be traced far through the endless meadows by its serpentine and smoking bed, and the little
silvery clouds of vapor which hung above the pools and
springs were beginning to melt in air as they felt the quickening warmth, which, pouring from the glowing sky, shed its
bland and subtle influence on every object of the vast and
unshadowed region. The prairie was like the heavens after the
passage of the gust, soft, calm, and soothing.

It was in the midst of such a scene that the family of the
squatter assembled to make their final decision concerning the

several individuals who had been thrown into their power by the fluctuating chances of the incidents related. Every being possessing life and liberty had been afoot since the first streak of gray had lighted the east, and even the youngest of the erratic brood seemed conscious that the moment had arrived when circumstances were about to occur that might leave a lasting impression on the wild fortunes of their semibarbarous condition.

Ishmael moved through his little encampment with the seriousness of one who had been unexpectedly charged with matters of a gravity exceeding any of the ordinary occurrences of his irregular existence. His sons, however, who had so often found occasions to prove the inexorable severity of their father's character, saw in his sullen mien and cold eye rather a determination to adhere to his resolutions, which usually were as obstinately enforced as they were harshly conceived, than any evidences of wavering or doubt. Even Esther was sensibly affected by the important matters that pressed so heavily on the interests of her family. While she neglected none of those domestic offices which would probably have proceeded under any conceivable circumstances, just as the world turns round with earthquakes rending its crust and volcanoes consuming its vitals, yet her voice was pitched to a lower and more foreboding key than common, and the still frequent chidings of her children were tempered by something like the milder dignity of parental authority.

Abiram, as usual, seemed the one most given to solicitude and doubt. There were certain misgivings in the frequent glances that he turned on the unyielding countenance of Ishmael, which might have betrayed how little of their former confidence and good understanding existed between them. His looks appeared to be vacillating between hope and fear. At times his countenance lighted with the gleamings of a sordid joy as he bent his look on the tent which contained his recovered prisoner, and then, again, the impression seemed unaccountably chased away by the shadows of intense apprehension. When under the influence of the latter feeling, his eye never failed to seek the visage of his dull and impenetrable kinsman. But there he rather found reason for alarm than grounds of encouragement, for the whole character of the squatter's countenance expressed the fearful truth that he had redeemed his dull faculties from the influence of the kidnapper and that his thoughts were now brooding only on the achievement of his own stubborn intentions.

It was in this state of things that the sons of Ishmael, in obedience to an order from their father, conducted the several subjects of his contemplated decisions from their places of confinement into the open air. No one was exempted from this arrangement. Middleton and Inez, Paul and Ellen, Obed and the trapper, were all brought forth and placed in situations that were deemed suitable to receive the sentence of their arbitrary judge. The younger children gathered around the spot in momentary but engrossing curiosity, and even Esther quitted her culinary labors and drew nigh to listen.

Hard Heart alone of all his band was present to witness the novel and far from unimposing spectacle. He stood leaning gravely on his lance, while the smoking steed that grazed nigh showed that he had ridden far and hard to be a spectator on the occasion.

Ishmael had received his new ally with a coldness that showed his entire insensibility to that delicacy which had induced the young chief to come alone in order that the presence of his warriors might not create uneasiness or distrust. He neither courted their assistance nor dreaded their enmity, and he now proceeded to the business of the hour with as much composure as if the species of patriarchal power he wielded was universally recognized.

There is something elevated in the possession of authority, however it may be abused. The mind is apt to make some efforts to prove the fitness between its qualities and the condition of its owner, though it may often fail and render that ridiculous which was only hated before. But the effect on Ishmael Bush was not so disheartening. Grave in exterior, saturnine by temperament, formidable by his physical means, and dangerous from his lawless obstinacy, his self-constituted tribunal excited a degree of awe to which even the intelligent Middleton could not bring himself to be entirely insensible. Little time, however, was given to arrange his thoughts, for the squatter, though unaccustomed to haste, having previously made up his mind, was not disposed to waste the moments in delay. When he saw that all were in their places, he cast a dull look over his prisoners and addressed himself to the captain as the principal man among the imaginary delinquents.

"I am called upon this day to fill the office which in the set-

tlements you give unto judges, who are set apart to decide
on matters that arise between man and man. I have but little
knowledge of the ways of the courts, though there is a rule
that is known unto all and which teaches that an 'eye must
be returned for an eye,' and 'a tooth for a tooth.' I am no
troubler of county houses, and least of all do I like living
on a plantation that the sheriff has surveyed; yet there is a
reason in such a law that makes it a safe rule to journey
by, and therefore it are a solemn fact that this day shall I
abide by it and give unto all and each that which is his due
and no more."

When Ishmael had delivered his mind thus far, he paused
and looked about him as if he would trace the effects in
the countenances of his hearers. When his eye met that of
Middleton he was answered by the latter, "If the evildoer is
to be punished, and he that has offended none to be left
to go at large, you must change situations with me and become a prisoner instead of a judge."

"You mean to say that I have done you wrong in taking
the lady from her father's house and leading her so far
against her will into these wild districts," returned the unmoved squatter, who manifested as little resentment as he
betrayed compunction at the charge. "I shall not put the lie
on the back of an evil deed and deny your words. Since
things have come to this pass between us, I have found time
to think the matter over at my leisure, and though none of
your swift thinkers who can see or who pretend to see into
the nature of all things by a turn of the eye, yet am I a man
open to reason, and give me my time, one who is not given
to deny the truth. Therefore have I mainly concluded that it
was a mistake to take a child from its parent, and the lady
shall be returned whence she has been brought, as tenderly
and as safely as man can do it."

"Aye, aye," added Esther, "the man is right. Poverty and
labor bore hard upon him, especially as county officers were
getting troublesome, and in a weak moment he did the
wicked act; but he has listened to my words, and his mind
has got round again into its honest corner. An awful and a
dangerous thing it is to be bringing the daughters of other
people into a peaceable and well-governed family!"

"And who will thank you for the same after what has been
already done?" muttered Abiram with a grin of disappointed
cupidity in which malignity and terror were disgustingly

united; "when the devil has once made out his account, you may look for your receipt in full only at his hands."

"Peace!" said Ishmael, stretching his heavy hand towards his kinsman in a manner that instantly silenced the speaker. "Your voice is like a raven's in my ears. If *you* had never spoken I should have been spared this shame."

"Since, then, you are beginning to lose sight of your errors and to see the truth," said Middleton, "do not things by halves, but by the generosity of your conduct purchase friends who may be of use in warding off any future danger from the law——"

"Young man," interrupted the squatter with a dark frown, "*you* too have said enough. If fear of the law had come over me, you would not be here to witness the manner in which Ishmael Bush deals out justice."

"Smother not your good intentions; and remember if you contemplate violence to any among us that the arm of that law you affect to despise reaches far, and that though its movements are sometimes slow, they are not the less certain!"

"Yes, there is too much truth in his words, squatter," said the trapper, whose attentive ears rarely suffered a syllable to be utterly unheeded in his presence. "A busy and a troublesome arm it often proves to be here in this land of America, where, as they say, man is left greatly to the following of his own wishes, compared to other countries; and happier, aye, and more manly and more honest too, is he for the privilege! Why, do you know, my men, that there are regions where the law is so busy as to say, 'In this fashion shall you live, in that fashion shall you die, and in such another fashion shall you take leave of the world, to be sent before the judgment seat of the Lord!' A wicked and a troublesome meddling is that, with the business of one who has not made his creatures to be herded like oxen and driven from field to field as their stupid and selfish keepers may judge of their need and wants. A miserable land must that be where they fetter the mind as well as the body, and where the creatures of God, being born children, are kept so by the wicked inventions of men who would take upon themselves the office of the great governor of all."

During the delivery of this pertinent opinion Ishmael was content to be silent, though the look with which he regarded the speaker manifested any other feeling than that of amity. When the old man had done, he turned to Middleton and continued the subject which the other had interrupted.

"As to ourselves, young captain, there has been wrong on both sides. If I have borne hard upon your feelings in taking away your wife with an honest intention of giving her back to you when the plans of that devil incarnate were answered, so have you broken into my encampment, aiding and abetting, as they have called many an honester bargain, in destroying my property."

"But what I did was to liberate——"

"The matter is settled between us," interrupted Ishmael with the air of one who, having made up his own opinion on the merits of the question, cared very little for those of other people; "you and your wife are free to go and come when and how you please. Abner, set the captain at liberty; and now, if you will tarry until I am ready to draw nigher to the settlements, you shall both have the benefit of carriage; if not, never say that you did not get a friendly offer."

"Now, may the strong oppress me and my sins be visited harshly on my own head if I forget your honesty, however slow it has been in showing itself," cried Middleton, hastening to the side of the weeping Inez the instant he was released; "and, friend, I pledge you the honor of a soldier that your own part of this transaction shall be forgotten, whatever I may deem fit to have done when I reach a place where the arm of government can make itself felt."

The dull smile with which the squatter answered to this assurance proved how little he valued the pledge that the youth, in the first revulsion of his feelings, was so free to make.

"Neither fear nor favor, but what I call justice, has brought me to this judgment," he said; "do you that which may seem right in your eyes, and believe that the world is wide enough to hold us both, without our crossing each other's path again! If you are content, well; if you are not content, seek to ease your feelings in your own fashion. I shall not ask to be let up when you once put me fairly down. And now, doctor, have I come to your leaf in my accounts. It is time to foot up the small reckoning that has been running on for some time atwixt us. With you I entered into open and manly faith; in what manner have you kept it?"

The singular felicity with which Ishmael had contrived to shift the responsibility of all that had passed from his own shoulders to those of his prisoners, backed as it was by circumstances that hardly admitted of a very philosophical examination of any mooted point in ethics, was sufficiently embarrassing to the several individuals who were so unexpectedly required to answer for a conduct which, in their simplicity, they had deemed so meritorious. The life of Obed had been so purely theoretic that his amazement was not the least embarrassing at a state of things, which might not have proved so very remarkable had he been a little more practiced in the ways of the world. The worthy naturalist was not the first by many who found himself, at the precise moment when he was expecting praise, suddenly arraigned to answer for the very conduct on which he rested all his claims to commendation. Though not a little scandalized at the unexpected turn of the transaction, he was fain to make the best of circumstances and to bring forth such matter in justification as first presented itself to his disordered faculties.

"That there did exist a certain compactum, or agreement, between Obed Batt, M.D., and Ishmael Bush, viator, or erratic husbandman," he said, endeavoring to avoid all offense in the use of terms, "I am not disposed to deny. I will admit that it was therein conditioned, or stipulated, that a certain journey should be performed conjointly, or in company, until so many days had been numbered. But as the said time has fully expired, I presume it fair to infer that the bargain may now be said to be obsolete."

"Ishmael!" interrupted the impatient Esther. "Make no words with a man who can break your bones as easily as set them, and let the poisoning devil go! He's a cheat, from box to phial. Give him half the prairie, and take the other half yourself. He an acclimator! I will engage to get the brats acclimated to a fever-and-ague bottom in a week, and not a word shall be uttered harder to pronounce than the bark of a cherry tree, with perhaps a drop or two of western comfort. One thing are a fact, Ishmael; I like no fellow travelers who can give a heavy feel to an honest woman's tongue, I—and that without caring whether her household is in order or out of order."

The air of settled gloom which had taken possession of the squatter's countenance lighted for an instant with a look of dull drollery as he answered, "Different people might judge differently, Esther, of the virtue of the man's art. But sin' it is your wish to let him depart, I will not plow the prairie to make the walking rough. Friend, you are at liberty to go into the settlements, and there I would advise you to tarry, as men like me who make but few contracts do not relish the custom of breaking them so easily."

"And now, Ishmael," resumed his conquering wife, "in order to keep a quiet family and to smother all heartburnings between us, show yonder redskin and his daughter"— pointing to the aged Le Balafré and the widowed Tachechana —"the way to their village, and let us say to them, God bless you and farewell in the same breath!"

"They are the captives of the Pawnee, according to the rules of Indian warfare, and I cannot meddle with his rights."

"Beware the devil, my man! He's a cheat and a tempter, and none can say they are safe with his awful delusions before their eyes! Take the advice of one who has the honor of your name at heart, and send the tawny Jezebel away."

The squatter laid his broad hand on her shoulder, and looking her steadily in the eye, he answered in tones that were both stern and solemn, "Woman, we have that before us which calls our thoughts to other matters than the follies you mean. Remember what is to come, and put your silly jealousy to sleep."

"It is true, it is true," murmured his wife, moving back among her daughters; "God forgive me that I should forget it!"

"And now, young man; you who have so often come into my clearing under the pretense of lining the bee into his hole," resumed Ishmael after a momentary pause, as if to recover the equilibrium of his mind; "with you there is a heavier account to settle. Not satisfied with rummaging my camp, you have stolen a girl who is akin to my wife and whom I had calculated to make one day a daughter of my own."

A stronger sensation was produced by this than by any of the preceding interrogations. All the young men bent their curious eyes on Paul and Ellen, the former of whom seemed in no small mental confusion, while the latter bent her face on her bosom in shame.

"Harkee, friend Ishmael Bush," returned the bee hunter, who found that he was expected to answer to the charge of burglary as well as to that of abduction; "that I did not give the most civil treatment to your pots and pails I am not going to gainsay. If you will name the price you put upon the articles, it is possible the damage may be quietly settled between us and all hard feelings forgotten. I was not in a churchgoing humor when we got upon your rock, and it is more than probable there was quite as much kicking as preaching among your wares; but a hole in the best man's coat can be mended by money. As to the matter of Ellen Wade here, it may not be got over so easily. Different people have different opinions on the subject of matrimony. Some think it is enough to say yes and no to the questions of the magistrate or of the parson, if one happens to be handy, in order to make a quiet house; but I think that where a young woman's mind is fairly bent on going in a certain direction, it will be quite as prudent to let her body follow. Not that I mean to say Ellen was not altogether forced to what she did, and therefore she is just as innocent in this matter as yonder jackass, who was made to carry her, and greatly against his will too, as I am ready to swear he would say himself if he could speak as loud as he can bray."

"Nelly," resumed the squatter, who paid very little attention to what Paul considered a highly creditable and ingenious vindication, "Nelly, this is a wide and a wicked world on which you have been in such a hurry to cast yourself. You have fed and you have slept in my camp for a year, and I did hope that you had found the free air of the borders enough to your mind to wish to remain among us."

"Let the girl have her will," muttered Esther from the rear; "he who might have persuaded her to stay is sleeping in the cold and naked prairie, and little hope is left of changing her humor; besides, a woman's mind is a willful thing and not easily turned from its waywardness, as you know yourself, my man, or I should not be here the mother of your sons and daughters."

The squatter seemed reluctant to abandon his views on the abashed girl so easily; and before he answered to the suggestion of his wife he turned his usual dull look along the line of the curious countenances of his boys as if to see whether there was not one among them fit to fill the place of the deceased. Paul was not slow to observe the expression, and hitting nigher than usual on the secret thoughts of the other, he believed he had fallen on an expedient which might remove every difficulty.

"It is quite plain, friend Bush," he said, "that there are two opinions in this matter, yours for your sons, and mine for myself. I see but one amicable way of settling this dispute, which is as follows: do you make a choice among your boys of any you will, and let us walk off together for the matter of a few miles into the prairies; the one who stays behind can never trouble any man's house or his fixin', and the one who comes back may make the best of his way he can in the good wishes of the young woman."

"Paul!" exclaimed the reproachful but smothered voice of Ellen.

"Never fear, Nelly," whispered the literal bee hunter, whose straightgoing mind suggested no other motive of uneasiness on the part of his mistress than concern for himself; "I have taken the measure of them all, and you may trust an eye that has seen to line many a bee into his hole!"

"I am not about to set myself up as a ruler of inclinations," observed the squatter. "If the heart of the child is truly in the settlements, let her declare it; she shall have no let or hindrance from me. Speak, Nelly, and let what you say come from your wishes, without fear or favor. Would you leave us to go with this young man into the settled countries, or will you tarry and share the little we have to give, but which to you we give so freely?"

Thus called upon to decide, Ellen could no longer hesitate. The glance of her eye was at first timid and furtive. But as the color flushed her features and her breathing became quick and excited, it was apparent that the native spirit of the girl was gaining the ascendancy over the bashfulness of sex.

"You took me a fatherless, impoverished, and friendless orphan," she said, struggling to command her voice, "when others, who live in what may be called affluence compared to your state, chose to forget me; and may heaven in its goodness bless you for it! The little I have done will never pay you for that one act of kindness. I like not your manner of life; it is different from the ways of my childhood, and it is different from my wishes; still, had you not led this sweet and unoffending lady from her friends, I should never have quitted you until you yourself had said, 'Go, and the blessing of God go with you!' "

"The act was not wise, but it is repented of; and so far as it can be done, in safety, it shall be repaired. Now, speak freely; will you tarry or will you go?"

"I have promised the lady," said Ellen, dropping her eyes again to the earth, "not to leave her; and after she has received so much wrong from all hands, she may have a right to claim that I keep my word."

"Take the cords from the young man," said Ishmael. When the order was obeyed, he motioned for all his sons to advance, and he placed them in a row before the eyes of Ellen. "Now let there be no trifling, but open your heart. Here are all I have to offer, besides a hearty welcome."

The distressed girl turned her abashed look from the countenance of one of the young men to that of another, until her eyes met the troubled and working features of Paul. Then nature got the better of forms. She threw herself into the arms of the bee hunter and sufficiently proclaimed her choice by sobbing aloud. Ishmael signed to his sons to fall back, and evidently mortified, though perhaps not disappointed by the result, he no longer hesitated.

"Take her," he said, "and deal honestly and kindly by her. The girl has that in her which should make her welcome in any man's house, and I should be loath to learn that she ever came to harm. And now I have settled with you all, on terms that I hope you will not find hard, but, on the contrary, just and manly. I have only another question to ask, and that is of the captain: do you choose to profit by my teams in going into the settlements, or not?"

"I hear that some soldiers of my party are looking for me near the villages of the Pawnees," said Middleton, "and I intend to accompany this chief in order to join my men."

"Then the sooner we part the better. Horses are plenty on the bottom. Go; make your choice, and leave us in peace."

"That is impossible while the old man, who has been a friend of my family near half a century, is left a prisoner. What has he done that he too is not released?"

"Ask no questions that may lead to deceitful answers," sullenly returned the squatter; "I have dealings of my own with that trapper that it may not befit an officer of the States to meddle with. Go, while your road is open."

"The man may be giving you honest counsel, and that which it concerns you all to hearken to," observed the old captive, who seemed in no uneasiness at the extraordinary condition in which he found himself. "The Siouxes are a numberless and bloody-minded race, and no one can say how long it may be afore they will be out again on the scent of revenge. Therefore, I say to you, go also; and take especial heed in crossing the bottoms that you get not entangled again in the fires, for the honest hunters often burn the grass at this season in order that the buffaloes may find a sweeter and a greener pasturage in the spring."

"I should forget not only my gratitude, but my duty to the laws, were I to leave this prisoner in your hands, even by his own consent, without knowing the nature of his crime, in which we may have all been his innocent accessories."

"Will it satisfy you to know that he merits all he will receive?"

"It will at least change my opinion of his character."

"Look then at this," said Ishmael, placing before the eyes of the captain the bullet that had been found about the person of the dead Asa; "with this morsel of lead did he lay low as fine a boy as ever gave joy to a parent's eyes!"

"I cannot believe that he has done this deed, unless in self-defense or on some justifiable provocation. That he knew of the death of your son, I confess, for he pointed out the brake in which the body lay, but that he has wrongfully taken his life, nothing but his own acknowledgment shall persuade me to believe."

"I have lived long," commenced the trapper, who found by the general pause that he was expected to vindicate himself from the heavy imputation, "and much evil have I seen in my day. Many are the prowling bears and leaping panthers that I have met, fighting for the morsel which has been thrown in their way; and many are the reasoning men that I have looked on striving against each other unto death, in order that human madness might also have its hour. For myself, I hope, there is no boasting in saying that though my hand has been needed in putting down wickedness and oppression, it has never struck a blow of which its owner will be ashamed to hear at a reckoning that shall be far mightier than this."

"If my father has taken life from one of his tribe," said the young Pawnee, whose quick eye had read the meaning of what was passing, in the bullet and in the countenances of the others, "let him give himself up to the friends of the dead like a warrior. He is too just to need thongs to lead him to judgment."

"Boy, I hope you do me justice. If I had done the foul deed with which they charge me, I should have manhood enough to come and offer my head to the blow of punishment, as all good and honest red men do the same." Then giving his anxious Indian friend a look to reassure him of his innocence, he turned to the rest of his attentive and interested listeners, as he continued in English, "I have a short story to tell, and he that believes it will believe the truth, and he that disbelieves it will only lead himself astray, and perhaps his neighbor too. We were all outlying about your camp, friend squatter, as by this time you may begin to suspect, when we found that it contained a wronged and imprisoned lady, with intentions neither more honest nor dishonest than to set her free, as in nature and justice she had a right to be. Seeing that I was more skilled in scouting than the others, while they lay back in the cover, I was sent upon the plain on the business of the reconnoiterings. You little thought that one was so nigh who saw into all the circumventions of your hunt; but there was I, sometimes flat behind a bush or a tuft of grass, sometimes rolling down a hill into a bottom; and little did you dream that your motions were watched, as the panther watches the drinking deer. Lord, squatter, when I was a man in the pride and strength of my days, I have looked in at the tent door of the enemy, and they sleeping, aye, and dreaming too, of being at home and in peace. I wish there was time to give you the partic——"

"Proceed with your explanation," interrupted Middleton.

"Ah! And a bloody and wicked sight it was! There I lay in a low bed of grass as two of the hunters came nigh each other. Their meeting was not cordial, nor such as men who meet in a desert should give each other; but I thought they would have parted in peace, until I saw one put his rifle to the other's back and do what I call a treacherous and sinful murder. It was a noble and a manly youth, that boy! Though the powder burnt his coat, he stood the shock for more than a minute before he fell. Then was he brought to his knees, and a desperate and manful fight he made to the brake, like a wounded bear seeking a cover!"

"And why, in the name of heavenly justice, did you conceal this?" cried Middleton.

"What! Think you, captain, that a man who has spent more than threescore years in the wilderness has not learned the virtue of discretion? What red warrior runs to tell the sights he has seen until a fitting time? I took the doctor to the place in order to see whether his skill might not come in use, and our friend the bee hunter, being in company, was knowing to the fact that the bushes held the body."

"Aye, it are true," said Paul; "but not knowing what private reasons might make the old trapper wish to hush the matter up, I said as little about the thing as possible, which was just nothing at all."

"And who was the perpetrator of this deed?" demanded Middleton.

"If by perpetrator you mean him who did the act, yonder stands the man; and a shame and a disgrace is it to our race that he is of the blood and family of the dead."

"He lies! He lies!" shrieked Abiram. "I did no murder; I gave but blow for blow."

The voice of Ishmael was deep, and even awful, as he answered, "It is enough. Let the old man go. Boys, put the brother of your mother in his place."

"Touch me not!" cried Abiram. "I'll call on God to curse ye if you touch me!"

The wild and disordered gleam of his eye at first induced the young men to arrest their steps; but when Abner, older and more resolute than the rest, advanced full upon him with a countenance that bespoke the hostile state of his mind, the affrighted criminal turned, and making an abortive effort to fly, fell with his face to the earth, to all appearance perfectly dead. Amid the low exclamations of horror which succeeded, Ishmael made a gesture which commanded his sons to bear the body into a tent.

"Now," he said, turning to those who were strangers in his camp, "nothing is left to be done but for each to go his own road. I wish you all well; and to you, Ellen, though you may not prize the gift, I say, God bless you!"

Middleton, awestruck by what he believed a manifest judgment of heaven, made no further resistance, but prepared to depart. The arrangements were brief and soon completed. When they were all ready, they took a short and silent leave of the squatter and his family; and then the whole of the singularly constituted party were seen slowly and silently following the victorious Pawnee towards his distant villages.

CHAPTER 32

And I beseech you,
Wrest once the law to your authority:
To do a great right, do a little wrong.
SHAKESPEARE

ISHMAEL AWAITED LONG and patiently for the motley train of Hard Heart to disappear. When his scout reported that the last straggler of the Indians, who had joined their chief so soon as he was at such a distance from the encampment as to excite no jealousy by their numbers, had gone behind the most distant swell of the prairie, he gave forth the order to strike his tents. The cattle were already in the gears, and the movables were soon transferred to their usual places in the different vehicles. When all these arrangements were completed, the little wagon which had so long been the tenement of Inez was drawn before the tent into which the insensible body of the kidnapper had been borne, and preparations were evidently made for the reception of another prisoner. Then it was, as Abiram appeared, pale, terrified, and tottering beneath a load of detected guilt, that the younger members of the family were first apprised that he still belonged to the class of the living. A general and superstitious impression had spread among them that his crime had been visited by a terrible retribution from heaven; and they now gazed at him as at a being who belonged rather to another world than as a mortal who, like themselves, had still to endure the last agony before the great link of human existence could be broken. The criminal himself appeared to be in a state in which the most sensitive and startling terror was singularly combined with total physical apathy. The truth was that while his person had been numbed by the shock, his susceptibility to apprehension kept his agitated mind in unrelieved distress. When he found himself in the open air, he looked about him in order to gather, if possible, some evidences of his future fate from the countenances of those gathered round. Seeing everywhere grave but composed features, and meeting in no eye any expression that threatened immediate violence, the miserable man began to revive; and by the time he was seated in the wagon, his artful faculties were beginning to plot the expedients of parrying the just resentment of his kinsmen, or, if these should fail him, the means of escaping from a punishment that his forebodings told him would be terrible.

Throughout the whole of these preparations Ishmael rarely spoke. A gesture or a glance of the eye served to indicate his pleasure to his sons, and with these simple methods of communication all parties appeared content. When the signal was made to proceed, the squatter threw his rifle into the hollow of his arm and his ax across his shoulder, taking the lead as usual. Esther buried herself in the wagon which contained her daughters; the young men took their customary places among the cattle or nigh the teams; and the whole proceeded at their ordinary dull but unremitted gait.

For the first time in many a day the squatter turned his back towards the setting sun. The route he held was in the direction of the settled country, and the manner in which he moved sufficed to tell his children, who had learned to read their father's determinations in his mien, that their journey on the prairie was shortly to have an end. Still nothing else transpired for hours that might denote the existence of any sudden or violent revolution in the purposes or feelings of Ishmael. During all that time he marched alone, keeping a few hundred rods in front of his teams, seldom giving any sign of extraordinary excitement. Once or twice, indeed, his huge figure was seen standing on the summit of some distant swell, with the head bent towards the earth as he leaned on his rifle; but then these moments of intense thought were rare and of short continuance. The train had long thrown its shadows towards the east before any material alteration was made in the disposition of their march. Watercourses were waded, plains were passed, and rolling ascents risen and descended without producing the smallest change. Long practiced in the difficulties of that peculiar species of traveling in which he was engaged, the squatter avoided the more impracticable obstacles of their route by a sort of instinct, invariably inclining to the right or left in season as the formation of the land, the presence of trees, or the signs of rivers, forewarned him of the necessity of such movements.

At length the hour arrived when charity to man and beast required a temporary suspension of labor. Ishmael chose the required spot with his customary sagacity. The regular formation of the country, such as it has been described in the earlier pages of our book, had long been interrupted by a more unequal and broken surface. There were, it is true, in general the same wide and empty wastes, the same rich and extensive bottoms, and that wild and singular combination of swelling fields and of nakedness which gives that region the appearance of an ancient country, incomprehensibly stripped of its people and their dwellings. But these distinguishing features of the rolling prairies had long been interrupted by irregular hillocks, occasional masses of rock, and broad belts of forest.

Ishmael chose a spring that broke out of the base of a rock some forty or fifty feet in elevation as a place well suited to the wants of his herds. The water moistened a small swale that lay beneath the spot, which yielded, in return for the fecund gift, a scanty growth of grass. A solitary willow had taken root in the alluvion, and profiting by its exclusive possession of the soil, the tree had sent up its stem far above the crest of the adjacent rock, whose peaked summit had once been shadowed by its branches. But its loveliness had gone with the mysterious principle of life. As if in mockery of the meager show of verdure that the spot exhibited, it remained a noble and solemn monument of former fertility. The larger, ragged, and fantastic branches still obtruded themselves abroad, while the white and hoary trunk stood naked and tempest-riven. Not a leaf nor a sign of vegetation was to be seen about it. In all things it proclaimed the frailty of existence and the fulfillment of time.

Here Ishmael, after making the customary signal for the train to approach, threw his vast frame upon the earth and seemed to muse on the deep responsibility of his present situation. His sons were not long in arriving, for the cattle no sooner scented the food and water than they quickened their pace, and then succeeded the usual bustle and avocations of a halt.

The impression made by the scene of that morning was not so deep or lasting on the children of Ishmael and Esther as to induce them to forget the wants of nature. But while the sons were searching among their stores for something substantial to appease their hunger and the younger fry were wrangling about their simple dishes, the parents of the unnurtured family were differently employed.

When the squatter saw that all, even to the reviving Abiram, were busy in administering to their appetites, he gave his downcast partner a glance of his eye and withdrew towards a distant roll of the land which bounded the view towards the east. The meeting of the pair in this naked spot was like an interview held above the grave of their murdered son. Ishmael signed to his wife to take a seat beside him on a fragment of rock, and then followed a space during which neither seemed disposed to speak.

"We have journeyed together long, through good and bad," Ishmael at length commenced; "much have we had to try us, and some bitter cups have we been made to swallow, my woman; but nothing like this has ever before lain in my path."

"It is a heavy cross for a poor, misguided, and sinful woman to bear!" returned Esther, bowing her head to her knees and partly concealing her face in her dress. "A heavy and a burdensome weight is this to be laid upon the shoulders of a sister and a mother!"

"Aye, therein lies the hardship of the case. I had brought my mind to the punishment of that houseless trapper with no great strivings, for the man had done me few favors, and God forgive me if I suspected him wrongfully of much evil! This is, however, bringing shame in at one door of my cabin in order to drive it out at the other. But shall a son of mine be murdered, and he who did it go at large? The boy would never rest!"

"Oh! Ishmael, we pushed the matter far! Had little been said, who would have been the wiser? Our consciences might then have been quiet."

"Eester," said the husband, turning on her a reproachful but still a dull regard, "the hour has been, my woman, when you thought another hand had done this wickedness."

"I did, I did! The Lord gave me the feeling as a punishment for my sins! But his mercy was not slow in lifting the veil; I looked into the book, Ishmael, and there I found the words of comfort."

"Have you that book at hand, woman? It may happen to advise in such a dreary business."

Esther fumbled in her pocket and was not long in producing the fragment of a Bible which had been thumbed and smoke-dried till the print was nearly illegible. It was the only article in the nature of a book that was to be found among the chattels of the squatter, and it had been preserved by his wife as a melancholy relic of more prosperous and possibly of more innocent days. She had long been in the habit of resorting to it under the pressure of such circumstances as were palpably beyond human redress, though her spirit and resolution rarely needed support under those that admitted of reparation through any of the ordinary means of reprisal. In this manner Esther had made a sort of convenient ally of the word of God, rarely troubling it for counsel, however, except when her own incompetency to avert an evil was too apparent to be disputed. We shall leave casuists to determine how far she resembled any other believers in this particular and proceed directly with the matter before us.

"There are many awful passages in these pages, Ishmael," she said when the volume was opened and the leaves were slowly turning under her finger, "and some there are that teach the rules of punishment."

Her husband made a gesture for her to find one of those brief rules of conduct which have been received among all Christian nations as the direct mandates of the Creator and which have been found so just that even they who deny their high authority admit their wisdom. Ishmael listened with grave attention as his companion read all those verses which her memory suggested and which were thought applicable to the situation in which they found themselves. He made her show him the words, which he regarded with a sort of strange reverence. A resolution once taken was usually irrevocable in one who was moved with so much difficulty. He put his hand upon the book and closed the pages himself, as much as to apprise his wife that he was satisfied. Esther, who so well knew his character, trembled at the action, and casting a glance at his steady eye, she said, "And yet, Ishmael, my blood and the blood of my children is in his veins! Cannot mercy be shown?"

"Woman," he answered sternly, "when we believed that miserable old trapper had done this deed, nothing was said of mercy!"

Esther made no reply, but folding her arms upon her breast, she sat silent and thoughtful for many minutes. Then she once more turned her anxious gaze upon the countenance of her husband, where she found all passion and care apparently buried in the coldest apathy. Satisfied now that the fate of her brother was sealed, and possibly conscious how well he merited the punishment that was meditated, she no longer thought of mediation. No more words passed between them. Their eyes met for an instant, and then both arose and walked in profound silence towards the encampment.

The squatter found his children expecting his return in the usual listless manner with which they awaited all coming events. The cattle were already herded and the horses in their gears, in readiness to proceed so soon as he should indicate that such was his pleasure. The children were already in their proper vehicle, and, in short, nothing delayed the departure but the absence of the parents of the wild brood.

"Abner," said the father with the deliberation with which all his proceedings were characterized, "take the brother of your mother from the wagon and let him stand on the 'arth."

Abiram issued from his place of concealment, trembling, it is true, but far from destitute of hopes as to his final success in appeasing the just resentment of his kinsman. After throwing a glance around him with the vain wish of finding a single countenance in which he might detect a solitary gleam of sympathy, he endeavored to smother those apprehensions that were by this time reviving in their original violence by forcing a sort of friendly communication between himself and the squatter, "The beasts are getting jaded, brother," he said; "and as we have made so good a march already, is it not time to camp? To my eye you may go far before a better place than this is found to pass the night in."

" 'Tis well you like it. Your tarry here are likely to be long. My sons, draw nigh and listen. Abiram White," he added, lifting his cap and speaking with a solemnity and steadiness that rendered even his dull mien imposing, "you have slain my firstborn, and according to the laws of God and man must you die!"

The kidnapper started at this terrible and sudden sentence with the terror that one would exhibit who unexpectedly found himself in the grasp of a monster from whose power there was no retreat. Although filled with the most serious forebodings of what might be his lot, his courage had not been equal to look his danger in the face, and with the deceitful consolation with which timid tempers are apt to conceal their desperate condition from themselves, he had rather courted a treacherous relief in his cunning than prepared himself for the worst.

"Die!" he repeated in a voice that scarcely issued from his chest. "A man is surely safe among his kinsmen?"

"So thought my boy," returned the squatter, motioning for the team that contained his wife and the girls to proceed as he very coolly examined the priming of his piece. "By the rifle did you destroy my son; it is fit and just that you meet your end by the same weapon."

Abiram stared about him with a gaze that bespoke an unsettled reason. He even laughed, as if he would not only persuade himself but others that what he heard was some pleasantry intended to try his nerves. But nowhere did his frightful merriment meet with an answering echo. All around was solemn and still. The visages of his nephews were excited but cold towards him, and that of his former confederate frightfully determined. This very steadiness of mien was a thousand times more alarming and hopeless than any violence could have proved. The latter might possibly have touched his spirit and awakened resistance, but the former threw him entirely on the feeble resources of himself.

"Brother," he said in a hurried, unnatural whisper, "did I hear you?"

"My words are plain, Abiram White; thou hast done murder, and for the same must thou die."

"Esther! Sister, sister, will you leave me! Oh! Sister! Do you hear my call?"

"I hear one speak from the grave!" returned the husky tones of Esther as the wagon passed the spot where the criminal stood. "It is the voice of my firstborn calling aloud for justice! God have mercy, God have mercy on your soul!"

The team slowly pursued its route, and the deserted Abiram now found himself deprived of the smallest vestige of hope. Still he could not summon fortitude to meet his death, and had not his limbs refused to aid him he would yet have attempted to fly. Then, by a sudden revolution from hope to utter despair, he fell upon his knees and commenced a prayer in which cries for mercy to God and to his kinsman were wildly and blasphemously mingled. The sons of Ishmael turned away in horror at the disgusting spectacle, and even the stern nature of the squatter began to bend before so abject misery.

"May that which you ask of him be granted," he said, "but a father can never forget a murdered child."

He was answered by the most humble appeals for time. A week, a day, an hour, were each implored with an earnestness commensurate to the value they receive when a whole life is compressed into their short duration. The squatter was troubled, and at length he yielded in part to the petitions of the criminal. His final purpose was not altered, though he changed the means. "Abner," he said, "mount the rock and look on every side that we may be sure none are nigh."

While his nephew was obeying this order, gleams of reviving hope were seen shooting across the quivering features of the kidnapper. The report was favorable; nothing having life, the retiring teams excepted, was to be seen. A messenger was, however, coming from the latter in great apparent haste. Ishmael awaited its arrival. He received from the hands of one of his wondering and frighted girls a fragment of that book which Esther had preserved with so much care. The squatter beckoned the child away and placed the leaves in the hands of the criminal.

"Eester has sent you this," he said, "that in your last moments you may remember God."

"Bless her, bless her! A good and kind sister has she been to me! But time must be given that I may read; time, my brother, time!"

"Time shall not be wanting. You shall be your own executioner, and this miserable office shall pass away from my hands."

Ishmael proceeded to put his new resolution in force. The immediate apprehensions of the kidnapper were quieted by an assurance that he might yet live for days, though his punishment was inevitable. A reprieve to one abject and wretched as Abiram temporarily produced the same effects as a pardon. He was even foremost in assisting in the appalling arrangements, and of all the actors in that solemn tragedy, his voice alone was facetious and jocular.

A thin shelf of the rock projected beneath one of the ragged arms of the willow. It was many feet from the ground and admirably adapted to the purpose which, in fact, its appearance had suggested. On this little platform the criminal was placed, his arms bound at the elbows behind his back, beyond the possibility of liberation, with a proper cord leading from his neck to the limb of the tree. The latter was so placed that when suspended the body could find no foothold. The fragment of the Bible was placed in his hands, and he was left to seek his consolation as he might from its pages.

"And now, Abiram White," said the squatter when his sons had descended from completing this arrangement, "I give you a last and solemn asking. Death is before you in two shapes. With this rifle can your misery be cut short, or by that cord; sooner or later must you meet your end."

"Let me yet live! Oh, Ishmael, you know not how sweet life is when the last moment draws so nigh!"

" 'Tis done," said the squatter, motioning for his assistants to follow the herds and teams. "And now, miserable man, that it may prove a consolation to your end, I forgive you my wrongs and leave you to your God."

Ishmael turned and pursued his way across the plain at his ordinary sluggish and ponderous gait. Though his head was bent a little towards the earth, his inactive mind did not prompt him to cast a look behind. Once, indeed, he thought he heard his name called in tones that were a little smothered, but they failed to make him pause.

At the spot where he and Esther had conferred, he reached the boundary of the visible horizon from the rock. Here he stopped and ventured a glance in the direction of the place he had just quitted. The sun was near dipping into the plains beyond, and its last rays lighted the naked branches of the willow. He saw the ragged outline of the whole drawn against the glowing heavens, and he even traced the still upright form of the being he had left to his misery. Turning the roll of the swell, he proceeded with the feelings of one who had been suddenly and violently separated from a recent confederate forever.

Within a mile the squatter overtook his teams. His sons had found a place suited to the encampment for the night and merely awaited his approach to confirm their choice. Few words were necessary to express his acquiescence. Everything passed in a silence more general and remarkable than ever. The chidings of Esther were not heard among her young, or if heard, they were more in the tones of softened admonition than in her usual upbraiding key.

No questions nor explanations passed between the husband and his wife. It was only as the latter was about to withdraw among her children for the night that the former saw her taking a furtive look at the pan of his rifle. Ishmael bade his sons seek their rest, announcing his intention to look to the safety of the camp in person. When all was still, he walked out upon the prairie with a sort of sensation that he found his breathing among the tents too straitened. The night was well adapted to heighten the feelings which had been created by the events of the day.

The wind had risen with the moon, and it was occasionally sweeping over the plain in a manner that made it not difficult for the sentinel to imagine strange and unearthly sounds were mingling in the blast. Yielding to the extraordinary impulses of which he was the subject, he cast a glance around to see that all were slumbering in security, and then he strayed towards the swell of land already mentioned. Here the squatter found himself at a point that commanded a view to the east and to the west. Light fleecy clouds were driving before the moon, which was cold and watery, though there were moments when its placid rays were shed from clear-blue fields, seeming to soften objects to its own mild loveliness.

For the first time, in a life of so much wild adventure, Ishmael felt a keen sense of solitude. The naked prairies began to assume the forms of illimitable and dreary wastes, and the rushing of the wind sounded like the whisperings of the dead. It was not long before he thought a shriek was borne past him on a blast. It did not sound like a call from earth, but it swept frightfully through the upper air, mingled with the hoarse accompaniment of the wind. The teeth of the squatter were compressed, and his huge hand grasped the rifle as if it would crush the metal. Then came a lull, a fresher blast, and a cry of horror that seemed to have been uttered at the very portals of his ears. A sort of echo burst involuntarily from his own lips, as men shout under unnatural excitement, and throwing his rifle across his shoulder, he proceeded towards the rock with the strides of a giant.

It was not often that the blood of Ishmael moved at the rate with which the fluid circulates in the veins of ordinary men, but now he felt it ready to gush from every pore in his body. The animal was aroused in his most latent energies. Ever as he advanced he heard those shrieks, which sometimes seemed ringing among the clouds and sometimes passed so nigh as to appear to brush the earth. At length there came a cry in which there could be no delusion or to which the imagination could lend no horror. It appeared to fill each cranny of the air, as the visible horizon is often charged to fullness by one dazzling flash of the electric fluid. The name of God was distinctly audible, but it was awfully and blasphemously blended with sounds that may not be repeated. The squatter stopped, and for a moment he covered his ears with his hands. When he withdrew the latter, a low and husky voice at his elbow asked in smothered tones, "Ishmael, my man, heard ye nothing?"

"Hist!" returned the husband, laying a powerful arm on Esther without manifesting the smallest surprise at the unlooked-for presence of his wife. "Hist, woman! If you have the fear of heaven, be still!"

A profound silence succeeded. Though the wind rose and fell as before, its rushing was no longer mingled with those fearful cries. The sounds were imposing and solemn, but it was the solemnity and majesty of nature.

"Let us go on," said Esther; "all is hushed."

"Woman, what has brought you here?" demanded her husband, whose blood had returned into its former channels and whose thoughts had already lost a portion of their excitement.

"Ishmael, he murdered our firstborn, but it is not meet that the son of my mother should lie upon the ground like the carrion of a dog."

"Follow!" returned the squatter, again grasping his rifle and striding towards the rock. The distance was still considerable, and their approach as they drew nigh the place of execution was moderated by awe. Many minutes had passed before they reached a spot where they might distinguish the outlines of the dusky objects.

"Where have you put the body?" whispered Esther. "See, here are pick and spade, that a brother of mine may sleep in the bosom of the earth!"

The moon broke from behind a mass of clouds, and the eye of the woman was enabled to follow the finger of Ishmael. It pointed to a human form swinging in the wind beneath the ragged and shining arm of the willow. Esther bent her head and veiled her eyes from the sight. But Ishmael drew nigher and long contemplated his work in awe, though not in compunction. The leaves of the sacred book were scattered on the ground, and even a fragment of the shelf had been displaced by the kidnapper in his agony. But all was now in the stillness of death. The grim and convulsed countenance of the victim was at times brought full into the light of the moon, and again as the wind lulled the fatal rope drew a dark line across its bright disk. The squatter raised his rifle with extreme care and fired. The cord was cut, and the body came lumbering to the earth, a heavy and insensible mass.

Until now Esther had not moved nor spoken. But her hand was not slow to assist in the labor of the hour. The grave was soon dug. It was instantly made to receive its miserable tenant. As the lifeless form descended, Esther, who sustained the head, looked up into the face of her husband with an expression of anguish and said, "Ishmael, my man, it is very terrible! I cannot kiss the corpse of my father's child!"

The squatter laid his broad hand on the bosom of the dead and said, "Abiram White, we all have need of mercy; from my soul do I forgive you! May God in heaven have pity on your sins!"

The woman bowed her face and imprinted her lips long and fervently on the pallid forehead of her brother. After this came the falling clods and all the solemn sounds of filling a grave. Esther lingered on her knees, and Ishmael stood uncovered while the woman muttered a prayer. All was then finished.

On the following morning the teams and herds of the squatter were seen pursuing their course towards the settlements. As they approached the confines of society the train was blended among a thousand others. Though some of the numerous descendants of this peculiar pair were reclaimed from their lawless and semibarbarous lives, the principals of the family themselves were never heard of more.

CHAPTER 33

No leave take I, for I will ride
As far as land will let me by your side.
SHAKESPEARE

THE PASSAGE OF the Pawnee to his village was interrupted by no scene of violence. His vengeance had been as complete as it was summary. Not even a solitary scout of the Siouxes was left on the hunting grounds he was obliged to traverse, and of course the journey of Middleton's party was as peaceful as if made in the bosom of the States. The marches were timed to meet the weakness of the females. In short, the victors seemed to have lost every trace of ferocity with their success and appeared disposed to consult the most trifling of the wants of that engrossing people who were daily encroaching on their rights and reducing the red men of the West from their state of proud independence to the condition of fugitives and wanderers.

Our limits will not permit a detail of the triumphal entry of the conquerors. The exultation of the tribe was proportioned to its previous despondency. Mothers boasted of the honorable deaths of their sons; wives proclaimed the honor and pointed to the scars of their husbands; and Indian girls rewarded the young braves with songs of triumph. The trophies of their fallen enemies were exhibited as conquered standards are displayed in more civilized regions. The deeds of former warriors were recounted by the aged men and declared to be eclipsed by the glory of this victory, while Hard Heart himself, so distinguished for his exploits from boyhood to that hour, was unanimously proclaimed and reproclaimed the worthiest chief and the stoutest brave that the Wahcondah had ever bestowed on his most favored children, the Pawnees of the Loups.

Notwithstanding the comparative security in which Middleton found his recovered treasure, he was not sorry to see his faithful and sturdy artillerists standing among the throng as he entered in the wild train, and lifting their voices in a martial shout to greet his return. The presence of this force, small as it was, removed every shadow of uneasiness from his mind. It made him master of his movements, gave him dignity and importance in the eyes of his new friends, and would enable him to overcome the difficulties of the wide region which still lay between the village of the Pawnees and the nearest fortress of his countrymen. A lodge was yielded to the exclusive possession of Inez and Ellen; and even Paul, when he saw an armed sentinel in the uniform of the States pacing before its entrance, was content to stray among the dwellings of the redskins, prying with but little reserve into their domestic economy, commenting sometimes jocularly, sometimes gravely, and always freely on their different expedients, or endeavoring to make the wondering housewives comprehend his quaint explanations of what he conceived to be the better customs of the whites.

This inquiring and troublesome spirit found no imitators among the Indians. The delicacy and reserve of Hard Heart were communicated to his people. When every attention that could be suggested by their simple manners and narrow wants had been fulfilled, no intrusive foot presumed to approach the cabins devoted to the service of the strangers. They were left to seek their repose in the manner which most comported with their habits and inclinations. The songs and rejoicings of the tribe, however, ran far into the night, during the deepest hours of which the voice of more than one warrior was heard recounting from the top of his lodge the deeds of his people and the glory of their triumphs.

Everything having life, notwithstanding the excesses of the night, was abroad with the appearance of the sun. The expression of exultation which had so lately been seen on every countenance was now changed to one better suited to the feeling of the moment. It was understood by all that the palefaces who had befriended their chief were about to take their final leave of the tribe. The soldiers of Middleton, in anticipation of his arrival, had bargained with an unsuccessful trader for the use of his boat, which lay in the stream ready to receive its cargo; and nothing remained to complete the arrangements for the long journey.

Middleton did not see this moment arrive entirely without distrust. The admiration with which Hard Heart regarded Inez had not escaped his jealous eye, any more than had the lawless wishes of Mahtoree. He knew the consummate manner in which a savage could conceal his designs, and he felt that it would be a culpable weakness to be unprepared for the worst. Secret instructions were therefore given to his men, while the preparations they made were properly masked behind the show of military parade with which it was intended to signalize their departure.

The conscience of the young soldier reproached him when he saw the whole tribe accompanying his party to the margin of the stream with unarmed hands and sorrowful countenances. They gathered in a circle around the strangers and their chief and became not only peaceful, but highly interested observers of what was passing. As it was evident that Hard Heart intended to speak, the former stopped and manifested their readiness to listen, the trapper performing the office of interpreter. Then the young chief addressed his people in the usual metaphorical language of an Indian. He commenced by alluding to the antiquity and renown of his own nation. He spoke of their successes in the hunts and on

the warpath, of the manner in which they had always known
how to defend their rights and to chastise their enemies.
After he had said enough to manifest his respect for the
greatness of the Loups and to satisfy the pride of the listeners,
he made a sudden transition to the race of whom the strangers were members. He compared their countless numbers to
the flights of migratory birds in the season of blossoms or in
the fall of the year. With a delicacy that none knew better
how to practice than an Indian warrior, he made no direct
mention of the rapacious tempers that so many of them had
betrayed in their dealings with the red men. Feeling that the
sentiment of distrust was strongly engrafted in the tempers of
his tribe, he rather endeavored to soothe any just resentment
they might entertain by indirect excuses and apologies. He
reminded the listeners that even the Pawnee Loups had
been obliged to chase many unworthy individuals from
their villages. The Wahcondah sometimes veiled his countenance from a red man. No doubt the Great Spirit of the
palefaces often looked darkly on his children. Such as were
abandoned to the worker of evil could never be brave or
virtuous, let the color of the skin be what it might. He bade
his young men look at the hands of the Big Knives. They
were not empty like those of hungry beggars. Neither were
they filled with goods like those of knavish traders. They
were, like themselves, warriors, and they carried arms which
they knew well how to use—they were worthy to be called
brothers!

Then he directed the attention of all to the chief of the
strangers. He was a son of their great white father. He had
not come upon the prairies to frighten the buffaloes from
their pastures or to seek the game of the Indians. Wicked
men had robbed him of one of his wives; no doubt she was
the most obedient, the meekest, the loveliest of them all.
They had only to open their eyes to see that his words must
be true. Now that the white chief had found his wife, he
was about to return to his own people in peace. He would
tell them that the Pawnees were just, and there would be a
line of wampum between the two nations. Let all his people
wish the strangers a safe return to their towns. The warriors
of the Loups knew both how to receive their enemies and
how to clear the briers from the path of their friends.

The heart of Middleton beat quick as the young partisan *
alluded to the charms of Inez, and for an instant he cast an
impatient glance at his little line of artillerists; but the chief
from that moment appeared to forget he had ever seen so
fair a being. His feelings, if he had any on the subject, were
veiled behind the cold mask of Indian self-denial. He took
each warrior by the hand, not forgetting the meanest soldier,
but his cold and collected eye never wandered for an instant
towards either of the females. Arrangements had been made
for their comfort, with a prodigality and care that had not
failed to excite some surprise in his young men, but in no
other particular did he shock their manly pride by betraying
any solicitude in behalf of the weaker sex.

The leave-taking was general and imposing. Each male
Pawnee was sedulous to omit no one of the strange warriors in his attentions, and of course the ceremony occupied
some time. The only exception, and that was not general, was
in the case of Dr. Battius. Not a few of the young men,
it is true, were indifferent about lavishing civilities on one of
so doubtful a profession, but the worthy naturalist found
some consolation in the more matured politeness of the old
men, who had inferred that though not of much use in war,
the medicine of the Big Knives might possibly be made
serviceable in peace.

When all of Middleton's party had embarked, the trapper
lifted a small bundle which had lain at his feet during the
previous proceedings, and whistling Hector to his side, he
was the last to take his seat. The artillerists gave the usual
cheers, which were answered by a shout from the tribe, and
then the boat was shoved into the current and began to glide
swiftly down its stream.

A long and a musing if not a melancholy silence succeeded
this departure. It was first broken by the trapper, whose regret was not the least visible in his dejected and sorrowful
eye: "They are a valiant and an honest tribe," he said; "that
will I say boldly in their favor; and second only do I take
them to be to that once mighty but now scattered people the

---

* The Americans and the Indians have adopted several words which
each believe peculiar to the language of the others. Thus "squaw,"
"papoose," or child, "wigwam," etc., etc., though it is doubtful whether
they belonged at all to any Indian dialect, are much used by both
white and red men in their intercourse. Many words are derived
from the French in this species of prairie nomaic. Partisan, brave,
etc., are of the number.

Delawares of the hills. Ah's me, captain, if you had seen as much good and evil as I have seen in these nations of redskins, you would know of how much value was a brave and simpleminded warrior. I know that some are to be found who both think and say that an Indian is but little better than the beasts of these naked plains. But it is needful to be honest in oneself to be a fitting judge of honesty in others. No doubt, no doubt, they know their enemies, and little do they care to show to such any great confidence or love."

"It is the way of man," returned the captain, "and it is probable they are not wanting in any of his natural qualities."

"No, no; it is little that they want that natur' has had to give. But as little does he know of the temper of a redskin who has seen but one Indian or one tribe, as he knows of the color of feathers who has only looked upon a crow. Now, friend steersman, just give the boat a sheer towards yonder low sandy point, and a favor will be granted at a short asking."

"For what?" demanded Middleton. "We are now in the swiftest of the current, and by drawing to the shore we shall lose the force of the stream."

"Your tarry will not be long," returned the old man, applying his own hand to the execution of that which he had requested. The oarsmen had seen enough of his influence with their leader not to dispute his wishes, and before time was given for further discussion on the subject, the bow of the boat had touched the land.

"Captain," resumed the other, untying his little wallet with great deliberation, and even in a manner to show he found satisfaction in the delay, "I wish to offer you a small matter of trade. No great bargain, mayhap; but still the best that one, of whose hand the skill of the rifle has taken leave and who has become no better than a miserable trapper, can offer before we part."

"Part!" was echoed from every mouth among those who had so recently shared his dangers and profited by his care.

"What the devil, old trapper, do you mean to foot it to the settlements, when here is a boat that will float the distance in half the time that the jackass the doctor has given the Pawnee could trot along the same?"

"Settlements, boy! It is long sin' I took my leave of the waste and wickedness of the settlements and the villages. If I live in a clearing here, it is one of the Lord's making, and I have no hard thoughts on the matter; but never again shall I be seen running willfully into the danger of immoralities."

"I had not thought of parting," answered Middleton, endeavoring to seek some relief from the uneasiness he felt by turning his eyes on the sympathizing countenances of his friends; "on the contrary, I had hoped and believed that you would have accompanied us below, where, I give you a sacred pledge, nothing shall be wanting to make your days comfortable."

"Yes, lad, yes; you would do your endeavors; but what are the strivings of man against the working of the devil? Aye, if kind offers and good wishes could have done the thing, I might have been a congressman or perhaps a governor years agone. Your gran'ther wished the same, and there are them still living in the Otsego Mountains, as I hope, who would gladly have given me a palace for my dwelling. But what are riches without content? My time must now be short, at any rate, and I hold it's no mighty sin for one who has acted his part honestly near ninety winters and summers to wish to pass the few hours that remain in comfort. If you think I have done wrong in coming thus far to quit you again, captain, I will own the reason of the act without shame or backwardness. Though I have seen so much of the wilderness, it is not to be gainsaid that my feelings, as well as my skin, are white. Now it would not be a fitting spectacle that yonder Pawnee Loup should look upon the weakness of an old warrior, if weakness he should happen to show in parting forever from those he has reason to love, though he may not set his heart so strongly on them as to wish to go into the settlements in their company."

"Harkee, old trapper," said Paul, clearing his throat with a desperate effort, as if determined to give his voice a clear exit; "I have just one bargain to make, since you talk of trading, which is neither more nor less than this. I offer you, as my side of the business, one half of my shanty, nor do I much care if it be the biggest half; the sweetest and the purest honey that can be made of the wild locust; always enough to eat, with now and then a mouthful of venison or, for that matter, a morsel of buffalo's hump, seeing that I intend to push my acquaintance with the animal; and as good and as tidy cooking as can come from the hands of one like Ellen Wade here, who will shortly be Nelly somebody else; and altogether such general treatment as a decent man might be supposed to pay to his best friend or, for that matter, to his own father. In return for the same, you are to give us at odd moments some of your ancient traditions, perhaps a little wholesome advice on occasions, in small quantities at a time, and as much of your agreeable company as you please."

"It is well—it is well, boy," returned the old man, fumbling at his wallet; "honestly offered, and not unthankfully declined—but it cannot be; no, it can never be."

"Venerable venator," said Dr. Battius, "there are obligations which every man owes to society and to human nature. It is time that you should return to your countrymen to deliver up some of those stores of experimental knowledge that you have doubtless obtained by so long a sojourn in the wilds, which, however they may be corrupted by preconceived opinions, will prove acceptable bequests to those whom, as you say, you must shortly leave forever."

"Friend physicianer," returned the trapper, looking the other steadily in the face, "as it would be no easy matter to judge of the temper of the rattler by considering the fashions of the moose, so it would be hard to speak of the usefulness of one man by thinking too much of the deeds of another. You have your gifts like others, I suppose, and little do I wish to disturb them. But as to me, the Lord has made me for a doer and not a talker, and therefore do I consider it no harm to shut my ears to your invitation."

"It is enough," interrupted Middleton; "I have seen and heard so much of this extraordinary man as to know that persuasions will not change his purpose. First, we will hear your request, my friend, and then we will consider what may be best done for your advantage."

"It is a small matter, captain," returned the old man, succeeding at length in opening his bundle. "A small and trifling matter is it to what I once used to offer in the way of bargain; but then it is the best I have, and therein not to be despised. Here are the skins of four beavers that I took, it might be a month afore we met, and here is another from a raccoon that is of no great matter to be sure, but which may serve to make weight atween us."

"And what do you propose to do with them?"

"I offer them in lawful barter. Them knaves the Siouxes —the Lord forgive me for ever believing it was the Konzas —have stolen the best of my traps and driven me altogether to makeshift inventions, which might foretell a dreary winter for me, should my time stretch into another season. I wish you therefore to take the skins and to offer them to some of the trappers you will not fail to meet below in exchange for a few traps, and to send the same into the Pawnee village in my name. Be careful to have my mark painted on them—a letter N with a hound's ear, and the lock of a rifle. There is no redskin who will then dispute my right. For all which trouble I have little more to offer than my thanks, unless my friend the bee hunter here will accept of the raccoon and take on himself the special charge of the whole matter."

"If I do, may I be——" The mouth of Paul was stopped by the hand of Ellen, and he was obliged to swallow the rest of the sentence, which he did with a species of emotion that bore no slight resemblance to the process of strangulation.

"Well, well," returned the old man meekly; "I hope there is no heavy offense in the offer. I know that the skin of a raccoon is of small price, but then it was no mighty labor that I asked in return."

"You entirely mistake the meaning of our friend," interrupted Middleton, who observed that the bee hunter was looking in every direction but the right one and that he was utterly unable to make his own vindication. "He did not mean to say that he declined the charge, but merely that he refused all compensation. It is unnecessary, however, to say more of this; it shall be my office to see that the debt we owe is properly discharged and that all your necessities shall be anticipated."

"Anan!" said the old man, looking up inquiringly into the other's face as if to ask an explanation.

"It shall all be as you wish. Lay the skins with my baggage. We will bargain for you as for ourselves."

"Thankee, thankee, captain; your gran'ther was of a free and generous mind. So much so, in truth, that those just people the Delawares called him the Openhand. I wish now I was as I used to be in order that I might send in the lady a few delicate martens for her tippets and overcoats, just to show you that I know how to give courtesy for courtesy. But do not expect the same, for I am too old to give a promise! It will all be just as the Lord shall see fit. I can offer *you* nothing else, for I haven't lived so long in the wilderness not to know the scrupulous ways of a gentleman."

"Harkee, old trapper," cried the bee hunter, striking his

own hand into the open palm which the other had extended with a report but little below the crack of a rifle, "I have just two things to say—firstly, that the captain has told you my meaning better than I can myself; and secondly, if you want a skin, either for your private use or to send abroad, I have it at your service; and that is the skin of one Paul Hover!"

The old man returned the grasp he received and opened his mouth to the utmost in his extraordinary silent laugh.

"You couldn't have given such a squeeze, boy, when the Teton squaws were about you with their knives! Ah! You are in your prime, and in your vigor and happiness, if honesty lies in your path." Then the expression of his rugged features suddenly changed to a look of seriousness and thought. "Come hither, lad," he said, leading the bee hunter by a button to the land and speaking apart in a tone of admonition and confidence; "much has passed atween us on the pleasures and respectableness of a life in the woods or on the borders. I do not now mean to say that all you have heard is not true, but different tempers call for different employments. You have taken to your bosom there a good and kind child, and it has become your duty to consider her as well as yourself in setting forth in life. You are a little given to skirting the settlements, but to my poor judgment the girl would be more like a flourishing flower in the sun of a clearing than in the winds of a prairie. Therefore forget anything you may have heard from me, which is nevertheless true, and turn your mind on the ways of the inner country."

Paul could only answer with a squeeze that would have brought tears from the eyes of most men, but which produced no other effect on the indurated muscles of the other than to make him laugh and nod, as if he received the same as a pledge that the bee hunter would remember his advice. The trapper then turned away from his rough but warmhearted companion, and having called Hector from the boat, he seemed anxious still to utter a few words more.

"Captain," he at length resumed, "I know when a poor man talks of credit he deals in a delicate word, according to the fashions of the world; and when an old man talks of life, he speaks of that which he may never see; nevertheless there is one thing I will say, and that is not so much on my own behalf as on that of another person.

Here is Hector, a good and faithful pup, that has long out-lived the time of a dog; and like his master, he looks more to comfort now than to any deeds in running. But the creatur' has his feelings as well as a Christian. He has con-sorted latterly with his kinsman there in such a sort as to find great pleasure in his company, and I will acknowledge that it touches my feelings to part the pair so soon. If you will set a value on your hound, I will endeavor to send it to you in the spring, more especially should them same traps come safe to hand; or, if you dislike parting with the animal altogether, I will just ask you for his loan through the winter. I think I can see my pup will not last beyond that time, for I have judgment in these matters, since many is the friend, both hound and redskin, that I have seen depart in my day, though the Lord hath not yet seen fit to order his angels to sound forth my name."

"Take him, take him," cried Middleton; "take all, or any-thing!"

The old man whistled the younger dog to the land, and then he proceeded to the final adieus. Little was said on either side. The trapper took each person solemnly by the hand and uttered something friendly and kind to all. Mid-dleton was perfectly speechless, and was driven to affect busying himself among the baggage. Paul whistled with all his might, and even Obed took his leave with an effort that bore the appearance of desperate philosophical resolution. When he had made the circuit of the whole, the old man with his own hands shoved the boat into the current, wish-ing God to speed them. Not a word was spoken nor a stroke of the oar given until the travelers had floated past a knoll that hid the trapper from their view. He was last seen standing on the low point leaning on his rifle, with Hector crouched at his feet and the younger dog frisking along the sands in the playfulness of youth and vigor.

CHAPTER 34

Methought I heard a voice.

SHAKESPEARE

THE WATERCOURSES WERE at their height, and the boat went down the swift current like a bird. The passage proved prosperous and speedy. In less than a third of the time that would have been necessary for the same journey by land, it was accomplished by the favor of those rapid rivers. Issuing from one stream into another, as the veins of the human body communicate with the larger channels of life, they soon entered the grand artery of the western waters and landed safely at the very door of the father of Inez.

The joy of Don Augustin and the embarrassment of the worthy Father Ignatius may be imagined. The former wept and returned thanks to heaven; the latter returned thanks and did not weep. The mild provincials were too happy to raise any questions on the character of so joyful a restoration, and by a sort of general consent it soon came to be an admitted opinion that the bride of Middleton had been kidnapped by a villain and that she was restored to her friends by human agency. There were, as respects this belief, certainly a few skeptics, but then they enjoyed their doubts in private, with that species of sublimated and solitary gratification that a miser finds in gazing at his growing but useless hoards.

In order to give the worthy priest something to employ his mind, Middleton made him the instrument of uniting Paul and Ellen. The former consented to the ceremony because he found that all his friends laid great stress on the matter; but shortly after, he led his bride into the plains of Kentucky under the pretense of paying certain customary visits to sundry members of the family of Hover. While there he took occasion to have the marriage properly solemnized by a justice of the peace of his acquaintance in whose ability to forge the nuptial chain he had much more faith than in that of all the gownsmen within the pale of Rome. Ellen, who appeared conscious that some extraordinary preventives might prove necessary to keep one of so erratic a temper as her partner within the proper matrimonial boundaries, raised no objections to these double knots, and all parties were content.

The local importance Middleton had acquired, by his union with the daughter of so affluent a proprietor as Don Augustin, united to his personal merit, attracted the attention of the government. He was soon employed in various situations of responsibility and confidence, which both served to elevate his character in the public estimation and to afford the means of patronage. The bee hunter was among the first of those to whom he saw fit to extend his favor. It was far from difficult to find situations suited to the abilities of Paul in the state of society that existed three and twenty years ago in those regions. The efforts of Middleton and Inez in behalf of her husband were warmly and sagaciously seconded by Ellen, and they succeeded, in process of time, in working a great and beneficial change in his character. He soon became a landholder, then a prosperous cultivator of the soil, and shortly after a town officer. By that progressive change in fortunes, which in the republic is often seen to be so singularly accompanied by a corresponding improvement in knowledge and self-respect, he went on from step to step until his wife enjoyed the maternal delight of seeing her children placed far beyond the danger of returning to that state from which both their parents had issued. Paul is actually at this moment a member of the lower branch of the legislature of the state where he has long resided, and he is even notorious for making speeches that have a tendency to put that deliberative body in good humor and which, as they are based on great practical knowledge suited to the condition of the country, possess a merit that is much wanted in many more subtle and fine-spun theories that are daily heard in similar assemblies to issue from the lips of certain instinctive politicians. But all these happy fruits were the results of much care and of a long period of time. Middleton, who fills, with a credit better suited to the difference in their educations, a seat in a far higher branch of legislative authority, is the source from which we have derived most of the intelligence necessary to compose our legend. In addition to what he has related of Paul, and of his own continued happiness, he has added a short narrative of what took place on a subsequent visit to the prairies, with which, as we conceive it a suitable termination to what has gone before, we shall judge it wise to conclude our labors.

In the autumn of the year that succeeded the season in which the preceding events occurred, the young man, still in the military service, found himself on the waters of the Missouri at a point not far remote from the Pawnee towns. Released from any immediate calls of duty, and strongly urged to the measure by Paul, who was in his company, he determined to take horse and cross the country to visit the partisan and to inquire into the fate of his friend the trapper. As his train was suited to his functions and rank, the journey was effected, with the privations and hardships that are the accompaniments of all traveling in a wild, but without any of those dangers and alarms that marked his former passage through the same regions. When within a proper distance, he dispatched an Indian runner, belonging to a friendly tribe, to announce the approach of himself and party, continuing his route at a deliberate pace in order that the intelligence might, as was customary, precede his arrival. To the surprise of the travelers, their message was unanswered. Hour succeeded hour, and mile after mile was passed without bringing either the signs of an honorable reception or the more simple assurances of a friendly welcome. At length the cavalcade at whose head rode Middleton and Paul descended from the elevated plain on which they had long been journeying to a luxuriant bottom that brought them to the level of the village of the Loups. The sun was beginning to fall, and a sheet of golden light was spread over the placid plain, lending to its even surface those glorious tints and hues that the human imagination is apt to conceive form the embellishment of still more imposing scenes. The verdure of the year yet remained, and herds of horses and mules were grazing peacefully in the vast natural pasture under the keeping of vigilant Pawnee boys. Paul pointed out among them the well-known form of *Asinus,* sleek, fat, and luxuriating in the fullness of content as he stood with reclining ears and closed eyelids, seemingly musing on the exquisite nature of his present indolent enjoyment.

The route of the party led them at no great distance from one of those watchful youths who was charged with a trust heavy as the principal wealth of his tribe. He heard the trampling of the horses and cast his eye aside, but instead of manifesting curiosity or alarm, his look instantly returned whence it had been withdrawn, to the spot where the village was known to stand.

"There is something remarkable in all this," muttered Middleton, half offended at what he conceived to be not only a slight to his rank but offensive to himself personally; "yonder boy has heard of our approach, or he would not fail to notify his tribe; and yet he scarcely deigns to favor us with a glance. Look to your arms, men; it may be necessary to let these savages feel our strength."

"Therein, captain, I think you're in an error," returned Paul; "if honesty is to be met on the prairies at all, you will find it in our old friend Hard Heart; neither is an Indian to be judged of by the rules of a white. See! We are not altogether slighted, for here comes a party at last to meet us, though it is a little pitiful as to show and numbers."

Paul was right in both particulars. A group of horsemen were at length seen wheeling round a little copse and advancing across the plain directly towards them. The advance of this party was slow and dignified. As it drew nigh, the partisan of the Loups was seen at its head, followed by a dozen younger warriors of his tribe. They were all unarmed, nor did they even wear any of those ornaments or feathers which are considered testimonials of respect to the guest an Indian receives, as well as evidence of his own importance.

The meeting was friendly though a little restrained on both sides. Middleton, jealous of his own consideration no less than of the authority of his government, suspected some undue influence on the part of the agents of the Canadas; and as he was determined to maintain the authority of which he was the representative, he felt himself constrained to manifest a hauteur that he was far from feeling. It was not so easy to penetrate the motives of the Pawnees. Calm, dignified, and yet far from repulsive, they set an example of courtesy, blended with reserve, that many a diplomatist of the most polished court might have striven in vain to imitate.

In this manner the two parties continued their course to the town. Middleton had time during the remainder of the ride to revolve in his mind all the probable reasons which his ingenuity could suggest for this strange reception. Although he was accompanied by a regular interpreter, the chiefs made their salutations in a manner that dispensed with his services. Twenty times the captain turned his glance on his former friend, endeavoring to read the expression of his rigid features. But every effort and all conjectures proved equally futile. The eye of Hard Heart was fixed, composed, and a little anxious, but as to every other emotion, impenetrable. He neither spoke himself nor seemed willing to invite discourse in his visitors; it was therefore necessary for Middleton to adopt the patient manners of his companions and to await the issue for the explanation.

When they entered the town, its inhabitants were seen collected in an open space, where they were arranged with the customary deference to age and rank. The whole formed a large circle, in the center of which were perhaps a dozen of the principal chiefs. Hard Heart waved his hand as he approached, and as the mass of bodies opened, he rode through, followed by his companions. Here they dismounted; and as the beasts were led apart, the strangers found themselves environed by a thousand grave, composed, but solicitous faces.

Middleton gazed about him in growing concern, for no cry, no song, no shout welcomed him among a people from whom he had so lately parted with regret. His uneasiness, not to say apprehensions, was shared by all his followers. Determination and stern resolution began to assume the place of anxiety in every eye as each man silently felt for his arms and assured himself that his several weapons were in a state for service. But there was no answering symptom of hostility on the part of their hosts. Hard Heart beckoned for Middleton and Paul to follow, leading the way towards the cluster of forms that occupied the center of the circle. Here the visitors found a solution of all the movements which had given them so much reason for apprehension.

The trapper was placed on a rude seat which had been made, with studied care, to support his frame in an upright and easy attitude. The first glance of the eye told his former friends that the old man was at length called upon to pay the last tribute of nature. His eye was glazed and apparently as devoid of sight as of expression. His features were a little more sunken and strongly marked than formerly, but there all change so far as exterior was concerned might be said to have ceased. His approaching end was not to be ascribed to any positive disease, but had been a gradual and mild decay of the physical powers. Life, it is true, still lingered in his system; but it was as if at times entirely ready to depart, and then it would appear to reanimate the sinking form, reluctant to give up the possession of a tenement that had never been corrupted by vice or undermined by disease. It would have been no violent fancy to have imagined that the spirit fluttered about the placid lips of the old woodsman, reluctant to depart from a shell that had so long given it an honest and honorable shelter.

His body was placed so as to let the light of the setting sun fall full upon the solemn features. His head was bare, the long thin locks of gray fluttering lightly in the evening breeze. His rifle lay upon his knee, and the other accouterments of the chase were placed at his side within reach of his hand. Between his feet lay the figure of a hound, with its head crouching to the earth, as if it slumbered; and so perfectly easy and natural was its position that a second glance was necessary to tell Middleton he saw only the skin of Hector stuffed, by Indian tenderness and ingenuity, in a manner to represent the living animal. His own dog was playing at a distance with the child of Tachechana and Mahtoree. The mother herself stood at hand, holding in her arms a second offspring that might boast of a parentage no less honorable than that which belonged to the son of Hard Heart. Le Balafré was seated nigh the dying trapper with every mark about his person that the hour of his own departure was not far distant. The rest of those immediately in the center were aged men who had apparently drawn near in order to observe the manner in which a just and fearless warrior would depart on the greatest of his journeys.

The old man was reaping the rewards of a life remarkable for temperance and activity in a tranquil and placid death. His vigor in a manner endured to the very last. Decay, when it did occur, was rapid but free from pain. He had hunted with the tribe in the spring, and even throughout most of the summer, when his limbs suddenly refused to perform their customary offices. A sympathizing weakness took possession of all his faculties; and the Pawnees believed that they were going to lose, in this unexpected manner, a sage and counselor whom they had begun both to love and respect. But as we have already said, the immortal occupant seemed unwilling to desert its tenement. The lamp of life flickered without becoming extinguished. On the morning of the day on which Middleton arrived, there was a general reviving of the powers of the whole man. His tongue was again heard in wholesome maxims, and his eye from time to time recognized the persons of his friends. It merely proved to be a brief and final intercourse with the world on the part of one who had already been considered, as to mental communion, to have taken his leave of it forever.

When he had placed his guests in front of the dying man, Hard Heart, after a pause that proceeded as much from sorrow as decorum, leaned a little forward and demanded, "Does my father hear the words of his son?"

"Speak," returned the trapper in tones that issued from his chest but which were rendered awfully distinct by the stillness that reigned in the place. "I am about to depart from the village of the Loups, and shortly shall be beyond the reach of your voice."

"Let the wise chief have no cares for his journey," continued Hard Heart with an earnest solicitude that led him to forget for the moment that others were waiting to address his adopted parent; "a hundred Loups shall clear his path from briers."

"Pawnee, I die, as I have lived, a Christian man!" resumed the trapper with a force of voice that had the same startling effect on his hearers as is produced by the trumpet when its blast rises suddenly and freely on the air after its obstructed sounds have been heard struggling in the distance; "as I came into life, so will I leave it. Horses and arms are not needed to stand in the presence of the Great Spirit of my people. He knows my color, and according to my gifts will he judge my deeds."

"My father will tell my young men how many Mingoes he has struck and what acts of valor and justice he has done, that they may know how to imitate him."

"A boastful tongue is not heard in the heaven of a white man!" solemnly returned the old man. "What I have done he has seen. His eyes are always open. That which has been well done will he remember; wherein I have been wrong will he not forget to chastise, though he will do the same in mercy. No, my son, a paleface may not sing his own praises and hope to have them acceptable before his God!"

A little disappointed, the young partisan stepped modestly back, making way for the recent comers to approach. Middleton took one of the meager hands of the trapper, and struggling to command his voice, he succeeded in announcing his presence.

The old man listened like one whose thoughts were dwelling on a very different subject, but when the other had succeeded in making him understand that he was present, an expression of joyful recognition passed over his faded features.

"I hope you have not so soon forgotten those whom you so materially served!" Middleton concluded. "It would pain me to think my hold on your memory was so light."

"Little that I have ever seen is forgotten," returned the trapper; "I am at the close of many weary days, but there is not one among them all that I could wish to overlook. I remember you with the whole of your company, aye, and your gran'ther that went before you. I am glad that you have come back upon these plains, for I had need of one who speaks the English, since little faith can be put in the traders of these regions. Will you do a favor to an old and dying man?"

"Name it," said Middleton; "it shall be done."

"It is a far journey to send such trifles," resumed the old man, who spoke at short intervals, as strength and breath permitted; "a far and weary journey is the same; but kindnesses and friendships are things not to be forgotten. There is a settlement among the Otsego hills——"

"I know the place," interrupted Middleton, observing that he spoke with increasing difficulty; "proceed to tell me what you would have done."

"Take this rifle, and pouch, and horn, and send them to the person whose name is graven on the plates of the stock —a trader cut the letters with his knife—for it is long that I have intended to send him such a token of my love!"

"It shall be so. Is there more that you could wish?"

"Little else have I to bestow. My traps I give to my Indian son, for honestly and kindly has he kept his faith. Let him stand before me."

Middleton explained to the chief what the trapper had said and relinquished his own place to the other.

"Pawnee," continued the old man, always changing his language to suit the person he addressed, and not unfrequently according to the ideas he expressed, "it is a custom of my people for the father to leave his blessing with the son before he shuts his eyes forever. This blessing I give to you; take it, for the prayers of a Christian man will never make the path of a just warrior to the blessed prairies either longer or more tangled. May the God of a white man look on your deeds with friendly eyes, and may you never commit an act that shall cause him to darken his face. I know not whether we shall ever meet again. There are many traditions concerning the place of good spirits. It is not for one like me, old and experienced though I am, to set up my opinions against a nation's. You believe in the blessed prairies, and I have faith in the sayings of my fathers. If both are true our parting will be final; but if it should prove that the same meaning is hid under different words, we shall yet stand together, Pawnee, before the face of your Wahcondah, who will then be no other than my God. There is much to be said in favor of both religions, for each seems suited to its own people, and no doubt it was so intended. I fear I have not altogether followed the gifts of my color, inasmuch as I find it a little painful to give up forever the use of the rifle and the comforts of the chase. But then the fault has been my own, seeing that it could not have been his. Aye, Hector," he continued, leaning forward a little and feeling for the ears of the hound, "our parting has come at last, dog, and it will be a long hunt. You have been an honest, and a bold, and a faithful hound. Pawnee, you cannot slay the pup on my grave, for where a Christian dog falls there he lies forever; but you can be kind to him after I am gone for the love you bear his master."

"The words of my father are in my ears," returned the young partisan, making a grave and respectful gesture of assent.

"Do you hear what the chief has promised, dog?" demanded the trapper, making an effort to attract the notice of the insensible effigy of his hound. Receiving no answering look nor hearing any friendly whine, the old man felt for the mouth and endeavored to force his hand between the cold lips. The truth then flashed upon him, although he was far from perceiving the whole extent of the deception. Falling back in his seat, he hung his head like one who felt a severe and unexpected shock. Profiting by this momentary forgetfulness, two young Indians removed the skin with the same delicacy of feeling that had induced them to attempt the pious fraud.

"The dog is dead!" muttered the trapper after a pause of many minutes. "A hound has his time as well as a man, and well has he filled his days! Captain," he added, making an effort to wave his hand for Middleton, "I am glad you have come, for though kind and well meaning according to the gifts of their color, these Indians are not the men to lay the head of a white man in his grave. I have been thinking too of this dog at my feet; it will not do to set forth the opinion that a Christian can expect to meet his hound again; still there can be little harm in placing what is left of so faithful a servant nigh the bones of his master."

"It shall be as you desire."

"I'm glad you think with me in this matter. In order, then, to save labor, lay the pup at my feet; or for that matter, put him side by side. A hunter need never be ashamed to be found in company with his dog!"

"I charge myself with your wish."

The old man made a long and apparently a musing pause. At times he raised his eyes wistfully, as if he would again address Middleton, but some innate feeling appeared always to suppress his words. The other, who observed his hesitation, inquired, in a way most likely to encourage him to proceed, whether there was aught else that he could wish to have done.

"I am without kith or kin in the wide world!" the trapper answered. "When I am gone there will be an end of my race. We have never been chiefs, but honest and useful in our way. I hope it cannot be denied we have always proved ourselves. My father lies buried near the sea, and the bones of his son will whiten on the prairies——"

"Name the spot, and your remains shall be placed by the side of your father," interrupted Middleton.

"Not so, not so, captain. Let me sleep where I have lived —beyond the din of the settlements! Still I see no need why the grave of an honest man should be hid, like a redskin in his ambushment. I paid a man in the settlements to make and put a graven stone at the head of my father's resting-place. It was of the value of twelve beaver skins, and cunningly and curiously was it carved! Then it told to all comers that the body of such a Christian lay beneath; and it spoke of his manner of life, of his years, and of his honesty. When we had done with the Frenchers in the old war, I made a journey to the spot in order to see that all was rightly performed, and glad I am to say, the workman had not forgotten his faith."

"And such a stone you would have at your grave?"

"I! No, no, I have no son but Hard Heart, and it is little that an Indian knows of white fashions and usages. Besides, I am his debtor already, seeing it is so little I have done since I have lived in his tribe. The rifle might bring the value of such a thing—but then I know it will give the boy pleas-

ure to hang the piece in his hall, for many is the deer and
the bird that he has seen it destroy. No, no, the gun must be
sent to him whose name is graven on the lock!"

"But there is one who would gladly prove his affection in
the way you wish; he who owes you not only his own deliverance from so many dangers, but who inherits a heavy
debt of gratitude from his ancestors. The stone shall be put
at the head of your grave."

The old man extended his emaciated hand and gave the
other a squeeze of thanks.

"I thought you might be willing to do it, but I was backward in asking the favor," he said, "seeing that you are not
of my kin. Put no boastful words on the same, but just the
name, the age, and the time of the death, with something
from the holy book; no more, no more. My name will then
not be altogether lost on 'arth; I need no more."

Middleton intimated his assent, and then followed a pause
that was only broken by distant and broken sentences from
the dying man. He appeared now to have closed his accounts
with the world and to await merely for the final summons to
quit it. Middleton and Hard Heart placed themselves on the
opposite sides of his seat and watched with melancholy solicitude the variations of his countenance. For two hours
there was no very sensible alteration. The expression of his
faded and time-worn features was that of a calm and dignified repose. From time to time he spoke, uttering some
brief sentence in the way of advice or asking some simple
questions concerning those in whose fortunes he took a
friendly interest. During the whole of that solemn and anxious period each individual of the tribe kept his place in the
most self-restrained patience. When the old man spoke, all
bent their heads to listen; and when his words were uttered,
they seemed to ponder on their wisdom and usefulness.

As the flame drew nigher to the socket, his voice was
hushed, and there were moments when his attendants doubted whether he still belonged to the living. Middleton, who
watched each wavering expression of his weather-beaten visage with the interest of a keen observer of human nature
softened by the tenderness of personal regard, fancied he
could read the workings of the old man's soul in the strong
lineaments of his countenance. Perhaps what the enlightened
soldier took for the delusion of mistaken opinion did actually occur, for who has returned from that unknown world to

explain by what forms, and in what manner, he was introduced into its awful precincts? Without pretending to explain what must ever be a mystery to the quick, we shall simply relate facts as they occurred.

The trapper had remained nearly motionless for an hour. His eyes alone had occasionally opened and shut. When opened, his gaze seemed fastened on the clouds which hung around the western horizon, reflecting the bright colors and giving form and loveliness to the glorious tints of an American sunset. The hour, the calm beauty of the season, the occasion—all conspired to fill the spectators with solemn awe. Suddenly, while musing on the remarkable position in which he was placed, Middleton felt the hand which he held grasp his own with incredible power, and the old man, supported on either side by his friends, rose upright to his feet. For a moment he looked about him as if to invite all in presence to listen (the lingering remnant of human frailty), and then, with a fine military elevation of the head and with a voice that might be heard in every part of that numerous assembly, he pronounced the word "Here!"

A movement so entirely unexpected, and the air of grandeur and humility which were so remarkably united in the mien of the trapper, together with the clear and uncommon force of his utterance, produced a short period of confusion in the faculties of all present. When Middleton and Hard Heart, each of whom had involuntarily extended a hand to support the form of the old man, turned to him again, they found that the subject of their interest was removed forever beyond the necessity of their care. They mournfully placed the body in its seat, and Le Balafré arose to announce the termination of the scene to the tribe. The voice of the old Indian seemed a sort of echo from that invisible world to which the meek spirit of the trapper had just departed.

"A valiant, a just, and a wise warrior has gone on the path which will lead him to the blessed grounds of his people!" he said. "When the voice of the Wahcondah called him, he was ready to answer. Go, my children; remember the just chief of the palefaces, and clear your own tracks from briers!"

The grave was made beneath the shade of some noble oaks. It has been carefully watched to the present hour by the Pawnees of the Loup and is often shown to the traveler and the trader as a spot where a just white man sleeps. In due time the stone was placed at its head, with the simple inscription which the trapper had himself requested. The only liberty taken by Middleton was to add: "May no wanton hand ever disturb his remains!"

Afterword

The literary reputation of James Fenimore Cooper has had a various career. In his own day his American contemporaries hailed him as the "American Scott," a designation that irritated Cooper by its implication that he was a derivative writer. No writer takes kindly to such a suggestion, but Cooper's fellow Americans meant it as the highest praise. Proud of being Americans, yet culturally self-conscious of the thinness of the aesthetic achievement of the New World, they meant to do high honor to Cooper by suggesting a comparison with Sir Walter Scott. Americans were, in other words, ambivalent in their bumptious nationalism; Europe was still their standard, whether they rejected it or promised to surpass it. The difficulty Americans have had in understanding the meaning of their national experience in relation to the Old World has proved also to be the theme that has given Cooper's writing enduring worth in our literary tradition.

Yet, before his place in the American tradition was firmly established, Cooper's reputation at first declined to that of being a writer of children's books, a curious fate that also overtook *The Adventures of Huckleberry Finn* and *Moby-Dick*. Like Twain and Melville, Cooper has kept a youthful audience; and the adventures of Natty Bumppo, the hero of the Leatherstocking series, are probably still a part of the reading experience of many young Americans. For that audience *The Last of the Mohicans* and *The Deerslayer* are the important books. Then in the twentieth century, as part of the movement toward defining the roots of our national culture, scholarship rediscovered Cooper, but it was not Cooper as writer of fiction but Cooper as social critic and observer of his times who emerged as important in this reassessment. Emphasis here fell more on Cooper's social criticism in such books as *The American Democrat* (1838) or on the travel books, which incorporated much social commentary, *Notions of the Americans by a Traveling Bachelor* (1828) and *Home as Found* (1838).

Until recently then, we have had two Coopers, one the writer of adventure stories, the romances of the woods, the other the conservative Jeffersonian gentleman troubled by the dangers of an uncouth democracy. Only now have we begun to see that the two are one, that is, that Cooper's social and political attitudes are at the very heart of his fiction and account for both its strength and its weakness. In this contemporary re-evaluation the Leatherstocking series is once again the center of interest, but such novels as *The Last of the Mohicans* seem far less important than *The Pioneers* and *The Prairie*.

The pattern of rise and fall in a writer's reputation may seem to suggest pure caprice on the part of his audience. Robert Frost, talking about poets today, used to ask puckishly, "Whose stock is up? Whose stock is down?"—as if reputation were the consequence of insiders' speculation. But the changing responses to Cooper's writing can better be understood in broader terms. He quickly ceased to be taken as a serious writer because the criteria of judgment changed markedly in America soon after he wrote. Realism, an ambiguous but necessary word for a tendency in writing, provided no categories to take account of Cooper's effects. In 1903 Frank Norris, in *The Responsibilities of the Novelist*, put the realist's case against Cooper: "Cooper, you will say, was certainly American in attitude and choice of subject; none more so. None less so, none less so. As a novelist he is saturated with the romance of the contemporary English storytellers. It is true that his background is American. But his heroes and heroines talk like the characters out of Bulwer in their most vehement moods, while his Indians stalk through all the melodramatic tableaux of Byron, and declaim in the periods of the border nobleman in the pages of Walter Scott." What had once been a comparison in praise had, by the end of the nineteenth century, become a term of opprobrium. Literary realism, despite protestations about its giving us the facts of life, derived from literary conventions, but the conventions were those of Balzac and Zola, a commitment to the ordinary and everyday in life and an adherence to plain speech. Mark Twain, part of whose great achievement was to make vernacular speech the stuff of great literature, had made the same point against Cooper in 1895 in an article in the *North American Review*, "Fenimore Cooper's Literary Offenses." The rules governing literary art, said Twain, "require that when a personage talks like an illustrated, gilt-edged, tree-calf, hand-tooled, seven-dollar Friendship's Offering in the beginning of a paragraph, he shall not talk like a Negro minstrel in the end of it. But this rule is flung down and danced upon" by Cooper. Cooper's tales of Indians and pioneers, what Twain called the "broken-twig" school of fiction, so outraged Twain that he parodied them hilariously; they violated his own practice and program for literature. Only children, and not too intelligent children at that, seemed Cooper's proper audience. "Cooper's eye," said Twain, "was splendidly inaccurate."

But there is a kind of accuracy and a dimension of reality that differ from a reality defined by plausibility of detail and adherence to the rhythm of the spoken language. D. H. Lawrence saw this clearly. Discussing the Leatherstocking series, Lawrence wrote: "Now let me put aside my impatience at the unreality of this vision, and accept it as a wish-fulfillment vision, a kind of yearning myth. Because it seems to me that the things in Cooper that make one so savage, when one compares them with actuality, are perhaps, when one considers them as presentations of deep subjective desire, real in their own way, and almost prophetic." The "yearning myth" Lawrence glimpsed beneath the bungled surface of Cooper's fiction was the dream of a new relation between man and man that first required a "cruel sloughing" of the past, to be followed by an emergence into an unencumbered new life. "The Leatherstocking novels create the myth of this new relation. And they go backwards, from old age to golden youth. That is the true myth of America. She starts old, old, wrinkled and writhing in an old skin. And there is a gradual sloughing of the old skin, towards a new youth. It is the myth of America."

Lawrence is making an extraordinary claim for Cooper. He

is saying no less than that Cooper somehow touched the quick of experience in America and fashioned in his stories the myth that gives shape and coherence to the meaning of American culture. If, with Norris and Twain, we are so put off by Cooper's stilted language and improbable events that we cannot for the moment suspend our disbelief, we will deny ourselves an awareness of what Lawrence glimpsed and recent critics, especially Henry Nash Smith, have revealed fully to be the reason for Cooper's present importance. James Fenimore Cooper has survived in our literary canon, has been rescued from children and social historians, because his fiction is an imaginative embodiment of a pervasive attitude in our culture toward the meaning of life in the New World.

George Santayana once remarked that we are condemned to live dramatically in a world that is not dramatic. We try to make sense, as we say, of experience, whether personally as biography or collectively as history. From the beginning there were two ways to read the meaning of the American experience. As the first settlers set out from the Old World to the New, they were both leaving an old home and seeking a new one. Universally, the voyage or the trip has lent itself to easy translation into the metaphor of the quest where the physical journey becomes a symbolic quest for the meaning of it all. One thinks of the wandering tribes of Israel in the Bible, Homer's Ulysses, Bunyan's Pilgrim, and Don Quixote. The metaphor is probably basic to shared human experience, but it has been especially characteristic of the American version; from Whitman tramping the open road to Saul Bellow's *The Adventures of Augie March,* the best of American literature has been organized around metaphors of setting out and venturing forth into the new and unknown. Until the twentieth century the metaphor hardly seemed metaphor at all; it conformed so closely to our historical experience that it seemed a fair description of the American reality.

But the meaning of the journey out of the Old World into the New always had a certain doubleness to it, an inevitable ambivalence. One valuation had it that the movement westward into a virgin continent meant the rejection of Europe and all it represented. In this reading of our collective experience, Europe stood for the snobbery of social classes, feudalism, rule by irresponsible aristocrats and kings, the craft of priests, institutional complexity, and social decadence; whereas the New World stood for the equality of all men, the abolition of social distinction, freedom, spontaneity, simplicity, and vigor. In short, Europe stood for the corruption of advanced civilization and America stood for the beneficence of nature. Yet at the same time, there was another way to read experience. Here, America meant the advance of the best of civilization, choice seed sifted from the Old World for planting in the New, as the Puritans put it, into a raw and savage continent. In this reading the American venture meant the progress of reason, order, enlightenment, and cultivation, an extension of civilization into a wild, untamed, savage continent where law was absent and barbarism posed a constant danger to the achievements of human order. Not only were the terms of evaluation different; they pointed in different directions. For the first the geographical *locus* of value was West, the frontier and, beyond it, the unfallen innocence of an Edenic world; for the second the point of reference was East, ultimately toward Europe and a developed society of urbanity and sophistication.

Such a stark formulation suggests an "either-or" appraisal, and we may ask impatiently, Which was it? But the question is a false one historically and may be a false one humanly. Americans saw the matter of their experience both ways; that is, they affirmed their culture at one and the same time both as a return to the simple harmony of the pastoral ideal as well as an advance in the achievements of high civilization. The late Professor Perry Miller explored this doubleness in the Puritans' conception of the meaning of their "errand into the wilderness," and the same ambivalence permeates American history from the politics of Thomas Jefferson to the historical writing of Frederick Jackson Turner. It even helps to account for the persistent nostalgia of our advanced industrial and technological society in the twentieth century. It is from the field of energy defined by the poles of Nature and Civilization that Cooper's power ultimately derives.

The Leatherstocking series, of which *The Prairie* is the narrative conclusion, was published by Cooper in the years from 1823 to 1841, but the chronology of publication does not follow the chronology of the narrative. If we place the two chronologies side by side, we see what Lawrence meant when he said that the Leatherstocking series, like the sequence of

American historical experience, goes backward in time.

Publication Sequence	Narrative Sequence
The Pioneers (1823)	*The Deerslayer*
The Last of the Mohicans (1826)	*The Pathfinder*
The Prairie (1827)	*The Last of the Mohicans*
The Pathfinder (1840)	*The Pioneers*
The Deerslayer (1841)	*The Prairie*

The series is held together by the presence of a central hero, Natty Bumppo, called according to his age either Deerslayer or Leatherstocking; the period covered is from his youth in the early eighteenth century to his death on the prairies in 1806. It is important that Cooper first imagined his hero at the precise moment when his simple code of natural justice ran athwart the institutionalized code of social justice, a conflict that defines the essential plot of *The Pioneers*. In that novel Natty and his Indian friend Chingachgook are old and living on the edge of advancing society, whose central spokesman is Judge Marmaduke Temple. Natty breaks man-made law, and Judge Temple, even while recognizing that by the standard of a higher law Natty is innocent, must, as the standard-bearer of social order, sentence him to jail. *The Pioneers* closes with Natty's escape from society and his flight westward into the setting sun to live out his last days, where we find him in *The Prairie*.

The Prairie is a difficult novel to read, if only because at first glance its plot seems to make no sense at all. The device of an abduction by which Cooper transports his socially superior characters, Inez and Captain Middleton, into the wilderness runs into the common-sense objection that Abiram White, the kidnapper, is hardly going to be able to collect a ransom for Inez from her parents if he cannot contact them; every mile his party proceeds farther west makes that increasingly improbable. Only in comparison with this central flaw in the plot do other matters seem less troublesome, such as Cooper's handiness in summoning up trees on the treeless Great Plains and the casual ease with which he disposes of escapes from the Indians. But if in Mark Twain's masterpiece, *The Adventures of Huckleberry Finn*, we have learned not to be bothered by the discrepancy of Huck and Jim floating passively farther and farther into slave territory when they are supposed to be fleeing for Jim's freedom to free territory, perhaps we can learn to allow Cooper the same freedom. Henry Nash Smith has suggested that Cooper "treats the portion of the Plains in which the action takes place as if it were an Elizabethan stage, a neutral space where any character may be brought at a moment's notice without arousing in the audience a desire to have the entrance accounted for." Cooper rather suffers in the comparison, but the suggestion frees us to see what *The Prairie* is really about.

The Prairie is a threnody over the passing of something fine and heroic in American life. From the moment that Leatherstocking appears framed in the setting sun before the startled eyes of Ishmael Bush and his band ("The figure was colossal, the attitude musing and melancholy . . ."), to the calm of his philosophic death at the end, *The Prairie* is about the passing of an ideal natural order before the inevitable advance of society. Despite the open, lonely spaces of the prairie, a considerable number of characters are involved. At one extreme we have the untutored, natural wisdom of Natty Bumppo, and even beyond him the ideal noble savage, Hard Heart; at the other extreme stand the delicate heroine, Inez, and her genteel lover, Captain Middleton. Between we have a remarkable range of social types, from the less socially elevated lovers, Paul Hovenden and Ellen, to the brutish yet moving figure of the violent outcast, Ishmael. Ishmael is a crucial as well as commanding figure in the book, and the first description of him bears careful scrutiny. By the standards of society, whose finest flower is the refinement of an Inez or a Middleton, Ishmael is animalistic in his powerful movements and savage in the bizarre confusion of his dress. A wanderer, as his name signifies, he has been expelled from society for crimes that began with his violation of the basic institution of ordered society, the rights of property.

As different as they are in all other respects, Ishmael and Natty Bumppo share one important similarity: both reject the law of the "clearings," as Natty calls the area on society's side of the frontier. At their first meeting, in response to Ishmael's rejection of legal property rights by an appeal to nature and higher law, Natty, himself an outcast because he has violated "legal law," can only concur, although Cooper, troubled by the difficulty he has worked himself into, tries to differentiate

Natty's position by saying it was somehow drawn from different premises. The problem posed by the agreement between Natty and Ishmael in their mutual rejection of society is touched again and again throughout the story and, in a minor key, by the advice Natty gives to Paul Hovenden toward the end of the book. He urges Paul to give up the anarchic freedom of "life in the woods" since "different tempers call for different employments." If Paul is to marry Ellen, his place is in society. "Therefore," counsels Natty, "forget anything you may have heard from me, which is nevertheless true, and turn your mind on the ways of the inner country."

In these two encounters, selected from the beginning and the ending of Cooper's tale, we can see clearly the problem that pervades the entire book. Cooper is committed to two conflicting systems of values, one that affirms the untutored wisdom and natural virtue of Natty and the other the manly refinement and civilized code of Middleton. But the two cannot coexist. Although Natty is the bearer of virtues that are in many ways superior to society, or perhaps beyond society, he is fated to vanish before the inexorable advance of civilization, which may be brutal at first in the ax-bearing hands of Ishmael and his sons, but which is good ultimately in the developed state of Inez and Middleton. Schematically *The Prairie,* as all the novels of the Leatherstocking series, is about the inevitable conflict between two species of good. The elegiac note at Natty's death at the end of *The Prairie* is to sound a mournful recognition that one good must give way to the other, even though in the process something heroic and grand is lost.

Roy Harvey Pearce, in a fine essay on the Leatherstocking series some years ago, pointed out that the basic situation was essentially a tragic one. If there is to be sorrow at Natty's passing, it is a sorrow that is to be borne and accepted, not only because it is somehow inevitable, but because the advance of civilized society represents a good of a different kind. To do justice to his theme, Cooper had to do two things. First he had to render Natty Bumppo and make him live in our emotions. The fact that the image of Leatherstocking still survives is a measure of Cooper's success with Natty. His job was relatively simple since it is on the level of straightforward action that Natty lives; his world is, by definition, not complex. Cooper's second job was to render the civilized society that inevitably destroys Leatherstocking's world. Cooper had to create in his fiction an image of an admirably sophisticated world so that we as readers can feel its worth and accept, even while regretting, the justice as well as the inevitability of the passing of Natty's world. It is here that Cooper fails. His civilized men, and especially his civilized heroines, are stock figures, stereotypes drawn from the tradition of the sentimental novel. We are not able to identify with them or believe in them. Further, Cooper fails to render the virtues of civilization in terms appropriate to it. If civilization stands for the order of reason as opposed to Natty's intuition, for a rich, subjective life as opposed to Natty's naïve straightforwardness, for an intense and valuable cultural milieu as opposed to Natty's lean and spare existence, then it had to be presented in its own terms; but Cooper presents the world of civilization as well as Natty's world of nature in terms of action, of pursuit and chase, so that one pole of the dramatic conflict is emotionally absent.

But literature is made up of more than *King Lear* and *The Wings of the Dove*. Cooper's theme was perhaps greater than his art, but a book like *The Prairie* has endured because it represents a flawed attempt to put down in writing an image of intense importance to American culture. Cooper's problem was to establish a dynamic and necessary relationship between nature and civilization, a potentially tragic relationship between the ideal and the real. The problem bristled with difficulties for the writer. Mark Twain produced one great book in the attempt to solve it, and Henry James translated it into an international theme in his complex explorations of the matter of America and Europe. The line of filiation from Cooper extends further to the best of American literature in our own time. It is fair to say that without having read Cooper no reader will catch the full resonance of the lyrical conclusion to Scott Fitzgerald's *The Great Gatsby* or the massive irony of Steinbeck's inversion of the westward movement in *The Grapes of Wrath*. In William Faulkner the relation of civilization to nature becomes a moral drama of man's inevitable fall, especially in "The Bear." The power of that fine long story derives in part from the memory of the American people, even in their cities, of the importance of nature in our historical experience. We still read Cooper today because he was the first of our authors to seize upon the dramatic possibilities of that unfallen western world that stands at the beginning of our national life.

JOHN WILLIAM WARD

SELECTED BIBLIOGRAPHY

OTHER WORKS BY JAMES FENIMORE COOPER

The Spy, 1821   Novel
The Pioneers, 1823   Novel (Signet CY746)
The Pilot, 1824   Novel
The Last of the Mohicans, 1826   Novel (Signet CQ707)
The Red Rover, 1827   Novel
Notions of the Americans, 1828   Social Criticism
The Bravo, 1831   Novel
The Monikins, 1835   Satire
Sketches of Switzerland, Parts I and II, 1836   Travel
Gleanings in Europe (England, France, Italy), 1837-38   Travel
The American Democrat, 1838   Social Criticism
Homeward Bound, 1838   Novel
Home as Found, 1838   Novel
The History of the Navy of the United States of America, 1839
The Pathfinder, 1840   Novel (Signet CQ674)
The Deerslayer, 1841   Novel (Signet CQ680)
The Wing-and-Wing, 1842   Novel
Wyandotte, 1843   Novel
Afloat and Ashore, 1844   Novel
Satanstoe, 1845   Novel
The Chainbearer, 1845   Novel
The Redskins, 1846   Novel

414 *Selected Bibliography*

The Crater, 1847   Novel
The Oak Openings, 1848   Novel
The Sea Lions, 1849   Novel
The Ways of the Hour, 1850   Novel

BIOGRAPHY AND CRITICISM

Beard, James Franklin (ed.). *The Letters and Journals of James Fenimore Cooper.* 2 vols. Cambridge, Mass.: Harvard University Press; London: Oxford University Press, 1960.

Boynton, Henry W. *James Fenimore Cooper.* New York and London: D. Appleton-Century Co., 1931.

Cooper, James Fenimore (grandson of the novelist) (ed.). *Correspondence of James Fenimore Cooper.* New Haven, Conn.: Yale University Press, 1922.

Cunningham, Mary E. (ed.). *James Fenimore Cooper: A Reappraisal.* Cooperstown, N. Y.: New York State Historical Association, 1954.

Dondore, Dorothy Anne. *The Prairie and the Making of Middle America: Four Centuries of Description.* Cedar Rapids, Iowa: The Torch Press, 1926.

Flanagan, John T. "The Authenticity of Cooper's *The Prairie,*" *Modern Language Quarterly,* II (March, 1941), 99–104.

Grossman, James. *James Fenimore Cooper.* New York: William Sloane Associates, Inc.; London: Methuen & Co., Ltd., 1949.

Lawrence, D. H. *Studies in Classic American Literature.* New York: Doubleday & Company (Anchor Books), 1961.

Lewis, R. W. B. *The American Adam: Innocence, Tragedy and Tradition in the Nineteenth Century.* Chicago, Ill.: University of Chicago Press, 1956; London: Cambridge University Press, 1955.

Lounsbury, Thomas R. *James Fenimore Cooper* (American Men of Letters Series). Boston: Houghton Mifflin & Co., 1882.

Paine, Gregory L. "The Indians of the Leather-Stocking Tales," *Studies in Philology*, XXIII (January, 1926), 16–39.

Parrington, Vernon L. *Main Currents in American Thought*. 3 vols. New York: Harcourt, Brace & Co., 1927.

Pearce, Roy H. "The Leatherstocking Tales Re-Examined." *South Atlantic Quarterly*, XLVI (October, 1947), 524–536.

Philbrick, Thomas. *James Fenimore Cooper and the Development of American Sea Fiction*. Cambridge, Mass.: Harvard University Press, 1961.

Ringe, Donald A. *James Fenimore Cooper*. New York: Twayne Publishers, 1961.

Rourke, Constance. *American Humor*. New York: Harcourt, Brace & Co., 1931.

Smith, Henry Nash. *Virgin Land*. New York: Alfred A. Knopf, Inc. (Vintage Books), 1957.

Spiller, Robert E., and others. *Literary History of the United States*. 3 vols. New York and London: The Macmillan Company, 1948.

————. *Fenimore Cooper: Critic of His Time*. New York: Minton, Balch & Co.; London: G. P. Putnam's Sons, 1931.

Van Doren, Carl. *The American Novel*. New York: The Macmillan Company, 1921.

Walker, Warren S. *James Fenimore Cooper*. New York: Barnes and Noble, Inc., 1962.

Waples, Dorothy. *The Whig Myth of James Fenimore Cooper*. New Haven: Yale University Press; London: Oxford University Press, 1938.

Winters, Yvor. *Maule's Curse: Seven Studies in the History of American Obscurantism*. New York: New Directions, 1938.

A NOTE ON THE TEXT

The text of this edition is based on the W. A.
Townsend and Company edition published in 1859
and reprinted in 1871 by the Riverside Press in their
collected edition of Cooper's works. Spelling and
punctuation have been brought into conformity with
current American usage.